I0572734

ISBN-13: 979-8-9993028-4-7

ISBN-10: 979-8-9993028-4-7

Cover design by: Myers Cover

Library of Congress Control Number: 018675309 Printed in the United States of America

Trigger Warnings

If you don't give a shit about triggers, boldly walk right into this war. I'll hold the door for you. I bet you love twisted surprises, don't you?

Trigger Warnings: Please take a moment to go over these if you are unsure about proceeding.

Explicit sexual language, Descriptive sexual acts, Vulgar language, Murder, Torture, Blood, Heavy graphic violence, Rape (not in detail), Hitting women, Sex Trafficking, Abduction, Gun usage, Divorce, Did I mention the torture?, Loss of parent, Power dynamics, Breath play, Anal sex, Male/Male scenes, Love wins.

****If you do not want to read about graphic torture, you can skip chapter 47. You will miss nothing in the storyline by doing so. It's just me giving a comeuppance to a rapist. He deserves it.**

This is not an exhaustive list as specific triggers vary widely between each person.

Love
like you've never
been Broken

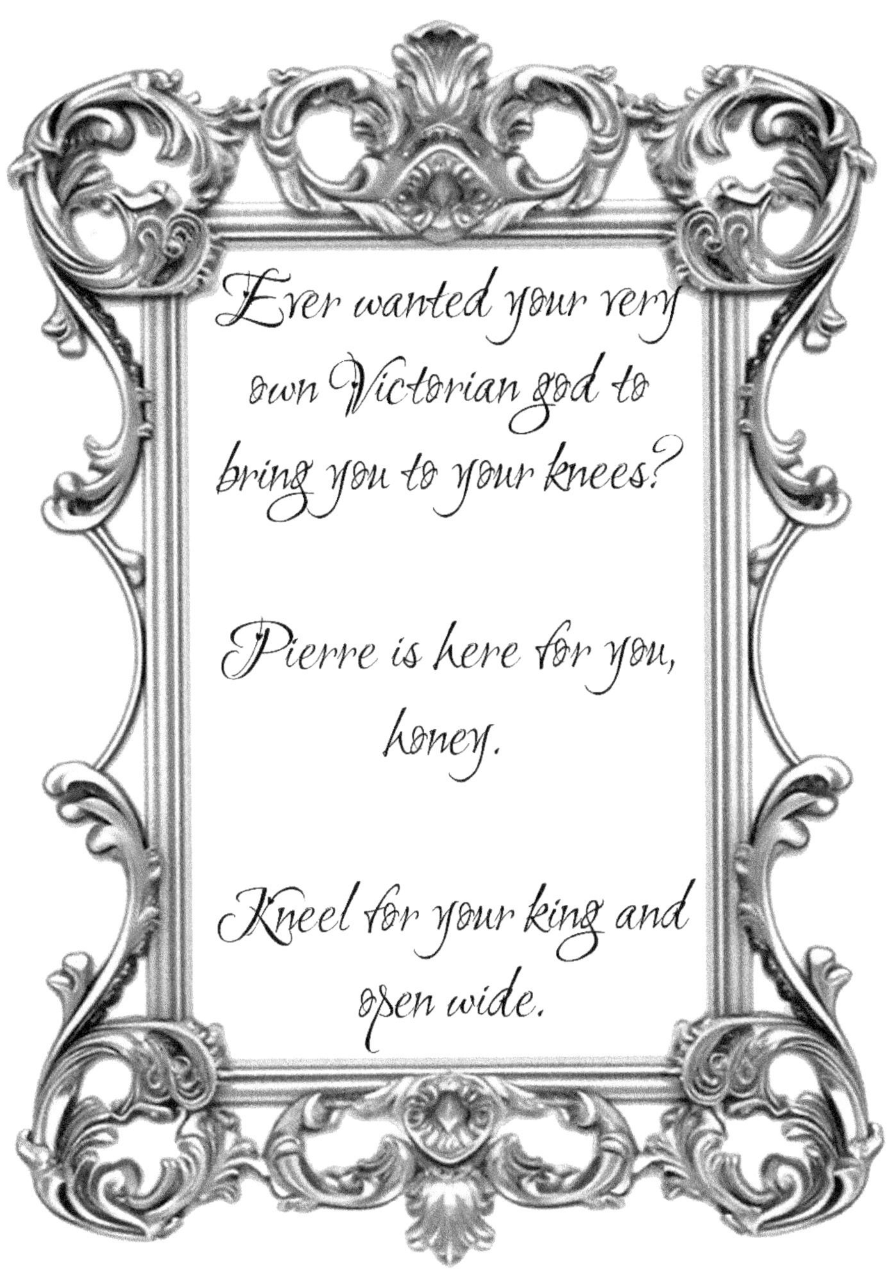

*Bethany - Chapters 13 & 14 are just for you.

This song was on repeat throughout the writing of Pierre's story. I encourage you to listen to it before reading any further. We'll wait right here while you do it. Get into Pierre's headspace before opening the door to his life.

Daylight – David Kushner

Chapter 1

Pierre

"I'm sorry, what?"

"Dude, keep up," Bam taps my bicep. "There was a guy…walking down the street—"

"Yeah, I got that part."

"He had no clothes on strutting down Canal Street. Methed out. Dick swinging in the breeze. Get this, he told the cops he was a member of the Lone Star Saints and was drugged, he thinks he was raped, and someone left him for dead."

Bam moves closer to me to lay out his conspiracy theory with his beer breath, *someone please save me,* "Now, why do you suppose they left him for dead when they didn't start the job in the first place? The guy was practically unharmed. We woulda finished the job." I want to scream I don't fucking know.

I have no idea why I'm being asked this. Sometimes I think I spend too much time at this biker clubhouse. Sure, the vibe is pleasant enough, maybe a smidge too rowdy for my tastes, my girls Zhar and Birdie are sometimes here, and there's no shortage of eye candy. There are some gorgeous bikers of all shapes, sizes, and colors here. I'm talking trip over my dick, hard as an iron railing looking men.

Not that I'm in the business of looking nowadays. Not since my husband, Seven, left a few weeks ago. I don't feel like shopping around for a new man. I'm still nursing a broken heart and don't give two fields of fucks about dating again.

Besides, I don't think I have anything in common with a biker. Except maybe tattoos, seeing as how I'm a tattoo artist.

I come to these functions because Birdie and Zharia expect it. They are almost obsessive in their drive to keep me from being sad about Seven and to get my dick wet again. It's exhausting constantly turning them down when they want me to go out.

I wouldn't be here tonight, crammed into a folding chair at the popular kids table, if it weren't for Birdie and Zharia begging me to leave the apartment and come to this charity Valentine's Day party the motorcycle club, the Southern Devils Society, puts on every year.

Birdie's dad, Rock, is the regional president of SDS. Her husband, Danger aka Lincoln, or Linx as she calls him, is the VP.

Oh yeah, Mr. Danger's also my stepbrother.

Zharia's men, yes you heard that right, plural men; I can't even get one to stay and she's got two hot as fuck men wrapped around her pinky, are at the end of the table with her, hovering near her. They pant and salivate every time they are around her. Both want her so bad and love her so hard they literally have hearts and moonbeams floating from their eyeballs. Birds and butterflies flit about the air around them.

They'll also kill anyone that comes too close to her. I'm one of the very few men allowed around her. Did I mention they are possessive?

Her guys are also part of the Top Five echelon of The Southern Devils Society. Shadow, my other guy friend besides Danger, is Sergeant at Arms, third-in-command. Zhar's other man is Gunney, aka Leo for her mouth only, and he is Secretary and fourth-in-command.

Rounding out the Top Five is Travares, the genius hacker who's fifth-in-command and the club Treasurer. Hot as sin. I mean H-A-W-T. Perfect eye candy to look at. I would be lying if I say I haven't thought about bending him over, gripping his hips, and fucking the sick out of him.

I shake my head, the guilt bubbling back up. I lusted after another man while married.

Whatever. Doesn't matter now anyways.

If you lined up the Top Five upper echelon, the inner circle, it would look like a group photo for a naked men's calendar come to life. Even Birdie's dad is in great shape, rocking that silver fox look hardcore. It's like he's just gotten better over the past twelve years I've known her as a bestie.

Don't tell her that though. She gets this look on her face, like she's just sucked a pickle flavored lemon and acts like she might throw up any time someone says her dad is hot.

Sometimes, when she's on my nerves extra special like, I ask her if her dad is into men and I'd love to find out. That usually shuts her up and she goes away and lets me stew in peace.

I'm here for charity. It's a fundraiser. That's what I keep telling myself. *Charity.* I'm not supposed to be gathering fodder for my spank bank later on. I mean, this is the very place to do it at so I look my ever-loving fill. Men in leather stand around talking or manspreading in chairs and all I can think about is bending over a few too many of them or ordering them to their knees.

I need laid. This is getting out of control.

Ugh. Jacking off is the only thing getting me through the lonely nights. Focus on why you're here.

I'm dropping money on the raffles, the fifty-fifty drawing, the silent auction, the pull tabs, and to top off my generosity— Zharia talked me into donating something to be raffled off. I put in a tap out tattoo session. Bikers will eat that one up. I used my cheapest rate for this charity. The bidding starts at three grand.

Do good shit, and it will return to you tenfold—or however the saying goes, just as long as I get some good shit finally. Here's me crossing my fingers for the good shit to start raining down in my very sad little life.

You hear that guardian angel? Put the crack pipe down and help rain down good shit on me.

Uhh, I want to clarify, not literal shit. Ok, got it?

I'm not supposed to know, but a faction of the club runs on vigilante shit. Like hardcore death and murder…but for a good cause. The notorious rival club, the Lone Star Saints out of Texas, are a thorn in everyone's side. I've already had a taste of their bullshit about two years ago when they kidnapped me and beat the shit out of me.

They are nasty men dealing in flesh and innocence. People go missing and you can almost guarantee the sick fucks over at LSS has stolen them.

However, the Southern Devils Society runs a non-profit human trafficking rescue and support system from here in Louisiana all the way around the Gulf to the Caribbean.

This is how the war started.

Using the elite task force, SDS intercepts the Saints' shipments of humans to sell into sex slavery and then the elite members swiftly whisk them off to a safehouse, to either find their family and send them back, or give them money and a chance for a new life. Either way, it's something I can get behind and respect. I gladly give to the Greater Louisiana Children's Society.

That's their corporate name for the vigilante shit.

While time has no bearing on my broken-hearted soul most days…what feels like a few short weeks ago, my husband of ten years, together twelve, moved out of our French Quarter apartment we shared while I was working and slinging ink at a tattoo convention in Florida.

The night I got back to New Orleans I noticed his stuff was missing. Everywhere I looked, his stuff gone. Just poofed. Seven left, taking all his belongings, leaving me alone to wonder what the fuck happened and how did it came to this point.

We hadn't taken down our Christmas tree yet—it was mid-January, give me a break, I was getting around to it—he made sure to take all the ornaments off, picking through to grab all his, then he took all the lights off, leaving them in a pile in the floor where the tree was…just so he could take his eight-foot black gothic tree.

How petty can you get.

Then! *Then*…he left me a voicemail while I was on a plane traveling home, breaking up with me all nonchalant, like it was no big deal to throw away our marriage, our life we have built. I didn't check my voicemail when I got off the plane, because for some crazy reason I had no voicemail icon on my phone nor a missed call from him.

I finally got home around midnight and he was nowhere to be found. I wondered why he wasn't answering my calls or texts. I thought he was asleep.

Nope. Once I was home on the wifi, all this shit started downloading to my phone and that's when the voicemail icon showed up.

It was totally possible to be pettier than the tree.

A fucking voicemail ended our twelve-year relationship.

I'm hurt, enraged, lost, brokenhearted, mad, sick to my stomach, anxious. You name it, I'm cycling through it.

I'm one big fat cycle of fucked up emotions. I'm not fit to be in the public.

That night, in a vulnerable, desperate state of mind, I called Zharia in the middle of the night. She and her men arrived and she held me the rest of the night. I'm afraid I might not be here if it hadn't been for Zhar and the guys. I was not in a good mindset. Seven's betrayal affected my manic depression instantly.

Zapping back to the present, exasperated, I tell him, "I don't have a clue, Bam. Have you seen Zharia?" I start to rise and Bam puts his big, meaty neanderthal hand on my shoulder, shoving me back down in the chair. I clench my teeth.

"Bam, I really need to get home, man," I sigh. I've put forth the maximum social butterfly behavior for the week. Fuck, the entire month. I'm tapped out after a few hours.

Bam, short for Bambino so he's said, has been sitting here talking my ear off for damn near thirty minutes with his drunken rambling. I love gossip as much as the next person but I don't know any of these people he's talking about and he's taking all these little side quests to tell me little tidbits about non-playing characters of the story; it's getting on my nerves. It's maddening the amount of useless knowledge he has about people.

Most times I entertain him, but tonight my heart isn't in it.

"Did I tell you about my hairdresser's little sister and the guy from the Jacksonville chapter?"

"No, and I'm not sitting here anymore to hear it." I pop up quicker than he can react, pushing the chair back, toppling it over and jumping away from him in one lightning quick move.

Ok, so maybe that was a little dramatic.

I manage to get away from Bam; however, my chair doesn't topple over like a normal chair, no, it levitates! It has some sort of spiritual awakening.

Fuck my life in slow motion.

It flies into Travares, somehow lifting itself just enough to catch him in the dick. His "umph" and grab for his crotch region, *yikes*, sends me into a panic. For some absolutely unknown to me, bizarre reason, I reach out and cup Travares's dick and balls too, repeating "Oh my god, I'm so sorry" over and over.

WHAT in the actual *FUCK* am I doing?

Then I panic even harder because I realize I've grabbed his crotch and wide-eyed, I yank my hand away like he's fire…in just enough space and speed to backhand Bam in the face who's sitting behind me now.

It just keeps getting worse.

Fucking make it stop.

Travares starts laughing through his groan as Bam jumps up snorting like a bull.

I turn wide frightened eyes on Bam. I sure as fuck do *not* want to tangle with him sober, let alone drunk.

Why are all these men so big?

Turning around, I put my hands up, I gush, "I'm sorry Bam, it was an accident. I didn't mean it." Only for Bam to hit me in the chest and shove me backwards…right back into Travares, who can finally stand up now…*uh shit,* just in time to catch me in his arms.

Have you seen enough, Karma? Does this not entertain you? This is bullshit.

I'm mortified at this point.

"Whoa, big guy, I got ya," Travares purrs in my ear in his rich timbre, sending a shiver through my body. His arm is snaked under mine with his open hand pressed flat against my chest. His other arm is resting low on my torso, low on my hip. My heart skips a beat.

That's interesting.

A picture in my head of him on his knees before me, mouth open and waiting like a good boy, flashes in my mind. Feelings and electricity shoot straight to my cock, through the embarrassment, through the hurt and anger. Lust snakes its way through my core.

Unbelievable.

Because time stopped for me weeks ago, sucked into the dark abyss, but the second hand just sputtered back to life inside my chest and the clock is ticking again.

I'm in another man's arms for the first time in twelve years, who's not my husband, and my body is reacting. *Reacting.* It's not done this for another man in over a decade. I didn't think it knew how to react anymore. My senses are on overload. An ember somewhere deep under the pain sparks to life inside me from being so close to him.

I must be losing my mind. After weeks of numbness, months prior to that of not being touched, Christ, I'm pathetic.

Travares is one of the handsomest men I have ever seen. Six-two, built like the rest of these knockouts around here, with his brown, longer on top, windswept beach hair, and his perfectly trimmed beard a shade darker than the hair on his head. Beautiful kissable full lips any woman would envy. His glasses don't hide his clear hazel eyes that are always watching everyone it seems. Ever so vigilant.

He has one long scar on his cheek making him look dangerous and villainous. It draws me in more. It does nothing to hinder his good looks, only makes him more intriguing.

Don't even get me started on his body. I could stare at him for hours, painting his every slope, dip, and hard curve onto canvas, in every light imaginable.

I found out Travares has a social media page with quite the following. He's a sexy masked man on a motorcycle with a stacked body and sizable bulge in his pants. Hundreds of thousands of followers. Who knows how many on his subscription page.

A flash in my mind of him above me in his mask, shirtless and shiny, one hand on my stomach, lowering himself on my...

No one, absolutely nobody has to know I have a fake profile and my secret hobby has been watching him and jacking off to his videos for some time now. Seven wasn't touching me, so I touched myself...to other men. I'm awful.

Him pushed up against the tiled shower, my hands flat against his perfect chest while I'm deep inside...

I always picture him shirtless because I've seen him shirtless before. He was soaked to the bone. A sudden southern thunderstorm caught him out in the French Quarter and he made his way to the studio because he knew we had towels. The effect of water glistening over those smooth, unblemished pecs and abs was chef's kiss and it's now a core memory of mine. Truly a work of art. It's rare to see a biker with hardly any tattoos. Doesn't matter, his body is still perfect.

I've seen Travares laughing with his brothers in the club and I've caught his eye a time or two in passing. He always smiles and dips his chin at me, respectfully, and I try not to let on that I can't get his wet chiseled chest and soaking wet jeans out of my head.

Which makes me blush any time I'm around him now.

However, right now, that chest is plastered against my back, solid as a rock, and his slightly heavy breathing in my ear is making it hard to think. Slowly I come to realize everyone is standing around watching this debacle happen. Yay! Front rows for everyone.

I quickly gather myself and right my body vertically where I belong. Away from his arms that felt too good around me.

Good gravy.

This night cannot get any worse.

I straighten my clothes since I've been manhandled and try hard to calm my racing heart and get back some kind of decorum.

I'm losing my fucking mind.

Bam shakes his head and sits back down. I'm kind of left standing here while Travares rights the chair I was sitting on, the one that decided to jump up and clobber him in the cock. Just my fucking luck, right?

Travares claps his hand on my shoulder, much like Bam did, but I don't mind this time. "At least buy me a drink for copping a feel of the family jewels." He laughs and winks at me, then pulls me along with him, walking between the tables towards the bar that sits along the wall of the clubhouse.

The Southern Devils Society clubhouse is a big warehouse set in the heart of the Central Business District in New Orleans. It has a fully stocked bar, pool tables, dart boards, axe throwing and a full kitchen. It's a sweet set up they have here and it's always packed with people. It's a sacred place to gather for bikers and they will defend it with their lives. The clubhouse is like a second home to some of these men and women.

It's got to be the safest bar around. Nobody's fucking with a shit ton of bikers that are always around here.

"Yeah, man, I can do that." I return a sheepish smile to him. Hey, at least he's being a good sport about it. I make sure I'm moving beside him and not stumbling around with my head in the clouds. Why am I so nervous?

I don't know, maybe it's because he looks like a romance novel cover model. He looks like he would be spread out on white sheets in a sun-streamed room in the afternoon light, beckoning you to come take a naughty nap with him.

He also looks like a true devil when he's decked out in his riding leathers, bandana and sunglasses. The most enticing look of them all—the bad boy image. And by fuck, he does this look very well.

Tonight, he looks like a nerdy biker with his glasses and his leather vest, his cut full of patches. He wears it over a black Henley and dark form fitting jeans. The bulge that my hand caressed looks real nice encased in those black pants.

Pierre, you are a married man.

Sorta.

It's complicated.

Jesus.

I'm just looking, ok!...and uh, also with some minor involuntary touching involved.

Seven had me served with divorced papers yesterday. Happy Valentine's Day to me, huh? Never thought I'd be a thirty-two-year-old divorcee. I'll just go punch myself in the face, it will hurt less. He cited irreconcilable differences.

I'm not at all clear what differences he speaks of.

I like Raisin Bran; he likes Lucky Charms. He doesn't sort his laundry; I do colors and whites separately. He prefers whole milk to my almond milk.

What kind of differences?? TELL ME, so I can fix them!

I guess there's no use wondering or trying. He has made it abundantly clear he is not coming back and there's no talking this out. He swears there's no one else but I have a sneaky suspicion about it all.

It was sudden, abrupt. No warning signs. I've wracked my brain for anything that could have flagged me as a warning sign of imminent doom.

I'm either blind or my rose-colored glasses are the wrong prescription because I saw nothing. Nada. Zip. Ziltch.

Seven has always been a moody fucker with his bi-polarism. He is either quiet or obnoxious. No in between. He swings between both, even with the medication he swears he takes like he's supposed to. Not very often is he right smack dab in the middle at a balanced disposition. We could only get so lucky.

It was a lot to deal with, especially having my own mental health issues and taking anti-depressants for it. But I loved my husband and I promised in sickness and in health I would be by his side, even if that meant riding out a storm every few weeks while he cycled in episodes.

A giant part of me wonders if this isn't a manic episode and he will come back. That's the shred of hope I'm clinging to. But if I listen to my girls, our Fab Four—Zharia, Tally, and Birdie—have all said, this is not an episode and he's gone for good, leaving me no answers and no closure.

Birdie said sometimes the closure we seek comes in the form of their silence and I felt that down to my bones.

Zharia and Tally said the fastest way to get over Seven is to get under another man. I'm not so sure that is a good idea. What kind of husband would I be then?

I still need to like, mourn my marriage, or something like that.

But I'm not a husband anymore, am I?

No matter how many times I call and get sent to voicemail, or my text messages sit on read, I still try. Maybe I should stop trying.

My dad says silence is still an answer, take it for what it is. He also said give people a chance to miss you.

It still doesn't make coping with this any better.

CHAPTER 2
TRAVARES

Holy fuck.

Never in my life did I think Pierre Lefèvre would end up in my arms but yet here we are. It happened. I'm not opposed to it. I mean it wasn't awful.

Dreams do come true.

The result has me thrown off my axis for a moment. It's like being starstruck.

The secret is I have always had a crush on Pierre.

I look back over my shoulder to see that Pierre is following me. I catch his eye and grin at him, giving a flirty wink to let him know I'm not mad.

I have no idea why I'm almost giddy. On missions I'm the broody, stoic type. At the clubhouse, I'm quiet, but sometimes playful with my brothers. Apparently, I'm all of a sudden in my flirty era.

I have electricity in my veins ready to shoot at anyone who steps between whatever's happening betwixt us. And there's definitely a betwixt going on.

I haven't had a good heartbreak in a while. I decide I got time for one with him.

Pierre is hot. H-O-T hot. And word on the street is he's single now. I have no problem being a rebound fuck for him if I can. I've wanted him since that first look.

I know if he wasn't married, I would have already moved in on him, making him mine somehow.

Pierre is elegantly beautiful. Not a lot of men draw me into their aura but Pierre does. His ethereal good looks and his attitude paired with his impeccable Victorian fashion sense is mesmerizing.

Seriously, who walks around, comfortable as all get out, dressed like the singer Prince?

I want to fuck the haughty out of him.

Bring him down to being a mere mortal.

Sometimes he reminds me of someone straight out of a vampire movie, a Dorian Grey crossed with Lestat, topped with the finest handlebar mustache I've ever seen and the best haircut. His steampunk-ish wardrobe includes ruffled blouses, nice form-fitting britches, satin vests with authentic pocket watches—I swear all his clothes are tailor made just for him. There's no way clothes look that good on a man.

Where do you even buy Victorian era clothing styles as good as his?

I wonder if he sleeps in a vintage nightgown like Scrooge McDuck wore? I snort to myself thinking that.

It all works for him though. The image he portrays is on point and I like it. A lot. He's not my usual type, but he does something to me. Fancy tremors run up and down my dick when he's near me. I think it might have a little bit to do with the fact that he was forbidden. It made me pine after him more. Made me want him more.

But now the door's blown wide open.

He's easily six-two, right up there with me. He's lean, like a swimmer's lanky body as opposed to my bulky, muscular frame. I felt his chest under my hand and he has definition just not as much as me.

I felt his heartrate skyrocketing too. It thumped in his chest in a panic, like a startled flock of birds trying to escape. His breathing was erratic and I'm not sure if it's because he was embarrassed or because I was holding him against my body.

It was doing something to me too that's for sure. It made my wounded, throbbing dick get hard and that was highly uncomfortable.

My body was responding even after being beaten up by a chair.

Pierre has always been reserved when coming here. A few times he's let his hair down after partaking in a couple of spirits with the girls and he has a great time. He was happily married to his husband, (so we thought) even though that guy never came around. Seven was too good to slum it with the likes of us or Pierre's friends.

I remember Birdie saying one time that Seven thought he was better than everyone and that's why he never wanted anything to do with Pierre's *fan club'*, as he called the Fab Four's three girls. It's their little clique from college. They've stayed friends for years since then.

Pierre's been on my radar since I met him four years ago when I was recruited for this club as a 'system analyst.' At the time, I thought he was a stunning man, too good for me. I didn't like it when I heard he was married.

There's been this magnetic pull to him that I can't resist. Like the uncanny knack of knowing where he is in the room at all times, or my eyes finding his at the same time he pans the room and lands on me.

I've had a big unrequited crush on Pierre for some time.

I know he's hurting right now. That's why I didn't get upset about the shitastic chair knocking me in the nuts, not that I would have anyways. I'm not the rage and yell kind of guy. I'm easy-going.

Not a lot bothers me.

Especially not a gorgeous man falling into my arms. I could have really done without the chair's dick punch but it was worth it to have him grab my balls.

Wow. I can't believe that happened. I chuckle to myself as we arrive at the bar.

Pierre smiles a genuine smile and it about knocks me for a loop. I've never had one of his smiles directed right at me. It's a sight to behold. He gestures to Dobby behind the bar.

"Well, get whatever you want, Travares."

"Declan."

He cocks an eyebrow at me. "Oh, we're going to first name basis now, are we?"

"I figure since your pretty hands have been wrapped around my balls we could be on a bit more friendlier terms than before."

His eyes widen and his nostrils flare. Maybe that was a little strong. I have a habit of being too truthful when I do speak.

To think, I was getting up to tell Danger goodbye and then I was heading out. Until Pierre happened. I'm not passing up this opportunity to talk to him. He's fascinating to me. This is the first time I have his attention.

Honestly, I'm kinda nervous.

"Ok then…Declan, have whatever you want."

"I'm not sure if what I want is on the menu."

Pierre blinks once. Then twice. Opens his mouth. Shuts it. I see his cheeks turn pink.

He gets a crease between his eyes. "Then, I, uh, would have to tell you to pick something on the menu." He licks his lips and I track his tongue along his bottom lip until it slips back inside his mouth. His eyes flick to the crowd out in the clubhouse.

Dobby appears before us, "What can I get ya, boss?"

I've repeatedly asked him to stop calling me boss but he calls all the Top Five boss. We've just stopped correcting him, it's no use.

"Hey Dobby, remember those three special drinks we worked on?"

"Sure do, I been pimping them out today. They're quite popular."

"Good, good." I look at Pierre with a sexy grin and say, "I'll have a Bend Me Over, please."

Dobby says, "Coming up, boss."

I watch Pierre's face closely. He's a well-controlled man. I respect that. His nostrils flare once more, his lips roll in and he bites them. That cute little blush has turned into a full flush from his chest where I can see the black and gray ink peeking out, up over the Death's-head moth tattooed over his Adam's apple, finally coming to rest on his flaming red hot cheeks.

I lean on the bar with one elbow, facing him. "So, Pierre, what was Bam talking about that made you jump out of your seat like the devil was trying to snatch your soul?"

He still looks shellshocked. He opens his mouth to say something but ends up just shaking his head instead.

Was that too direct? I'm sure he's picking up what I'm putting down.

Maybe he doesn't welcome what I'm putting down.

If he wants a revenge fuck, or a get-over-someone fuck, or an I-just-want-dicked-down fuck, I'm down. I'm the man for the job.

Dobby the Club Elf magically appears and hands me my drink, "Try this one, T."

I sip, looking over the rim into Pierre's bright blue eyes. I pull my lips back and smack them together, licking my lips. "You did good, Dobby. Almost as good as the real thing."

As if Pierre was coming out of a stupor, he hands his card to Dobby and clears his throat, "I'm buying his." Dobby takes the card and bebops down the bar to the card reader as 'Pink Pony Club' plays through the clubhouse speakers.

I know Bam is behind this song. It screams his brand of fuckery.

I make up the playlists that are played in the clubhouse. It's mainly rock, sometimes some techno rock remixes are thrown in. But nothing that reminds you of glittered unicorns and pink tutus are added to my lists…no matter how catchy they are and if I might like them.

Damn him. I'm never getting this song out of my head.

That means this amateur, just baby stage hacker, Bam, snuck in and added this to the playlist for tonight. He keeps me on my toes.

He may not look like a computer nerd, like at all, but he truly is one. He's in his senior year of college for computer science. Bam will graduate with high honors in a few months. He's also one of my closest friends.

The federal government *aka* the Army, through the G.I. Bill, paid for my schooling to be a master, most sought after in the industry 'Systems Analyst'. They call me The Ghost.

Also, I studied all the online tutorials, forums, and dark web information I could gather since my early teens to learn what I know.

God, I love technology. Joining this club for such a good cause was the best move I've ever made. I'm grateful to Rock for this opportunity.

I came highly recommended.

I wait for him to meet my gaze again. He's trying his best not to look at me. I watch his Adam's apple bob once, twice, denoting his nervousness. He drums his fingers on top of the bar with his black polished fingertips. The smooth skin of his jaw ripples as he swallows again.

I'm not trying to make him uncomfortable. This is not how an interested guy reacts.

I straighten up and tell him, "Thanks for the fondle and the drink, Pierre. I'll leave you be. Have a good night, man."

I go to move by him, when I come abreast of him his arm darts out and his slim fingers wrap around my forearm. He looks over at me with a fire in his eyes and says, "Wait."

Chapter 3
Pierre

What am I doing?

My breath shudders in my chest. With what little bit of air seems to be getting into my lungs and bloodstream, I'm so dizzy and not acting myself.

I can't believe this gorgeous man wants me. Me…the odd guy, the alt dude everyone thinks is cool, or as some of them in the club whisper: the artsy faggot. Yeah, there's a few old-school-mentality guys around here.

Travares has made it clear to me that he wants me. I'd be blind to miss the blatant flirting. Mind blown.

I'm trapped here, in my panic, holding his arm, not wanting him to leave. Part of me really wants him, the other part still believes I'm a married man and it would be cheating.

"Yes, Pierre?"

His eyes are just as beautiful as the rest of him. I've never seen them so up close. Specks of yellow gold, blended with forest green, like glittering sunlight shining on the moss on ancient tree bark. They're stunning.

"I-I," I can't even get it out. Just say it! "Were you serious?"

His smile widens and his predatory canines flash, "Oh yeah, I definitely want to get bent over by you, whenever you're ready."

The air's been knocked out of my chest. He's serious. He wants me. I bite my bottom lip in thought. I scan the people out in the clubhouse. No one's paying attention to us. I sign the receipt and pick up my card, pulling my chained wallet out and replacing it in its spot.

"My place or yours?" I ask him.

"I do believe you're closer. I'm all the way over in Metairie."

My hand lowers to his, tangling our fingers together briefly, then slips free, "Let's go then."

He downs his drink in two gulps and lays the plastic cup on the bar top then gestures for me to lead. One last look at him and I'm weaving in and around people to get to the door.

I step out into the chilly February night air and I'm not entirely sure if my shiver is from the cold or the sexy biker following me out.

When the door shuts behind him and I turn around to ask him which car is his, he closes the distance between us in two strides. He grabs my face, caresses my cheekbones, and next thing I know, his lips are crashing into mine and I'm opening for him.

It's wild and exhilarating. Breathtaking. Intense. Soul awakening.

My heart slams in my chest and I groan in my throat. My hands, that I don't know what to do with, instinctively wrap around his waist on their own accord.

His tongue sweeps through my mouth and it tickles as it glides across mine. He tastes like his fruity drink from the bar which makes it that much more intoxicating.

Declan pulls his tongue away and immediately I miss the invasion. My lips feel the cool night air as he pulls away with his boyishly good-looking smile, "You have no idea how long I've wanted to do that." He lets out a soft laugh, "Way better than my imagination."

He's fantasized about kissing me?

One day I'm going to look back and know that this is a pivotal moment, a core memory forming. Pierre is getting his groove back. Right now, I'm so nervous and my heart's beating out of my chest but goddamn, I feel alive. So fucking alive. Finally.

Fucking finally, I feel something other than crushing grief and loneliness.

I feel the smile forming before it unfurls on my lips. I bite my lip and nod, breathier than I anticipated I manage to say, "Glad it exceeded your fantasies." I know I'm blushing. I can feel the heat on my cheeks, especially in the cool night air.

Matter of fact, all of me feels like it's burning up in situational awareness. Our bodies are so close and I can feel his words breathe across my lips as he still has my face cupped in his hands.

"Whose car?" he breathes out.

I panic. "I do rideshare everywhere. There's no parking at my place. Well, there's street parking if you can find it."

"We can take mine and hope for the best." He slips his hand into mine as he pulls me towards a blacked-out Range Rover, whose lights came on as the engine turns over from the remote start.

I'm busy pushing away the thoughts that scream I'm cheating on my husband.

I hear Zharia in my head with her lilting tone, '*He abandoned you and he's not coming back. Live a little and get some dick.*'

I haven't had sex in so long. It was never something important to Seven. He never had any interest in fucking after we were together for a few years, so it was rather sporadic when we finally did have it. I've just learned to live without.

A loveless, fuckless marriage.

In this moment, I am very, very interested in sex. And I'm tired of going without. I'm ravenous.

I want to be selfish with Declan and accept the offer of his body.

I barely get the apartment door unlocked and thrown open before Declan's mouth is back on me, kicking the door shut behind him. Tongues slide against each other and our breathing grows heavy. One or both of us moan, I don't know, I'm lost in the moment. I've never been kissed like this before. I feel tingles clear down to my toes.

What a shame to live this long and never find this kind of fire.

Oh, how I've missed the thrill of the chase. Missed being touched. It's the anticipation of a good fuck that's killing me.

Declan can be summed up in three words: intense, passionate, and sexy.

As nervous as I am, I'm not backing out. This is what I need to get over Seven.

I'm so tired of living in a silent wasteland of darkness and depression. It's time to move forward in life. If sticking my dick in this hot as fuck biker will help, then I'm on board.

Put me on the ass train to Poundtown, I'm here to be mayor.

In more comfortable surroundings, my body responds willingly, soaking up every touch to my skin. His tongue clashes with mine as I reach up and pull his leather vest off, dropping it to the floor. His fingers are busy unbuttoning my waistcoat as I unbutton my front and sleeves. I grow harder the faster we try to hurry and strip each other.

His teeth nip at my lips and he sucks my tongue into his mouth. I should be repulsed at the slurping sounds filling the living room but I'm not. They spur me on and amp up my desire, groaning like a man in danger of losing his sanity.

Because I am. Already I want to dive off the cliff with him.

Our ragged breathing echoes around the apartment when suddenly, I'm stripped of my waistcoat and hear it hitting the floor beside us.

Next, my dress shirt is quickly pulled down over my shoulders and it flutters to the floor at my feet. I grab the hem of his shirt and start to lift..oh.my.god..over the rock-hard abs and up his ribs and pecs muscles, where I stutter and stop, hands on his skin. Holy fuck, I've never felt a body like this.

"I'm going to die if I don't get those nipple piercings in my mouth, pronto," he says. He knows how sensitive they are for me.

Declan's a god. Chiseled from marble and come to life. Perfect artistry. Poetic.

We break apart so he can finish yanking his shirt over his head. His eyes are like molten lava, warming me up everywhere his gaze touches as he stands in front of me, his chest heaving.

I look my fill down his naked torso and admire his excellent physique. I'm impressed he can sit for hours on a bike or computer and still look like this.

My tongue peeks out to touch my lips where he was. I feel him all around me, in my personal space, in my head. His cologne is in the air, wrapping around my head making it spin. I swear it has some special pheromones in it sucking me into his orbit and putting a chokehold on my senses.

His hungry eyes eat me up and I bask in his appraisal. I'm not self-conscious even a little bit about my body. I want to show him. He unabashedly stares at me through his lashes and slowly rubs his thumb over his bottom lip. Like he's sizing up his prey. Ready to pounce.

The sexual tension between us is insane.

"You look like one of those old-school bare-knuckle fighters and I want to eat you up. I need you inside me."

Arousal bubbles up inside me at his words. The nervousness and guilt inside of me is quickly fading away and I feel the old me creeping to the surface after years of being suppressed. The part that wants unleashed again.

I look into his hazel eyes and ask, "You sure you want this?"

CHAPTER 4
TRAVARES

I mean the tent in my pants aggressively suggests so.

"Abso-fuckin-lutely." That came out as breathy as I meant it to.

Pierre takes my breath away with his beauty. He's completely covered in ink. Everywhere I look. It's amazing to take in. I can't wait to run my tongue and hands over it.

I only have two tattoos but Shadow owes me one for going on a mission in his place. I've just never been one that feels like I need to be inked up. But standing in the presence of such greatness makes me want more, makes me want to decorate my body.

Pierre is a work of art. I want to cover him in my cum and lick it off his pierced nipples, feeding it back to him off my tongue.

I plan to do so many filthy things to him.

In a much rougher tone, husky in arousal, Pierre gives me a command, "Get on your knees for me like a good boy, Declan."

Damned if that authoritative tone didn't make my balls quiver with delight.

I grin at him as I lower myself to my knees in front of him. I tilt my face up, waiting for the next command. He doesn't disappoint.

"Take me out and stroke me. We'll see how good you can follow directions." He gives me a playful smirk, but those smoldering eyes hold me captive.

"Yes, sir." His breath hitches at my response.

I'm quick to undo his belt, the button and drag his zipper down. The bulge in his pants has me excited. I can't wait to feel this big cock up my ass. This is going to be so much better than I ever imagined.

I free his cock and get my first glimpse at his piercings. Holy mother load! Pierre's cock stands proudly wearing jewelry and leaking at the tip. He's pierced damn near everywhere. It's glorious to behold. I run my hand over his Jacob's ladder down the underside, then with my thumb I caress his magic cross around the tip, spreading his precum around the swollen head and the metal balls of the jewelry.

Any man that can get his dick pierced is hardcore in my book. This many times? God level pain tolerance.

Hot as fuck though.

I lick my lips in anticipation. My eyes lift back to him. His baby blues are almost all black, dilated with desire. His skin is so hot and flushed and I'm drawn to the heat. Like a moth to a flame.

"Show me how well you can suck cock, baby boy." His thumb drags across my lips. I open my mouth, waiting like a starving baby bird.

As soon as his fingers leave my skin, I wet my lips and then I have him in my mouth. Gotta say, I've never sucked a man off with this much metal in his dick but I'm up for the challenge. So far it's tickling my tongue and I feel the barbells grazing over the surfaces of my mouth.

Pierre lets out a groan as my mouth works over him. He threads his slender fingers in my hair, pulling me closer.

"Such a good cocksucker. Your mouth feels so good." I hum out my appreciation of his male form and it makes him hiss when I wrap my hand around his girth not in my mouth.

I suck him in harder, deeper and his breathing becomes heavier, more erratic. He's losing himself. I love that I'm bringing him to the edge. I love that this is his reaction to me.

There's no denying that once we'd come together like this, it would be like a bomb going off inside me. I may not get another shot so I'm going to make the most out of this one time.

I take him in the back of my throat and swallow around him, humming the entire time. I gag and tears spring to my eyes. Still, I continue.

"That's a good boy. Take me deep in your throat."

Still Pierre holds me there until I think I might actually throw up and then he yanks me away, chest heaving.

"*Fuck*," he pants.

I take in gulps of air and watch his face above me. It's like a different Pierre. The hardness that he's carried around melts away from his shoulders, his face softens and when he smiles at me the world stops moving.

"That was close. This isn't how I'm coming. It's going to be deep inside your sweet ass."

Pierre loosens his fingers from my hair and offers me a hand. I take it and rise off the floor, landing a searing kiss with lots of hands, then I follow him to the doorway off the living room.

We come into a very generous-sized bedroom with a king-size bed. Pierre walks into the room toeing off his shoes and pulling his pants down, along with his boxer briefs. He strips his sock off and turns to look at me, hard cock jutting out proudly from his completely shaved area. He grips his hard dick and strokes it a few times while looking at me with lust filled eyes.

Oh, sweet baby Jesus.

Gorgeous. Spectacular. Stunning. I'm out of words to describe Pierre. *Goddamn*, stars above.

I close my mouth and quickly shed the rest of my clothes and stand in front of him.

Not that I'm one to compare cocks but I see we are evenly matched. It's still going to burn when he slips into me though. The precious, sweet burn I crave from him.

"Ok big boy, show me what you got," I taunt him.

He chuckles and says, "Come closer."

Before I can even think about saying no and play hard to get, my body is in motion. He reaches for me, cupping his hand on the back of my neck, pulling me in for another deep kiss. When I step up to him, our dicks slide together and it's one of the most erotic featherlight touches I think I've ever had.

His hand is there to wrap around me, jacking my dick, right next to his in his hand, making precum leak out and onto both of us. I groan low in my throat at his touch.

He wipes our precum all over us, up and down, grazing his fingers across the sensitive tips. I can feel how slick it is and his piercings gliding over my sensitive skin feel wild. I love it. It's nothing I've ever experienced.

He breaks our kiss and leans back, still gripping my cock. "Please tell me you have condoms."

"I have two in my wallet."

"Good. Get one. I'm going to fuck you within an inch of your life and make you forget every man before me." The lazy, sexy grin he gives me makes my blood pump harder to my dick. I'm already so hard it's almost painful.

While I dig in my wallet, Pierre goes to a nightstand and produces a bottle of lube and turns down the blankets, pushing them out of the way. The excitement continues to build. I can't believe I'm about to get fucked by my man-crush.

"Get on the bed, hands and knees, baby boy."

Gah! When he calls me that, I just, I just, *fuck*. I should hate being called a boy but how he says it makes me weak in the knees. I love it. I'll be his bad boy, his baby boy, whatever he needs.

A zing of electricity shoots up my fingers into my chest as I hand him the condoms before I climb onto the huge bed, ass up in the air. I've been told my ass is to die for. We'll see if he agrees.

Pierre turns on music that flows through the room, just loud enough to be a soundtrack to us fucking. I'm good with Artemas playing. Fits the mood.

He runs the palm of his hand over the curve of my ass a few times. He pulls my cheeks apart. I know he's just standing there looking over me, I can feel his hot gaze on me, searing my skin with want and need.

I take a peek over my shoulder, "Like what you see?"

A moment later I feel his breath across my puckered hole. Is he…? Yeah, that's it, I feel his tongue slide over my rim. He most definitely is eating my ass. His tongue tickles my entrance and I arch more into the display. I want his tongue on me there and everywhere.

His tongue probes at my hole, causing goosebumps over my skin. I love getting my ass ate and he's surprising me with his skills.

"God, it feels so good," my voice low and husky.

My moaning is completely involuntary. It seems to spur him on. He's making me out of my mind with lust.

"Pierre…"

When he pulls away I immediately miss the heat of his mouth.

My legs are spread wide enough for him to slide his hand between them and run his fingers over my engorged cock from behind. I hiss at the touch overwhelming my senses.

"Does it feel good, my bad little biker?"

I suck on my lip and groan deep in my chest when his grip firmly encircles my shaft.

"Yes, god yes."

"God can't save you here, Declan. I am your king now."

"Please let me worship you. Let me show you how much I want you. I need you inside me. *Please*."

He pours lube over his fingers and more onto my back door. I feel his fingers rubbing over the rim, gauging when to slip in. I'm ready, fuck, I'm so ready.

Pierre's smooth voice gives me another command I'm more than willing to obey, "Beg for my cock. Tell me how long you've waited for it."

Almost taking the air from my lungs, he slips two fingers in my ass as I begin to say, "Fuck, Pierre! Since I first saw you four years ago and you were off limits. I've wanted you." He adds another finger as I stutter over my tongue. "You're the most beautiful man I've ever seen."

He slips in another finger and I about come then.

"Please fuck me, Pierre, put me out of my misery of waiting. I want your thick cock inside me. Fuck my ass."

The condom wrapper ripping open makes me take a deep breath, reveling in the fact I'm going to get what I've wanted for quite some time.

My heartbeat resembles a hummingbird, thrumming quickly through my veins. Scorching me from the inside out. I don't think I've ever been this excited to get fucked.

Pierre climbs up on the bed and settles himself behind my upturned ass. He gently runs a hand down my back, the barest of touches sending chills over my skin. His hands roam over the dip of my spine, coming to rest on my hip.

"Who's fucking you tonight, Declan?"

"You are," I breathe out.

He lines up at my entrance and applies pressure. "What's my name, baby boy?"

I feel the pressure in my entire body. He slips past the ridge of his head, surpassing my tight ring. My breath gets caught in my throat.

He asked me a question.

"Pierre, my king," I say breathlessly.

"Very good. That's who you are calling for as I take this ass. Tonight, you're mine."

He pushes in until our thighs are touching and the burn is delicious, almost unbearable but I crave more.

So much more.

"Fuck, oh fuck." I practically pant.

"Are you ready?" he taunts above me.

Am I ever.

Chapter 5
Pierre

"Yes, take my ass. Fuck me, Pierre. Make me your bitch."

"Such a potty mouth for such a cute Prince Charming. I love it, tell me more." I slap his perfect ass cheek and I exhale harshly through my nose and my nostrils flare. I pull out just enough to slam back into his ass harder.

"Fuck, harder! Do your worst, big guy."

Something tells me Declan can take how I like it. Rough, fast, detrimental.

I dig my fingers into his hips as I pull him back to me, pushing in deeper.

"I love this ass already, naughty boy. Fuck, it feels so hot and tight."

I pick up speed at this already hard, demanding pace. I feel like my body's going to combust into dust and starlight.

I'm so close already. There's precum stringing all over the sheets below Declan. He grips his cock while trying to balance on one arm, which is hard to do since I'm giving him the railing of a lifetime.

Declan is hard, unbelievably hard as I fill his ass to the brim. It's addictive. Don't get me wrong, it feels amazing and I want to come but I want this feeling to last.

"Yes, Pierre, fuck me just like that, baby. Fuck, I'm so close."

I positively growl as I lean forward and thread my fingers in his hair and pull, effectively making him sit up on his knees, his back to my front, without breaking pace. I'm floating on cloud nine.

I feel so alive!

Hell, how I've missed fucking like this.

Primal, brutal, animalistic.

By the sounds falling out of Declan's mouth he loves it too. I love that he's so loud and vocal, his moans spur me on. Thank fuck, I have no neighbors.

I pull his head back so it's resting on my shoulder. I bite the side of his neck then suck, making him cry out. His scent fills my nostrils and drives me even more crazy.

"Such a good boy," I compliment him in a low voice. He whimpers in return.

Reaching around the front of him, I cover his hand that's jacking his cock. I feel how slick and wet it is from the impressive amount of precum oozing out of his tip.

"Do you want to come, Declan?"

"God yes," he sobs.

"God's not here, Dec, only me."

"Pierre, my king," he pants, "Please let me come."

"Yes, Prince Charming. I'm going to make you come like a good boy. You want to be my good boy, don't you, Declan?"

"Yes, more than anything," he whimpers breathlessly.

His breath catches in his throat when I squeeze harder on his hand and make him speed up. I reach down to cup his balls, rolling them around in my hand and the moans I elicit from his beautiful mouth sends fire down my spine.

"I'm going to come deep in your ass. I want you to take every bit of cum you can. Fuck, Declan. Come with me, gorgeous."

I can't hold back any longer. I flex my hips and snap hard into his ass, making him cry out. Hot spurts of cum shoot from his tip all over the bed as he hollers and sobs my name.

His tight ass squeezes the remains of my climax out of me. I bite his shoulder and shudder as the orgasm continues to rip through me. Goddamn, it lasts forever. I feel like I'm floating, zinging through space and time, weightless.

I collapse on his back with a grunt once I stop moving. Holy fuck.

As I soften I slide out of him. I dive over to the side of the bed and wrap an arm around him, bringing him against me, away from the mess we've made. We lay suspended with each other as we catch our breath.

I run my fingertips down his cheek, "Are you ok?"

He's quiet at first until he says, "Yeah. I'm good. I'm pretty sure that's the hardest I've ever been fucked in my life."

My brow furrows, "Did I hurt you?"

"Nahh, only the good kinda hurt. I loved every bit of it."

"Good." After I lay here another minute, I tap his leg that's thrown over me and tell him, "I need to get up. I'm going to run us a bath."

I scoot out of bed, pulling off the condom and on my way to the bathroom, I stop to admire his body. The plains of his sculpted muscles catch in the lowlight with shadows. I commit this image to memory.

I have the most overwhelming desire to paint him on canvas.

One day, it's going to happen. His image will live forever on canvas.

That way I can keep this moment alive forever. The sinful night Declan set me free.

Chapter 6
Pierre

Birdie, one of my besties in the Fab Four, sits across from me in her station at the tattoo studio we run together. My three besties—Birdie, Zharia, and Tally—and me that make up the Fab Four, are closer than ever. We are family. We met back in freshman year of college in this city and have been inseparable since.

They've been with me even before Seven was in the picture. I can tell the girls have always been leery of Seven. They didn't love him, but they tolerated him for my sake.

None of them were happy when I announced at twenty years old I was going to marry the guy I had been dating for three months. They thought I was insane. They don't know the half of it.

They know about Seven's mental illness, the half ass taking his medicine when he's supposed to, and his outbursts and temper. But what they don't know is how bad it really was. I've not divulged how unsettling it was to live with him.

In a fucked up way, it's been kinda nice to have peace and quiet. To have the order and control I crave in my life.

I was always in a constant state of anxiety. I never knew which version of Seven I was going to get when I'd walk in the door home from work. Or when I called him or he showed up to the studio while I was working unannounced.

The first few weeks of Seven's abandonment, I lived in a heightened state of anxiety and desperation. I made myself sick with it.

It wasn't until a few nights ago with Declan that the anxiety that's been eating my soul alive deflated to a manageable level.

I can survive this.

My night with Declan was eye opening.

It was also magical and didn't end until three in the morning, when he received a call from Rock, waking both of us up.

We exchanged phone numbers and he kissed me goodbye, reminding me he's a text away.

Have I reached out? No.

Why, you ask? Because I don't know why.

I'm a chicken shit, ok.

I need to reach out. At least to say thanks. Is that a thing? Thank you texts after fucking someone? I don't know the new rules for hookup etiquette.

Birdie snaps her fingers in front of my face and I snap back to, "Where did you go? Come back here and tell me what's going on inside your head. Spit it out, Lefèvre."

Birdie can play hardball when she sets her mind to it. Sure, she's sweet and motherly, but on the flip side she can be a banshee from hell when the people she loves are threatened or hurting.

I continue to stare at her, giving her nothing. I'm not sure I want to tell anyone just yet. If you tell one of these girls anything, you might as well tell them all with the way shit spreads between them.

I say that acting like I don't get excited about their henhouse gossiping. *Hypocrite*, my mind whispers to me.

It's mine and Declan's secret. Our wonderful night of debauchery getting lost in one another is something I've been secretly smiling about the past few days.

But on the other side of that self-doubt coin, Birdie can help me muddle through some of the feelings I'm having.

Utilize your friends.

That's what I would tell any one of them. *Take your own advice.*

I set the tablet I was drawing on down on the desk. Today I'm playing front desk bitch since my client cancelled and our new receptionist came down with the flu yesterday and was sent home.

Birdie has spent some major time in here disinfecting every surface. She was not scheduled to be here today, but she wanted to come clean. She didn't want us or clients to get sick.

"Ever the bossy princess," I casually throw out to her and she snorts.

She hates to be called princess, unless it's by my brother. Birdie's dad is the president of the Southern Devils Society and he is like a god around here. A king among men. That makes her a biker princess and she finds the title ridiculous. I guess he's still her bodyguard, just now his obsession is on full display.

My stepbrother is insanely obsessed with his wife, with good reason. My best friend is an amazing woman.

My daddy fell in love with his momma at a class reunion about seven years ago. They got hitched, which made me and Lincoln aka Mr. Danger, stepbrothers. We fell into brotherhood with gusto and now he's one of my closest friends and confidants, a true brother from another mother.

Even with this confusing issue, I didn't want to go to him.

However, his wife has no problem badgering me to death over it. "I know something's bothering you. But something is also making you smile more. Your eyes give you away, Pierre. You're torn about something so spit it out. Plus, you've been quieter than usual. You've got those little worry lines between your eyebrows going on." She squishes the skin between her eyebrows together—it still doesn't wrinkle like she thinks it does—"Ya know, the ones you get when you're stressed about something. You can't hide from me. Lay it out for me. Let's talk, fren." Then she tries batting her eyes at me like that's going to butter me up.

I sigh and look out the shop window at Jackson Square. It's a beautiful spring day. The sun is shining through the tree branches. The leaves dance in the breeze from the Mississippi river. It casts moving shadows on the ground that remind me of glitter. It looks like an idyllic day for a carefree spirit to wander the French Quarter.

I have no idea what that would feel like anymore. All I do is work. Yeah, it's made me rich beyond my wildest dreams growing up as a live-by-the-penny family.

But where's my time for living?

I look back at Birdie, who's moved to sit on the corner of the desk.

"I slept with someone."

Birdie's mouth drops into an O and she gasps, more firmly she nods and says, "Good for you, Pierre. How do you feel about it?" *Nice recovery, girl.*

"Conflicted. Guilty. Relieved. Confused."

"There's nothing for you to feel guilty over. I hope you know that. You're going through an emotional divorce. You are allowed to have fun and take pleasure in someone else. You know that, right?"

I shrug. "I've been married so long it's hard not to think of myself that way anymore. I don't feel single. I feel like a cheater."

Her eyes narrow and she stands up. "Please tell me you haven't been tearing yourself up like this. Your mind is lying to you. You aren't a cheater. For fuck's sake, you got served divorce papers." She kneels beside the office chair I'm sitting in. "You know it's over Pierre. Seven's gone. You have to take care of yourself now. And sex is one of those needs. It's a healthy part of life."

"I suppose."

"Did you have fun?"

"Yeah, I did," I get that goofy grin on my face. I can't stop it even if I tried. The one that happens when I think of Declan.

"Do I know him?"

"Yeah."

"Oh my god, I saw you talking to Travares at the bar. Oh shit!" she gasps, loudly. "It's him, isn't it?" She gets a huge smile on her face.

I full on smile right back, trying to hide it behind my hand.

Her breath catches in her throat and she practically shrieks, "Pierre Armond Lefèvre! You bagged yourself one of the finest! Oh boy! Please tell me it was the best ride of your life because that man is as fine as the best wine in the world."

"Shame on you, married lady," I admonish her, laughing. "Your crazy ass husband would kill Declan if he heard you right now." I point up to the camera in the corner of the room that Danger has control over. You betcha he uses it to stalk his wife under the guise of protecting her.

Part of me looks at Birdie and Zhar sometimes and wonders, what would it be like to be loved so completely, with such passion and obsession. Is it as powerful as all the books make it out to be?

"I may be married but I'm not fucking blind," she laughs.

True. Even when I was married, I still noticed Declan. He's hard not to notice.

"So, his name is Declan." She cocks her head and scrunches up her nose, "It always sounds weird to me to find out their real names. I'm so used to their road names. Hell, I thought Shadow's was Shadow for the longest time until Zhar told me it was his real name."

"Don't worry, me too."

"Will you be seeing him again or was this a one-time thing?"

I shrug again. "I don't know. I haven't talked to him since then."

Her brows drop and she practically growls at me, "What the fuck you mean? You left him hanging? Gawwwd damn it, Pierre." She hits herself in the forehead.

My eyes blow wide. "Should I have texted him? What do I even say?" I ask her. Fuck if I know what I'm doing. I haven't dated in forever. It's not like I had a lot of practice in that department anyways. I had two serious relationships before I got with Seven, and one of those was a puppy love short saga in high school as I was coming out.

"Yes! You should have. How long's it been? Jesus, if it was the Valentine's party that was three days ago." She shakes her head at me, "Unless you meant to hit it and quit it, then that's acceptable."

I groan and lean my head back, closing my eyes. "That's the thing. I don't know what I want." I lift my head and look at her startling blue eyes, not so unlike my own, "I don't have a clue what I'm doing."

She stands up and goes to her station to get her rolling chair. She parks next to me, holding her hand out, "Gimme your phone. We are going to see where this is leading. You don't even know what his intentions are. You're both probably waiting for the other to text and trying not to look needy to the other one."

She types away on my phone and when she finally says, "There. Now we wait." She sets my phone down on the desk and as soon as her fingers leave the device, it chimes.

We look at each other before she picks it back up.

As she reads, her eyes start dancing and a slow satisfied smile takes over her face. She starts punching in letters while she bites her lip. She hits send and with a smug look sets the phone down again.

Chime.

"Go ahead and read it. I guarantee you have a date tonight and your old fuddy-duddy ass needs to go buy condoms. You're going to have company tonight. I'd go so far as to bet my pinky on it." She's preening in her seat, happy with herself. I almost dread seeing what fucked up shit she sent.

I open my phone to the message thread.

Me: Hey handsome! You've been on my mind the past few days.

Declan: Oh yeah? You've been running nonstop in my mind too. You have to be exhausted by now <winky face emoji>

Me: Would you be interested in coming over tonight?

Declan: I would love to. 7:30 sound good?

Birdie did what I didn't have the guts to do. Now, I have to decide if I'm going to follow through.

Do I want to do this?

Yeah, I really do. I loved getting lost in his body.

I loved wrapping myself around him and falling asleep tucked in behind him. I hadn't realized how much I missed human contact…even before Seven left.

I also have to decide on boundaries. How far am I willing to take this? Is this just sex or the start of something else? Am I ready for something more? My mind is in turmoil.

Me: *7:30 sounds good.*

Declan: *See you then, big guy xoxo*

I can't keep the grin off my face when I look up from my phone to Birdie. I'm met by that devious smile of hers.

"Sooo?"

"He'll be here at seven-thirty," I tell her.

She does squeal now. She grabs my hands and squeezes them, "I'm so happy for you, *Mr. Irresistible*." She winks at me and sighs. "Oh! We have to call Tally and Zharia! Zhar's going to die."

I can only sit with this goofy ass grin on my face while she bounces around dancing to no music with her phone up to her face. Wait! Call the others?

"No, not ye—"

"Hola, chickie!"

"Howdy, frens!"

The three screens show some of the people I most cherish in my life.

"Guys…you won't believe this. Pierre might have a boyfriend!" Birdie blurts out with no preamble.

All three of them squeal now. I just shake my head.

"Details, mister!! ALL of them, right now. We deserve this juice," Zharia says over the other two, clapping her hands and bouncing in her seat. We managed to catch her in her office.

Tally looks a little put out that I hadn't confided in her yet. We seem to be a little closer within the friend group. I just hadn't gotten around to it.

Clearly, since this call is being forced upon me. A simple text would have done in the group chat.

Birdie quickly slides into her rolling stool and props the phone up so we are both in the picture.

"Who is it? Inquiring minds need to know." Tally's face is full of curiosity.

I side eye Birdie. It's always easier when it's one of them in the hot seat while they sniff out issues like a bloodhound. There's no use trying to deny anything to them. They are vicious and relentless.

"His name is Declan, but you know him as Travares."

Zharia gasps and pumps her fist and hisses, "YASS!"

"Wait! Isn't he the other Top Five cutie?" Tally asks. "The sexy one with the face scar?"

Birdie answers, "Yes, that's him and Pierre fucked him like a bat out of hell." She dissolves into a fit of giggles.

I sit back in the office chair and cross my arms over my chest with my lips twitching. "Oh, you were there for it? You know how it went down? You got all the deets?"

Birdie blinks at me and cocks her head. "Oh, come on, Pierre. You must know you give off big-dick Dom vibes."

I almost choke.

"Pardon?"

"Mm-hmm, yeah, babes, you ooze sex appeal if you haven't noticed. It gives bend-them-over-and-do-damage energy meanwhile they never forget you."

I snort at the two of them when Tally speaks up, "They ain't wrong, muffin. You totally look like sex on a stick and I'm sure there's more than just Declan out there that wonders how hard you fuck. I bet it's like a spiritual experience."

"I bet he leaves bruises and says the filthiest things in his authoritative, calm voice."

I can only stare at them.

"I'd go so far as to say Pierre likes a little BDSM on the side and sprinkles that shit heavily on his dick." Zharia is nuts.

They all look at me while I sit here shaking my head at these feral women. "Ladies, a gentleman never kisses and tells."

"Lies! Fables! You better come off with some deets or we will show up at seven-thirty and get them from the other willing party," Zharia threatens while wagging her eyebrows up and down.

"I'll be there in spirit!" Tally singsongs.

"Well actually, I have Travares's number and I can just text him to get a play-by-play."

Birdie moves like she's going to grab her phone again and I grasp her arm, "That won't be necessary."

"Ohhhh. Shivers girl! Pierre just gave you the stern daddy voice. That was hot as fuck, Pierre. I hope you gave it to Declan too. God, gay sex is so hot." Zharia fans herself. I hope she's at her home office.

"Eww, Zhar, I'm like your brother," I retort when it finally clicks what she said.

"I meant in general and I don't discriminate. I'd watch any one of you fuckers fuck someone."

"Hard pass for me, sis," Birdie pops off.

"Anywaysss…did you enjoy yourself, Pierre?" Tally butts in.

"I did." I tell them honestly. "It felt magical. I haven't had sex like that in so long. How I like it, like there's fire inside me and I surrender to the force of nature that sex is."

Tally gets a dreamy look on her face, "I'm so happy for you getting dicked down finally."

"I'm not sure if this will lead to anything. I'm not sure I want a relationship right now. I mean, I'm supposed to be mourning my marriage, right? If I can move on so quickly, what does that say for the love I hold for my husband? How sacred I held our marriage?"

Staying single sounds like the best course. I can just live in the now and do some friends-with-benefits stuff. That sounds like a good plan. I need to stop panicking over it. I don't regret doing it. I'm just not sure if I can give myself fully to whatever this is.

"Just sex seems like the safer option."

I can give hella dick, but other than that, my well of feelings is dead. There's only darkness and now a spark in my loins that Declan reignited.

Tally smiles and sighs with an *Aww*. "I'm so thrilled for you anyways, Pierre." She hugs herself. "You deserve all the good things. Live your best filthy life and get some sweet ass." She lifts her arm to cheer in triumph.

I chuckle at something so dirty coming out of Tally's innocent looking mouth. She's far from innocent though. *Bad influence* in the dictionary has her picture beside it.

Birdie leans forward and looks into the camera and says, "Travares is coming over tonight too."

It's physically impossible for her to stay quiet about some things.

Zharia throws up spirit fingers and adds in another squeal. "Yay for sexy time! I can't get enough!"

This woman gets plenty of sexy time. She's fucking the Sergeant-At-Arms *and* the Secretary of the motorcycle club either separately or all together. Their throuple is Zharia's dream life and they are giving it to her one day at a time. That bitch is in hog heaven.

It was only a month ago Zharia was rescued by her two men from where she was kidnapped and held hostage by the rival biker club, Lone Star Saints. She was missing for nineteen days and during that time we were all on pins and needles searching for her, going out of our minds.

Now, every chance Zharia gets to love on her guys, she grabs them and disappears somewhere. No hate here. She deserves some happiness.

"I guess your old ass should grab some condoms before going home."

"Hey! I'm the same age as you guys!"

"You might need more than one and I know it's been a while since you last used them," Birdie says as she lays her hand on my arm, "I just want you safe."

I love how she always mothers us. For the life of me I have no idea how she became such a great motherly figure when her own mother was a shitty person who only cared about herself. Birdie got dealt a shit ass hand in the mom department.

Then again, so did I. At least Birdie's mom stuck around.

"Yes, babes, I plan to. We used them last time too."

Birdie smiles. "Great job, Pierre. See, you're already making better choices than I did."

"Samesies," Zharia slides in.

"I'm a born-again virgin; there's no bad decisions for me to make." Tally cracks me up. She's just very picky when it comes to lovers. "My hymen's grown back."

"Girl, not the hymen," Zharia shakes her head, rolling her eyes with a smile.

On that note, I lightly clap my hands together and say, "Welp, let's just hope my three PM large piece doesn't run over on time so I can go grab some. I should have done it earlier when the morning piece cancelled."

"I'll go get them for you, I don't mind," Birdie says, looking at me with sincerity.

"You don't have to do that."

"You would run and get tampons for any one of us. Matter of fact, you have. This is no different. Let me do this for you so you are less stressed about your time commitment."

It would be a huge favor and save me so much time fighting French Quarter horrendous traffic. It could take an hour to go fifty feet.

Would it be so bad to accept her help? She's right, I have gone to the store and bought each one of them private things like this. I've even bought condoms for them.

But we're talking about me and my personal needs. They've never had to buy me things like this.

"Let us repay you," Zharia says softly.

"It's settled. Text Birdie what kind and she'll be right back in a jiffy with them. I love it when a plan comes together," Tally replies, using her no-nonsense voice. The one you don't argue with.

"Yay for teamwork!" Zharia giggles. "We are so going to win best friends of the year."

"Thanks, B."

"Am I getting Magnum fat or English cucumber size?" Her sizzling grin gets even better when I tell her, "Magnum is fine," with barely a straight face. I can feel my handlebar stache twitching.

I know I'm blushing because I feel the heat spreading into my hairline.

Zharia and Tally gasp and start giggling and Birdie just drops her mouth open and breathes out, "Pierre!"

My lips tug into a shit-eating grin.

"Pierre's been hiding an anaconda in his pants the entire time. Who knew. It's always the quiet types, isn't it? Like my Leo." Zharia shakes her head and sighs.

"Great talk, girls, looking forward to the next one," I say before Zhar launches into a dick comparing conversation. I reach up and end the three-way video chat.

Nope, not going there.

CHAPTER 7
TRAVARES

I push the doorbell that's to the side of the door. It's the door that's leading upstairs to the apartment over the tattoo studio. Birdie used to live here until she moved in with Danger. She gave her coveted apartment to Pierre and his husband. Now I reckon Pierre lives here alone.

At least he doesn't have a far commute to work.

The door buzzes and unlocks allowing me to enter. I walk up the stairs and come to a landing that has another door and as I reach the top steps, the door is swinging open and there stands the man who has my heart racing.

"Hey," he says with a smile.

"Hi." Do I rush into his arms? 'Cause that's what I really want to do. *Cool your jets, Dec.*

He steps aside and with his arm he gestures for me to step inside. On the way by him, I can't resist, I stop and brush my lips against his. I feel his lips quirk up in a smile.

"Hey sexy," I whisper across his lips.

"Hey handsome," he replies, meeting my eyes.

I move further into the apartment while he shuts the door. I love how beautiful this place is. It's decorated tastefully. There are pieces of art hanging and you can clearly tell which ones are done by Pierre and which ones are Birdie's.

Birdie is a color fanatic. She's a walking rainbow. That's her specialty so it's easy to deduce the brightly colored ones are hers.

Pierre paints in shades of black, white, and gray, just as he tattoos. His specialty is muted tones with a pop of one singular color to showcase. The one I'm admiring now; the highlighted color is magenta.

I've seen some of the black and greys he's done. He's a master tattooist. Absolute perfection. Even before this bloomed around us, whatever it is, I had already made up my mind Pierre will be doing my next tattoo with electric blue as the showcased color.

"You want something to drink?" he asks as he heads into the open concept kitchen. He turns to me and raises his eyebrows.

"Sure, surprise me. I'm good for whatever."

He busies himself with pouring sodas in glasses. I watch him as I sit on the couch in the living room. My lips quirk up. Damn, in his beige linen pants slung low on his hips and his tight black t-shirt, he looks delicious. His normally styled hair falls onto his forehead, as if he's been running his fingers through it one too many times. I've never seen him this dressed down.

I like it too.

Still hot.

Still want to fuck him.

Still want to rock his world.

He brings over the drinks and hands off mine. Our fingers touch and that exhilarating zing goes up my arm. Does he feel it too?

He sits at the other end of the couch and throws his arm on the back of the couch. "I'm sorry I didn't message you sooner. Honestly, I didn't know if I was supposed to until Birdie ripped my ass for not texting you. Pardon me, I didn't know the current post-*fucking* etiquette."

I can't help but smile. I love the way he talks with his bayou twang.

"It's all good. I'm not sure where I stand; therefore, I didn't text. I figured you'd reach out if you wanted to see me again."

He sits forward with his elbows resting on his knees. "Yeah, I'm not sure how I feel. It's been an internal battle." He twists around, sitting back with one leg drawn up. It dawns on me, he's restless, nervous. "I kinda feel like a cheater if that makes sense. Don't get me wrong, I loved every minute of it and I don't regret it one bit…but still makes me feel like a selfish bastard."

I'm hesitant to ask, but I do anyways. "Do you not want to see each other again and leave it as a one-night stand? Or you want to keep going and see where the spark between us goes?"

"You feel it too?"

"Yeah, I do, Pierre. I want to get to know you. For fuck sure I want fucked like that again."

He smirks and says, "I was hoping you'd say that. I can't offer you more than friends with benefits. I want to make that boundary clear."

I roll my tongue on my cheek and nod, watching him, gauging his emotions, feeling out the moment. I worry this is just his rebound and I've already had dozens of conversations in my head about how I can't allow myself to fall for him.

I'm already halfway there. I think I'm dickmatized after one good ass fucking.

He won't be able to give me what I need. I shouldn't expect it. He's not healed from Seven and I don't want to be the replacement but if that's the only way I get to have him, I'll fight like hell not to catch feelings. I'll fuck him until this spark runs its course and then I'll move on.

Will it break my heart? Most likely.

Will I still go through with this? You betcha.

I'll take whatever he'll give me.

"Ok," I finally answer him. "I accept those terms."

"Have you eaten?" he asks while observing me.

I could totally give a snarky, flirty comment right now, but I really haven't eaten much. One tuna fish sandwich at Shadow's house wasn't enough. But I'll be damned if Gunney doesn't make the best tuna fish concoction around. And it's on the most perfectly toasted sourdough bread he's learned to bake.

Shadow and Gunney are learning to cook now by watching YT videos and a 1980's Home and Garden cookbook Zharia found at a thrift store.

I've been to dinner a few times. I don't mind being the Guinea pig. So far everything's been good. They're so domesticated now. Pussy whipped looks good on them.

"I have not," I answer.

"That's good, because I have food arriving soon. I hope you like po-boys."

"I do, but um, I'm kind of allergic to shellfish," I hesitate to say. I don't want to shit all over his surprise but I also don't want a reaction.

"I got a chicken one and a shrimp one. I have no problem eating the shrimp. It's my favorite anyways. I'll make sure to wash my hands and brush my teeth afterwards so you won't have a reaction." He smiles at me and it melts my insides a little more. *No no, tsk tsk.*

Just then there's a buzz by the door. "Speaking of."

He jumps up and pads to the door in his bare feet. I watch as he presses the button to disengage the lock down below. Then his few steps to the front door, his graceful movements as he walks and opens the door. A few words are exchanged and the door shuts with him heading back this way.

I'm struck by how relaxed he looks. Maybe he's not as affected as I am.

I need to simmer the fuck down.

"What made you go into the Army?" Pierre asks as we finish up eating.

I shrug. "It was an opportunity. I didn't have enough money to go to college and my parents couldn't afford it, so I found a way to pay for my schooling. Who knew I was really good at being a soldier? I moved through ranks rather quickly."

"What did you do while in there?" Pierre sits back into the couch cushions facing me with his leg bent. His arm lays on the back of the sofa, absently rubbing at the fabric.

I sit on the other end of the couch opposite him, angled towards him with my ankle resting on my knee. Our half eaten sandwiches still sit on the table.

"Cyber Operations Officer. It's a fancy title for a computer geek who waged war from a desk. I made a name for myself online under an alias and became one of the best hackers in the world. For me it was all legal since the United States government was ordering me to do it. It was all in a day's work."

I don't normally share what I did in the Army. Some of it wasn't on the up and up though. Please don't think our government plays fair. Rules are merely suggestions in cyber warfare.

"Wow, that sounds interesting actually." He leans forward, "So can you quietly rob a bank and leave no trace?"

I grin at him and say, "Something like that."

He sits back with a whistle then smiles at me.

"I also helped Danger develop the tracker that's in Birdie and Zharia."

He has an impressive look across his face. "I'm beginning to think they should have put one in me too. Either way that tracker is cool ass shit. Good job."

"If you were mine, I'd have one in you. This world is too crazy without one. My sister and niece have them too," I tell him.

I almost forgot the rival motorcycle club Lone Star Saints kidnapped him too at the same time they took Birdie. Both of them were held for ransom. They really worked Pierre over and he spent some time in the hospital, then recuperated at home when he got out.

That was almost two years ago and Danger has told me Pierre still has nightmares from it.

I remember Danger being out of his mind there for a while. His wife *and* brother taken…we annihilated every LSS member there the night Danger went to get his woman rolling a hundred deep of Devils behind him.

"Tell me about having three best friends that are girls. I'm sure you hear some of the most bizarre shit from them," I finish with a laugh.

He shakes his head and smiles. "Ohmigod" he groans under his breath. "You have no idea."

I love how his face softens at the mention of the women. His girls. His bitches, as they lovingly refer to themselves.

Pierre truly loves them like they are his family. I find their dynamic fascinating. Maybe I need a gaggle of girly friends to keep me humble and happy. I mean I do have my sister and she's a super truthful brat.

He lets out a long breath, then smirks. "Well, they are certifiably crazy, as we all know." He shrugs and spreads his hands out in front of him and laughs. "You know it's true. If you tell one something, all the others know immediately in group text. We keep no secrets amongst us and we are brutally honest with each other. We've talked about heartbreak, sex, recipes for cookies, dating nightmares, more about sex positions, which fast food place has the best fries. Stupid shit, and lots of not-so stupid shit, we've talked about it all. But they're my ride or die. I can count on them for anything; they will have my back, day or night, no questions. Just show up with a shovel and duct tape, down for revenge or anarchy shit. I trust them implicitly and would lay my life down for any one of them."

I will give their group props, they are tight knit. "That's some beautiful friendships to have. You're one lucky fella. Have you told them about us?"

"I have." A cute blush graces his cheeks.

I can't help but smile. "And?"

He looks at me through his lashes and grins, "They are very much in favor of." The twinkling in his eyes is adorable.

A slow smile spreads across my face. I passed the first best friend test. Sorta. I'm sure they are more than ok with him fucking someone in order to move on. I know of at least two that are most likely happy it's me helping him get over Seven.

I keep brushing off the feelings of being used. I knew what I was signing up for.

I'm having fun, right?

As long as I can keep my yearning under control and not catch strong feelings, we should be good. I'm already finding it hard not to fall any further than lust and infatuation.

Pierre makes it difficult not to fall. He's great. The aura surrounding him draws you in and sucks you right into his orbit. He's always been an enigma to me. I'm loving this, sitting here and getting to know him better. We've been talking a couple of hours now. It's like a special treat. I'm finding that I like talking to him and just hanging out.

"I'm really happy for you. Friends like that are hard to come by. I should find me a girl posse to keep me in line." I wink at him.

"My only warning is when their periods sync up, make yourself scarce," he deadpans.

I chuckle at that. Sounds like a nightmare. Having an older sister was bad enough; I couldn't imagine three at a time. Fuck that. Not worth all the money in the world. Pierre's a saint or sadist, hard to tell.

Chapter 8
Pierre

"I wish I could say I'm joking. They're like vultures sometimes." He shakes his head with a haunted look in his eyes. This is a man who's dealt with a lot of women shit.

"Anyways," enticing predatory smile, "I invited you back over so I could fuck your sweet little ass again. Once wasn't nearly enough for me." I have no problem stating what I want…now that I know the proper etiquette for fucking in modern times.

I want more.

Declan recovers quickly at my bluntness. He scoots to the edge of the sofa, hanging on my every word.

I let out a pent-up breath and hold up a finger, "I don't have a lot to offer you right now, Declan. I don't know what you want out of this, what you're expecting, but you deserve so much more than I can give, so this has to be casual for me. I'm not ready for anything more. I hope you understand. I want to be upfront and honest with you."

My hands are shaking. Declan's dangerous for my battered heart. He's so likable once he lets his guard down. I've had a great dinner with him and I love getting to know him more.

He looks like he's concentrating and finally he nods, "Ok. I'm ok with it, Pierre." Suddenly his boyishly handsome grin pops out, "Try not to fall in love with me, pretty king."

I can't. I won't.

I lick my bottom lip and suck it in, biting its plumpness between my teeth to halt my smile at his pet name for me. I like it.

I release it when I say, "The same could be said back to you. No catching feelings."

"Just fucking and hanging out then?"

"I'm fine with that arrangement," I say.

"Are you a switch? A verse?" he asks.

"No, I'm not, I'm a top through and through. I'm not versatile like some."

"I don't care to top so this arrangement works out. I'll be your tasty bottom."

"Do you want condoms or tests?" I ask.

I consider this too. The only man I have fucked bare was my husband. I know I have no sexual transmitted diseases but can the same be said for Declan?

"Condoms for now, tests when we can," he replies.

"You need a safe word, baby boy."

"Hmm, that sounds nice. How about tangerine?"

"That will do. Tangerine it is."

A feral smile spreads across his face, "All this sex planning is just making me want you more. Do you feel it in the air? Because I can smell your pheromones working overtime. You have me, all you have to do is say when."

"This is me saying when, Prince Charming."

Declan jumps up and puts his hand out to me, waiting. Have I really agreed to this? Yes, because I want this man with a fiery passion. The way he makes me feel is addictive.

Even in the beginning, it never felt this way with Seven. The way Declan makes me want him is straight up scary.

I place my hand in his and stand up. He steps into my space, placing his other hand on my cheek, rubbing the apple with his thumb. His head dips and his beautiful lips settle over mine.

We're gonna break the bed tonight.

It's a commanding kiss, full of promise, full of fire. I get lost in his mouth and moan out my pleasure. This makes him pull back with a half-smile and he says, "Lead me to your kingdom and let me bow before you. I want you so bad. Take me to your bed, pretty king."

I lean forward and peck his lips again before I pull him to my bedroom as he wishes. The anticipation builds with every step. Shivers skitter across my spine and my cock strains painfully in my pants.

We quickly shed out of our clothes and when he faces me, he has nothing but lust written in his hazel eyes. Declan drops to his knees in front of me and grips my hard rod.

"Do you enjoy seeing me kneel in front of you, worshiping your cock?"

A sudden case of heart palpitations renders me momentarily breathless at his words…because, fuck yes, I enjoy the sight. A lot. It makes me weak in the knees to see him like this.

But it rips the air from my lungs to watch his lips wrap around my rock-hard shaft and my soul tries to leave my body with the first stroke of his tongue over the crown. My slit weeps at the contact.

I suck in a ragged breath and Declan takes me clear to the back of his throat.

"*Oh my fuck, Declan,*" I barely get through my trembling lips. "It feels so good, baby boy. More."

He doubles down and sucks harder while he starts humming, making my toes curl. I'm not going to last long if he keeps doing that.

Declan's lips pop off my cock and he dives in for my balls, licking, kissing and sucking. I use this opportunity to yank him back up to me. I throw my arms around his neck and kiss him with all the arousal building in me. Our tongues wrestle, breathing heavy, chests heaving together, cocks touching. I pull back and tell him to lay on his back in the middle of the bed.

He starts at the bottom of the bed and crawls his way up to the headboard. I watch his perfectly built ass sway as his body moves like a panther up the bed. Sleek lines, muscles working, veins standing out. Fuck he's a wet dream come to life.

Slowly he slides his long, muscular frame around in the bed until he's laying on his back, hands to his sides, cock jutting into the air.

When he grips his cock at the base and gives me a teasing smirk, I feel my own dick surge with more fortifying blood. I didn't think I could get any harder.

Before I set my phone on the dresser I queue up his favorite album he just told me about over dinner—'*Take Me Back to Eden*' by Sleep Token.

I hurry to the closet and pull out the surprises I procured for this very scene about to happen.

"I bought you some things," I tell him over my shoulder.

"Oh yeah? Show me." When I turn around and look at him, he licks his teeth from one side to the other and I see a flash of his predatory canines. I can't wait to feel them bite my flesh.

I saunter over to the bed, dangling the black silk blindfold between my fingers.

Declan crooks his finger at me and taunts, "Bring it on, King Daddy, I'm ready for whatever you dish out, big guy." I love that spark of brat in him.

I breathe out a dark chuckle and smirk at him, "We'll see." I lay the blindfold on his chest and set the g-spot stimulator and bottle of warming lube on the bedside table. I made sure to get the tingly kind. I'm about to set his ass on fire and ramp up his climax game. I'm about to make sure Declan never forgets me.

"I need consent. Are you ok with the blindfold? And are you allergic to anything such as specialty lubes?"

These questions cause a wicked smile to unfurl on his kissable, succulent lips. "I'm ok with a lot of things, Pierre. I'm not ok with fisting though. I'm not allergic to anything except shellfish." He lays back down seductively, hands to his sides. "Fuck me how you want."

"Good. That's real good to hear," I murmur in his ear while I slip the blindfold over his beautiful eyes. I lean over him, brushing his lips with mine, "Be a good boy and yell loud enough to make the heavens shake." His breath hitches. He bites his bottom lip and smiles.

"As you wish," he breathlessly says.

Grabbing the lube and vibe off the table, I trail my fingers down his torso as I make my way down his body.

I slide between his legs and kiss down the inside of his thigh until his legs lay splayed apart.

"I've dreamed of being between these legs again," I rub my hands up the sides of his thighs. He still has a grip on his cock and I lean up enough to lick the precum off.

Declan hisses, *"Fuckkk."*

My tongue continues to swirl on his tip. He lifts his hips, canting his pelvis at my face. I take him deep for a moment then pull off.

He groans and says, "Goddamn that was nice."

I spread him further, taking in the beautiful sight of his puckered asshole. I want to run my tongue across it.

After I lube up my fingers, wiping the excess on his hard cock, smearing it up and down over his balls down to his ass, making sure there's plenty there to get it good and tingly.

"That feels good."

When I breach his tight ring with my two fingers he hisses through his teeth. "That feels even better."

I haul his legs up higher so I have a better view. Watching my fingers disappear into his ass is like looking at heaven. Goddamn, he's so sexy. And he's into me.

He grabs behind his knees to pull them up to give me better access.

"You're so beautiful, Declan."

He whimpers when my third finger slips in, stretching him. I fuck him with my fingers and lap up every moan that slips from his throat. "Pierre..." he breathes.

"I can't wait to be balls deep in your ass. You took me so well the last time." I push in and out with my fingers, loosening him up for my cock. We're both hard as steel.

I reach for the vibrator and lube it up with my fingers. When I push in, he gasps.

"Oh shit, Pierre!" he cries when I turn it on. I listen to him whimper and blubber while I milk his g-spot and he leaks precum all over his abdomen. Like lots of precum.

"Yes, baby boy, just like this."

His head starts turning side to side, lost in the feeling. "I'm ready. Goddamn, I'm ready. Fuck me now, pretty king. Please. Fuck, *please*."

I about lose my mind when he says *please* so prettily.

CHAPTER 9
TRAVARES

Every nerve in my body is a live wire set to kill level. Everywhere Pierre touches me is set on fire. I'm ready to combust.

Flames lick all over my balls and up my shaft. It feels like my cock has a snake slithering all over it. Chilled yet burning up. It's one of the most interesting sensations I've ever had. The lube he's wiping all over my cock and balls and all around my ass must be one of the warming ones.

It works.

I'm being driven wild.

Primal instincts are kicking in and my mind narrows to being lost in feral lust.

Of course, this is all heightened due to my inability to see what he's doing to me. Surrendering to him. To the feelings. To the submission.

I trust Pierre won't hurt me. Not intentionally.

The sound of a foil wrapper pierces over the music of my favorite band. I can't wait to be fucked wild while the Great Vesselonious Marie Token sings Vore to us.

His cock replaces his fingers at my entrance. The feeling of emptiness is short lived as he rubs his bulbous head back and forth across my very warm, tingly back hole, teasing me.

"You look gorgeous like this, Prince Charming." Pierre starts pushing into me and my breath catches in my throat when the first pinpricks of the burn start in. I grip my cock tighter.

I breathe through my nose, my chest rising as I stretch to accommodate his girth. Pierre's cock is definitely an ass-full.

"Oh fuck, baby boy. *Goddamn*," Pierre grits out.

"Don't stop, please don't stop," I beg him through breaths.

Our thighs meet and I feel him pulse deep inside me. He only waits a heartbeat for me to adjust before his long hard dick starts working in and out of me, slow, smooth, through my tight hole.

I can only imagine how majestic Pierre looks above me fucking me, stealing my breath like he's the conductor of my body.

"*Fuck, fuck, fuck*," I chant as he quickens his pace.

Pierre wraps his large hand around my hand gripping my aching cock. "Does this feel good, Declan?" he asks rough and low over top of me, applying pressure to my hand.

Best I can do is make a pitiful excuse of a whimper of his name.

He hitches my ass up more, resting it on top of his bent knees. Enough to hit deeper and milk my prostate. It feels so fucking good. I'm spiraling in my mind.

I've never experienced something so intense with anyone else.

This is a spiritual experience.

I am forever changed because of this moment.

Pierre set the bar so high it's impossible for another man.

In this position, he rails me hard, then slows his pace to do some really good, sensual hip work. Then repeat. Repeat again. Until I find myself yelling with need, the need to come. The need that's crawling all over my skin.

I hear my loud moans filling the room and I can't stop them. Nor do I want to. He said be loud. Not a problem.

No one else has ever fucked me with such passion or determination. Pierre is on a mission to send me into the stratosphere.

My other hand, the one not tugging on my cock, rubs all over him, over his nipple rings causing him to groan, all over his arm, his ribs.

Pierre's other hand slides up my chest, over my pecs, circling my nipples, coming to rest at my throat. He wraps those slender artistic fingers around my throat and applies pressure. It sends a shiver down my spine. Shit. Just when I thought this couldn't get any better.

"Fuck me, pretty king, choke me. Fuck my ass harder, Pierre." I don't care that I'm begging, digging my fingers into his skin, trying to pull him to me while I ride his cock. "*Please.*" I don't care that it comes out practically as a sob.

Christ, I can't last much longer.

"If you don't leave marks, I'll push you until you do," Pierre hisses on top of me. He's bent over so far he can't really be that far from my face. His fingers around my neck tighten.

I dig my fingers into his hips, pulling him closer, holding him there, just trying to get every bit of him inside me that I can, legs spread as wide as I can manage. My other hand continues to slide up and down on my cock. Every nerve ending from root to tip is screaming with pleasure.

The sounds, the feelings, the smell of him—I'm in sensory overload with this blindfold on.

When Pierre growls low in his throat and clamps his hand harder on my throat the tingles fly through my asshole, through my balls and shoot out my cock.

"Pierre…fuck…I'm coming—PIERREEE, *FUCK,* fuck me!"

"Declan, yes baby boy…I'm gonna come in your ass, baby," Pierre says loudly in his lust filled hoarse tone as he topples over into the same blinding, weightless abyss as me. He roars with his orgasm and I feel it rip something apart in his chest. Together we spiral down until there's nothing left in our balls.

He pulls the blindfold up and suddenly I see his beautiful face, his eyes happily lit up, a smile in place just for me and his jaw relaxed, satiated by tremendous sex.

He collapses on top of me, panting. Only our joined heavy breathing is heard in the room while the music still plays.

I'm so fucked.

I should never have agreed to no strings.

Chapter 10

Pierre

Zharia, legs planted shoulders width apart, sways her ass side to side leaning over my island while she stuffs her face full of strawberries. She's forever moving to her own music in her head. I don't think her big doctor's brain ever settles down. No wonder she needs two men to tire her out.

In this instance though, she does have music to sway to. Florence + The Machine plays softly in the background to Wine Wednesday.

We are gathered in my apartment located in the heart of the French Quarter over mine and Birdie's tattoo studio. It used to be Birdie's apartment until she moved in with my stepbrother in his penthouse. Technically she's my landlord. It's hard to believe I've lived here for a year and a half now.

Come to think of it, there's been nothing remarkable that's happened in this apartment since we moved in. It was a stale, beige, wasteland, aligning with Seven's bland choices. I've never much cared how the apartment looked. I spend most of my time in the studio, surrounded by art. The apartment was a place where I slept and ate dinner.

Until it came alive in the past two weeks since I've been fucking Declan in it almost daily.

Mmm. Fucking Declan.

My new favorite past time I've become obsessed with.

He's addicted just as much as I am.

There's not a spot or surface in here that I haven't bent him over or laid him out and had my way with him. He's my very own bad boy who loves filthy things.

While Birdie and Zhar finish laying out the food, with their friend Cherry, I check my phone. No messages.

Cherry is a new face here. She is the dedicated ride share driver Zhar and Birdie met some time ago. She's a senior in college, going for nursing. Zhar and Birdie have taken a shine to her and invited her to our friend get together.

I check my phone again.

Am I expecting a message?

It's been since last night that I've seen him. His last text today was a kissy winking face when I sent him a good morning text, hours after he left my bed.

"Pierre?"

I blink up from my phone and Birdie stands there with her hand on her hip, leaning up against the island with her brow cocked.

I missed something.

"Can you run that by me again?"

Zharia giggles and Birdie tries to hide her smirk. Cherry just stands there blinking because she's new here and apparently doesn't realize how catty these bitches can be.

"I said we are happy to see new faces and make new friends and not to worry, she's welcome in your house as you said before."

Doh. "Right, yes, welcome Cherry." I stand, slipping my phone in my pocket. I come over to the island with the girls. "Are we waiting on Tally?"

Talullah Belle Montellosi lives in New York as a wildly successful fashion designer and she always video chats us for Wine Wednesdays. The Fabulous Four stick together like glue and we always make time for one another.

It's rough having her live so far away, but she does take numerous trips back to see us and her mom.

She's originally from North Shore. Her mom currently lives in Aurora Gardens, outside of the French Quarter. So, her family is not far from here and we love it when Tally comes home to see all of us.

Suddenly, my phone chirps in my pocket. My heart skips a beat.

First off, I should not be having this reaction to someone who is a simple fuck and I have no feelings of attachment for. I have to shut this shit down quick.

Second, I feel the blush creeping across my face as Birdie and Zharia just stand there staring at me expectantly.

"Go ahead, big daddy, answer the text," Zharia purrs, wagging her eyebrows.

"Yesss," Birdie slithers with a devious grin, "Do tell what the plans are for tonight after us. From my understanding, there's been nightly visits every night for the past two weeks."

My eyes narrow at her. "Did your stalker husband forget to take a camera out of this place when you moved out?"

Birdie waves dismissively, "No, there are cameras on the outside of the building. Linx just happened to notice there was movement at night. Nothing nefarious. Not stalking. Just merely an observation." She winks at me.

"So, you been knocking boots every night with your man-candy hot computer geek?" Zharia gets that crazy look on her face. The one that comes before she starts asking a bazillion questions and plotting people's lives. I was hoping this aspect of her would gone away, settled down, completely disappeared when she got with her two men, but noo, by the look on her face it's still alive and well.

And it's my life she wants to meddle in.

I decline to answer.

Her face lights up, "I'm so happy for you, Pierre! No, really I am. Fuck yeah, it's those daddy vibes." Zharia actually growls.

I chuckle because she's ridiculous. "I guess so. Whatever vibes it is, he likes it and keeps coming back for more." I shrug, hoping they will let me off the hook.

Saved by Birdie's phone ringing. That'd be Tally. Great. Another one to bust my balls.

Tally sits in her living room. She has her tablet propped on the back of her couch, while she's huddled up under a blanket in the corner of her couch with a glass of sweet red. Her brown and blond highlighted, super chic New York hair is piled high on top of her head with a pair of chopsticks. She's already taken out her contacts and her glasses are perched on her face.

Without them she's blind.

Zharia waves and blows kisses at her on the screen causing Tally to smile and blow them back to her.

"I've missed y'all!"

You can take the girl out of the South but she will still sound like a Southerner.

We have the big screen TV equipped with a high-resolution camera that we have aimed at the sitting area of the living room and the kitchen island a few feet beyond that.

Declan was actually the one to set it up when me and Seven moved in at Birdie's request just for our Wine Wednesdays.

"I can't wait to come down on my next visit!" Tally says through a smile.

Zharia throws her super long black hair over her shoulder and cocks an eyebrow at Tally, "Things are escalating with Big Daddy over here. We were just about to get the details out of him. Isn't that right, Pierre?"

"No, that's not right. I'm not going into detail about my sex life." I pop an olive in my mouth.

"Ok, then we will make up stories and you can tell us if we're on point. Or not. Orrrr we can just call Travares…" Birdie chimes in.

"Ohh, I love a good story time!" Tally giggles and claps. I know my blush is clearly visible on the apple of my cheeks. I feel the burn.

"Cherry, it's lovely to see you again." I reach out my hand to take hers in mine and squeeze them. "I hope you can hang with these clucking hens."

Birdie slaps her thigh and says, "We aren't that bad!"

I lift eyebrows at her.

I know they can be like that. Bossy, pushy, meddling. I know they mean well. There are times where I do need a little push and their meddling is helpful. It gets me out of the box where my emotions are compartmentalized.

But they've not had a lot of opportunities throughout the years to meddle in my life so they're soaking it up while they can.

Part of me wants to unleash all the sordid details they crave. That would be uncharacteristic of me. I normally don't kiss and tell.

"Things are going well." There, I gave them something.

Birdie snorts and Zharia gasps and says, "You think that will pacify us, don't you?"

Birdie turns to Cherry, "Pierre over here is knocking the dust off his cock finally and he's never told us about his sex life with his ex-husband. He's listened to our stories plenty of times, while we don't even get a crumb from him. We are dying to know how things have been going the past two weeks with his new boyfriend."

"We aren't in a relationship."

"…his friends with benefits then," Tally says from the TV.

I absently nod at her label. Sure, we are friendly…when I'm not dominating him on top.

For the most part, Declan and I get along very well. He says I have geeky vibes that match his. We like a lot of the same shows, music and movies. He games while I read. He likes to cuddle and so do I. He loves takeout while I love to cook.

One thing we both love and can agree on is fucking each other. We can't get enough. My sex drive is through the roof right now.

I can't stop thinking about Declan. And the way my heart swoons at the sight of him or upon hearing his voice, oh lordy, somebody fan me.

After two weeks fucking around, today is the day I started feeling something more. Like a nudge. Telling me to open my heart just a teensy bit wider.

But I can't allow that. That's how Pierre ends up on the short end of the stick. That's how a person ends up hurt.

Cracking open the gate to my heart sliver by sliver is how it gets to be open too wide. I will never get married again. I'll never give myself completely to someone else, just so they can use my love to destroy me. Love should never be weaponized but I feel like that's exactly what Seven did.

If I let no one in like that, I don't have to worry about breaking my own heart.

Have some fun and get fucked. This is my rebound as Zharia so eloquently put it.

"Friends with benefits sounds accurate," I say, then pop another olive in my mouth. I'm reaching for a cracker and the knife when Zharia grabs my forearm.

In a stunned voice she says, "Do you think you'll ever want more?"

"More dick? Or more Declan fucking? Because I'm kinda hoping that stays a constant thing in my life either way." I shrug.

"More…as in a relationship with him," Birdie supplies.

I wrinkle my nose as I place the cracker in my mouth and start to chew, shaking my head.

"Is he not good boyfriend material?" Cherry asks quietly. It's the first time she's spoken.

I take a drink of my wine then set the glass firmly back on the island. Looking up to all their eager and waiting faces, I opt to go with my honest feelings.

"He's definitely boyfriend material; I'm not and I'm not going to be."

Zharia's face falls. Birdie's lips are drawn into a narrow line. Tally silently shakes her head, because she knows.

Since she and I are a little closer than I am with the other two, I've confided in her about being adamant I'm not boyfriend material. Tally and I speak every day practically. That's not saying I don't speak to Birdie and Zhar frequently, I just have a deeper connection with Tally.

I head into the living room sitting area and claim my corner of the couch. I'd rather be sitting down for this conversation I know Birdie and Zharia are going to pull out of me.

With her wine dangling between her two fingers, Zharia prowls into the living room and perches on the chair across from me. She stares all motherfuckingly at me and she can't resist a head tilt in my direction. Birdie takes the other section of the sectional sofa and Cherry sits in the seat beside Zhar. We are all in front of the TV with Tally nibbling on a snack up on the screen.

Here it comes. Zharia's eyes narrow on me with a precision only a surgeon has.

"Pierre, please tell the friend group why you think you're not boyfriend material. I'd like to hear your side first. We have all night. Spill it, so then we can prove how wrong you are."

CHAPTER II
TRAVARES

Club meeting nights have been moved to Wednesdays since that's when the 'other halves' meet and we know they're safe and sequestered away. Hopefully not getting into too much trouble.

Nobody has come right out and asked if I'm fucking Pierre, but *they know*, especially the others in the Top Five. I can tell when they look at me, with their knowing eyes. They want to ask so bad.

It doesn't help that I can't stop thinking about Pierre, or Pierre fucking me, or what my cock looks like in his mouth. Jesus. I can't focus the past few weeks we've been together…doing whatever we're doing.

Three out of the Top Five guys have significant others at Wine Wednesday and it made sense to switch our meetings from Tuesdays to Wednesdays. At least Danger, Shadow, and Gunney don't have to worry what their spouses are up to. They are at Pierre's apartment and I guarantee there's a guard at the door and a handful of associates stationed around Jackson Square, silently watching, listening. Guarding.

The ladies and Pierre always have a tail. I doubt Pierre even knows he has one. He's never said anything about it to me.

Tonight, we are here meeting about the surge of Lone Star Saints in our areas across the home base state of Louisiana. More have infiltrated New Orleans. Lake Charles seems to be overrun by them.

Lone Star Saints think they can come into our territory and steal our people and sell them to the highest bidders. This shit has to stop.

They've already kidnapped Birdie, Pierre and Zharia. Everyone's on high alert knowing these cold-hearted bastards are around. They give no fucks. They're dangerous. And now they are desperate.

Last month when we rescued Zhar, we wiped out their entire security team at the makeshift doctor's office they had her imprisoned in. We killed everyone there except three people.

Zhar.

Shawn, Zhar's friend.

Bonnie, Panhead Pete's wife.

Super unfortunate was the absence of Pete himself and his two right-hand people when all the killing was going on.

It would have literally solved like ninety-nine percent of all our problems if he had been there and died.

"Does anyone have any new business?" Danger asks, his voice carrying throughout the clubhouse.

The clubhouse is a big insulated metal building, finished to look like an office building, nestled in the heart of the Central Business District of New Orleans.

Upstairs is one big apartment with a hoard of bedrooms and three bathrooms. It's for associates going through a rough patch and who need a place to lay their head.

The full bar is being manned by Dobby and Wildman while Slim Jim is sitting at the bar annoying the hell out of them.

I'm seated on the stage, along with Gunney, Shadow and Danger. Rock, our club President, stands beside Danger, rounding out the Top Five. All here and accounted for.

Rock is a force of nature. A hurricane in his own right. That's one man you sure as hell don't fuck with. Sharp as a tack, smooth like butter, and savage enough to run a criminal empire and slay his enemies. He's talking to the probies now, our newly pledged. Probies haven't been initiated yet nor received a patch. They are earning that right through whatever rites we put them through.

This is a chapter wide meeting, so the room is packed. New Orleans chapter is the biggest chapter in the region.

Our club is split into two separate factions.

The majority of the club is just your average biker club. We ride, we have fundraisers for our 'project', we volunteer within our community. We do good things.

The other side, the darker side, is a vigilante group, a small army if you will, who have banded together to stop our rivals, The Lone Star Saints, from sex trafficking in our area. Our area encompasses the entirety of the southern United States, most of the ports along the Gulf coast and those all the way around the Florida peninsula and up the East coast.

Our Elite team, about twenty-five of us, fuck the Saints up on a regular basis.

We kill them.

We destroy their plans, intercept and steal back the stolen in a warped Robin Hood kind of way and make them pay for their atrocities against humankind in spilled blood. All in a day's work.

We take all the poor souls they steal from homes, schools, bus stops, or the streets; we rescue them and give them a fighting chance. As a collective, we are not afraid of getting bruised and bloody for our cause.

There have been hundreds, even thousands of people saved from human trafficking by our efforts.

The rescue comes first, but what comes after that is the true service. It's called *The Project.*

We try to locate their families. A few Sorters are stationed at one of the numerous safe houses all over the territory. They gather information from the rescued folks. That info comes to me and Bam.

While the safe house Mothers are making sure the survivors are clean, clothed and fed, we are already coordinating on different sites trying to locate where they're from. Meanwhile, they are treated fairly, given proper medical care and they are given a comfortable bed to sleep in.

Bam and I take the information and we try to track down where the people need returned to, if they wish. We have a great success rate with children because of the National Crime Info Center's database. Any missing kid goes into it so they can be searched for nationwide.

Unfortunately, that doesn't help the foreign people they traffic on U.S. soil.

Of course, we are searching for any AMBER alerts, present and expired. Somehow—definitely noy by legal means—we have access to lots of shiny things behind the firewall and safety net over at the National Center for Missing Children's database.

If the teen or adult survivors do not wish to return, they are given a safe stay up to a month in the safe house and two thousand dollars in cash to find a place to live or go wherever they choose.

Rock has been known to give a few of them jobs on his docks or at his shipping company. And he recently bought an entire block of apartments, just to house the influx of survivors we intercept from boats or ports on their way to Texas, who actually want to stay in New Orleans.

Lone Star Saints have gotten a fuck ton braver in the past two years. First with Birdie and Pierre, then their brazen abduction of Zharia right from the parking garage of her hospital in broad daylight. We can't figure out their angle.

If they were going after the women of the Top Five they are going to be sadly mistaken when they find out I prefer dick and they'll have to kidnap a whole grown ass man instead of a woman they can overpower easily.

That doesn't seem to be their angle though. Birdie wasn't Danger's when LSS threatened to take her. Zharia said she was told by the Saint's new leader, Panhead Pete, that she was taken because she was a doctor and they needed one on staff.

As they do with everything else, they just stole themselves one.

That was the most agonizing nineteen days when Zharia was missing. Everyone was on high alert and edgy.

Rock's wife died a few years ago, so he has no one to steal besides his pride and joy daughter. That leaves me, and as far as anyone knows, I'm happily single.

Only family I have is my older sister Lily, and her daughter, my eight-year-old niece, Poppy.

That's all I have in this world and I guard it with my life. Our parents died within a week of each other from Covid back when it was a wild and scary time. We lost them early in the beginning of the pandemic when it ran rampant all over the world. My parents were victims of the horrible disease and that left just me and Lily.

I make sure I take care of her and Poppy. Their rent is paid on time, Poppy is at the best school, Lily's tuition to night school is paid. With the money I make from working for Rock and the freelance jobs I take, I'm set.

I live simply. I spend the most money on takeout and food delivery services so I don't have to leave my place.

Hermitting myself away is a very real problem for me. I do make sure I leave my apartment and go to the gym. I'm still vain enough that I want to look good.

I know when you picture a computer nerd you think overweight, pale, living in their parents' basement. Surprise!

I figure I have to spend the money on something. Since I have no real material wants and with my investments and my side hustle with a couple big name firms, I'm golden. I can retire right now and live comfortably the rest of my life. And take care of Lily and Poppy.

But Lily is struggling. I can't imagine how hard it is to be a single parent. My sister carries stress around like a hundred-pound rucksack. It weighs her down and I hate seeing it.

She lost her job almost two months ago and can't find another that will work with Poppy's school schedule and night courses. I've asked her repeatedly to let me talk to Rock and see if he has any open positions in his companies.

Of course, she refuses to let me do that.

Oh Lily, can't do things the easy way. She has to make sure she earns it. I'll tell her tomorrow when I see her for lunch, she's going to have to accept more help, and that help will be me asking Rock about jobs.

"Travares?"

I snap out of my musings and blink at Danger.

It must be comical because he smirks and says, "The treasury report?"

I look at Gunney and Shadow sitting beside me wearing matching smirks.

"Right." I nod and stand up. "Greetings brothers." I clear my throat and look at the manilla folder in my hand that has the monthly report on it.

I just recently got promoted to Treasurer, making me fifth-in-command. Not that I care about being in the Top Five. I think they gave it to me because I've become an invaluable asset to this organization.

I technically worked for Rock as an employee before I became an associate.

Once I give our monthly finance report, I sit back down, trying to keep my mind on business. I have to stop thinking about dick twenty-four-seven.

Holy shit, I've been dickmatized.

Danger stands at the mic, giving the room a sweep before beginning. "I-10 is now where the action is happening for Lone Star Saints. This is the new/old mode of trafficking. Truck drivers are the biggest problem. I guess too many boats have been intercepted for their liking."

The low rumble of chuckles dies out before Danger continues, "We are actively monitoring I-10 and the weigh stations. Last parting thing, make sure you watch your women and kids extra hard in these times. LSS is growing desperate. I've spoken to New Orleans finest and they have noticed disappearances are up six percent from last quarter. We can't confirm it's LSS, but we all know how they are."

That remark received lots of grumbles among the crowd.

"They're up to something again; I can feel it. Just be a little extra vigilant to the women and kids in your vicinity, even at the grocery store. Let's protect women and children out there. Be the eyes in the back of her head that she desperately needs. Peace be with you, brothers. Have a good night and thanks for coming.”

The clubhouse erupts into applause and whistles and clapping. These men are fed the fuck up. I’ve lost count on how many have motioned during one of these meetings to just go wipe their headquarters in Houston off the map. Flush every one of them out and kill them.

We can’t go on a killing spree for obvious reasons, but that doesn’t stop them from suggesting it all the time.

“Hey Hacker, you got a minute?” Rock asks.

The five are left standing in a circle on the stage. Well, all except me who was halfway to the stairs already.

I halt in place and slowly turn around, “Yes, sir.”

I walk back over to where the guys and Rock are standing. Why does this feel like an intervention? Like they’re about to spring some shit on me and it’s not work related. I brace for it.

“We need to know your immediate family so they can be placed under protection. I remember you bringing your sister a few times to the kids’ fun days with your niece.” This man forgets nothing. I’m impressed. “Are they the only ones?”

This is not what I was expecting so I’m a little caught off guard. They want to put a tail on my sister and niece. To protect them. In case Panhead goes after them.

I nod, “Yes, they are the only ones, sir.”

“Ok. Text me their address and a pic of them and I will set it up ASAP. You can choose to tell her about the security or not, either way, I want your family protected. There has been an increased number of small attacks on our members here lately. Petty shit mostly, but you never know when it’s going to escalate.”

I look around at the faces of the men I’ve come to look at as brothers, chosen family. They have been through some shit and come out on the better side of it, but not without some trauma and scars.

I pull out my phone and text Rock the address along with a pic I took about two weeks ago with all three of us at City Park.

"I appreciate your efforts, Rock," I say, "I'll let Lily know when I see her tomorrow for lunch."

Rock claps me on the shoulder, "Excellent. In the meantime, if you need something else for them, please let me know."

I nod and take his hand he's offering for a shake. "Is there anything else, sir?" I happen a quick flick of my eyes to each one as Rock drops my hand.

"Yeah, what's your intentions with my stepbrother?" Danger pipes up.

My eyes snap to him and I watch as his jaw ticks. Being on the bad side of Mr. Danger isn't advisable. Not just because he's my Vice President and superior, but because he's one bad ass motherfucker and as built as I am, there's no way I'm winning that fight. I know my limits.

I'm not sure how Pierre will feel about this, so I go the politest way I can, "That's between Pierre and me."

I watch Danger's eyes darken and feel the ire rolling off of him from feet away. Maybe that was the wrong thing to say. I'm not good with confrontation.

Danger leans in and points at me, "Pierre is family. Don't even fucking think about hurting him." His Cajun accent getting thicker with his threat. Definitely the wrong thing to say.

But I told the truth and now I'm getting aggravated.

"Noted. Are we done here?" my eyes narrowing at Danger.

His fist clenches and he takes a deep breath. He breathes out of his nose and it reminds me of a bull getting ready to gouge out your innards. "Look, Travares, I like you, I'm happy to call you brother. But so help me god, you hurt my brother, I won't be nice about it when I hunt you down."

"Understood. I get it, but I don't know how comfortable Pierre is with me saying anything. I have no intention of hurting him. It's not serious anyways, that's what he wants." I try not to sound like being casual hurts me. I knew what I agreed to a few weeks ago. *No strings, no feelings.*

Thinking back over the late-night cuddles, the conversations in the dark, holding each other and watching TV or just reading. All the loving, intimate moments. I think it's too late for me.

I'm the one going to get hurt in all this.

I should be worried about me, but I'm not. I'm caught in the spiral and I'm riding the funnel until it spits me out. I'll worry about picking up the pieces then.

Chapter 12

Pierre

"Seriously? Who's going to want a broken man?" My hard eyes challenge Zharia's heated gaze.

We've been sitting here discussing all my self-doubt, anger and loneliness.

Birdie quickly reaches to pat my hand and interject, "But you're not a broken man, honey, you're a hurt man. There's a difference." Birdie holds my hand and squeezes to reassure and soothe me.

"I refuse, flat refuse, to let Seven have this much power and control over your happiness anymore. He doesn't get to win this time. Fuck Seven." Zharia flips her wrist around and lurches forward to go on some more, "And furthermore, good riddance to Seven. He did us all a favor by leaving. With how shitty he was to you all the damn time, I'm glad he's not here to continuously slice you open and watch you bleed to death by his dickish fuckery. No, fuck that. Suck a pox covered dick, Seven."

That visual turns my stomach as I give her a dirty look. We all had agreed not to talk shit about Seven.

The group is quiet. Zharia's outburst lingers in the silence.

Tally clears her throat, "We don't need to make Zharia feel like the bad guy, she's only speaking out loud the things we all wish we had the nerve to say." Zharia slumps back into the chair and brings her wine up to sip on. I know her fury over Seven simmers right beneath her skin and I love her for her loyalty and urge to protect me. "She speaks the truth all three of us feel. Am I relieved not to have to speak to Seven ever again? Yes. Am I relieved Pierre can finally start to heal from the trauma Seven's caused him? Yes, again."

Tally looks directly into her camera lens and leans forward, "Pierre darling, I wish you nothing but happiness. And you deserve *sososo* much better than what you have been given. Scraps of love and affection are no way to live. Seven wasn't your happily ever after. But what if Declan is?"

I watch my best friend on the giant TV screen waiting for my response. I look away from the TV to Zhar and Birdie who look just as sincere as Tally does in their concern for me. I sigh and pinch the bridge of my nose. "I'm not ready, ok? I'm just not there yet. Please, let's not disparage Seven."

Zharia sighs in frustration, "Fair enough. It's only been like a month. We just don't like that you're sad and we can't make it better."

"I'm happy Declan can make you smile again," Birdie says with a half-smile of her own, "No matter what it is between you two, I'm glad you're getting what you want and need for the time being."

No matter how much these ladies annoy me, get under my skin, suffocate me with love, I can never stay upset with them. My sisters from other misters. They mean well.

I'm drying the last plate when the door buzzer sounds from the intercom. Declan is right on time.

The ladies left almost an hour ago and I know his meeting ended roughly the same time. The men came to grab their two ladies and I know while they were here they were sniffing out how I was.

It's not just the ladies of the Fab Four who've been worried about me. My brother, Shadow and Gunney are concerned too. Danger, or Lincoln as I know him, has been watching me like a hawk and checking in often. I'm not saying we don't talk or see each other often, but there's been a noticeable uptick in his visits to the shop, or invitations to lunch or dinner, or random texts.

We've probably scared off poor Cherry. She didn't know what to expect and I seriously doubt an emotionally charged feelings dump onto the coffee table in front of her was her idea of a good time.

Once I buzz Declan up, he bounds up the stairs in thirty seconds and I pull open the door to his gorgeous face. Even though I just saw him this morning as he crawled out of bed early for his gym appointment, I find myself missing him more and more and wanting to be around him lots more.

"Hey, handsome," he slides across the threshold to excitedly take me into his arms, placing his plump kissable lips across mine in a sensual, longing kiss which makes me melt into him. When he's near me, all the agitation from the past few hours just dissolves. His touch resets my mood and finally I feel the quiet that his presence brings.

Perhaps that's why I crave his presence. He calms the storms inside me. My mind and body recognize him as a bringer of peace.

"Hey, sexy," I answer between nibbles.

Declan pulls back with a sly smile, "How was girls' night? Talk about anything interesting?" Releasing me with a wicked grin across his mouth, he toes off his boots, leaving them by the door. He caresses my cheek, giving me a sexy wink as he walks off into the apartment.

He knows he was a long-lasting topic tonight.

Once I've locked the door, I swing around towards the kitchen and notice the two bags he's carrying. One's an overnight duffle, and the other is from a grocery store.

"I know you're probably wined out, so I brought over your favorite IPA," he says as he opens the fridge and puts the beer on the top shelf, leaving two out on the island for us.

"How thoughtful." I gladly accept the pale ale from him and ask, "Have you eaten?"

"You wanna feed me, Daddy?" His playful half smile wraps around the neck of the bottle and his eyebrows wagging up and down. I shake my head with my own smile at his taunting. The only time he calls me daddy is when he's in a playful mood. I'll show him daddy if he keeps it up.

"I just need to make sure you're well-nourished for what I have in store for you later."

His eyebrows shoot up, "I like the sound of where that's leading to. But yes, I ate at the clubhouse. Rock has meeting nights catered."

I know from Birdie they only have meetings like tonight's size once a month and there are subcommittees and event planners that have their meetings in the clubhouse throughout the week too.

I also know that Declan has a total of three meetings a week for the club. Some are during the day and he is able to take them on a video call.

And he always comes over here afterwards. He's been here more often than not, although I've been to his massive house a few times. We've been spending a lot of time together and some of it we even have clothes on for.

I love hanging out with him. He's so cool and smart. He told me his IQ once and I told him I didn't realize the scale went that high and it's no wonder he has the job he has. He told me he holds a couple degrees and he anonymously does good things online and left it at that.

I gesture to the couch and we both go sit down with our beers. I want to give him a chance to decompress from his meeting before I jump his bones.

"How was your day?" I ask him as I toss a few throw pillows into the chair. I don't know why we had to have so many fucking pillows on one couch. This was Seven's decorating idea and I just realized I can change this. I can change all of it if I want.

Remodel is placed on the back burner in my mind.

"It was good. I mainly worked on our budget today so I could present any budget changes to the committee chairs. Wasn't hard. How was your day?"

I pick at my label for a bit, still sorting through the emotions of Wine Wednesday and say, "It wasn't bad, but it's better now." I meet his eyes with a warm smile. I'm truly happy he's here.

Like too happy. Tone it down.

Remembering this weekend is a club event, I ask, "Are you going to Family Day on Saturday?"

I drain a few gulps of my beer to settle my nerves. I didn't drink but one glass of wine the entire night. Wasn't feeling it. But all that's forgotten now since he's here.

Sometimes I don't even remember why I'm sad when he's around.

If I'm not careful, I'll become addicted to that feeling.

"Yeah, it's my turn to volunteer. I usually bring my sister and niece."

"Lily and Poppy, right?" I ask.

"That's right, you remembered." I love the smile that spreads across his face. I like how he was happy that I remembered.

"I listen."

"Are you going on Saturday?" he asks me.

Shaking my head, I tell him, "I don't really have family to bring. It's more for the people who have kids. Thankfully I have none of those crotch goblins." I work really hard at not shuddering.

Children.

Hard pass.

They are loud, messy, and destructive.

If I want that, I'll get a cat or a dog, they don't live as long as kids.

Zharia and I are on the same page about this. I don't want to give up my life for child rearing. I like slinging ink all hours of the day and night and not being responsible for another human.

Just the thought of a mouthy teenager trying to sneak out. Knock me in the head with a hammer, I think I'll handle that better than an angsty teenager.

Declan sits up in his seat with his elbows on his knees, "Would you like to go to lunch with me tomorrow? I'm meeting my sister and my niece at *Ochellic* and we would love to have you."

I can't help but swallow past the lump in my throat. Isn't it too soon to meet family? His sister is the only family he has left. This is like meeting the parents, only it's the sibling's approval you are trying to get.

"Uh, I…" I don't even know what to say. It's not like we put labels on this. And now he wants to leap to the stage of meeting family. Do casual hookups meet family members?

Is this really casual anymore?

I'm not dwelling on that hot thought right now. Stick with the current issue.

"It's just lunch. Even if you just go as my friend. You can say no, it won't kill me," he chuckles lightheartedly and it eases some of the constriction in my chest.

"Can I think about it?"

"Absolutely."

I stand up and hold my hand out to him. His eyes glitter with desire. He places his hand in mine and rises from his seat.

"I can't wait to be inside you."

CHAPTER 13
TRAVARES

My neck and face flush at his words. I've been waiting all day for him to be inside me again. Dying to feel him, kiss him, be near him. My skin crawls when I'm away from his touch. I need him so bad it's scary.

I shouldn't feel this way.

He pulls me towards him, sliding his toned body up next to mine and softly, reverently trails his hand down my jawline from my chin to my ear with the back of his knuckles.

Very romantically.

Very lovingly.

Every morning that I have to leave his bed is like the longest day ever until I see him again.

Pierre leans in and as soon as his soft lips touch mine, I'm a goner. I let the wave take me further down, drowning in my feelings. The fire he's igniting in my blood sings hotly through my body when his tongue meets mine.

It's like the waves crashing into the rock. I grab on to him as my lifeline while I gasp for air, running my hands all over him. I'm rock hard in my jeans and the zipper is uncomfortable; fuck, I need to undress and like soon. But I will suffer for one of his hot as fuck, out of this world kisses.

Pierre pulls back and looks deep into my eyes. His eyes are blown dark with arousal. I see this look in his eyes often. Damn near every time I see him. He can't get enough.

I don't know if it's of me, or of the sex.

We seem to see a lot of each other for this being no strings. We definitely spend way too much time being intimate for this to be casual any longer. We both feel the pull to each other. This is different than just a hook up.

At least now it is for me. I want more.

I have to admit it. I'm falling hard for Pierre.

"Take me where you want me, my king, I am yours."

He emits a low groan and gives me a quick kiss before stepping back and pulling my hand to follow him. Of course, I follow.

I'm like a lost puppy and he's my favorite person.

"Take your clothes off. I want to see what's mine."

Pierre stands by the bed looking at me in his lightweight dark blue lounge pants and his black V-necked t-shirt. Goddamn, he looks so good. His arms are crossed in front of him and his thumb absently rubs on his chiseled jaw.

He's so beautiful.

Right, I'm supposed to be undressing not staring and shooting heart shaped laser beams at him.

When my clothes lay in a heap on the floor is when Pierre comes over and holds up the blindfold. That's one of my favorite things Pierre does is take away my vision to enhance my other senses.

He holds up a textured masturbation glove, a stainless steel prostate milker, and an electrically charged silicone flogger.

Holy fuckoli! The night's just got super interesting.

I'm so excited I could do the cha-cha right now.

Pierre holds up blue satin ropes.

Oh gawd. He's trying to make me pass out with arousal. I just know it.

"Is there anything in the gifts I bought you that you're not sure of using? Please tell me and I won't use them on you."

"I'm down for whatever you have planned, pretty king," I hear my voice coming out breathier than intended. Just goes to show how much I want this. *Need* this. My heart stutters in my chest and my breathing turns ragged from excitement.

"That's the spirit, baby boy," he pats my cheek playfully with a grin spread across his face. "On the bed with that tight ass. Lay on your back, Prince Charming."

He swats me on the ass when I turn away and I dutifully crawl across the bed, making sure my ass is in the air and he can see the sexy, swaying invitation. *Come get me, big guy.*

As soon as I lay down, Pierre is over me, one arm resting on the headboard, smiling a devious smile at me. I look up into his dark gaze and heat coils and slithers in my core, clear down my spine.

He puts his other hand under my chin, his thumb resting on my bottom lip. "I'm going to test your limits. Any time you want me to stop, say the magic word. What's the word, Declan?"

"Tangerine," my voice husky and hoarse with need.

He pats my cheek, "Good boy."

God, that does something to me every time. I die to become his good boy always. Something about it coming from his mouth, in that tantalizing voice, drives me crazy.

He puts the blindfold on me and I immediately miss my vision. I hear him moving around in the room, then I hear music. Whiskey Myers plays their bluesy, sultry music and Pierre hums while I feel the bed dip beside me.

It's wild having my vision taken away. It makes everything else so vivid. It heightens the entire experience.

Pierre is beside me, smearing my cock with something wet and slippery. Lube. The air on my cock feels cold, until it doesn't and things start heating up. He's used warming lube on me again. And he's blowing on my dick to speed it along. Pierre steadily blows on the lubed area, intensifying the sensation.

Damn, I love when he uses the feisty lube. Or spicy lube as he likes to call it.

"How does that feel?"

"Mmm, it feels intense." I sigh as the sensations take over.

I feel him everywhere around me but he's not even touching me. His energy: I want to drown in it. Overflow, stretch my skin, turn inside out for him.

His lips, a feather light touch on my inner thigh, causes me to gasp as it turns to a love bite.

My loins truly feel like they are being licked by flames.

I'm hard as a rock and feel myself leaking on my abdomen. How did I miss the sadist side of Pierre? I'm here for it. I want to whine I want to come so bad, but this is blissful torture. I know he'll take care of me in the end.

Tonight is about sharing and fucking until we can't walk. Seeking pleasure, giving it in return, reveling in feelings and sensations.

"Feels so good," I whisper to him, wherever he is around me.

Pleasure races down my spine when Pierre firmly grasps my hard cock and strokes it once. It's enough to make me shiver and goosebumps to break out across my skin.

"*Ohh*, fuck."

Ohh, oh, what is that? *Ohmigod*, he has the masturbation glove on. I almost lose it right then and there. The many, many silicone nubs and soft spikes sliding all over me with the warming lube.

Holy fuck. OVERLOAD.

I whimper and bite my lip, holding my breath, terrified if I take even one small breath I'll come and it will all be over before it can really begin.

"Pierre!" It bursts out of my chest. I grit my teeth.

I'm riding the edge of not enough and fuck, it's too much.

I'm about to break. He must sense it because he backs off, but he doesn't let go. He leaves his hand wrapped around me just enough to keep me trembling.

He has to know I don't need all this to turn me on, he's enough, but fucking hell, this is sweet torture.

His other hand trails down my cheek, down the column of my neck, across my chest. He's all over me.

He pauses and pinches my nipple. My hips cant upwards, eager for his touch on me again. His hand feels like electricity on my skin. He squeezes my cock again finally and my breath shudders in my chest.

"I think baby boy loves when I touch him like this," Pierre softly says across my lips.

He's so close, I want to reach out and touch him. "Yes," I gasp as his hand slides up my painfully hard dick and comes back down agonizingly slow to cup my balls and roll them around in the glove.

His lips brush over mine and the light touch makes it that much more intense. I feel his soft pants on my skin as he wrestles for control of himself.

He's barely tethered to this realm too.

This is my first go around with someone like Pierre and I'm loving it. I think I'm ruined for any other man. Utterly ruined. I'll never find another Pierre.

That thought constricts my chest. But not for long because Pierre is moving on the bed and speeding up my heart rate for what's next.

He's at the end of the bed. That's where I feel him. I feel his energy radiating up the bed to me. I'm very aware of where he is.

The hair on my arms raise up in anticipation.

Pierre's hands encircle my ankle and he pushes up my legs up so I'm spread wide for him.

I hear him sigh and say, "Beautiful."

I groan with need and want.

"Please Pierre…"

"What do you need, Prince Charming?" Pierre asks as his fingertips trail over my calf to my foot, making me shiver as it tickles the hair on my legs.

"Please fuck me, I don't know how much more I can take," I beg in a hoarse voice that I don't even recognize as mine. I don't think I've ever been this turned on in.my.life!

I want this all the time. With him.

I want how I feel with him to last forever.

But I can't tell him that. Never. I've fallen and it's detrimental to my heart at this point.

He doesn't want me like that no matter what his actions say.

No matter what his body says to mine…he doesn't want me that way.

There were rules in place. I need to play my role and stick to that.

I have no time to dwell on that passing thought for Pierre is at my back entrance with a cold, steel ball pressed against me.

The prostate toy.

I spread my legs wider in invitation.
Here we go.

Chapter 14

Pierre

I tried to warm up the steel prostate toy by sitting on it while teasing Declan beside him but I don't think I got it near warmish by the little jump he gave when it touched his skin.

"Declan," I groan while I rub my hard cock on the edge of the mattress. "We'll get to the part where I fuck you within an inch of your life," I can't stop the vibration that goes through my body, it makes my voice husky, "but right now I want to play with you. I want to take my time."

Removing the toy, I hear his ragged breathing. He's on the brink, right where I want him. Anticipation is killing him. The arousal flowing off of him is exhilarating. His need is intoxicating. It's me he needs.

I shouldn't want him like I do.

But god, oh god, I can't fucking stop.

If the pulsing of his throat is any indication of his heart rate and how much he wants me, I'd confidently say he's edged perfectly and I'm consuming his mind totally.

I crawl back onto the bed beside him. I look down on him and smile to myself. I can give heart eyes at him when he's not looking. I'm playing a dangerous game.

I begin pushing my lubed finger through his tight ring, getting him ready for the toy. He knows it's coming and that's part of the reason his legs are trembling.

He takes a sharp intake of breath and I feel him clench then sigh and relax.

That doesn't stop me from moving my finger in and out of him. "I need you riding the edge, Declan, I need to know you're mine. You want to be my bad boy, don't you? My own personal nerdy biker built like a fucking Greek god who fucks like a savage hurricane. Say it. Say you're my Prince Charming."

"I'm yours," he pants. "All yours, my king." He clenches as another wave of pleasure sweeps through him.

When he relaxes again, I add another finger, making him purr deep in his chest. Its rumble is music to my ears. There's so much precum gathered on his stomach. All for me. I did this to him.

I can't resist leaning down and running my tongue through the puddle on his stomach.

Fuck. It's so good. I groan at the same time as Declan. My tongue licks his seeping slit, back and forth across the tip and he whimpers right before he moans deep in his chest, "*Oh, god, Pierre.* I'm yours."

And it's beautiful. His voice is like an angel singing to me.

"I love hearing that. *Mine*," I growl.

"Yours," he rasps.

A fiercely strong protective urge overcomes me. All of a sudden I want to cross a boundary and throw caution to the wind. My chest is dying to burst with it, the feeling I refuse to name. It's surprising to me, it came out of nowhere, but it burns, locked away in there.

Another time. Focus.

"My very own bad boy to do what I want with. Mmm." My fingertips glide across his ribs, leaving a trail of goosebumps. "How very fortunate of me. Do you want to be my baby boy, Declan?" I scissor my fingers inside him while I pick up the electrified flogger. The tendrils of silicone soft, like a caress. But once turned on…

After turning it on, I drag it over his chest.

Declan lets out a cross between a moan and a sob. Bless his heart. "Yes, god, *yes*, please fuck me now!"

I pull my fingers out and he whines.

"Ohhh," I whisper over him. "We've only just begun," I finish in a rich, deep tone, amused at his impatience.

Declan asked me last night for the beast inside of me that I keep held back. Said he can handle it.

We'll see.

I slide the flogger down his legs and his trembling legs jerk. His chest rises and falls with labored breaths. The juice on the flogger is only dialed up halfway, but it's still enough to give a little razzle dazzle to the skin.

With my left hand I place the cold ball of the prostate milker on his hole. He stiffens but relaxes when I softly say, "Declan, you're beautiful. I wish you could see how stunning you look right now. Breathe, baby."

I push, he hisses.

"That's it, Prince Charming, bear down, don't fight me. Let me in."

When the toy is in and his ring clamps around it, I drag the electrified flogger up from his ass, over his cock to his stomach, and he cries out in pleasure.

"Oh my god, Pierre, fuck that feels amazing," he gasps.

I smirk to myself.

Watching him under me steals my breath.

With the right amount of tension, I find his g-spot and begin rolling the toy over it. His hips rise off the bed and his cock jumps. He's jerking his hips, looking for anything to sink his dick into. His moaning is getting louder and my dick leaks precum all over his side.

"Pierre! Fuck, please. *Please*," he begs.

"Goddamn," I sigh, then inhale long and low, "I love to hear you beg, bad boy. A little too much. You want to come?"

"Yes, god yes."

"You want to come on this toy," I give a few slow, firm swipes across his magic spot, "or on my cock?"

"Your cock, always your cock. Fuck my ass, Pierre. I'm begging, babe, make me scream."

I gently pull out the toy and toss the flogger aside. I leave on the textured glove. This is what's going to push him over the edge. It's going to get loud, folks.

I quickly crawl between his legs and push his knees up to his chest, opening him wide for me.

"I want to fuck you so bad, Declan." I rasp.

"Do it, fucking do it now," he demands in a hoarse voice while I lube up nice and good, wiping a good bit on his waiting hole. How sweet and hot it looks. I can't wait to be in there.

My cockhead lays at his opening and his weeping rod jumps between us.

"Yes, bad boy, take my cock, Dec," I hiss as I push in.

"Oh, fuck," his breath catches.

"Open up."

His ring relaxes as he bears down on me. I slip in smoother. Nice and snug fit.

"There's my good boy," I praise him. "My good bad boy."

When my thighs meet his ass cheeks, the warmth of coming home, I pull out almost to the tip and push right back in, stealing his breath.

I bite my bottom lip and groan, "You feel divine, Prince Charming," I suck in air, "so fucking good, baby."

"Pierre, I love how you feel inside me," Declan barely gets out through his pounding heart and ragged breathing.

I quickly grab the warming lube again and squirt a healthy amount in the gloved hand. I wrap my hand around Declan's hard cock and give it a good squeeze. His ass clenches and his breath gets caught in his throat as he loudly moans. "Oh, fuck, Pierre, fuck me…I can't last," Declan loudly begs. His moans echoing off the walls mixed with the low music and my hard breathing as I fuck him.

I snap my hips forward, taking his ass, owning him, hopefully ruining him for anyone after me. I imprint myself firmly in his memories. I waste no time and begin fucking him in earnest.

I tip my head back and groan. His dick is so hard it has to be painful for him. I take pity on him.

"Tell me whose ass this is, bad boy, and I'll let you come."

"Yours, Pierre, fuck, I belong to you," he pleads and sobs.

I feel the familiar pull in my balls. My orgasm is rolling through them and about to barrel out of me into him. I know he's close, ready to tip over the edge.

"Come with me, Declan," my voice a husky command.

He cries out as he shudders, "Oh god, yes, my pretty king."

Declan erupts in my gloved hand, cum shooting out onto his abdomen, hollering my name, the tendons in his neck standing out, losing himself in pure carnal pleasure.

"FUCK," I roar as I come the hardest I've ever done in my fucking life. Jesus fuck. My toes actually curl. He sucked the soul straight from my body out of my cock.

I love looking at the mess of cum he's made on himself while I catch my breath.

Both of our chests struggle for air. For a minute all that's heard is heavy breathing while Florence + The Machine lulls us back to Earth. Holy fuck, how long has it been?

"Are you ok?" I ask him between deep, aching breaths.

"Yeah," he croaks. "I think I died for a minute. I know I was airborne." He huffs out a small laugh.

"Same."

I pull out of him and watch the cum leak from his well-used hole. I love this fucking sight.

I can't wait to untie him, clean him up in the shower and hold him close to me for the rest of the night while he sleeps like a baby.

I remove the blindfold and I get lost in the forest in his eyes.

I memorize the look in his eyes. Sated, pleased, and something else I can't pinpoint.

That flutter in my chest is back when he smiles up at me.

CHAPTER 15
TRAVARES

I try not to be fidgety sitting at this really nice restaurant table. I tap my fingers on my bouncing thigh. Nope, not nervous at all.

This morning Pierre told me he would be here at lunch to meet my sister and niece.

I'm so fucking nervous.

This is a big deal to me. Maybe not to him, but it is to me. I want my sister to know who I'm brokenhearted over so she will understand better when I want no one else for a very long time. Because when all this is over, and it does have an expiration date, so he says, I'm going to need Lily to get me over my first broken heart.

Although, he sure doesn't act like it's going to end. It only appears to be getting better actually. I'm pretty sure this isn't how casual hookups are supposed to work.

Lily and Poppy arrived a few minutes ago. After I receive my hugs and we sat down, my sister snaps her napkin and lays it across her lap. She helps Poppy and turns to me, "Soo, little brother." Her eyebrow cocks up, "What's new?"

She knows exactly what's new. I've been hashing out my complicated feelings with her as a sounding board.

My sister is my best friend. There's no one else I'm closer to. Sure, I have brothers in patches, but nothing beats a sister. Sisters are special. She's soft and motherly, but will straight cut a bitch if needed.

My eyes narrow at her and flick over to Poppy quickly and back to Lilly. I clear my throat, "Nothing's new. For you anyways."

The hostess appears by our table, Pierre beside her. I stand—struck dumb, because *HE SHOWED UP!*—as he comes around to the empty seat in our four-seater, taking the seat across from Poppy, who is looking at him with open curiosity.

I grab the back of my chair and lower myself back into it, facing my sister across from me.

I clear the clog in my throat, goddamn my heart is beating too fast. My mouth is parched and I feel a little faint.

I should not be having this reaction to my *friend with benefits* meeting my sister. *Like he's my boyfriend.*

Like something he doesn't want to be.

This was a horrible idea. I see that now.

I can't leave well enough alone. I just keep pushing his boundaries and skirting near lines to blur them.

"Lily, Poppy, this is my friend Pierre."

Pierre puts his hand out to Lily. She places her hand in his and he raises it up slightly to kiss the back of her hand. "Pleased to meet you." He offers his hand to Poppy and does the same thing.

Her little nose wrinkles up and she giggles, "Your mustache tickles."

Pierre chuckles as he settles back into the chair, "Sorry about that."

I like it. I love when it tickles me. But I can't tell an eight-year-old that. I don't have kids but even I know you don't talk about things like that until they're like twelve, right? Or is it like sixteen? This is why I don't procreate.

Lily is watching me with her eagle eye and processing every little movement and facial feature. I can practically watch the steam pop off the top of her head as she downloads all the data she can gather from this encounter. Which just makes me look around the restaurant and take big gulps of ice water.

What in the fuck is wrong with me? I force myself to look at him. Sitting there so demure, so regal, like he isn't the hottest man in the room, like he isn't turning my blood to lava.

"Declan tells us you're an artist, a very good one."

He turns to pin his stare on me. I melt under his gaze. I'm a puddle at his feet.

Fuck, I'm drowning.

Anything he wants.

He looks at Lily and smiles, "That's very nice of him to say. Yes, I draw, paint and I'm a tattoo artist here in the city."

"I draw too," Poppy interjects. "What do you like to draw mostest?"

"Drawing is serious business to her. She loves drawing in her sketch book. At eight, she's not bad. I mean you can tell what she's drawing so that's good to me," Lily supplies. Then looks at Poppy and says mostest isn't a word, it's used as *most* in your sentence structure. Ok?"

"Yes, Mommy. Thank you." Poppy turns to Pierre and says, "Wanna see my art?"

He looks to be studying her. Like she's a miniature puzzle he's trying to put together. I don't think Pierre's had much interactions with kids.

We aren't to the having kids talk. Damn, I'm barely at the *let-me-call-you-mine* stage.

Boyfriend stage is within my grasp, I think. I'm still far from that line though. Perhaps one day.

"It's so silly that my favorite is a secret. I can't tell another soul or I will perish."

"Like a banana?"

Pierre looks confused for a minute, then chuckles, "Yeah, something like that."

She leans forward and covers her mouth with her hand and whispers loudly, "You can tell me. I won't tell," she points to us over here and jerks her eyes over to her mom with a nod.

She thinks she's being smooth.

Then again knowing her smart ass, she's probably being facetious.

That brings a smile to his face. He puts his hand up and whispers in a conspiratorial tone, "I like drawing silly animals."

Poppy's face lights up. Her favorite thing to draw is animals.

Her eyes assess him before she softly says in awe, "Me too." I just served up her next favorite person to her on a silver platter.

I will kick myself in the ass if she gets attached to him after the first meeting and this doesn't work out.

God, it's like a kick to the balls to think of not having Pierre in my life every day like he is now. I don't know how long it would take to recover from something like that.

I refuse to allow the tidal wave of apprehension to overtake my senses. Now's not the place nor time. I'll reserve the freakouts for when I'm alone in my apartment.

Poppy crosses her arms and leans them on the table in front of her. She narrows her eyes, "Are you my Uncle Ducky's boyfriend?"

Out of the mouth of babes.

I choke on my water and my sister's mouth drops open. After last night, I have no idea how he's going to answer that.

Through the H2O dripping into the wrong pipe trying to drown me, I try to sputter, but Pierre beats me to an answer.

He calmly says, "No. Your uncle is a friend I care about deeply. He's a very good friend of mine. However, I heard you were his best friend."

"Are you jealous?" she asks with curiosity.

This kid, man.

"Yep. Declan's a good friend. Sometimes I want him all to myself. I'm honored to be his friend."

Her face screws up a little and she cocks her head slightly, "Are you one of those fae lords with the golden ring?"

I almost laugh out loud at his perplexed expression.

Lily pops off with a laugh and throws her hands up, "Whoa, little momma," she leans over by Poppy, "we don't throw *fae lord* out in nice restaurants for the muggles to hear. It's rude to ask the fae if they are real in public," Lily winks at Poppy, who nods sternly with a touch of embarrassment at her faux pas.

Lily straightens and looks at Pierre and says, "We are reading The Lord of the Rings series. She's partial to the fae characters."

Poppy nods and says, "And the dwarf. I like him too. Mommy says I have to read the books before I'm allowed to watch the movies. We're almost done."

It dawns over both of us what my niece is talking about then.

Pierre crosses his arms over his perfect chest and hums, resting his thumb on his chin. "I only tell the closest of humans. Perhaps on our second meeting I will tell you my secret." He winks at her and his moustache twitches.

That makes Poppy smile so big and my heart jerks in my chest, making me very aware of the situation I've gotten myself into.

As they begin talking about tattoos and ink and machines, and he holds her rapt attention, I realize holy fuck, this was a bad idea.

Pierre is perfect.

This is really going to hurt.

I'm a fucking idiot.

Back at my house, my phone is ringing beside me in the center console of the car as soon as I turn my car off. It didn't take her very long. She must have seen I arrived at home with her little family stalking app she installed on my phone and calls it family security.

If she only knew how much I can tell about her with that tracking chip she let me put in her. I know how many breaths she takes a minute.

Lily thinks she's sneaky but I know she checks in on that app more than she'll admit. She worries about her little brother.

She has very good reason to worry considering the absolute shitshow going on with this club and the Lone Star Saints and people disappearing.

"Yes, sister," I drawl down the line.

"You got it bad, lil bro. It's written all over you. Your heart is bleeding on your arm. There's no hiding it from me. Does he know?"

I let out a breath with a bit more force than intended as I unlock my house and walk in through the side door, into the spacious foyer and kitchen.

My home is an antique, vintage Victorian. It's a three-story, five bedroom, four bath, white brick home sitting on a large city lot. We pay for all that space too. It even has a white picket fence around the meticulously manicured lawns. The inground pool in the back had Poppy come to mind when I purchased the house a few years ago.

The plan was to move Lily and Poppy in. Lily's been reluctant to the idea. Her crazy driving need to be fiercely independent barely lets her accept small help, let alone me buying a whole damn house and moving them in. It was way too overboard for her. I've been trying to butter her up since.

This area of New Orleans is one of the safest in the city, better than where her apartment is. Its houses are from old money and not many of them come up for sale often. I got extremely lucky snagging this big guy. The neighborhood is lined with beautiful houses, expensive fences and cars and flower boxes on windows sills.

Right out of a Thomas Kincaid painting.

I'm greeted with silence. Until my alarm system says, '*Welcome home, Declan.*'

"I was afraid of that, I tried to hide it, and no, he doesn't know. If he were to find out, we would be done." I answer Lily as I reset the alarm. No way in this town, regardless of how safe the area is, am I leaving doors unlocked or the security system unarmed.

"When are you going to tell him or are you just gonna keep trying to hide it? You're doing a piss poor job of hiding it from me, Dec, I don't know about your other friends, but you aren't fooling me, little bro."

She means the club. The club I've basically forbidden her from including in the dating pool. Not that she dates a lot.

She can come to events but a big fat hell no on dating within my club. I don't want to have to whip a brother's ass if he hurts her or Poppy.

"Fucking hell."

"Yeah, fucking hell and everything else around it. I didn't know it was this bad. I mean you said you were really into him, I didn't think it was head over hills, irrevocably, deeply invested in love with him. Jesus, I don't think you did either. Declan, he's going to hurt you. He's going to break your heart. You're already breaking your own heart."

"You don't know that," I grumble quietly.

"You're right, I don't, but my gut is telling me that and I always listen to my gut. It's never steered me wrong. You're going to have to make a difficult choice in the future." I hear the apology in her voice.

I know she's into all things cosmic and metaphysical and she's learned the hard way to trust her instincts, so when she tells me in all seriousness, "I got a crystal for this," I can't help but snort a laugh.

"I'm sure you do, sis. Do you have a matching candle for it too?" I shake my head because I already know the answer.

I dare not call it her witchy-woo-woo *shit* again, but sometimes she's right. Her little hunks of rocks help. They remind me of her and I smile every time I find one in my home, tucked away while I wasn't looking while on one of her frequent visits.

After every time we hang out for dinner and a movie, I've found little scraps of paper with symbols hidden in plain sight, folded up under a book, a lamp, and even my desktop speakers one time.

The most recent one I've found a few weeks ago, coincidentally about the time I started fucking Pierre, is a small, printed photo of the goddess Aphrodite with a male symbol drawn over it in red Sharpie. It was stuck under my mousepad.

My sister is trying to manifest a man for me.

It's cute. If I wasn't so pathetic in the dating world maybe I would already have a boyfriend and my sister wouldn't have had to use her so-called magic on me. I'm not a put-yourself-out-there type of person. I have the occasional hookup and that's all I need.

Or so I thought.

"Of course, I have a matching candle. Don't forget the needed herbs too."

I don't knock her ways. She believes in it too much for me to mock it. But I do like to tease her about her crystals and herbs.

Sitting on the couch, I lean my head back and it hits the wall behind me. "Couldn't you have manifested me a man who doesn't have commitment issues and who isn't going through a divorce?"

She sighs through the line, "I apologize, I should have closed those loopholes. When I prayed over the photo I asked for the usual: have a job, is nice, loves music and nieces, and can talk about the hoard of romance novels you read nightly." My mouth pops open, as if she doesn't speak truth and I'm not attacked by that. So I like romance…"I was trying for an *enthusiastic compatible partner* I believe were my exact words."

Well, that he is.

"Oh shit, maybe you are compatible with a commitment-phobe and traumatized divorcee. Yikes, I'm so sorry."

"I hardly doubt your gods sent me someone else's husband as my one true love. Especially one that refuses to love again. That would be pretty fucked if you ask me," I argue.

"There's not a soul out there who could deny your feelings while watching the emotions storm across your face when you saw him. You lit up, Dec, you truly came alive. It was good to see. Fuck, I almost teared up. I just wish it could turn out how you deserve." Lily puffs out a reserved breath. Yeah, it's a no-win situation.

"I know," I rub my forehead, "I know. You're right."

"Can you say that last part again? I'd like to record it for playback when I feel like shit about myself." She giggles softly.

It makes my chest rumble with my own laugh.

"I'm scared to bring it up to him. It's been almost a month. I don't even know if he wants this to be exclusive, I just have out of respect. I don't think he's been with anyone else because I'm with him almost every night now. I talk to him all day. Goddamn it, what have I gotten myself into?" I groan, knocking my head back on the drywall a few times like it will knock some sense into me. Too late now, dumbass.

I'm never going to be able to let go.

He'll be free and be fine at the end of this roller coaster, meanwhile I'm left behind destroyed.

He laid these hard lines when we started this journey.

I'm the one deviating from the agreement. I'm the one wanting more.

I should walk away right now if I know what's good for me. This is a dirty and dangerous game neither one of us are going to forget.

This is a different kind of danger and my head is spinning. This has all moved too fast. I keep losing my footing when I'm around him.

"I love that you love so hard, and you're so happy with him. I'm happy you get to meet the love of your life."

My heart hurts for her while it soars for me.

Her husband, Poppy's father, died in a car wreck on I-10 when Poppy was three. Tragic. It almost killed Lily. I almost lost her. I think I did there for a while. She just checked out. Myles was the love of her life. He was one of the best dudes to ever have entered my life.

I've never seen a more perfect couple. They were so happy together and their relationship was goals. I looked up to them and wished for the day I could have a love like that.

"Don't feel sorry for me, Ducky," she whispers brokenly. "I'm happy for you. This feeling is what I've always wanted for you. Love him hard while you can, Dec, but don't lose yourself. Walk away with your head held high when the time comes. Save some of you left over for me and Popsicle."

I can't imagine my life without them in it.

"Never. Always and forever, Lil."

"I love you. Always and forever," she replies softly.

Chapter 16
Pierre

As soon as I arrive at the clubhouse I see Rock's theme for the Mardi Gras Family Fun Day is a circus. And holy fuck balls, circus it is. It's straight pandemonium.

I have no idea how he's managed to get the proper permits to have a whole ass freaking circus in the parking lot plus the neighboring property's lot. And he has two streets shut down.

There's a kid-sized Ferris wheel in the middle of the one street. This is over-the-top. Such a Rock thing to do and I guarantee Birdie had a hand in the planning.

God, money really can buy anything.

I swing my gaze to the petting-zoo in the neighboring building's parking lot. Money can also rent like twenty llamas for kids to ride. Oh, and I see a few camels.

Where the fuck do you even get camels at in New Orleans?

I should have known it would be this ridiculous. Rock goes all out for Mardi Gras Family Fun Day. He loves kids and puts on quite a bit of events geared towards families.

I step out from between cars and the sound of kids squealing and laughing hits me full force then. I try not to dread this part. I'm not a person who likes loud noises. Kids are loud little beings with no respect for personal space and they never fail to *not* listen to their parents trying to correct them.

Kids just don't mind the same way we used to.

Already the screams are making me flinch. I promised Declan. I can suck it up and do this.

Goddamn it, I hate the loudness of it all.

The only loudness I will tolerate is Declan's kind, when he's crying my name as he comes. Yes, that's an acceptable loudness level.

Declan said he would be somewhere in this mess with Lily and Poppy. The chore of finding them in the throng of people is daunting. I start off in the general direction of the petting zoo. Poppy strikes me as an animal lover. As am I.

Now that I think of it, I can finally get that dog I've always wanted but couldn't have due to Seven's allergies. Suddenly there's a peppier step in my gait.

I can do what I want.

I guessed right. Sure 'nuff, there's Poppy in the middle of the goat enclosure hugging a baby goat to her chest, while a few others mill around her bleating in her hair. She's laughing and loving it. Lily's taking pictures of her while Declan laughs at whatever Lily is saying.

You can see how close they are. How much he trusts her. Loves her. He will slaughter anyone harming those two. He won't mind spilling blood over them and I can respect that. I'm glad he has someone in his corner like that.

I hang back and observe them and Poppy. It's almost like I fit in with them.

I want to be in that circle of trust. I yearn for that kind of family unit.

Seven ruined that for me.

I swear I will never trust another man with my heart. Love fucking sucks.

But that's a different love. Watching Declan and Lily makes me feel like I missed out on something as an only child.

Lincoln is the only sibling I have and he's a step. We are just as close as actual blood brothers. Lincoln has saved me many times over with his gentle, soothing voice, pulling me back up to land when I'm drowning in my own thoughts.

I'm super close with my dad but it's not the same as a sibling, not one you've grown up with.

I would still give my life for Lincoln if needed. No need for full blood, he's chosen family. And family is family.

I have four sisters in my chosen family and I like to believe I would kill for any one of them and Lincoln. When I was kidnapped, I was beaten for not giving up Birdie's location. I was willing to die to keep her safe.

I understand Declan's need to protect his family though. He's a target which makes everyone in his known circle a target. I love people that are loyal and protect their own.

That's the kind of loyalty we have. Does Declan have that kind with someone outside of his family? Is it possible?

Really, I shouldn't be wondering if he would ever be that loyal to me.

I see Declan scanning the immense crowd so I head their way. Poppy is the first one to see me. She points and loudly announces, "The Ringmaster is here! Hello, Ringmaster! Over here!" Almost like a cockerel crowing the sun up in the East, Poppy loudly makes my arrival known. People start turning towards us to see what the fuss is all about. *Perfect*, I groan inwardly.

Can't say I was expecting to arrive this way with such a herald. So much for sliding in unnoticed.

Just go with the flow, Pierre. This kid's actually not too bad. Could be worse.

I bow at her, "Lady Poppy, tis a pleasure to see you again, mi'lady."

"Oh, he's good, Mom," she squeals. "Hi, Pierre!" She clammers to the edge of the enclosure so she can get out to greet me.

As soon as she's out of the gate she rushes up to me. She smells just like I imagined a barn full of animals and shit would smell like.

She gives not one fuck because she waves me down to her, closer to the smell. I end up just crouching low because the angle wasn't right and she whispers in my ear, "Do I get the answer to the secret yet?"

She pulls back with a big smile and her eyebrows hover in her hairline.

Ok, this kid, I like this one. She's cool and crafty.

I whisper back, "I'll tell you what I am, if you tell me why you call him Uncle Ducky."

She seems to think it over, then sticks out her hand and says, "Deal."

I shake her little hand and she says, "I couldn't say Declan when I was a baby and it came out sounding, funny, like I had snot on my tongue…but it came out like ducky. You know, like a duck. It just stuck. Ha! You made me rhyme. But sometimes he'll quack for me and he buys me little ducks to add to my collection. Ducky sounds way cooler than Declan anyhow."

I can't help but throw back my head and laugh. Yeah, I like this kid. There were a couple deep breaths in all that but she powered through to the end to perfect her story.

I glance at Declan and he's unreadable right now. I can usually tell his moods, sometimes his thoughts, but his eyes have gone darker and his body seems tense.

"Now, tell me before I pee my pants," Poppy urges.

"If you insist. I'm a Sindair Elf of the Woodland Realm. Don't tell anyone. It will put my life in danger."

She immediately puts her finger over my mouth and whispers, wide-eyed, "Shhhh. We musn't speak about the Faries." She mimics her mom's voice as she says it.

"Your secret is safe with me, Ringmaster. Are you like Legolas's brother or cousin?"

I shrug, why not? "Sure."

"Oh! Do you know Arwen?"

I simply smile like a Cheshire cat. I love this game.

Her mouth drops open, "Wooow," she says in awe, "I know a real-life fairy. Does Uncle Ducky know?" She is quiet like we're hiding secrets, murmuring behind her hand, breathing her little child breaths into my ear when she leans in to talk to me.

She is not as quiet as she thinks she is.

I shake my head and she nods. "Our secret then."

"Yup."

I stand up and face Declan and Lily, who just watched that entire exchange with amusement. Poppy slides her hand in mine and it startles me. I look back down at her and she smiles and turns the imaginary key on her lips.

Ok, then. We have a secret pact.

Looking back at Declan, I say, "Hi. I've arrived in case you didn't hear my royal announcement. I do have one question, why am I the Ringleader or whatever?"

"Ringmaster," Poppy pipes up to correct me.

"I'm sure it's the mustache. The guy playing the Ringmaster has a handlebar. Fake I presume. Not as epic as yours," Lily replies.

"Ahh, that makes sense now."

Declan watches me with hooded eyes and everywhere those hazel eyes touch feels scorching hot like a sunburn from a day at the sunny beach. It gives me the same ooey gooey warm feeling basking in his light.

I'm keenly aware of his roaming eyes.

I try not to preen under his gaze. Or squirm. Or scream "Fuck me now." Or beg to sneak off.

I'm in so much fucking trouble.

So much.

I'm never going to recover from this.

I want to pull him away and take him home with me. Sequester us from the world. I want to throw him on the bed, wrap him up and have my way with his muscular hot-as-sin body. Then take care of him in every way I can, cuddling him all night afterwards.

Basically, the same thing we do every night.

I'm not sure what to do if Declan wants something more. We kinda just fell into this…whatever this is…friends with benefits? Situationship? I don't consider him my boyfriend but I do care about him deeply. That wasn't a lie.

I'm a *love-being-in-love* kinda guy, but I can't allow myself to do that. That would be stupid to do right now. My heart hasn't mended and there's no way I'm going to trauma dump on someone else. These are my hangups, not his and he deserves better. That's why I plan on telling him we need to cool down, back off a little.

Like maybe not fuck every night and have sleepovers all the time.

Like not winding our bodies together on the couch chillin' with the TV.

Or lose ourselves in our books while we lay tangled up with each other.

Or fuck like a storm that rages all hours of the night.

Every cell in my body rebels at the brain's decision. My mind screams that this is lunacy as my cock throbs for him.

We'll start that line of thinking tomorrow. Tonight, he's coming home with me and I will continue my debauchery and worship of his perfect body.

Tomorrow.

It really is horrible of me to keep leading him on for my own selfish needs. I'm using him to escape. More like using his body.

But my mind is using his mind to wake me up, come out of the fog. In him, I've found a new friend. I love hanging out with him. He's easy to look at too, so that helps.

I don't think I could hang out with him without wanting my hands on him, touching him in some way.

His mind is the most beautiful thing about Declan.

Sharp, witty, highly intelligent. Conversations with him are always memorable. Deep discussions about everything under the sun while we lay in bed or cuddle on the couch. I love his rich laugh and how it's so spontaneous. I love his fascination for herbology because of his sister's wanting to try natural remedies. His keen interest in making money and buying properties to build wealth. But most of all, his passion, the fire in his blood about all things techy.

Declan melts when he explains how important his laptop is to him. He likens it to his co-worker, an extension of himself, a teammate, something that he would miss terribly if broken or missing.

He makes me laugh at corny jokes. Like some of the worst dad jokes, seriously. He makes me feel alive and excited about life. Mostly, Declan drives away the numbness I've been walking around with.

Numbness that surrounded my heart, my head, my dick.

Long years of a piss poor excuse of a marriage takes its toll.

I didn't realize how numb I was until Declan kissed me like I was Sleeping Beauty and my life depended on it. He breathed new life into me.

"Do you like cotton candy?"

Poppy's question shakes me back to reality.

"Yes, I do."

The impish smile she gets when I look down at her tells me how much she loves cotton candy too and that's where I should take her next.

I'm picking up your hints, child.

"When you buy yours, will you share half with me?"

"Poppy Maeve!!"

Poppy looks up at her mom, who is turning three shades of red by the time she drops in a crouch in front of Poppy. "We do not ask people to buy us things. You ask me to buy it and not manipulate people into giving you things. It's not nice. Are we crystal clear on that?"

"Yes, Momma," Poppy says softly.

Lily sighs. She puts a lock of stray hair back into Poppy's crazy Mickey Mouse bow on the back of her head. "Ok, do you want your own cotton candy?" Lily asks.

"Yes, please."

Declan's sister stands and sheepishly looks at me, "I'm sorry, Pierre. Don't let her trick you into that," Lily apologizes.

"All good. No harm. But I still want my own cotton candy." I grin at her and she gives me a genuine smile back.

Lily nods and says, "Well, if you're a good boy you can have your own."

As soon as it slips from her lips her blush deepens. "Oh god! I didn't mean that to sound so flirty, I swear to god."

"Nobody thought it but you sis," Declan chuckles.

"Yes, you were! You have such a filthy mind." Lily turns back to me and says, "If you be a good, respectful man you may have your own and not share with a messy kid. There, fixed it. I'm going to stop now. Shutting up."

I can't help but laugh. Her embarrassment keeps digging deeper but it's so cute. She blushes just like Declan.

"Lily. It's ok. All good. Let's go get our treat." I smile at her to make her feel better. I'm not offended. I thought it was funny.

Declan has shared Lily's tragic story with me. He's spoken of how she's been locked away inside herself and how her only focus has been Poppy for the past five years.

Once we procure the precious fluff, Poppy sits next to me on a bale of straw, while her mom and Declan go stand in line at the ice cream truck. She puts some fluff on her tongue and lets it dissolve. This brings her so much joy.

She looks over at me and says, "I like how it melts. Science is cool."

I concentrate on her statement and agree with her, "Yes it is, kiddo."

Here I am, sitting on the straw bale, eating straight sugar while her mom and uncle eat their ice cream cones and talk about her date on Tuesday night. I'm trying hard not to fuck Declan with my eyes. I guess Declan is babysitting Poppy that night and they are planning for it to be a sleepover.

"Do you stay at my uncle's house too?" Poppy pulls my attention back to her.

I look over and down at her. Good gravy, she's covered in cotton candy. How the fuck? So fast.

Poppy is an adorable child. She has eyes a darker green than Declan's and her mom's. She has a splattering of freckles across her fairylike nose. Her caramel-colored hair waves slightly in the breeze. I realize in this moment, this is what Declan's child would look like.

Why does that thought both excite me and make me sad?

I clear my throat. "No, I can't say that I do."

Technically not a lie. The very few times I've been there, I do not spend the night. I always come back home.

I imagine Lily has taught her daughter about gay relationships considering her uncle would have a boyfriend and not a girlfriend. I can't tell if Poppy knows about things like that so it's best for me to stay as PG as possible.

I mean, she did ask if we were boyfriends so she must know something. I don't know what age people have those talks with their children. Why would I need to know that?

Poppy leans in closer to me. She whispers with her cherry flavored breath on my cheek, "I heard my mom talking on the phone. She said she was sure you were a nice man and all, but you were going to hurt Uncle Ducky." Her green eyes bore into mine with all the curiosity of a child. "Are you going to hurt him?"

Fuck. What a gut punch. By an eight-year-old, no less.

In the peripheral, I'm cognizant that it's grown quiet and eyes are on me. I knew Poppy's whispers weren't whispery enough. Kids, man.

Making sure I swallow the sugar on my tongue before answering, I flick a glance over to Declan and back, giving Poppy my full attention as I say, "I promise you, I have no intentions of hurting your uncle." I take my pointer finger and X over my heart, "I swear. Cross my heart."

Goddamn. It's getting hotter out here or it's just me in the hotseat right now, melting under curious stares and the fierce protective energy coming off his niece.

"My mom watches shows where they bury bodies. Don't hurt him." Said in all seriousness with a high level of threat, well, as much as a kid can muster. The psycho killer kid has the audacity to smile at me like a lunatic.

Noted.

Chapter 17

Pierre

Declan's barely through the door before I have him slammed up against it, kissing him with a fervor that's been locked away inside me while I had to innocently walk around a circus holding his niece's hand.

He groans and grabs my hips, anchoring me to him.

My chest hurts with emotions burning through my veins. Emotions I refuse to acknowledge, refuse to accept.

REFUSE.

Tonight, I tell him.

Afterwards.

I grip his hair and pull his lips off mine. I stare into his wild eyes, glassy with lust. His breath comes in ragged gulps. Goddamn, he's so beautiful.

"I want you so bad," I tell him.

"I'm yours, take me," he replies.

I take a step back and start throwing clothes off at the same rapid pace he does. Clothes are flung all over the floor as we make our way back to the bedroom.

I stop him with a hand to his chest, "No, here. Bend over the couch, baby boy. Stretch out and spread 'em."

He gives me a cocky smile then walks over naked to the back of the couch that's positioned in the middle of the living room. He arches his back and bends gracefully over the cushions, reaching his arms down towards the carpet. He spreads his legs, planting his feet more than shoulder width apart.

The last thing he does is, fuck if it doesn't almost send me into a flurry of shoving my dick in his ass, he rocks his ass side to side in invitation.

Ohh, fuck.

Stunning.

I quickly grab the bottle of lube we have stashed in the side table drawer.

I stroke myself as I walk up and station myself behind him, where something sharp thrums through my chest at the exquisite sight.

Declan brings his arms up to the edge of the couch. He pushes up like he's doing a push-up.

"Did I say for you to rise?" I admonish him.

"No, sir." I hear the smirk in his tone.

My hand smacks across his right ass cheek and the sound echoes through the apartment.

"Umph!" is his response and he lowers his chest to the couch again.

Don't feel sorry for him. He loves it.

I take my hand and slowly push him back down by my fingertips. He goes willingly.

"Pierre…" Declan pleads.

I love when he ramps himself up into a tizzy with want and need and he becomes putty in my hands. My same hands that love to run over the dips and plains and curves of his body.

I've been slowly working on a piece starring his body. I keep it in my studio upstairs and I don't plan to show it to him. It's my selfish piece of him.

Long after me, when he settles down with his soulmate, because he totally believes in soulmates, when my sheets grow cold and my heart seals the door shut, I'll remember how he looks in the morning light.

How he looks in the moonlight.

How he looks in candlelight.

I need him because I'm fighting demons tonight and every fucking night. I'm fighting myself, the fucked-up part of my brain that allows people in. Where's the guard to the gate? I'm my own worst enemy.

Declan deserves better than me—a broken man.

Pushing the self-hate away, I lay my hands on him. He sucks in a breath. "Declan, you're so beautiful it hurts to look at you sometimes. I lose my breath."

My fingers trail over his back, over the swell of his ass. I watch the goosebumps form on his skin. "Does my bad boy need a good spanking?"

"Oh fuck," he moans low in his throat. "Yes, I've been a naughty boy…*sir*."

I bite my lip and suppress the grunt fighting to leave my throat. God, I love his sass. Makes my dick harder.

"Hmm." The crack of my hand on his other ass cheek reverberates in the open space. His body stiffens and his body shudders with a grunt that tapers into a sigh.

I raise my hand to his pinkening ass and slap the first cheek, alternating back and force a couple of times. I'm sure it stings.

Lubing up my finger, I find his entrance and start pushing in. His breath catches in his throat and he moans, "Fuck, that feels good." Already his breathing is ragged.

He gets just as excited as me. We're both desperate for one another.

Sliding two fingers into his tight ring makes him groan louder. I push the third finger through the barrier.

"Oh god, fuck…I need you inside me."

"I can't wait to be inside you," I rasp. Because I can't, I truly just want to be buried inside him. The sweet relief he gives me is what I'm craving right now. Along with a good distraction from being in my own head, I love sharing this with him. I want no one else like this.

"Please, Pierre. Make me come on your pretty white couch, king."

I rub more lube on my cock, getting it slick to enter him. He's been giving me fuck-me-eyes all day and evening. It's about time he gets what his eyes have been begging for.

I line up to his entrance and feel him bear down as I enter him. "It's stainproof," I tell him through my groan.

"Shit. Fuck." Declan breathes through the stretch and burn like a champ.

"You're taking my cock so good, Prince Charming." My thighs touch and he knows I'm seated to the hilt. I'm as deep as I can get.

He pulsates around me. I can feel his inner walls fluttering around me.

I barely pull out and Declan hisses and arches his back as I settle in behind him with a slow pace.

I grab his hip as I pull out until just the tip is left in him. I love the sound he makes. I let his ass pull me back in and when I slam home he cries out.

Leaning over him, I reach up to his open mouth and shove two fingers in, hooking his chin and pressing on his tongue. He arches his back up, angling back to me and half sobbing, as he grabs the couch cushions.

This is the whole reason I'm in this spot. There's a large mirror on the opposite wall. I pull his face up and force his chin in that direction.

"Look how gorgeous you are. Look how well you take my cock and beg for more."

The couch starts shaking with our movements.

"You love taking my fat cock. You fucking live for it. Dirty boy, always ready to bend over for me."

I move my hand away from his face, into his hair, and I give a small yank. It's enough to expose his throat and he growls.

My eyes meet his darkened gaze in the mirror. "I love looking at you. Listen to you pant with arousal."

A sheen of sweat coats us both, but in the light, the sweat glistens and shines and my mind goes feral for his heat. I run my hand up his wet back, up to his hair, straight around to his throat. Gripping his throat, I haul him back against me.

My breath catches at how beautiful we are together.

I bite the side of his neck, never taking my eyes off of him and he cries out.

"Oh my god, Pierre, you feel amazing."

In between thrusts and his cries, I tell him, "Stroke your big cock for me, naughty boy. Watch yourself give you pleasure."

"Oh god," he sobs. He touches himself and cries out again. He's so hard it's painful. "Fuck, Pierre, I..please, I need to come."

"Watch us."

With hooded eyes ripe with desire, he watches us. I whisper by the shell of his ear, "Your king owns you."

He breathes rapidly through his nose and mouth, lost in the lust, "I love knowing I belong to you."

"Every moan, every breath, every shudder, it's all mine, Declan."

I know the angle I'm at, he won't last long, not with my cock milking his prostate like that. He's at my mercy.

But I want to see him shatter and he's so fucking close.

I pull him back and take in a deep breath. I try to get it out of my mouth through my own ragged breathing while I pound away at him, "Come for me, Declan. Your king demands it."

It's exquisite when I hold him in my arms and he unravels.

"Scream for me, baby."

He gasps, great heaving gulps of air while he shoots jets of cum all over my couch, crying out for me. His loud screams fill up the living room and bounce around the walls, landing right in my chest.

His pleasure sets off my own. While Declan dirties my couch and hoarsely yells my name, my spine shoots electricity out my ass and I come so hard buried deep in his body.

He watches my face as I come and say his name like a prayer. My whole body shakes with the force of it.

Fuck, I may pass out.

Being with him is beyond anything I could ever imagine.

When my soul slams back into my body and Declan sags into the lush couch, I pull out and I stagger a bit.

My heart is in trouble.

I'm in trouble. I keep fucking warning myself yet I do the exact goddamn opposite.

This whole thing is nothing but complicated trouble.

The mantra still goes round in my head, *Don't do it.*

But do I fucking listen?? Hell no.

My stupid fucking heart is doing it. It's skipping beats thinking about him, it's fluttering in my chest running my hand down his chest.

STOP IT!

It's bleeding when I tell it no. It's hemorrhaging when I say this is not for us and he's not ours.

We don't deserve his goodness.

CHAPTER 18
TRAVARES

The vibration of my cell phone wakes me up. Pierre has an arm flung over my waist and his legs are tangled around my leg. He's a human starfish with an extremely high body temperature most of the time.

Sleeping next to the man is like sleeping in a toaster oven.

My cell phone keeps vibrating on the nightstand. I reach over and connect the call. I sleepily say, "Yeah."

"Clubhouse, one hour." Then Danger disconnects.

This means one thing—we have a mission.

Since we never know the Lone Star Saints' schedule for transporting their victims, when we do hear about it and can locate movement, we head in as swiftly as we can.

Time is of the essence when people's lives are at stake.

Before I lay my phone back down, I peep the time; it's just after two in the morning. I lay my phone back on the nightstand and I take a moment to gently squeeze Pierre and hold him before I have to wake him so I can leave. I commit to memory once again the feel of his skin touching mine, the soft breaths lingering over my chest from his sleepy time lips, and the smell of his soap from our shower earlier that does sweet, molten things to my innards.

I want to lay here forever with him.

This moment is everything I ever dreamed of. Laying in my lover's arms, who's also my best friend now, and feeling such contentment that it steals my breath and knocks my heart around.

How could he not want this?

I would be the luckiest man on Earth if he finally let down those walls and let it happen. Hell, I already feel like I'm his. And he is mine, whether he wants to admit it or not. I see the way he looks at me. I feel it in his touch, the way he caresses my skin, there's sparks where he leaves a trail. It's in the way he takes care of me, just listens to me when I need it, and most importantly, it's in the smile he has reserved just for me.

I melt inside every time he smiles at me.

I gently shake his shoulder, making his mustache tickle my chest. He rouses, but not enough. I do it again and whisper, "Hey, baby, I have to go."

He immediately hugs me to himself tighter and sleepily whines, "What's wrong?"

"Danger called. I have to go. Club business. I'll see you in a bit, ok? I'll be back soon. I'll use my code to get in."

His precious bottom lip sticks out in a pout in his sleep. It's so cute. "Ok," he mumbles.

I move off the bed and regret it immediately. It's fucking cold in here. Pierre keeps the damn thermostat on frozen tundra setting, meanwhile he's like a ball of fire consuming all in its path with heat from the sun.

After I quickly dress, I kiss him on the temple, and I head for the door. One last look at my man and I disappear into the darkness.

"Bonnie has died. Sources say Panhead is losing his mind."

Oh shit. Panhead, the rival club's fearlessly stupid leader, his wife was stabbed and shot at her job as a night security guard. Panhead brought her to the building they were holding Zharia and demanded she save his wife.

Before we left that building, an ambulance was called to take Bonnie to a real hospital. Zhar did an admirable job getting her that far and saving her.

"What happened?" Slim asks. The cantankerous bastard doesn't give a shit about her; he wants any info for gossip. Whatever word of mouth drama he can get to fuel his endeavors.

Slim Jim, Wild Bill, and T-Bone are our resident gossip hounds. That's because they are ancient and have been around forever, and they have one of the largest networking rings I've ever had the privilege to see in person.

It's crazy how many people they know.

However, they're my eyes and ears in the trenches for in person data gathering. I handle everywhere else. I have eyes everywhere. I'm always listening.

Or at least my military grade spyware programs do the listening.

My fingers are flying away across my laptop while Rock, our club President, breaks the news to us. Panhead is beside himself over the loss of his wife from her blood going septic and the doctors not being able to stop it. She died being toxic to herself. I can't say I'm upset. Anyone who can support a man like that is a waste of fucking air.

So, the biggest piece of his life died.

A loss he blames us for.

Because we took Zharia back, thus taking the doctor they stole, who was treating Bonnie. Even though Zharia told him she needed a real hospital. He refused to send her.

Strange that a man who's the head of a lucrative, repulsive human trafficking ring could be such a loving and caring husband too. Make it make sense.

We break up into our designated teams. I hand out the earpieces to all personnel suiting up for the raid.

"Sound check," I say into my mic. All of them turn and give me a thumbs up.

My place is usually yards away, in a black candy van, looking at body cameras and any others I can tap into. I have the radar pulled up and I'm tracking the semi by satellite. I can tell how far it is away exactly, I can tell exact speed and the time of arrival within a few seconds.

This mission is going to take some maneuvering. There're a lot of moving parts and at any second we may have to pivot and change plans.

We have already been briefed on every scenario and what we are expected to do.

"There's an overpass here," I say, pointing to the laptop screen while everyone huddles around. "We are going to end this there. We begin it by surrounding him, causing him to slow down or do something stupid. Let's hope it's the former."

"Target is moving approximately seventy miles per hour on interstate ten. He's approaching the New Orleans area, coming from the East. We will intercept in T-minus fourteen minutes. Typical detain, snatch and grab," I confirm.

The spot is by an overpass. Men are stationed all over that area by the freeway exit. Ditch lines, vehicles on the off ramp that can't be seen until it's too late, under the trusses under the bridge, because there are civilians who are still driving by. It probably won't go unnoticed there's a military team wearing Kevlar and toting guns wandering around a freeway exit.

"We are trying to do everything we possibly can to not make this semi flip on the freeway. Right, Shadow? There are innocents in the trailer and their safety is main objective. Got it, Shadow? Driver is to be detained only," Danger adds.

Man, Shadow flips one U-Haul truck and he never lives it down.

The guys climb in the big black SUV's, and I sit at my desk in the candy van Bam and I occupy for missions.

"Oh, in case there are guards in the back, it's shoot to kill at first sight. We take no prisoners," Shadow informs us and everyone else wearing an earpiece. Basically, everyone on the team.

I love a good killing to herald in the dewy morning light. When the sun rises and shines on the fresh blood of the evil, I know it will be a blessed day.

Fuck these guys with a rusty, dull steak knife.

Bam shows up at the open back doors of the candy, err, I mean mission van. We have to stop calling it the candy van.

"Hey, hacker, does it make your dick stiff when a deadly plan comes together?"

"Not now, Bam."

He climbs in and takes a seat at the other laptop. As far as computer geeks go, Bam is definitely not your average stereotyped nerd. Neither am I, but he looks more like a stupid jock with air for brains.

Acts like it too.

It's hard to tell by looking at him, or even talking to him half the time, he's one of the smartest people I've ever met. He just acts stupid.

Bam has one of the sharpest minds I've run across in a long time. I head-hunted him from Tulane and Rock brought him on after I put Bam through the paces and tested every angle of his mind.

I never saw the crazy though. He unleashed that after the fact.

"Don't be moody, Dec, it doesn't suit you."

"Sorry, *Kill*, I'll work on my customer service can-do attitude in the middle of a serious rescue mission." I roll my eyes while looking at my monitor that's hooked to the side of the van. I'm running a program that will give me the best possible outcome with the most updated intel we have on the semi-truck.

Killian Montellosi tries his hardest to get me riled up whenever he can. Says it takes the edge off, like a good jack off session, to get the blood pumping. Not the visual I needed.

I also didn't know he was cousins to Pierre's best friend, Tally. I never paid attention to her last name, which is the same as his apparently. Her company's called Tally Blue Belle and she never goes by her last name in any interviews or magazine articles. She's always referred to as Tally Belle.

I've heard Pierre on the phone with Tally and you can just tell they are super close. It's an easy flow between them, one that's perfected over years of friendship.

Does it make me jealous his closest friend is a woman? No. I know Pierre. He's not the least bit bi.

Actually, he says when he was a teenager he jokingly convinced himself that vaginas had teeth on the inside that would bite gay dicks off if they're stuffed somewhere it doesn't belong and that's how he steered clear of women.

Alrighty then.

Terrifying.

Anyway, I've only ever met Tally at Danger and Birdie's wedding and even then it was just in passing.

"Matter of fact, I think you should work on being a team player and handing over that program to me. I could do so much more with it."

"We aren't using my program to try and stalk available women for you to plow through. Not happening, kid."

"Not a kid, old man."

I love that it bugs him when I call him kid. He's in his senior year of college and he'll be graduating in two and a half months in June. I happen to be thirty-four, ten years his senior.

We finally set off towards the stretch of road where a huge semi is barreling down the interstate, headed right into our trap. Unbeknownst to the driver, he will most likely die tonight.

We don't normally let human traffickers and their cohorts live. It's just not the Devils' way.

During missions I tend to get quiet. I focus hard. There's a lot riding on my observational and technical skills. Lives depend on my intel.

Bam queues his mic, "Alright gentlemen, let's one and done this truck so we can get home and get some middle of the night dick."

"Shut the fuck up, Bam!" "I'm getting pussy!" Laughter and remarks ring through the speakers. Bam sits there laughing into his mic.

It's not just me he fucks with. It's everybody.

I look over to the monitor where Shadow, Gunney, and Danger ride in silence in their SUV. The triple threat guys.

I know they try to include me but I'm not out there in the field like they are. It's always them. But each one of them has told me they wouldn't be here if it weren't for me being the eyes in the back of their heads, calling shots.

I've heard stories about them from their women. Those guys are fucked. There's no going back for them. They love and obsess over their women. It's amazing they let them breathe without being on bended knees supplying pure oxygen to them. They spoil Birdie and Zharia so much and it's light heartening to see them with their women and how gentle they are. These guys are some rough motherfuckers but the ladies bring out the softies inside of them.

It's been fun to watch them fall. I swear Danger's never getting his head on straight ever again. He takes it all in stride though.

All three men have changed since falling in love and living their lives authentically, how they want. They haven't lost their hardness in situations like this. If anything, it's made them more determined and I think that's because their women were abducted by the same scum of the Earth we are stopping tonight. They're even more invested in stopping the Lone Star Saints and their merry band of accomplices.

I watch body cams get into trucks and SUVs. It will take them approximately four minutes to reach where the truck will be detained on the interstate. They will arrive three minutes before the truck. The moving team boxing in on the truck is already in position on either side of the truck.

At this time of night hardly anyone is out on the roads, which makes it better for us. Less innocent casualties.

I'm monitoring the trucks speed and direction by satellite and the team starts sounding off letting us know they are in position.

"T-minus three minutes," I warn.

Bam sits behind me humming '*Icky Thump*' under his breath. I just shake my head.

He's watching the backs of our men in the vehicles surrounding the truck. He's watching a broader view from satellite, one where we can see if there's anyone following our entourage.

When our guys reach the truck, who's driving in the center lane of the three-lane highway, our men surround the semi. The Hummer cuts in front while two blacked out SUVs pull up beside the rig, one at each door.

Danger pops out the opening of the Hummer at the same time Gunney and Shadow pop out of the sunroofs in the SUVs.

Mr. Danger points his gun at the driver and signals him to pull over. For a very tense few minutes it seems the driver isn't going to comply. Slowly he eases the truck to the berm and comes to a stop, holding up his hands from the steering wheel.

Men swarm the truck at all angles. It's happening so fast you almost can't keep up with all the movement.

Almost.

I have a tracking system in the earpieces and on the screen to my right I can see all their forms moving as a computer program maps their movements. To the untrained eye, it probably looks like a video game.

"We have incoming. Six o'clock, an SUV headed your way," Bam warns them.

We watch as the SUV slows down and comes to a gentle stop alongside the trailer of the semi-truck, right by Danger.

Suddenly, Danger's voice comes through the tiny speakers in our ears, "Detective Berry, how lovely to see you tonight. It might be best if you drive on by and pretend you never saw us."

Detective Berry can be heard speaking, "How many this time, Danger?"

Detective Berry is the only cop we trust. He's one of us but turns a blind eye to the Elite Team. He's more of a charity kinda guy. I'm sure he heard through the grapevine a mission was being done tonight. This is not a coincidence, him appearing like this.

"Almost sixty," Danger informs him.

I check the police scanner to track where the rest of them are hiding and prowling the city. We are still good. They are a good ten minutes away. By then we will already have the victims loaded in the buses that just pulled in behind the truck and are ready to whisk them off to the safe houses.

It looks like this batch came from Cuba. It burns my ass these sick fucks get away with more than what we can catch.

The buses are getting fuller by the minute.

Everything is going as planned. Most of our missions run smoothly. We rarely ever have a hiccup. We are in and out in less than ten minutes.

There's usually an interpreter on the buses waiting for the victims to pile in. We've ran across instances where the people don't speak English. Now an interpreter is mandatory.

Of course, he's part of the Elite Team and has sworn with his life to secrecy. Also, a nifty, iron tight NDA, just like everyone else signs.

Rock doesn't sue snitches. They die.

"Incoming. A car coming up from the rear," Bam warns again. His eagle eye is trained on the screen watching the car approach.

Thankfully they pass by, no brake lights.

Once the buses are full and pulling away and the driver is detained, we all let out a big sigh of relief and pack up to head back to the clubhouse.

"You gonna go fuck your boytoy when you slip back in at dawn?" Bam taunts me.

"Don't call him that."

"Ohh ho, pretty boy's done caught feelings. You know, that's a big no-no with FWBs?"

I practically growl at him, "I'm aware. Mind your own business."

"I can't wait to see how this pans out. I'd like to go on record now and say I told you so when he breaks your heart."

Bam's words echo through my mind when I slide between the sheets and pull Pierre's sleeping form to me. In the blacked-out room I can almost imagine the rest of the world doesn't exist and he's all mine.

I have a sinking feeling he'll never be mine though.

CHAPTER 19
TRAVARES

I can't sleep that well, tossing and turning, so I'm up by eight. Pierre is still sleeping soundly as I tiptoe out of the bedroom, softly closing the door.

I fiddle with the coffee maker and finally get it to work. It's been a few weeks since Pierre and I have been on much *friendlier* terms.

Fucking, that's what we're doing. Lots of it.

I spend the next few hours completing my report for last night on my laptop at his dining room table. I make sure to catalog every move and use the timestamps from the videos. I need this report completed by one this afternoon, where I have to send it to Rock, encrypted of course, so when we have our meeting at two we have an accurate account of the mission to review.

Honestly, I don't think it could have gone any smoother than it did. It was a classic textbook Fuck Up LSS mission.

The bedroom door opens and it pulls me out of my trip down memory lane. For now, it relieves me of the duty of clipping together videos for the review.

A smile spreads across my face as a flash of heat hits my loins upon seeing him.

Pierre comes out rubbing his eyes in nothing but a pair of sleep pants, slung low on those slim hips. That V has me biting my lip. His well-defined tattooed torso and arms on display make my janky heart stumble and fall. Jesus, he's gorgeous. That sleep tousled look is working for him.

He comes over and kisses the top of my head and I put my arms around his waist. He rests his arms around my neck.

"What time did you get back in?" he runs his fingers through my hair and I close my eyes, soaking up his affection.

"A little after five."

"Damn. What time did you get up?"

"Around eight."

He tsks to himself, and possibly me. "You should still be asleep." He yawns to drive his point home. Still so cute. I want to crawl inside him and hum with happiness. Ugh, stop.

My ass is sore and I can't be provoking him to bend me over again so soon. I need a little recovery time. Pierre is a fucking god in the bedroom.

With that said, it was a damn fine excellent night.

"It's eleven, Pierre. Your kingdom awaits. If you want to show up to work on time today you should get a move on. While you're in the shower, I'll fix you something to eat." I pat him on the ass as he bends over to kiss me. His lips linger just a while longer than expected. A small hesitation.

"You take such good care of me."

Normally he doesn't work on Sundays, but he has a big high-profile client that wants absolute privacy. The shop must be shut down and the blinds pulled. The guy is willing to pay out the ass for this.

Pierre's the best in the business for black and gray tattoos. No one can match his skill—competition proven, nationwide voted. He's won Best B&W Artist of the Year four times. His clients are prepared to throw down a huge chunk of dough to sit in his chair.

I casually lean against the counter, sipping my coffee, contemplating how my life has ended up here. This coffee tastes a lot like existential crisis and anxiety.

The time reads eleven-oh-nine. I pop his secret sin into the toaster—his frozen waffles. I'm stretching with my arms up over my head when a knock sounds at the door.

It's not even ten minutes after Pierre goes into the bedroom. I wait to see if Pierre hears it and comes to answer it.

I'm not sure he wants me to answer his door.

But the knock comes again, more urgent this time. Not that I'm one to normally answer someone else's door, but the third impatient knock drives me to open the damn thing.

I pull it open and a man inches shorter than me, blond mussed up hair, dark circles under his eyes, stands there staring me up and down.

There is a look of shock on his face. His eyes travel down from my face to my bare chest then basketball shorts—that hide nothing without my underwear on—and back up.

His gaze lingers on my shirtless chest just before he snaps out of his perusal of me and a scowl takes over his face as it registers to him that I'm not Pierre. His mouth gapes open.

"Who the fuck are you?"

I cock an eyebrow at him and wait.

His mouth snaps shut and that's when the anger simmers around him, slithering like a snake, ready to strike.

"Who are you?" he tries again, slower, lower, with veiled fury.

"Did you really come here to find out who I am?"

Instantly he sneers, "No. I came here to see my husband."

Ahhh, this is Seven.

"But I clearly see why he's been too busy to answer his phone."

I give a calculated smile. "That he has. He's been very busy. I been fucking him like you wouldn't."

There are flames in his eyes and I watch his jaw work. I'm sure there's plenty he wants to say to me but he's too intimidated to say it. I've got a good six inches on him and I have way more bulk than him. He doesn't stand a chance starting shit with me.

But he wants to. It oozes off of him.

He wants to swing on me. Rip my face off in jealousy. For someone who wants nothing to do with his spouse, jealousy is a surprise reaction to me.

"Are you going to let me into my own house?"

"I don't think I can do that. I shouldn't let anyone into *his* house that Pierre doesn't want here. That includes you."

He's furious.

I'm giddy.

Damn. I've always wanted to see the jerk Pierre was married to.

Seven's the mystery man. He never came to club events with Pierre. That would have been the only opportunity to have been introduced to him.

He's nothing to look at. Pierre is upgrading, tooting my own horn if I may.

I instantly hate him. Not just on principle, not just because from the grave of their dead marriage he's still ruining Pierre's life, or I should say the one he could have if he'd open up to it. I hate this guy because he's an asshole.

"Where's Pierre? I demand to talk to him right now."

Oh? We demand, do we?

The entitled attitude flowing off this asshole…makes me want to punch him right in his self-righteous mouth.

"In the shower," I reply with another sly smirk.

"Get the fuck outta my way, gym rat. Or whatever other gutter he pulled you from."

I have to hand it to him; he has guts saying shit like that to someone like me. He doesn't know I'm a government trained killer. He's just going to pop off the mouth and start making demands like a petulant child.

"That's not going to happen without Pierre's permission and we both know it."

His lip curls into a snarl. Now he's really mad.

And I'm still giddy.

Tickled pink at annoying him.

I should be nice. He did me a favor. A huge solid when he left Pierre and left him wide open for someone who will treat him as he deserves. The trash took itself out.

But yet here he is on the doorstep, like a stubborn piece of dogshit on the bottom of your shoe.

"Declan, baby?" Pierre calls from within the apartment. "Where are you?"

"At the door, my love, you have a visitor."

Seven looks like he's having a coronary now. His face is flushed red and his face is a mask of hatred. Oh, this guy immediately hated me before, now he positively loathes me.

"Who is it?" Pierre stops dead in his tracks coming around the island into the living space upon seeing Seven in the doorway.

"What are you doing here, Seven?" Pierre asks, shocked to see him. He has one of his peasant tops on with a pair of black slacks and his wing tipped dress shoes. He looks smashingly fuckable right now. And the cologne floating over to me makes my cock twitch in these not-fit-for-public shorts.

It's going to be a situation here soon if I'm not careful.

"Your fucktoy here won't let me in my own house." Seven's just going to start rage whining. Not his best move.

I level him a lethal look, gone is my nice, playful side. "Watch your fucking tone with him," I growl at him and his eyes go wide.

He continues in a hurry, "I need to talk to you. Let me come in."

"This isn't your house any longer and I don't have anything to say to you, Seven."

"But I have stuff to say to you." You can tell he does not like being told no, like Pierre probably never told him no.

My eyes stay locked on Seven on the doorstep. This elitest prick never deserved Pierre. I don't know what he saw in this fake ass jerk.

Pierre sighs. "Let him in, Declan."

I expected this. I knew Pierre would cave. He wants the closure he feels he deserves so bad. But he won't recognize that Seven is too shallow to ever give it to him.

Yet here he stands. More like breezing right past me. He stops just inside the living room.

I shut the door and make my way around Seven, and the discarded clothing from last night—that Seven is gaping at now—which are trailing straight for the bedroom. Coming alongside Pierre, I run my hand across his chest and tell him by his ear as I lean into him, just loud enough for Seven to hear also, "I'll be in the shower."

My eyes on Seven, I lean in and kiss Pierre's cheek.

One last withering glance at Seven and I strut to the bedroom.

Once the door closes, I don't move away from it. Yes, absolutely, I plan to eavesdrop on this conversation. No shame.

Pierre's muffled voice comes through, "Why are you here, Seven?"

"I would ask how you've been but I can clearly see you're just fine." I can picture the sneer on Seven's face.

"Get to the point." Pierre sounds exasperated.

"Who is he?"

"None of your business. Just tell me what you have to say and then leave."

"I want to know who's in my house."

"Once again, not your house and not your business."

"I need you to sign the divorce papers."

So, that's why he's here.

"I'm not giving you half a million dollars, Seven, absolutely not."

What the fuck? That's a shitload of money to ask for in a divorce. I knew Pierre was a master at his art but I didn't know he was rich from it. I can see that though. I'm not with him for his money, I have my own, so it never made a difference to me how much he was worth.

"There was no prenup and I'm entitled to half a million dollars per my attorney. You're worth way more than that and you know it. Give me what I earned and I'll be gone."

"Do you even hear yourself right now? How selfish you sound? Earned?" I hear the incredulous tone in Pierre's voice as it grows louder.

"I don't give a fuck what I sound like, Pierre, just give me what I'm due. You can have everything else."

"I'm not signing them. No way."

"It's because of him, isn't it?"

Oh, do I detect jealousy with a dash of venom in those words? I hope it eats him alive every minute of his pathetic life when he walks out of here that I'm the one bringing Pierre happiness unlike he ever gave him.

"He has nothing to do with this."

"What's he doing here then, half naked like he belongs here."

"Jesus fuck. It's none of your business, Seven. Is that all you came here for?"

"Is he one of those trashy ass bikers you always hang out with?"

"Don't fucking call him that ever again. You done?"

"Yeah, but—"

Pierre doesn't even wait for him to be finished. "Then get out. Now before I call the cops. At this point you are trespassing."

"If we go to court, I'll get more than half a mil and you know it. Just sign them if you know what's good for you."

"Are you seriously fucking threatening me right now?"

"I'm advising you it's in your best interest if you settle for this amount instead of taking it to court and having to give me more. I don't want to spend more on an attorney than I already have if you fight this. I'm saving us both time. Sign them by tomorrow, Pierre. Let's get it over with. We both know it was over for quite some time, why drag it out."

"Go fuck yourself, Seven." I hurry over to the shower and turn it on just as I hear Seven's parting comment, "Always a pleasure, Pierre."

Quickly undressing and getting into the shower I let my mind wander to why Pierre is dragging his feet over this as I work like The Flash to wash my body. It's pretty clear Seven is not coming back, and from the tone of that conversation, he's not apologetic either.

Man, fuck that arrogant dickwad.

Pierre appears outside the glass shower doors. "It would have been less subtle to piss on my leg in front of him."

I grin to myself. Yeah, Seven got the memo.

I shut the water off and get out, grabbing the towel off the hook. I don't start drying myself until I'm sure he's had his fill. His eyes roam my body and I feel every inch of his gaze across my heated, wet skin. God, I want to sink to my knees and let him take my mouth.

He leaves the bathroom while I finish up drying and dressing. I meet him back out in the kitchen while I grab my boots.

He looks nervous. This isn't good. I did something wrong and he's pissed.

"Look, Declan, I think I need to take a step back from this," he moves his hand around between us, "whatever this is. I need to slow down. Maybe not every day." He anchors a hand on his hip and grabs his forehead with the other. "I'm overwhelmed and I need a break."

This is definitely not what I wanted to hear. Especially as number one prick of the city just left.

I stand with my boots on but unlaced. I watch his face; I look into his eyes. Pierre is spiraling but he's set in this decision.

"If that's what you wish."

"It is. I'll call or text you…if that's ok." He gathers up his sweater and stands in the doorway. "Thanks for making my waffles how I like them."

"You're welcome," my mouth is dry as death when I answer. My heart is crashing around in my chest like a frantic bird.

The moment is here.

It's happening now.

Like it was foretold.

I run my fingers through my damp hair and resolve myself that this is most likely it and he doesn't even want to fight for what we have.

I walk through the bedroom and grab my duffle. I breeze past him and stop at the front door.

One more time I look at him, standing by the island where he stopped after following me out of the bedroom.

"Yeah, you can call me Pierre, I'd like that."

He promised me nothing and I can't get mad at losing everything with him.

Feeling gut punched, I walk through the door and away from the man I've fallen madly in love with…who doesn't want me.

"I fucked up."

"No, you created a boundary," Cherry argues. "You called time out. It's ok to step back and realign."

I half smile over at her, "How did you get so wise?"

"Must be that smarty pants college I go to with my big, bad-ass brain." She smirks at me and that does make me smile for real then.

Cherry reminds me so much of Tally, it's uncanny. It's like they are long lost sisters. Except Tally has dark hair with caramel highlights, and Cherry has bright orange hair and rosy cheeks. She's a vivacious carrot top and her face and arms are full of freckles. Her baby blue eyes stand out from her pale skin and speak of her kindness.

Cherry looks like a porcelain doll…with the mouth of a sailor. She's apparently good at decent advice too.

"I read a lot of self-help books. That's the secret. My absolute favorite is *The Invitation by Oriah Mountain Dreamer*. Life changing stuff in those pages. You should give it a shot. Matter of fact all of you should. It makes you really take a look inside yourself to help love yourself more," Cherry says, waving her wine glass around us sitting in my living room. Of course, Tally is on the TV.

Zharia has her phone out already looking up the book to read. She's in her era of being a *Yes Woman* and keeping her mind open to new possibilities. Zhar is definitely enjoying her journey of self-discovery with Shadow and Gunney. She'll read anything to help keep her blissful life intact.

Birdie leans forward and I notice her wine glass still sits there but she has covertly been sipping on a bottle of water. "Pierre, you're allowed to pump the brakes. I doubt Travares is holding that against you."

I've kept my distance for a week and a half thinking through the mess in my head.

I miss him.

I still can't make him promises but I still call him mine.

This is only making it worse. I'm the problem. I'm like the whole problem. My head is not right. He's done nothing to warrant being used like this but I also made myself very clear when we embarked on this fling—I do not want attachments or strings. I can't get involved with someone again with a heart so broken.

However, my heart doesn't feel so broken when I'm with him or thinking of him.

It feels like I'm soaring through the clouds when I think of him.

He's probably confused.

I'm confused. I suck at this.

I treat him like he's mine, I tell him he's mine, but I won't let myself be his. I turn him down every time he asks me out on a date. I've been to his place twice and stayed the night with him only once but left early in the morning.

I love sitting around and cuddling him for hours in bed or on the couch, which is clearly intimate and indicative of a relationship. Running my fingers through his hair, my fingertips down his beard and hugging him to my chest is not something someone just wanting sex would do.

I miss hanging out with Lily and Poppy for brunch and game night.

This was not at all how it was supposed to be.

"You are deserving of love, Pierre," Tally says softly from the TV.

Wine Wednesday is turning into *Happy Hour starring Pierre's love life*. I'm not for it. Don't recommend. Not with these women. Sharks circling, sniffing for blood, they are.

"Why can't you commit? What's going on in that beautiful mind of yours? What's holding you back?" Zharia holds her phone and her wineglass in her hand while she smooths down the ultra-soft blanket around her tucked in legs. She's made herself perfectly content in the corner of my couch.

I just stare at her. How dare she come right out and ask me. How dare she call me out like this. Who needs enemies when you've got friends that will drag you under the bus to make you spill your guts to them, unwillingly.

That might be a tad dramatic. Zhar is just good at getting people to share their problems. Aggressively.

"I have my reasons."

"Well, so far your reasons suck." Zharia gives a challenging few blinks at me over her wine glass with her perfectly arched eyebrow lifted.

I see Zharia is 'choosing violence' as she calls it.

There's no getting out of this. If something is wrong, Zhar will not stop until we purge the negative and start the healing process. She's done it enough times to each of us. She calls them breakthroughs.

I'm just real tired of it being me every time here lately.

With a deep, reserved sigh I cautiously begin, "I'm broken. My marriage has broken me. Obviously I wasn't a good enough husband and—"

Birdie and Zhar open their mouths to interrupt. Birdie lets out a little squeak to begin speaking and I silence her with a hand up.

"If you want me to spill then give me a chance to finish. No interrupting me, you know that's my pet peeve."

Birdie sits back and motions zipping her lips with her fingers. Zharia nods, just like Tally does. Cherry blinks in rapt attention like I'm the messiah delivering the most profound sermon.

She's still learning the ropes around here. She's got a lot to learn when it comes to personalities. She hit the jackpot of attitudes when she showed up as Birdie and Zharia's rideshare driver that night…the night when Zharia went to meet her fake/real husband. I can only imagine Cherry's face when she heard them two bickering in the back seat.

"I feel like I should be mourning my marriage harder than I am. I've come to learn in the past five weeks of having Declan around that I almost feel relieved that Seven is not around anymore, that he had the courage to call it quits and walk away. I was content to let us suffer and suffocate each other. Those heart stopping moments when I would walk in the door after work where I wouldn't know which version of Seven I was getting are missing and I love that for me now. It was nerve wracking to live in a volatile environment. Constantly being gaslit and blamed for everything wrong, that wears a person down. I became numb to it all. I thought if I just coast the rails Seven would be ok and there would be no outbursts or fights and he'd get his shit together finally."

I stop, holding up my hand asking for a moment, and the other hand lifts to rub my eyes with my thumb and middle finger, pinching the bridge of my nose to hopefully will away the tears that are stinging and threatening to come.

One deep, calming breath later. "There are lots of things I've hidden from you. I didn't want you seeing Seven in a bad light." Zharia snorts. She was not his biggest fan, like ever, straight from the beginning. "I feel I should be sad more often, or even be some level of sad, but the more days that go by, I feel like I can breathe better than the day before. I can finally stand up straight and hold my head up. I'm ashamed I put so much time and energy into something, *someone*, and they tossed me away, along with everything we've built for over a decade and I'm not fucking sad. I just feel like I'm expected to mourn longer. I don't know why, maybe it's society that has ingrained that notion into my head. Let's not even touch how hurt my heart still is at not being enough and being an epic failure."

I finally look up at them. I scan each one of their faces. There's no judgement there, not that I expected any. Only concern and love are etched on their beautiful faces.

It is not lost on me that I have some of the most gorgeous best friends.

Birdie is the first to speak after a few moments. "That's a lot to unpack, Pierre." She comes over to sit beside me on the couch and takes my hand in hers. "But we are right here beside you, to walk with you through this, and we will help in any way that we can. I promise you; we have no judgement and fuck anyone who does. You are a wonderful human being, full of love, compassion, loyalty and everything else that's good in this world. I'm so sorry you weren't loved how you should have been for so long and that you carried that burden, that sorrow and sadness alone."

Now the tears do well up in my eyes as I watch Birdie's thumb slide back and forth across the back of my hand.

I hear Zharia stand up and come over to us. She sits down on the other side of me on the couch. She takes my other hand and holds it in both of hers.

"We love you so much and only want the best for you. You're our brother and we are your sisters. We take care of our own. Let us. Seven was not the best for you; we can all agree on that. You deserve to have someone who doesn't make you fear coming home. You deserve a grand love story, a sweep-you-off-your-feet and make-your-heart-skip-beats kind of love story. You are deserving of love. So much fucking love," Zharia ends on an almost growl.

Cherry clears her throat and I glance up at her and a lone tear streaks down my cheek. Birdie is there to wipe it off, always the motherly one of the bunch. "Mr. Pierre, I know I don't know you all that well yet, but I firmly believe everyone should feel safe in their own home and everyone should feel love in their lives, *especially* from their partner. You do deserve an epic love story and you do deserve the love that's out there waiting for you regardless of how long it's been since your last relationship. Grief has no levels for time or limit on the power of those feelings of loss. You are only putting more stress on yourself if you are holding yourself to the standards of society on anything. Don't do that to yourself. It's not nice."

Out of the corner of my eye I see Tally wipe tears from her eyes with a tissue.

"Cherry is absolutely right, *Compagno*, there is no set limit. You are holding on to some archaic limitations that's toxic to your brain. What, are you supposed to wear a black veil and not date for a year? This isn't *Gone With The Wind*, we don't have to abide by that shit anymore. Personally, I am thrilled you're already out there getting you some good dick," Tally declares.

I can't help but chuckle while Birdie and Cherry giggle. Zharia says, "Fuck yeah, me too, homie. Well said, Tal."

"Speaking of that hot piece of ass you've snagged," I just shake my head and roll my eyes while looking at the ceiling while Tally continues, "Why haven't you claimed him as your boyfriend? Y'all are so cute together and he seems to really make you happy."

I've given them teasers of things Declan and I do and what we talk about. If I don't give them little sips of tea they get restless and start circling. It's best to hold them off with scraps. But Tally can see straight through my bullshit and I've shared more with her than the others.

"I don't want a relationship. I'm done with that. I just want to come and go as I please. Declan is well aware of the arrangement that he's agreed to."

Zhar clicks her tongue and as she rises and returns to her nest on my couch, she says, "Someone should tell that poor guy then, because he looks at you like he's going to eat you alive at any minute while batting those gorgeous eyelashes I envy and shooting you full of heart-eyes."

I shake my head. "No, he knows. I was very clear about it." Maybe I do need to remind him. That means I would have to talk to him and it's been so long already…

Tally pipes up, "Why don't you want a relationship?"

I look over at the TV and camera, "I just got out of one. I want to be free for a while. It's been over a decade that I could do whatever I wanted. I don't want tied down again. I don't want to answer to anyone. This heart is on high alert and closed up, we aren't doing that shit again. I let one man ruin my heart, I'm not about to have it half-assed mended and broken again."

I sound like an idiot to myself. A conflicted one, but still an idiot.

Tally nods like she knows I'm blowing smoke up everyone's ass.

That does not stop Zharia though. "I call bullshit. You can't snap me cute couple pics and tell me there's nothing there."

My eyes narrow at her and her tone. I don't have it in me to put up with Zhar's shit. Not tonight.

I raise my hands and shrug. "That's how I feel."

Zharia shrugs too, but it has some sass with it. "Suit yourself, but just know I'm on your team, however, I'm also Team Declan now. He's good for you. I think if you let him in, you could have an epic love story, the kind that comes by once in a lifetime. Take the risk, I know from experience. He wants you, Pierre, like way more than FWBs."

"I'll take your advisement under consideration."

"So, when are you going to tell us how the sex is?"

I should have known Zharia was going to bring that up again.

Chapter 21

Pierre

It's been over two weeks since I've touched him. It's been days since I've heard from Declan. He sent me a 'hey, thinking of you' text. I still have yet to answer him.

What am I supposed to say?

I never got a chance to remind him of the rules concerning our hookups because I just blurted out we-shouldn't-see-each-other-so-much bullshit.

I can't let myself get sucked into another soul sucking relationship. Because that's what relationships do to you. They start out great and slowly over time your soul starts to wither and die. Or they cut you to your core and traumatically hurt you. I'm ok being alone. I've started distancing myself hard the past few days. It was inevitable.

We were two sinners burning out of control, running away with the flames. I love it and I hate it at the same time. I'm not fighting the attraction, just the commitment.

Glancing around the clubhouse, with a whiskey neat in my hand that I probably won't finish because I'm not a big drinker, I covertly search for Declan's head in the crowd. It's the annual Easter Egg Hunt. Another family gig.

Rock and Birdie went all out. The clubhouse is decorated with pastels and rabbits everywhere. The playground Rock had installed out in the closest corner of the parking lot is full of screaming crotch goblins. Why do children feel the need to scream like someone's murdering them?

Do parents really put up with this shit all the time? Hard no for me, dawg. No way in hell I can deal with loud and messy demons, no matter how much I love them. In my eyes, parents are a different breed of people.

This is why Seven and I agreed to no kids as a whole. We didn't want to be parents. Sure, we could have adopted or fostered but we chose not to.

Personally, I can tolerate older kids, you know, when they reach like twelve or older. They don't scream as much and they can be taught how to clean up after themselves. They're more trainable at that age, like a good dog.

Like I love Birdie and Danger's son, Denver, that's my nephew, but even he sometimes grates on my last nerve.

But goddamn, he's the cutest. I just love him to bits but I'm happy to hand him back over to his parents.

He's currently chewing on a frozen lion head teether hitched up on his momma's hip. Birdie is telling me I need to wipe my scowl off my face and start looking less mean, more cheerful. She's threatening to put bunny ears on me and make me help with the egg hunt that's happening in about ten minutes.

Declan and I didn't talk about being here at this event. I don't even know why I'm looking for him. He's gotten so far under my skin, thoughts of him carousel in my head nonstop. Always coming back to him. This can't be healthy.

I really need to end this completely before it spirals further out of control. Fuck, it's already out of control. In no way, shape, or form do I have any handle on the emotions that march in circles throughout my body and mind.

I didn't quite end things totally, there's still an open end to how we left things. Maybe I need to cut ties completely, like tell him it's over and I will feel better. My mind will go back to normal and thoughts of him won't consume me and I won't obsess over them.

We should have ended this before it was too late. As soon as feelings got involved, I should have cut it off no matter how good the sex is. I've caught 'the look' on Declan's face a few times but said nothing. This is getting too close to the dreaded L word. He's already falling and I'm going to have to be the bad guy and shove him back up. No falling, no feelings, no strings.

Tell yourself that too!

I'm fucking trying here!

I could walk away right now and have no scars from it.

Sike. Keep thinking that, buddy, my heart whispers.

Although, the past few days of silence have been upsetting to me. I don't know why. After all, this was all my idea and

I'm the one adamant about maintaining some level of control and distance.

I never felt this way with Seven. Not even in the beginning. It's downright fucking scary and too intense for me. I could have loved Declan in another lifetime, but not this one.

Right now, I don't feel worthy of love. Seven's done a number on my self-esteem, on my head in general, but Declan was there to give me hefty boosts of dopamine.

He's served his purpose: got me out of my slump after a breakup.

Two weeks ago, at another Sunday brunch, a date Declan asked me out on with his sister and niece, I conceded to come to it because I really like Lily, and Poppy loves me. I kinda missed the kid and that's when I knew I was in too deep and I was drowning.

It was after that brunch I put the brakes on harder and distanced myself even more.

Lily told me I needed to take better care of my guts if I wanted to have more serotonin and dopamine to feel good overall. She's convinced a lot of problems with humans can be solved by making sure our guts are taken care of.

I've been taking these supplements and herbal mixture she's texted me about and I can say they are definitely doing something in there. My guts are clean, squeaky fucking clean. I'm sorta thankful I haven't had Declan over more this week because his sister is fucking up my gizzard.

Nothing like a good system cleanse to wipe the slate clean.

Or as Lily calls it *rebuilding your digestive tract.*

I call it shitting through a screen door.

This shit better work.

Don't get me wrong, Declan makes me happy, to a degree, but my stupid battered heart isn't one hundred percent yet and I don't actually trust it around him currently.

I don't trust my head or heart at this moment and both of them betray me by wanting to jump right into this, gung-ho and all that shit.

I'd rather walk away than jump into another relationship.

Clearly I am not the marrying type if my husband left me.

Zharia raises her eyebrows, "How's the vitamin routine going?"

I roll my eyes. "Jesus. My colon is clean. I've shit out my spleen in the process." Zharia laughs. "I don't know if I feel lighter because I've lost half my body weight to the toilet or if it's because I really have boosted my dope."

"God, I'm sorry I asked." She wipes away a tear that leaked out while she completely laughed about my discomfort.

I shrug and sip on my whiskey. "You asked and if anything, I'm honest."

"You let me know the minute it works great. I'll take a week off work to shit my guts out, literally." She's such a bitch she starts laughing again. "I can always use more happiness, even by worshipping the porcelain god."

Birdie snorts. "I think you get more than enough happiness." Her smile stays in place as Zharia smirks at her.

Unbeknownst to me, Declan is walking up behind me. I suddenly feel an arm come around my waist and haul me over to a hard body. His laundry fresh, taunting leather and definitely manly smell hits my nose, registering it's him.

Even knowing who it is, it still doesn't stop my reaction. I recoil, cringe, and jump away.

My very bad reaction.

The dreadful look of rejection fans across his face.

"Stop it," I practically hiss at him, shaking my head. "Just don't."

Birdie, Zhar and Cherry stand there with mouths dropped wide. At least Cherry had enough manners to cover her mouth with her hand and try to disguise her squeak of *Oh*.

He steps back, taking his soothing energy away from my aura. I guess we know what my provoked reaction will be.

Honestly, I'm not even sure why I did it. I was craving his touch not even five minutes ago. Unconsciously my mind has decided this is not happening and rejects the affection. That sounds like a plausible excuse.

I'm a horrible person.

Throwing his hands up, he says with a hard edge to his voice, "What, I'm not yours in public at all?" The angry flush spreads through my body.

When I don't say anything, he nods and rubs his chin and looks down, shaking his head with a scoff. His face rises to mine, his jaw set hard, unrelenting, and I see the immense hurt, the hurt I'm causing. I'm breaking his heart.

It needs done.

"Oh right, I'm just your plaything in darkness. The dirty little secret you keep hidden and strung along. The fuck buddy unworthy of PDA. No feelings, remember? Thanks for checking me, I forgot my head there for a minute, *sir*."

A loud clang beats in my chest. A silver lining is building in his eyes, the despair, hurt and anguish is going to spill over and I see his desperate need to control his emotions right now.

The rejection seared in his expression. His heart is written across his face and for the first time I see what I've done to him.

Where his heart is.

Where I didn't want to believe it had gone.

The feelings he's holding back are clearly written in his eyes and it utterly terrifies me.

But it doesn't stop my heart from cracking because I'm a horrible person.

He looks me in the eye and quietly, lethally says, "Tangerine. All of it, tangerine."

I would have been less shocked if he had slapped me. I physically jerk. My eyes go wide and I feel my heart cracking in my chest.

What have I done? Immediately, I regret my decisions.

You wanted this, my mind screams. *Here's your fucking bloody chance.*

I barely recover to lift my hand out, "Declan…"

But he's already through the throng of people, headed for the door with Lily and Poppy chasing after him.

He's through the door with my heart and a piece of my soul before Zharia let's lose a deep breath and says, "What the fuck was that, Pierre? You broke that man's heart hardcore."

I turn my face to her and all she does is glare at me.

"Not cool, Pierre," she says and starts to walk away. "I need a refill," she throws over her shoulder.

Birdie's eyes are wide and she looks shocked. Fuck, I'm shocked! And I'm the dumb fucker that did it.

Danger appears beside her, "Hey Princess, it's time." He kisses the side of her neck and smooths Denver's hair down.

The perfect picture of a happy marriage, of the perfect life.

Once again I ask myself, what have I done? I could have, no I should have handled that better.

I'm a dick.

CHAPTER 22
TRAVARES

"What the fuck was that, Dec? Are you ok? What the hell does tangerine mean?" Lily grabs ahold of my arm as she runs up behind me. She jerks me to get me to stop marching to my SUV in the parking lot and getting the hell out of here before I explode.

I'm pissed.

I'm hurt.

I'm shocked.

And I'm desperately confused.

I stop abruptly causing Lily to smack into me. "What just happened, Dec?" she says again as she steadies herself and steps back, holding Poppy to her. I can see the concern on her face. I'm sure she can see all the emotions raging on mine.

Putting my hands on my hips, I chuff while shaking my head looking at the ground, "I have no fucking clue."

"Clearly it was something powerful."

"I don't want to talk about it right now. Thank you for coming. I'm sorry, I have to get away and screw my head back on straight."

Lily grabs my hand, "Don't you dare shut me out, Declan." Her tone is serious, not brooking any argument from me. "What does tangerine mean?"

I pinch the bridge of my nose. Fuck. This all went to shit. I planned on telling him tonight how I feel. I thought maybe he had feelings for me too. He shows it in his actions but clearly I misinterpreted that. I could have sworn on my momma's grave that he had started having feelings for me too.

I wanted to explore where this could go.

Jokes on me, big time.

I can't go on like this. I want him in all ways. I guess some PDA is his limit. Not being public is killing me. I want to show him off, I want to be claimed.

That shit stops now. I need to leave here. I need to start hardening my heart and chalk this up to a lesson learned. I need to start getting over him.

This week I've taken some time to reflect on everything. I discovered the desire to be with him but if he doesn't want the same things as me, I'll have to let him go.

I don't want to spend my time being someone's toy any longer. There has to be a level of respect I have for myself no matter what I agreed to. Things change.

Looking at Lily, I can see she's waiting to intercept the meltdown I'm about to have.

"Lily, please. Finish here and meet me at home." I turn to go.

"Absolutely not, brother. I'm leaving now. We need to go home and talk about this. Something big just happened back there and it's affecting you gravely."

I can't have Poppy losing out. She needs this time in a safe space to do kid things.

"Did you just end things with one word, Declan?" Lily asks, horrified.

I hang my head and nod, fighting back the burn of tears.

"So that's what tangerine means. Dec, honey, I'm so sorry."

"I have to go," I hoarsely rasp. I have to get away, especially if Pierre tries to come out here.

Before she can grab me again, I turn and march to my vehicle, leaving it all behind. "I love you, Lil, but I have to go," I throw over my shoulder.

I leave Pierre behind, where he wants to be. Stuck in his head, that's poking down into the sand, while the world continues on without him.

I'm such an idiot. I should never have gotten this close. I fucked up.

I see things clearly now.

This has run its course.

And now it's over.

This song came to me one day at this point in the story. Through Declan's heartbreak, the melody haunted me until I played it. I urge you to take a listen before proceeding. Share in Declan's pain. We'll wait, take your time.

Needed Me — Rihanna

CHAPTER 23
TRAVARES

Four weeks later

Something screwy is happening. There's been hits all over the city tonight. Member's wives or partners are being threatened. Associate's houses and vehicles are getting vandalized. Two wives and one girlfriend have been attacked and put in the hospital, one with a stab wound.

Shit is crazy right now and has me and Bam working double time tracking things.

All the things coming across the police scanner are related to associates of The Southern Devils Society.

An SUV came flying through a parking lot, aimed directly at Birdie and Denver, then it slammed to a stop very close to them. But before anyone could get out of the strange SUV, Birdie's security detail was shooting at the vehicle as it squealed out of the mall parking lot. They ended up getting away.

At the same time, two men escorted Zharia by gunpoint out of the front door of the hospital where they were intercepted by her security team, mere feet from the waiting car. Two dead men now sit in the hospital morgue. Unfortunately, that incident included the police to make a report. Birdie's did not.

I know of at least three men who are absolutely furious right now.

In each instance a calling card is being left behind. A simple LSS is on the business card dropped on the property. They've basically declared war again.

Revenge is their motive after their leader's wife died. I'm sure Panhead's out for blood since he thinks we are the reason she's dead. It's his own damn fault but he's too stupid to realize it.

I had hoped we were done with these assholes and they would realize we are going to best them at every angle.

My phone rings in the middle of this fuckshow. I look down and see that it's Poppy's school and my heart immediately speeds up and trips over itself.

Tonight's not a good night. Dread fills my guts in a hot/cold flush.

"Hello?"

"Mr. Travares? Declan?"

"Speaking. What's wrong?" The panic is there, right on the cusp of my throat.

"Poppy is still here, and it's just that… Lily has not called or shown up yet." I look down at my tactical watch and see it's after seven. Lily never misses picking up her daughter by five. Never. "Mr. Travares, see, we would like to go home, but we're worried."

This is unheard of. Lily would never let Poppy stay this long. She would have called me to go get her if she was going to be tied up.

"Thank you. I'll be there in fifteen minutes. I'm on my way."

My guts are churning...Tonight's fucked up already.

Once I'm in my SUV, I try calling Lily's phone a couple of times. It just rings and rings and goes to voicemail. My heart is starting to sink.

I dial Shadow next. I'm closest to him. He's like my best bud in the club. I mean all the Top Five are close to me, but I'm more partial to Shadow.

"What's up, Prince Charming?" he snickers into the phone.

I sigh, "I swear to god, you guys need to stay off my social media."

He's referring to the post I made a few weeks ago with my helmet on, shirtless, leaning up against my bike at dusk. I was unbuckling my pants and they were open enough, especially since they were pushed down low on my hips.

It was captioned with—*Prepared to kneel for you, Your Prince Charming.*

It's an old post and really should be taken down now that everything's done and over with but I just can't bring myself to do it. Plus, the engagement is off the hook. Everyone wanted to know who I was kneeling for.

"I can't help it if you're a supremely popular thirst trap and you got recommended for me...and then I matched up your bike and tattoos. For someone that knows you like I do, it wasn't that hard."

"Sure. I bet. That's how all of you know then, you just stumbled upon me, is that it?" I did not want them to know about my side gig I do for shits and giggles. I have quite a following on social media where I show off my muscles and buff body while wearing some type of mask or motorcycle helmet.

Men and women love me.

I get paid lots of money to show my body off. I also do workout videos and do some influencer stuff for fitness companies. I've done teaser videos of where you almost see my face and the comments fly off the page.

Gunney does the same shit I do but I never hear him giving him shit about it.

Then these idiots go and stumble upon it '*innocently.*'

"Anyways asshole, Lily isn't answering her phone and she didn't pick up Poppy from school. I'm on my way to get Pops but I think I need Zharia's or Birdie's help watching Poppy while I track down Lily. Do you think that's a possibility?"

"Yeah, man, sure. Do you need some help? Me and Leo can come along," Shadow offers.

"I'd love any help. You know it's been a strangely volatile night. I'm trying really hard not to think the worst. I mean, I'm nobody. Why would they go after me and mine? I'm not like you guys."

"You're still you, and that happens to be a high-ranking hacker in the Top Five of the most notorious motorcycle club on the continent. Of course, they're coming after you too. Come get us, we're at Danger's penthouse. It's got the most security. Danger will be here with the women and his son. We'll help you look for Lily."

I'm so grateful for the brotherhood I lucked into with these men. I consider myself fortunate to call them friends and brothers.

After I got a very scared Poppy settled with Birdie, Zhar and Cherry, I took Shadow and Gunney back to my house. I

woke up my machines and started running the trace for her tracker.

Gunney has never been to my house and he's busy picking up things to look at.

"We mustn't touch things that don't belong to us, Leo."

"Ixnay on the name-aye," Gunney says. We all know Zharia and Shadow are the only ones allowed to use his government name. I do it to annoy him sometimes.

Pulling up my apps I start plugging in info to do a search with. The first couple of times nothing pulls up.

Kinda like it did when Zharia went missing.

Next, I tap into her phone to find its location. When the dot starts blinking, I zoom in. It shows her still on her college campus.

After I hack into the college's security footage, I run a trace with her photo.

"What's it doing now?" Shadow's standing behind me watching the display of six monitors, rapt fascination on his face. Things are running on all the monitors I have displayed on the walls trying to find my sister.

"AI is searching through all the footage from the past few hours looking for Lily's face. It will start displaying clips where she's at and timestamp them. I'm going to use those to see which way she went." I pull up yet another program. "This is the tracker that's imbedded in her car. It shows me it's in the parking lot of the school too. Exact same place as her phone. It's weird. It's like she's just sitting in her car."

"Is she taking a nap?" Gunney asks from my couch. He's going through the many gossip groups across the city to see if there's a buzz there.

"Doubt it. She has just as much trouble shutting her brain down as I have. We only sleep a few hours a night. I've never known her to take a nap."

I point to a screen on the top row, upper far right. "That's the police scanner running, the ones they use inside the cars and it also pulls in nine-one-one calls. AI is working to pick up any calls with keywords to pull those calls for me to review."

"Damn. You really are a whiz," Shadow says as he claps my shoulder. "We'll find her. We won't stop."

That makes me feel marginally better. Where the fuck is her security detail?

I helped search for both Zharia and Birdie. These are programs I've built and patented and sold to the military for a tidy sum. I know how well they work.

It's well past dark by this time. I've been at this for fifteen minutes when suddenly a call pops up in the program. I hurry and click it, replaying it.

A woman is crying, saying she found a body of a young woman with shoulder length brown-blond hair. She's in an alley by Saint Charles Avenue.

I immediately start searching for the business the caller is saying where the body is at. The woman says she is an employee of the coffee café on the corner and she was taking the trash out and happened to see a woman's foot when she opened the dumpster.

I hear the nine-one-one operator offering reassuring words to the caller and letting her know units are in route. I can hear the caller saying "Ma'am, are you ok?" repeatedly, trying to rouse the victim, just in case.

She is met with silence and the operator tells her to hang tight; the first unit is set to arrive in less than two minutes.

The police scanner gets a hit and I run both programs' sound so I can hear the in-car audio and ambulance communications. The operator is relaying information to them on where to find the woman on the phone.

Gunney has moved off of the couch to stand behind me next to Shadow. We sit here and listen to the mayhem unraveling on my screens and plowing through my speakers. My heart is in my throat.

Sure, I feel guilty for not being out there right now looking but I'm searching in the best way I know how.

There's a lull in the police chatter. Gunney asks, "Her tracker has not popped up yet right?"

"Correct. It should show me her vitals at least."

I feel Shadow and Gunney behind me give an apprehensive look between them. They both know all too well how these trackers I designed are meant to work. My sister and niece were the first to get the trackers embedded. Lily always had so much faith in my ideas and was gracious enough to let me test on her and Popsicle.

Clearly a signal jammer will render them useless, such as in Zharia's case.

My fingers are flying across the keyboard running yet another program on finding any cameras in that alley. So far the sweep is not working. Either there are none or I can't connect for some reason. I dig in a little harder and come up with nothing still.

I'm getting frustrated and it's showing.

The location of the body is not far from my house. I live in Uptown, right on Octavia Street. I'm not far from Tulane or Audubon Park. I almost have Lily convinced she needs to move in with me and occupy some of these five bedrooms and four bathrooms. I have a yard compared to most homes around this neighborhood. It's perfect for Poppy to run around and get fresh air in, two things important to Lily. But then again, the jarring million+ I paid for it, the house better come with a yard.

I bought this house two years ago hoping one day I could raise my own family here. I haven't found Mr. Right yet to have that life with, but I thought I had that man in Pierre.

Instead, last week at brunch, I asked Lily to move in with Poppy into my house. Lily still has a year left of school and I can help more with Poppy already here. It will be less stressful for both of them and it makes me feel better about where they live. Lily's barely making it by with her two-bedroom apartment and measly pay from the deli she works at for a few hours as a server.

The one thing she wanted to pay for herself was her rent. She has no idea she's paid a month ahead…every month…just in case. The landlord makes her think she's right on time, even when the landlord lets me know it's a few days late.

"Do you want to race over there and poke our nose into this? Or is this something we're going to wait on?" Shadow asks.

I turn around in my chair and look up at both of them. I'm antsy, I gotta move. There's a bad feeling growing in my core.

These two are some intimidating motherfuckers and wherever we are going, I'll need them as back up or as support. Then again, I'm the same size as them and I bet there's lots of people who say I'm intimidating.

God I wish I knew what to do!

Where the fuck is my sister?

"We head to her car now."

Pierre

"Hey, Bird. What's up?" I say as I answer my phone.

I just changed into pajama pants and I'm about to get settled in for the night with a good horror book I picked up at Clover Corner, the newest cute bookstore over on Dumaine Street.

"Pierre, I really need you to come to the penthouse. Like now."

I go on high alert in a heartbeat. That's a mighty demand from my best friend. Not something she normally asks for, especially this late at night.

"What's wrong?"

She fills me in on the attacks and about her and Zharia's interactions and almost abductions again. "Crazy shit is happening tonight with LSS. We are under attack. I'm not sure if LSS has put you and Travares together yet, but you're in danger by just being Lincoln's brother. We would feel safer if you were here with us at the tower in the sky. Please say you'll come." I hear the fear in her tone. This is serious business.

Then I hear my brother in the background. "He doesn't have a fucking choice in this," then louder from what sounds like a different room, "Get here now, Pierre, I can't lose you."

"You heard him, P, we need you safe. Up in The Tower is the safest."

I'm honestly shook.

Going to the tower is my only choice. The sky-high penthouse they live in is often referred to as The Ivory Tower. The Tower for short.

"S-Sure, I'll come. I need to get dressed and grab a few things and I'll come there. I need to get a rideshare set up so let me get off here and do that."

"No! Don't worry about it. There will be a car for you in…uhh," I hear my brother muffled in the background again, "about five minutes Linx says. Find Jonesy, he has Daddy's car." Birdie's voice wavers and she takes a deep breath. I can audibly hear the tension in her breath.

"Another thing you should know, P…Poppy's here. Lily is missing."

Jesus fuck, no! NO! My stomach just dropped out my ass. Gut punched. No, this can't be happening. Declan must be out of his mind and Poppy is probably scared to death and worried.

"Oh my god. How is Poppy? How's Declan?"

On speakerphone, I'm running through my bedroom to the closet to grab an overnight bag. I'm shoving shit into it when I hear Poppy's little voice in the background, "Miss Birdie, when will Uncle Ducky and Mommy be home? I'm hungry."

"Birdie, put me on the phone with her please."

I hear rustling and a tiny voice says *hello* tentatively.

"Poppy, sweetheart, it's Pierre."

"Hi, Pierre. Where have you been? Can you come get me? I don't know where Mommy and Uncle Ducky are."

Grabbing my night meds, I throw them in the bag. It's been three minutes. I set the phone down quickly and in the calmest voice I can muster, I continue talking to Poppy, "Honey, I'm going to come stay with you tonight, is that ok? Want to be besties and have a sleepover at Aunt Birdie's house with me? We can eat all her snacky snacks."

Poppy giggles and my nervousness slips for just a second but she still has a stressful and sad undertone. This poor baby. I shudder thinking about where her mom could be and what's happened if LSS has her while they are on a warpath.

I remember all too well what can happen at the hands of those so-called Saints. They beat the living dog shit outta me and I spent a week in the hospital. Thank fuck the bones in my hand healed well enough for me to still tattoo with.

"Ok," she says softly.

"I'll be there soon, sweetheart. Hugs and kisses. Give the phone back to Aunt Birdie, please."

Having managed to change my clothes into a pair of sweats that don't reveal as much as the pajama pants and a T-shirt with a hoodie over it. I slip on my black Crocs.

Not a word from you. They are my comfort item. Crocs are the hill I will die on. The most comfortable shoes I've ever worn. I dare you to try them. Laugh all you want, I don't care.

Once I set the alarm and lock up, I sling my bag over my shoulder and go in search of Jonesy, the Chavanet family driver. I've known him since I was twenty, when I first met Birdie.

Sure enough, Jonesy is double parked with the flashers on, standing by the passenger side, waiting on me.

I walk up holding my hand out. He takes it into both his hands and we shake.

I nod and say, "Jonesy."

"Pleased to see you, Mr. Lefèvre."

I dare not correct him to call me just Pierre…again. He won't listen.

I slide into the sleek expensive car and the scent of leather and sandalwood permeates my senses. It sends a pang to my heart. A despairing wave of sadness from the scent washes over me from missing Declan so badly. I didn't expect it to be this bad.

The sadness has taken me by surprise. The past few weeks I've come to realize just how deep I had fallen. I resisted so hard. I cut him off to bleed him out of my system and all it did was burr him under my skin more.

On the way to Birdie's, I call Tally and let her know what's happening. She's super worried about us here in the city. She tries to get us to move away all the time but it's not like her city, New York, is any better.

This is home and there's always going to be violence. It's everywhere you go, so why not stay home?

When I reach Lincoln and Birdie's building I see the security men stationed around the perimeter. They are trying to blend in but they stick out like a sore thumb with the Kevlar vests and tactical clothing.

I see my brother is sparing no cost in protecting his loved ones. There're even guys stationed across the street and I'm sure there are others on the rooftops of the surrounding buildings.

I nod to a few and continue into the building, stepping up to the executive elevator that leads up to the penthouse. There are extra measures and precautions installed on this elevator.

The night guard at the expansive ornately decorated counter waves at me and reaches to pick up the phone before I'm even off the giant doormat at the big glass entrance.

Considering my brother owns the biggest security firm in the country, I'm pretty proud of the innovative ways his team has come up with to vet people going to the penthouse.

Not everyone has access to the top. They are very picky who they let up.

I let the box beside the elevator scan my eye. Once it flashes green the doors open. Once inside I have to use my eight-digit pin to access the floor.

When I hear Lincoln say "send him up" to the night guard, the doors close by a code Raul has and uses at the desk. It doesn't matter that Rual knows me well, it's still about safety. There are very, very few people who know how to get up to the penthouse and there's only one way there.

Pictures of who has access are hanging behind the counter. As soon as they see us enter the lobby, they pick up the phone that has the direct line to the penthouse to get permission. Regardless of who we are, they still have to get permission and verify no one is under duress or coerced into the elevator.

My brother Mr. Danger is not fucking around when it comes to his family's safety.

When the elevator doors open next, Birdie has the front door open and welcomes me in. Poppy hears me talking to Birdie and comes around the corner to see me. Oh, my heart.

Her sad little face is tear streaked; she looks exhausted. Behind her stands a very tired Zharia hugging herself. I crouch down and hold open my arms. For a second I doubt my little friend will hug me. But Poppy comes running and my heart melts.

Her arms wrap around me just when her little body slams into me. She snuggles her head on my shoulder and a small sob escapes. "I missed you, Ringmaster," she breathes. "Brunch isn't the same without you."

I pat her back to soothe her and tell her, "I missed you too, Poptart."

That earns me a small squeeze.

I let Poppy release me first. I let her decide how long she needs comforted. I don't want to cut short the time she needs to process her emotions. I'm sure they are wildly all over the place. Such as mine are.

"Have you eaten?" I smooth down her unruly brown-blond hair that falls in waves around her shoulders.

Birdie pipes up, "We did but she didn't eat much."

"We even tried fruit snacks." Zharia seems to think kids only like fruit snacks as a snack.

I look at Poppy and she seems to shrink into herself again. I tilt her face up, "Hey. I won't let anything happen to you. Do you believe that?"

Her bottom lip pouts, but she gives a small yet brief nod while looking at the moth tattoo on my neck. She's killing me with her trembling bottom lip.

"Uncle Ducky is doing everything he can." Let her believe I know that as fact. Because even though I haven't been told, I know Declan is tearing this city apart looking for his kin.

He'll leave a trail of corpses and burn every building down until he finds her.

"Come on, let's go sit down." I take her hand, but she stands there, doesn't move, face down and it completely rips my heart out. Instead of pushing her, I just bend down and scoop her up and carry her into the kitchen, her tired head laying on my shoulder.

Poppy trusting me enough to carry her, or run into my arms, means the world to me. I deposit her onto one of the chairs at the island. She looks so small and scared.

I've never had that paternal urge. I've never once felt the need to procreate or be a parent.

However right now, all I want is to protect and comfort this little girl. I feel my best participation in her mother's search is to take care of Poppy. I'm familiar with her now and you could visibly see her stiffened shoulders relaxing at the sight of me. Birdie's nice and all, but she's not familiar like me.

For me not liking kids, Poppy sure does mean a lot to me. We've bonded like besties.

"Do you want some Mickey Mouse pancakes?" I ask her. I know she's a huge Disney fan.

"I do!" Zhar sings.

A smile creeps onto Poppy's lips. She cocks her head and questions my skill, "You can make those?"

"Psst! Yep, sure can, itty bitty. Girl, we will have some of the best pancakes."

"He's the best!" Thanks, Z.

"And they taste delish!" Birdie verifies, coming to sit on the barstool next to Poppy at the island. "That's it, we're having breakfast for dinner! Well, our snack anyways."

I get to work mixing the ingredients. I know my way around my best friend's/brother's house well enough to find all the stuff I need. Birdie sits at the island with Poppy showing her funny animal videos on some app she has on her phone. It keeps Poppy's mind busy and off the very adult issues going on around her.

I pour three dollops of batter on the greased griddle and watch them form bubbles. The dollops spread and link into the famous mouse ears.

Hey, if this helps Poppy eat, then so be it.

Plating a big pancake, I add a few pats of butter on top and slide it over to Poppy who just beams at the plate. "These look amazing, Ringmaster! Thank you!"

Hearing her call me Ringmaster again makes me chuckle and constricts my heart.

"Ringmaster?" Birdie asks with a quirked eyebrow.

"Yeah. Something about me reminding her of a circus Ringmaster in the big top at your dad's Mardi Gras circus."

"I love this! Yes, I see it. I always thought old English boxer but Ringmaster works too. It's cute." I slide her plate in front of her as she smiles at Poppy. She runs her fingers down Poppy's hair.

"Ringmaster definitely fits," Zhar agrees.

Birdie wiggles her fingers like a mad scientist in front of her and asks Poppy, "Say…when we get done here, would you like to take a bubble bath in my grossly humongous bathtub?" She beams at Poppy like they are *bestest friends* at a sleepover and staying up past bedtime is the new cool. Birdie's perfect with kids. I knew she would make a great mother.

Operation: Keep Poppy Calm is well underway.

CHAPTER 24
TRAVARES

The world is too heavy for me right now. I'm losing my mind and trying so hard to reign in my shit. I'm numb with dread. I can't sit still. My skin crawls. I'm antsy.

Shadow and Gunney rode their bikes here since the weather is mild. The itch to ride is worse when there's been a cold spell, like there has been lately. We need some throttle therapy ASAP.

I'm going straight to my sister's car parked in the college lot. That's where we start.

My brothers are going to ride with me. I really appreciate their support and I've told them such, many times, I'm amazed, no grateful is the word, that I have these kinds of people in my life. It means the world to me. I knew it was a good idea to accept Rock's very generous offer of employment and to become part of this chosen family.

I pull my Indian Springfield Dark Horse, aptly named Hades, out of the garage and hurry to start him up. His deep, penetrating rumble echoes between the houses, bouncing everywhere. Snapping my phone in the dash holder, I fine tune the programs running so I can still hear all of them at once.

I have a feeling the neighbors are going to complain again. Fuck them. None of these posh privacy fences are going to stop that sound from shaking your lungs when I hop on and rev.

Throwing on my helmet, I key it up for the interconnected audio system to connect each of us together so we can talk. Absently, I notice that while Shadow and Gunney are sitting on their bikes, we all look like clones. You won't be able to distinguish which one of us is which if we're all covered up and helmets on. We're that close in build, like true brothers.

Shadow keys up and asks, "Hey Dec, can you still hear the police scanner? What's it saying?"

"Nothing useful. Body has no ID on it. They are having to do good ole fashioned detective work," I reply.

"Oh no, they have to work for it," Gunney mocks and chuckles as he clips his phone into its holder on his bike.

There are detectives who are notorious for relying on modern techniques to solve things, and if that doesn't work, they don't bother doing old school police work to solve shit. Basically, they're lazy fucks.

"Exactly. I've gotten no other hits on all the other programs," I tell them as I pull ahead of them, leading the way to Lily's car.

I'm extremely worried about why her tracker isn't working.

We make it to the college parking lot in record time, definitely due to breaking a large handful of traffic laws. Don't give a shit.

I roll up beside Lily's car, the only one in the parking lot this late.

Suddenly my thoughts run to Poppy and how she's handling this. *God, I hope Poppy hasn't been too much trouble for Birdie. I need to check on her but I know she's safe and Birdie will take care of her.*

Once I'm off my bike, not taking my eyes off the car, I'm immediately searching for any clues. I reach in a saddlebag and pull out a pair of surgical gloves to touch the car with.

I don't trust a fucking thing about this situation. Did someone drug her door handle and cart her off afterwards? Did they sneak up behind her?

The car door is shut all the way. There's nothing outside the vehicle. No powders or oils on the door or handle. No sign of forced entry or any signs of a scuffle. Gunney and Shadow are looking below and all around the car for clues, evidence, anything to go on.

Gunney nods to me after using the digital sweep across the car for any bombs or triggers. You can never tell with LSS.

Peering into the car, I see Lily's purse and backpack on the passenger floorboard where it looks like it was tossed. I hesitantly open the driver's door, swinging it wide open.

I feel Shadow move up behind me to see around me into the car. Gunney opens the passenger door and bends down to look in the car too.

"Is this her stuff?"

"Yeah, that's her backpack and that's the purse I bought for her birthday last year." Clearly robbery is not the motive.

My heart is hammering in my chest. I can't lose my sister. I just can't! She's all I have left beside Poppy. She's like my other half.

Think positively, Declan!

"Do you want me to pull her bags out from my side?" Gunney asks.

"Just her purse. I want to see if her stuff is still inside."

Gunney picks it up off the floor and hands it to me across the console. I set it on the seat and use the glow from the streetlamp above to rummage through her purse. Her wallet, phone and ear buds are still in her purse. There's still cash and all her cards are still there.

Plus, her five-hundred-dollar purse is still here.

This wasn't a robbery like I had hoped.

"Fuck," I grunt in frustration.

I yank her purse up and bring it over to my bike, setting it on my seat and begin to look through it more. What I'm looking for I have no idea. There's jack shit in here to tell me where she is.

I shove the purse in my saddlebag and turn to look at my brothers. Gunney and Shadow are going through her backpack. I'm so lost. I don't know what to do. Where do I go after this?

"Nothing in here. Just books and notepads." Gunney tosses it back on the floorboard.

It doesn't make much sense to go to her apartment. How was she going to get there? Her car and keys are here. Besides, if she was at her apartment she'd likely have Poppy, and clearly she doesn't.

I must look hopeless because Shadow comes over and grips my bicep, "Hey man, I get it. Your mind is going to all kinds of dark places. You can't let doubt slither in and take over. You know her best. Think bro, where would she be?"

Standing here with my hands on my hips, I tilt my head back staring up at the night sky, working my throat hard not to scream.

"She would be at my place, school, or her apartment. Can we split up and quickly run through this area?"

"Sure, man. Be back in five, that good?"

"Yep." I take off running, dodging tree roots and benches, constantly sweeping my eyes here and there for any signs of my sister. I don't even know what she's wearing to say what to look out for.

We find nothing. She's gone without a trace. No clues. No nothing.

Just like the others.

Just like *thousands* of others.

I feel sick.

The chatter on the police scanner has been quiet. I've been keeping one ear on that.

"Should we go to the scene of that girl's body?" I choke up asking that. I can't help it. I'm a cunt hair away from losing my shit right now.

"I'll call Danger," Shadow says as he slips away, phone up to his ear.

I have the immense desire to call Pierre and have him talk me off the edge. Hear his voice and let it soothe me. The big gaping hole in my chest grows smaller every time I hold myself back. Lily says that's healing.

But I can't call the only other person who could comfort me besides my sister. He doesn't want that type of relationship. And I'm mad at him for ghosting me and just ignoring me rather than manning up and breaking it off completely. Instead, he left me hanging on for his next call or text. Until I stopped waiting. No matter how much I miss him, I can't allow myself to lean on him for support.

One hand on my hip and the other pinching the bridge of my nose against the heat of stinging tears that are burning my eyes up, I just stand here finding my center of balance again. I have to get a grip.

Lose your shit after she's found.

I feel the energy coming upon me right before I feel Gunney wrapping his arms around me, hugging me. Just this simple gesture almost makes a sob break through.

If anyone knows how I feel right now it's these two. I saw how distraught they were when Zharia was kidnapped by the Lone Star Saints. They were a fucking mess, but yet united in their shared mission and goal to find their woman and steadfast with determination to make sure who stole her would pay the ultimate price.

I'm determined to find my sister.

I wrap my shaky arms around Gunney and hug him back. "Thanks, brother," I mutter.

"Anytime." He leans back and his hands grip the sides of my face, his steady eyes gaze into mine, "We know. We understand, and we are here with you ready to do whatever needs done. You are not alone. We have your back. Lead the way." Gunney pulls my head down and kisses my forehead. "Let's go to the scene, hacker."

I blink away more fearful tears as I bite my top lip. I nod to Gunney then just over his shoulder, I nod to Shadow as he gives me one of his fierce, empowering looks.

This is what I needed to steel my spine to do what needs done.

"Ok. Let's go."

Chapter 25

Pierre

"She's out," Birdie whispers from the overstuffed chair in her living room, right beside the couch I'm sprawled on. We crashed here after eating our pancakes.

I look over at Birdie who is smiling a sad, small smile. Birdie knows the outcomes that happen when LSS is involved. We went through some pretty traumatic shit together at their hands. If the guys are still looking, then there's a very high probability the Saints have taken Lily in retaliation.

"Does Declan know I'm here yet?"

The small shake of Birdie's head is all I need as confirmation. Zharia looks like she's about to burst into tears.

"I never thought I'd see you with a child asleep on you. Well besides your nephew Denver that is. It's sweet." Birdie says with a wistful twinkle to her eyes. We are both on overdrive with empathy.

"It really is, P, it looks good on you."

"Yeah, me either, but I actually like this one. She doesn't poop on me." I wink at Birdie through my exhaustion. It's past Poppy's bedtime but we let her sit up and watch *How To Train Your Dragon II.* She said it's far superior to all the other kid movies because of the dragons. Heh, the dragons *are* really bad ass. I wholeheartedly agree, kid.

Hey whatever. Anything to take her mind off what's happening currently.

What *is* happening is a whole lotta shit. Birdie gets updates from Danger, who is holed up in his home office down the hall, tracking attacks and locations, fielding calls and helping her father run an empire at war.

We just let him be.

They have not found Lily yet and it's been a couple of hours.

Poppy has been quiet, snuggled into my side, under my arm. She's wrapped with a super soft fleece blanket Birdie had on the back of the couch. I'm fairly certain she's drooled on my shirt.

She's attached herself to my hip. Almost literally.

I twist my torso and slip my arms around her and one under her legs and stand up, cradling her. Birdie jumps up, followed by Zharia, together they race ahead of me to open the door to one of the spare bedrooms.

Birdie already has the bed turned down and a nightlight is plugged in, casting shadows around the room. I see one of Denver's plush teddy bears laying on the bed. The nightlight is a moon in a wooden holder and quite frankly, it's super cool. Poppy loves the moon and the solar system. Such thoughtful touches.

I know from brunch-time table secrets we have between us that Poppy's afraid of the dark. We have that in common and bonded over our shared fear. It's our secret because a grown ass man can't lose street cred over something so silly. At least that's what I told her. She's sworn to secrecy by her most scared vow: spit in the hand and a shake.

I was very taken aback when she proposed that as our method of binding. I suggested a pinky promise and she said I wasn't to that level of trust yet.

Fair enough, little one. Spit in my hand, I did.

The walk over to the bed feels like a mile as the weight of what I'm doing hits me. I'm putting Declan's scared niece to bed, without his permission, while her precious mother is missing and he's desperately trying to find his beloved sister. The gravity of the current events...*Fuck man, this shit just got real deep*, I think as I choke up.

Declan will be destroyed if Lily is gone.

Poppy will grow up without a mother. She'll be orphaned.

As I lay her on the bed, Birdie is unwrapping her from the blanket so she won't overheat. I pull up the covers, tucking her in and Poppy whimpers in her sleep, lifting her hand slightly, "Don't go, Pierre. Please don't leave me." Her childlike voice is haunting in the quiet room.

My heart truly breaks right now. I feel a crevice crack wide open. This is the kind of memory that will last a lifetime for me, the vulnerability and the urge to protect. I'm surprised at the strength of the urge. I will do anything for this tiny princess at this moment to keep her safe and calm.

And the sad fucking part of that is she's no longer part of my life on a regular basis and I don't know if she ever will be again.

My gaze swings over to Birdie and Zharia in the shadows. Birdie's wiping a tear off her cheek and biting her knuckle. I see Birdie has hope for Lily, but it isn't limitless. We know the score.

Zharia has both her hands over her mouth, shoulders slightly shaking and tears wet her cheeks too.

"I'm right here, Poptart." My voice holds a hoarseness I don't often hear, so wrought with emotion. I hold her hand in mine, rubbing her knuckles.

"Please stay with me. I'm scared," her sleepy voice pleads, like she's ready to burst into tears. Well, she probably is.

I hear the girls behind me backing up towards the door with a few sniffles, then the soft click of the latch as they silently slip away.

I can see in the dark with the faint glow of the nightlight. I walk to the other side of the bed and lay on top of the blankets. The poor baby scoots next to me and curls up into my side and sighs.

Strange how this little human was able to get past all my defenses and distaste for children and pry her way into my heart. This is the hard part of getting attached. I was never supposed to have met her. She wasn't part of the plan.

I found myself missing her too these past weeks Declan and I have been separated. And her cool ass mom, I missed Lily too.

Poppy keeps Dec on his toes, as well as me. She was like this weird, little quirky friend I'd made that sometimes at inopportune moments spouted random facts she learned in school. It was brilliant and impressive to me.

Now granted, I've only been around her about a dozen times—a few brunches, a few club events and twice a dinner over at Declan's.

Looking back at it, that was a lot like dating.

Needless to say, we've had enough time to have this friendship we have. I'm humbled she feels this comfortable with me. I know she doesn't let just anyone in and the fact she accepted me and let me in almost instantly as a guarded kid, is not lost on me. Her trust is one of my most valuable things.

I pull up my phone and snap a pic of her asleep next to me. This might be the last time I see her. I'm sure as soon as Declan finds out, he'll yank her away, protecting her heart, just like his.

I put this on myself. I blame me. Like I said…I'm the problem. I brought this all on myself.

I pull the discarded blanket over me as I scoot down and settle in beside her. Pop's little poofs of air whisp across my t-shirt.

I will hold her as long as she allows it to keep her safe and keep the worry at bay. She deserves to have people who care about her in her corner. And I do care about her.

"Sweet dreams, Poptart," I whisper into the still silence. Her even breathing is the only response.

As soon as my kickstand is down, I'm moving swiftly to our contact—Lead Investigator Patrick O'Connor, or as we know him, Paddy. O'Connor is a cop and part of the Irish Catholic community here in the city. He's also aware of what we do and fully supports us, usually by providing valuable info.

He holds his hands up and says, "Boys, Danger already called. I can't just let you in a crime scene," Paddy says.

I try to go around him but he's damn near as big as me. I know if I really wanted to get by him I could. Shadow and Gunney would have my back and hold Paddy while I walked on by.

But I'm trying to do this in some sort of calm, grown up manner.

However, my patience is wearing thin.

"Pad, I need to see who it is. My sister is missing."

"We got shit all over the city tonight thanks to Panhead. Shit is crazy," Paddy grunts as I press in on him, "I can't let you in…here…at this entrance." He cocks an eyebrow, willing me to catch his drift. He gets low and quietly tells me, "You're gonna have to go 'round and come in from the back. I can let you in there but not with the rats and their cameras out here." I glance over at the news crew already milling about.

I pat Connor on the arm and say, "I'll be there in a few."

Heading down the block, we cut across so we can come up in the opposite direction, where it seems the city's finest are awkwardly standing, watching us approach.

I lead us through the flashing lights, Shadow and Gunney a step behind me, flanking me on the sides. Uniformed and street clothed officers stop talking and stand to watch us pass by.

I see…they know why I'm here.

And they know who we are.

They know how very important we are. They know we run this city.

They also know we are under attack tonight. All of them are on high alert for our retaliation.

We approach the yellow tape surrounding the area and an officer holds up the tape as we duck under. The crunch of our boots on the gravel seems to be just as loud as a firecracker in my overworked brain.

Dread and ice-cold fear coil in my stomach like a lead weight. Nerves seize the breath in my chest, yet I keep moving.

I'm terrified of what I might find in the body bag that's laying on a gurney twenty feet away. But still, I move forward to that black plastic bag.

I think I already know what I'm going to find.

I think my world is about to fracture and break apart into a million pieces.

I can barely breathe. Shadow's hand comes up to rest on my shoulder.

If my sister is in this bag, I don't think I'll survive. I try to drown the noise inside of me, screaming in panic, so I can do what needs to be done. I swallow the huge lump in my throat and reach for the body bag. I'm vaguely aware of the crowd of police personnel surrounding us.

Paddy comes rushing up and says, "Travares, wait, now I have to tell you, I need you prepared to view the body."

"I've seen plenty of dead bodies, Pad. Kindly move out of the way." I move around him and continue my assent.

I continue to reach for the bag's zipper; only then do I realize how much my hands are shaking.

Now or never, Dec.

I hold my breath and pull down the zipper.

The first thing I notice is the long brownish-blond hair seeped in blood laying everywhere. The face of the girl is bloody and bruised and beyond recognition. She was beaten severely.

My eyes travel down to her chest, where her shirt was ripped open. Carved into her flesh across her chest are the initials **LSS**.

This is a calling card. We are meant to find her.

Lifting my hand to move her hair from her face, Paddy snatches my wrist. "I can't have you touching her, T. You know that."

I do know that. But I can't help it. I need to see her face, her whole face. Lily had a beauty mole under her left eye. She complained about it all the time, how she wanted to cut it off herself.

By the looks of this girl's face, I wouldn't be able to tell if there was a mole or not.

The horror she must have felt, the pain and suffering.

I will never understand how someone could do this to another person, especially a woman this size.

A woman, Detective Laurens, makes her way up to us. As she grows closer, she nods to us, "Gentlemen." She pins her gaze on me. "Mr. Travares, we all know why you're here so let's not beat around the bush. As you can see our victim's face is unrecognizable. We are unable to get fingerprints, because of physical reasons."

"What reasons?" I can't help but ask.

"That's classified."

"That's bullshit is what that is, Nicole."

Her jaw clenches. She knows she better just give up the info or I'll find a way to get it without her. "If you must know, the killer cut the pads of her fingers off." She practically hisses at my lack of respect. "He wanted her left anonymous. Either that or make it extremely difficult to identify her." She tosses her ponytail over her shoulder and then looks in the bag.

"However, there was one thing the vic had in her hand, clutched tightly, that might be an ID of some sort for us if possible." She holds out a manilla envelope and tips it up to pour something out.

I open my hand, palm up, and hold it under the pouch with some of the worst heart palpitations I've ever had. I swear I'm going to pass out.

A piece of jewelry slides the length of the envelope and the cool metal of a necklace slithers into my hand. A flashlight beam appears on the jewelry.

My heart stops.

No. No. Fuck no.

It's a golden necklace with the name Poppy in cursive script and a red ruby inlaid as the O. I bought it for Lily when Poppy was born. She never takes it off.

Never.

Ever.

Not once.

In all the ways they tried to make her a no one, a nobody, she held on to the one thing that was everything she had so I would know her without a doubt. It's the one thing that would scream her name from the other side. She could scream her name in death and I would hear her.

Maybe that's me screaming her name.

Someone's screaming her name.

There's not enough air as I drop to my knees and everything goes black.

Chapter 27

Pierre

I rouse awake by the bed shifting, the sound of sheets sliding together. Thinking it's Poppy moving, I instinctively pat her beside me and whisper '*shhh, it's ok.*'

But when I open my eyes I see a shadow slipping into the bed.

On an instinctual level I know it's Declan.

And on a deeper level I know Lily's gone. His sadness and sorrow are palpable. I fight the urge to throw up and sob for her lost life. I feel it in my soul.

"Dec…" I groggily croak. "What's…"

"Not now, Pierre," his voice shaky and soft. Wounded, full of pain. Vulnerable.

He wraps his big arm around Poppy's sleeping form, that's still right up next to me, and pulls her over to him across the space, tucking her under his chin. He buries his face in her hair and a small sob escapes him.

My arm drifted over with Poppy's body when he slid her over and automatically my hand reaches for him and comes to rest on his head. My thumb slowly slides back and forth through his hair, trying to comfort him.

"Don't touch me, Pierre." Declan says it in a calm, quiet, deadly way that brooks no argument.

Immediately, I lift my hand off his person and swing my legs off the bed. I snatch my phone off the nightstand and head for the door. Reserved. Guess I did this to myself so I shouldn't be too mad about it. Hurting him was never on the table, yet by his tone I can tell that's exactly what's happened. Any idiot can see I've hurt him.

He's not going to allow me to comfort him, no matter how hard I want to.

I know where I'm not wanted and I don't need to be here. Trudging through the shadows, I make my way out of the room as silently as possible.

As the door closes behind me, I feel a thud in my chest, one of loss. Walking down the hallway to the sound of hushed voices, I start getting anxious. Bad news awaits me.

Birdie, Danger, Zharia, Shadow and Gunney stand around the kitchen island. I look over at the microwave and see it's near two in the morning. They all turn to me and watch as I walk up to the island where they're gathered. We all kinda stand there looking between us, not sure what to say.

I finally speak. "Lily's gone, isn't she?"

They nod in unison and my heart plummets and I can't help but gasp a sob back. Birdie puts her hand on my back and rubs circles.

Lead settles in my gut, realizing the weight of the situation. Declan's life changed overnight.

My heart yearns to comfort him, to hold him, whisper to him it will be alright. My arms ache to wrap around him and shield him from the ugly he's going through.

I care for him more deeply than I ever thought I wanted. I love him. Plain and simple.

I feel like I've ruined everything. He needs me but he's too wounded to allow it.

It will never happen if he's like he was to me a few minutes ago. I can't imagine what's he's going through. I know Danger and I have only been stepbrothers for a few good years but I would be devastated to lose him.

Lily was all Declan had left. Her and Poppy. That was his best friend, his therapist, his ride or die. They had one of the closest bonds I've ever seen. The astronomical void left behind will never be filled.

Unless Poppy heals the pain of loss for him but that's a lot to put on a child. I'm sure Poppy will become his world now and he will lay his life down to protect her. I have no doubt Declan can finish raising her and be there for her every step of the way and every important milestone of her life.

What feels like devastation in my heart is that I realize he won't allow me to be a part of her life. I will always be an outsider now.

Unless…but what if…No.

"What happened?" I quietly ask instead of following my train of thought. My thoughts seem to be slightly erratic here lately. Definitely not in character for me the past twenty-four hours.

Shadow clears his throat. Gunney puts his hand on Shadow's shoulder in support. These two have had a helluva bad night supporting Declan on his search. I'm sure it brought back memories of nightmare experiences and emotions from Z's disappearance.

Everyone looks at me before Shadow takes a breath to tell me the terrible news.

Oh god, this is bad.

"She was found in a dumpster, throat slashed," he took a steadying breath, "raped, and *LSS* carved into her chest."

I grab at my stomach as it rolls and my heart punches my ribcage in rage and despair. I cough to cover the sob breaking out of me. My friend. Lily, oh god Lily, I'm so sorry, you did not deserve that.

My eyes burn as they tear up. I gasp to catch my breath after the first sob escapes me. I can't look at any of them any longer. I bow my head and struggle so fucking hard to maintain my composure.

Birdie puts her arms around me. Zharia comes up on the other side and wraps her arms around me too. Their touch comforts me more than they know. Maybe they do know.

Shadow continues, "We heard the nine-one-one call and went to the scene. He ID'd her by a necklace. She was beaten too bad…" he clears his throat again, trying not to choke up. "Travares is obviously devastated. He's been quiet the entire way here after he discussed with Laurens where to take Lily."

Christ, Declan saw all that. There are no words how awful my heart feels. My chest is caving in. Everything inside me burns. I want to rip apart the person who did this.

If Declan doesn't burn the city down looking for her killer I'll be amazed.

Instead of screaming, I absently nod in thought, biting on my thumb nail. What do you actually say in the face of such tragedy?

What am I going to say to Declan in the morning?

My anxiety ratchets up a few notches. What about poor Poppy? How's she going to handle being told the news?

He's made it clear he does not want me around, but I'm not giving up this time. Somewhere between two AM and five AM I decided I need to get my ass in gear and win him back. I was so fucking stupid.

My five AM reality call was accepting how deeply in love I am with Declan. I was all along.

The bleeding heart inside my chest screams, *FINALLY.*

I'm sick and tired of allowing Seven to rule my life, and that includes loving freely.

I just gotta get him to talk to me first.

My southern upbringing will not allow me to be rude and blatantly ignore his pain and not give condolences, so whether he likes it or not, I'll be talking to him when he gets up.

But after that…I will still support him. Silently, from afar, but still close enough if he needs…This isn't the right time to hash out the details of our broken relationship.

I have to fix this soon.

I miss him and I want him back and I need him. I want to word vomit all that in an outpouring of emotions that I've kept repressed. That would be entirely inappropriate at this time. *So, shut the fuck up, Pierre.*

But I know the name of this powerfully overwhelming feeling, don't I? I know what this is and I need to get with the program and admit it fully. I love Declan and I can't live without him. I tried so hard to resist. He's everything I need, want and then some.

He's everything I never knew I needed.

But he doesn't need that dumped on him right now. And he sure as hell sounds like he doesn't want it from me.

Patience, Pierre.

For the second time in a few hours, I'm roused by the shifting of blankets and the surface I'm lying on dipping under the weight of something. I'm confused for a moment.

Since I must have drifted off on the couch after talking to Birdie, Zhar and the guys earlier, I lay here clawing at sleep for just a second more.

Fuck I'm so tired. I haven't slept on a couch in ages. Not since my dad and I didn't have enough money to buy me a bed when I was growing up. I should be grateful to whomever was kind enough to throw a blanket over me.

I'm jostled again. Before I crack open my eyes, I smell her strawberry scent. Poppy's tiny form climbs in beside me and settles in the crook of my arm. Her face lays on my chest, snuggling up against me.

I'm sure that's Declan I feel staring a hole in the side of my head. Someone stands at the back of the couch over top of me and I can only assume it's him from the angry vibe they're giving off.

I lift my arm and smooth her hair back from her temple. Her eyelashes flutter on her cheeks and my heart crawls up into my throat and rests there. I try to push past it.

"Good morning, Poppy," I lightly say to her as I hug her. My heart is completely broken for her. Does she even know yet?

I feel the room filling up with nervous energy. She does a sniffle, shaking her little body. Oh, man. It's like I went from my warm cocoon of sleep to having a bucket of ice water dumped on me.

I hear another sniffle behind me, towards the kitchen. Birdie. They're listening to us. I guess it is odd, me and a child. I've never really had an opportunity like this to become close to a kid before now. I have a strange sensation in my chest.

There are soft sounds of coffee being made, a cabinet lightly opening, the swish of the barstool gliding over the hardwood floor. All normal morning things for a completely abnormal morning. It dawns on me that Poppy woke up this morning and sought me out, choosing to come lay with me. Her friend.

She feels safe with me and that to me is the most important thing in my life as I hyperfocus on the trust I've earned.

"Morning, Ringmaster," she quietly says. She lays here a few heartbeats more before softly speaking again. "Uncle Ducky found Mommy. She's dead."

Hugging her tighter, I whisper in anguish, "I'm so sorry, Poppy."

"I'm scared, Pierre. What if Uncle Ducky doesn't want me? Where would I go?" Her small sob shoots a bullet straight through my hurting heart and it covers up a much deeper voiced sob in the background.

Declan.

My wounded heart whispers and calls for him.

Jesus fuck. I have no guts left. Poppy's done ripped them out and burned them alive. Donkey shit. This is how much this sucks right now.

"Shh, I'm right here. Turn over here and look at me. I wanna see you." She rolls towards me and I push the tendrils that are flying everywhere out of her face. Our eyes lock and I tell her, "Uncle Ducky loves you very much. You hear me? More than anything. Until all the stars burn out in the skies. Of course he will want you. I promise you he will do anything to keep you with him. You don't have to be scared. Com'mere," I pull her to my chest to hug her.

"And I promise, if Uncle Ducky can't take care of you, I will. I will come get you and you will live with me."

Just like that, my heart changes. Everything changes.

I've promised a child I would take care of them, not knowing if I can keep that promise, but I'll try with all my might and every resource if something happens to Declan.

"Can I have Mickey Mouse pancakes again?"

"Sure, you can. Will that make you feel better?" I ask hesitantly. I'm not sure how to deal with kids. I'm basically winging it with this one.

But I know how to be a friend to just about anyone, so that's the route I take.

She jumps up and her eyes drift to the kitchen where I know Birdie, Danger and Declan are. I feel the tension coming off of them. I sit up and gather the motivation to stand. Wiping my hands down my face, I rub my eyes and yawn. Ok, let's start this shitshow of a day.

I rise and slowly make my way around the couch. When I raise my eyes they lock with Declan's. There are so many emotions churning in there, like an angry, choppy sea, dead set on rage and destruction. The overwhelming sorrow overrides it though. My Dec always wore his heart on his sleeve and I can see his sadness surrounding him like a cloak.

He has every right to be angry right now.

His anger at me has taken a back seat to Lily's death. We knew what we agreed on, the conditions and limitations. He agreed. I reminded him. He still agreed. I no longer wanted to invest in our relationship—cough—catch feelings—cough—and decided to walk away.

But I've changed my mind. Totally. Completely.

Seeing him right now makes my chest flutter and breaks my heart at the same time. I'd love nothing more than to walk up and put my arms around him.

He needs a hug just as much as I do, I'll wager.

Instead, I walk up to him and put my hand out and say, "I'm so sorry, Declan, I really am. If there's anything I can do, please let me know how to help."

I'm so close to him I can breathe in his essence like smoke. I can feel his energy crawling across my skin, igniting feelings. He stares at my hand and when I go to put my hand down, he lifts up and takes my hand.

His intense gaze stays on mine and I'm flooded with so much at once.

Baby steps, Pierre.

The longer I stand here the stronger the urge gets to reach out and pull him to me. I'm not sure how that will be received so I stick with the handshake. Seems safer.

"Thank you, Pierre," he softly says.

Pressing my lips together, I drop his eyes and nod. I can't keep staring into those depths. Slipping his hand out of mine, I move to go around him.

He grabs my bicep and leans in and tells me in a low gravelly tone where only I can hear, "Don't break her heart too. Your time around her is finite." His lips are moving right on the shell of my ear, "Thanks for taking care of her last night." He releases me and steps away from me, locking eyes with me again.

"Uncle Ducky, do you want Pierre's pancakes?"

My eyes skate down to Poppy as she climbs onto the island barstool and makes herself at home, tapping her fingers on the countertop. She's either ignoring the tension or children don't pick up on it.

I look back up at Declan. While looking at me he says, "No, popsicle, I don't want pancakes right now. Duck has to make a few phone calls but I'll be back in a jiffy." He raps his knuckles on the countertop while kissing her on the top of her head and hurries off towards Danger's office.

I notice Birdie hovering at the end of the island with Danger behind her. He's rubbing her arms and she has tear tracts down her reddened, puffy face.

Feeling shellshocked and stripped raw in a matter of a couple of blinks is no way to start the day, so I try hard to hit the reset button and grab for coffee. Nothing's changed. Sweet Jesus, hand over the bean water if I'm going to get through this day.

Only then can I make some mean Mickey Mouse pancakes for a special little girl.

CHAPTER 28
TRAVARES

Hanging up the phone with the funeral director, there's a knock on the office door, and I automatically say 'Come in' thinking it's Danger. I know they are trying to give me privacy to do what needs done.

I didn't expect Pierre to enter and shut the door quietly behind him.

"Declan."

I study him hard. He still looks exactly like the man I fell in love with. He's also the same man who ghosted me and broke my heart. He sort of has this lost look about him though, that's new.

I don't give an inch. I learned no matter what I did, what I said, how much I cared, at this time Pierre is incapable of loving someone else. His heart is too firmly shut. Seven is stealing his happiness from him still and Pierre is letting it happen.

He proved it by letting me go. I know what I bring to the table. I know my worth. It was fun while it lasted but in a way I have to thank him because he stopped it before I could jump off the ledge straight into the bottomless abyss.

I may believe I've found my soulmate, and I may have fought to keep it, but even hope has a time limit. Best to walk away. I've spent weeks wondering why I'm not enough, why he would destroy everything we'd built. I've hardened my heart and patched it up best I can.

Now I have to find some way to deal with how much Poppy has attached herself to him. Just fucking great. She's been asking for him for weeks now. This is a volatile situation with her just losing her mom, her only parent left. If I take Pierre away from her too, how will that affect her now and in the long run?

Either way, Poppy pulls us together, nothing more.

Leaning back in the office chair, I ask him, "Do you need something?"

He takes a few steps into the office, coming to rest behind the chair in front of the desk. His hands rest on the back of the chair while he looks at me with hope and compassion in his eyes.

He's probably just happy I'll talk to him after he told me he felt 'like being alone for a while' and he appreciated the time we spent together but he was no longer interested.

"Yeah, I, um, wanted to say I can take Poppy back to my place and keep her occupied while you need to do what needs done. I'm not sure what all encompasses something like this but I know you'll be busy and I want to help. I want to be here for you…and Poppy. I'll do what I can for you."

So that irks me. "Don't let my sister's death make you feel guilty and start caring. We'll be fine. Thank you for the offer but Poppy is safe and ok right here. Is that all?"

I can tell that is not what he wanted to hear, but exactly what he expected. The tick in his jaw indicates his anger spiking but he's working really hard at keeping his shit together. He's the one who cut this off.

How exactly does he expect me to act?

My main objective is taking the best care of Poppy and not allowing anything to hurt her further. Unfortunately, I didn't foresee them bringing Pierre over here last night. I'm going to feel like the biggest dick when I have to keep Pierre away from her.

She won't understand and she'll most likely fight me over it, but I feel like it's for the best right now.

"I swear I won't let anything happen to her, Dec. She's scared and at least I'm familiar to her. She's comfortable with me and I don't mind. Let me help." His eyes plead with me.

A surge of tiredness falls over me. It would be so easy to let him help but I have to remember how easy it was for him to lead me on and then disappear. I can't let him use a revolving door in and out of Poppy's life. Plus, I don't want him to be a constant reminder that I'm not enough to love.

If it wasn't love, he's lying. I felt it. He felt it, but it doesn't matter now.

I tap my pointer finger on the desk twice before I say, "You're not interested in us anymore, remember? We're fine, Pierre." I stand up and gather my things, "You can help by leaving me alone. I gave you that respect when you requested it, now I would like the same. I won't be here much longer. You should use this time to tell Poppy goodbye." I move past him and make it to the door before…

"I never meant to hurt you." The words are so soft I almost missed them. But I didn't.

I scoff and look at him with my hand on the doorknob, "Hey, it's cool. It meant nothing, right? Just passing time and our time has passed. We owe each other nothing. Take care, Pierre."

I walk out of the room on shaky legs and vow to get away from him as fast as I can before my traitorous heart bursts and drags me back.

"I don't understand why he can't come over. He's your friend. He's *my* friend. *We* are friends! News flash, Uncle Ducky, friends are people too."

Poppy stands in the living room with her hands on her hips, where she stopped after walking into my house. She's on her shit about Pierre coming over to watch a movie since he promised her he would.

I'm not sure why she thinks friends aren't people but that's a thought for another time. I'm just not following eight-year-old logic right now.

I'm trying hard not to sigh in exasperation. Short of telling her the ugly truth…I close my eyes and breathe in. As an alternative, I calmly say, "Pierre and I aren't friends anymore." Hopefully leaving it at that.

Nope. Not Poppy. For sure as fuck, not Poppy. She has to push the subject until she has all the answers. Her most infuriating quality that she inherited from her mother.

God, I hated when Lily would do the same thing to me.

"But he IS my friend and I want to watch a movie with him," she insists, crossing her arms over her chest in defiance.

Do not snap at this child, Declan.

"Poppy. I don't want him here at my house." In my own agitation I face her with my hands on my hips too.

Be the adult.

"Fine, then take me to my house and he can stay with me there. Then he won't be in your house at alls."

I rub my eyes and sing-song the theme song for *Digimon* in my head to clear the irritation. I need to smooth this over. She doesn't understand the complexities of the situation.

"No, Poppy. Final answer."

I expect her to yell, stomp her foot maybe.

In lieu of that, her lip pouts out and it trembles while her eyes fill with tears. I have no idea where this is coming from. I know they were growing closer before the breakup, but I had no idea she liked him this much. He always made time for her. He always answered her questions with patience and grace. He never treated her like a dumb, annoying kid.

Honestly, it shocked the shit out of me because I distinctly remember him saying how much he dislikes children of all ages. He was hoping Denver would cure him of the 'unsavory trait' inside him.

I don't know what his angle is here and it's got me off center to tell the truth. When shit got real, he bailed. Well, shit's really real now and I'm just trying to manage the fallout with Poppy when it inevitably happens.

He's already said he's coming to the funeral in a few days. She's going to see him there anyways. Which if I had my way would be the final time she sees him. Me too, for that matter. I can't stand the gut-wrenching pain of loss every time I see him and my traitorous broken heart leaps for joy. It doesn't understand his rejection when his actions and words spoke a love language that weaved the two of us together in our own love story.

Stop dwelling on stupid shit.

"Look, we'll see him in a few days, ok? Can I have you for a few days by myself?" I feel my eyes fill at the same time my sinuses burn. I take a few steps to Poppy and crouch down, clamoring to my knees. I hold open my arms as the first tears trail down my face. "Come cry with me."

The dam breaks.

She starts sobbing and runs to me. She wraps her small arms around my neck and buries her face in my neck while her little body shakes and heaves in sobs.

I gently smooth down her hair as my tears spill over and her hair soaks them up. I whisper how much I love her, and want to keep her, and how we're going to be ok.

Poppy needs to know how much I'm hurting too. She needs to know she's not alone in her grief. I won't hide how I'm feeling from her where her mother and our grief is concerned. She needs to know men cry too. Men hurt too.

Some of us just show it more than others.

Chapter 29

Pierre

The sun is high in the sky when Danger agrees to let me go back to my apartment. He's had a security team installing all kinds of techie shit I'll have to learn how to use.

He's been rambling about old buildings in the Quarter and how hard they are to fit modern things, such as home security systems.

I mean, he did have one in here when his wife lived here before me, but he respectfully took it out when I moved in. Guess he didn't want to see his brother walking to the kitchen with his swinging dick.

Now I have no choice. Shit's got too real.

Mine and Birdie's studio downstairs is getting fitted with new technology too. She had to relent. Danger was going to do it anyways so it's best she just agrees. He will do whatever it takes to keep her safe but still let her live her life on her terms.

There's a new door installed at the bottom of the apartment stairs that lead up. It's metal and it's solid and it has a reinforced glass window. It has one of those handy dandy retinal scans too, just like at Danger's place.

Me: Your husband is overkill

Me: He is acting like an army of ninjas are going to slip in through the water faucet.

Birdie: LMAOOO

Birdie: Soooo true

Me: Call him to come home. He's driving me crazy. He's already checked the French door ten times.

Me: Hell, the workers are already finished and gone. Lincoln is just obsessing now.

The ringing of a phone from the hallway can be heard coming closer to me just as my brother appears in the living room. He looks at the screen and hurries to answer it.

"Hey babe. What's wrong?"

He nods his head and does the required 'Mm-hmms' when needed.

"Ok, be there in a few. Love you lots, Princess."

Thank YOU, B!

Danger looks up and sees me just chilling at the kitchen island. He slips his phone in his pocket and makes his way over to the kitchen. His steps are hurried and I know he's going to be gone soon.

Right on target.

I'd really love a shower in my own place.

"Hey bro, gotta go. Ole Lady wants to go to the park with Denver while it's a nice day. I have to gather about twelve men." He rubs his chin, staring off into space. "That might not be enough."

"Ok."

He raps his knuckles on the island surface, "Call me if you need anything. I mean it."

I put my hands up in defense, "I will, I promise."

"Anything. There will be a detail outside. They will follow you anywhere so make sure you ain't trying to shake them. Understood?"

"Yes, Lincoln, I get it. High alert. Head on a swivel. Be aware of my surroundings. I don't plan on leaving anyways. Tomorrow the shop will reopen. Everything for today was rescheduled and I'm taking the rest of the day for myself."

"Right. I'll be checking in regularly too. Like every couple of hours. Get used to it. I'll talk to you later. Make sure you reply or answer timely. Got it?" God, when he goes into protection mode he is an insufferable asshole to deal with.

After my nod, he pulls me into one of his bear hugs and walks out the door.

Finally.

Alone.

Shower.

I quickly put my phone on charge with the bedside charger. Undressing as I make my way to the bathroom, I toss my shirt on the bathroom floor as I walk in. I drop my sweats and reach in the linen closet and my eyes land on the bottle of body soap Declan had here. He didn't take it when he was last here.

That's because he thought he was coming back.

A need, a yearning so bad comes over me. It makes me physically shudder. I want him so bad. Fuck. I miss him.

Against my better judgement, I reach for the bottle and pop the cap open. Don't do it.

I fill my lungs with the scent of Declan and my chest constricts, then swells. It makes my knees weak.

The worst fear was fucking this up. And then I went and did it because I let fear step in and destroy what we built.

And what a beautiful thing we built together. I can freely admit I loved every minute I spent with him. In our short period of time, we became inseparable and best friends immediately.

It's important to me to be best friends with your partner. At one time Seven was my whole world, my best friend and partner in crime.

Whoa. Whoa. He's not our partner. Partners are for committed relationships and we've got a really rocky situationship going on now.

His anger is too sharp towards me right now.

That's why you're alone right now and he's dealing with his sister's death on his own.

Self-mental torture is a beast of its own.

This is the freedom I so stubbornly wanted and my oh my, how much it tastes like bitter ash melting on my tongue.

Yet I still breathe in the soap and let the shiver work its way through my body. It's the reaction I have whenever I think of him, definitely whenever I'm around him.

I take it to the shower with me. Once the water's warm, I step under it and the sigh that comes out of me bubbles up straight from my soul.

Fuck. What a night.

The past twenty-four hours have been fucked up. I'm soul-tired. Bone weary.

Smelling Declan does something to me. It feels like there's electricity racing across my skin in the warm water. I can imagine his hands rubbing across my skin. It's a memory. Here in this shower. Our bodies rubbing together.

My cock stirs and I hang my head, putting my hands on the tiled walls. I'm fighting here. I can't. Now's not an appropriate time to fuck my hand.

Why not? He's not here. Lean into it.

I can't resist the pull of arousal in such a sad time.

Even under the tragic circumstances and then the rejection, Declan makes my body light up with want and need. Fuck, the desire I have for him is off the charts.

Gripping his soap bottle in one hand, I pour a good amount in the other hand. My dick is already at half-mast growing fast. That's just from smelling it.

As soon as I wrap my hand around my cock it's already hardened and ready. It wants something more than this pitiful release. It wants him. It wants his ass, his body, his mind.

Gripping tighter, I begin to stroke up and down to the memory of how his skin feels under my hands. How his smile lights up his face and when he bites his bottom lip because the thought of me fucking him crosses his mind.

"Fuck," I groan into the shower and it reverberates back at me. "Declan, baby, I miss you," I choke out.

I think of the dips and curves of his spectacular body. I remember running my tongue over him, kissing all over his body. The roughness in places, smooth as a baby's ass in others. All of it feels so good against my lips and skin. It makes me shiver under the hot water with the memory of how good it was.

The smell is overpowering the shower, the whole bathroom. Possibly into my bedroom as well. Good. I want to smell him everywhere.

I'm in the mood to torture myself tonight.

Quickening my pace, I run my fingers over the tip, spreading the slippery precum over the head. I suck in air through my teeth at the sensation.

"Declan," I moan as if he could hear me.

I replay the memory where he was laughing and playing around and decided to push me and see how long it would take for me to bend him over.

It didn't go as planned for him.

I yanked his basketball shorts off, he had no underwear on underneath. I spit on my fingers and pushed his leg up to his chest. Just as his ass lifted off the couch, I was pushing my fingers into his ass.

He let loose a cross between a yelp and a moan. I quickly stretched him and just as fast, I pulled him onto my lap as I sat back. He straddled me as I pulled lube from the side table.

We were frantic for each other. Couldn't get enough. Bodies burning up and ready to combust. I remember so well.

My breath catches and I groan when I think of when Declan positioned himself over me, hovering for a few seconds before he lowered himself on my shaft with that tight ass. It felt like a warm wave crashing over me as he slid down my length. So hot and tight.

I gripped his cock between us as he rode me. It was one of the best times of my life. Hearing him above me, moaning my name, catching his breath, shuddering at the filthy things I said to him.

Suddenly, my balls draw up and I feel the lightning bolt strike down my spine. My cum shoots out of me as I yell Declan's name. My knees shake and almost give out.

Oh fuck, I pant to myself, holding myself up against the wall while my head hangs.

I thought this would make me feel better, but all it's done is made me feel like a bigger piece of shit.

"We have a lead."

My head snaps up from my laptop where I was working on hacking the phone of a notorious Saints member. Well, more like their top three officers' phones.

"Please clarify."

"On where Pete is and who may have hurt Lily," Rock speaks up. "And where her security detail was. They were bought by Pete's blood money and were nowhere near the scene."

I do a great job holding back the roar I want to let loose.

Our Wednesday night Elite Team meeting is underway and we have much to discuss. Namely the attacks of the womenfolk and the death of my sister. Sunday's club meeting put everyone on high alert after the shitshow that happened last week.

My sister's memorial was a few days ago. I spoke of growing up with my best friend and how supportive we were of each other; about how much I loved her and what she meant to me. Using past tense words to speak of her was the hardest.

In the quietness of my house that night, I secured Lily's necklace around Poppy's slender neck. I almost lost my head and started sobbing when I was doing it.

It's been at a jeweler's fitting it with one of the rarest, smallest trackers built by man. I helped design the programming with Danger, specifically with Poppy in mind. Now the ruby has a tracker under it.

I'm still not sure why my sister's stopped working. The last marker where it pinged from was two blocks over from the college and her body was found a few more blocks away after that.

Even if I went to look for the tracker, I would never find it. It's so small it could be anywhere. The only feasible explanation I can come up with is they cut it out of her on the way to where they killed her. They crushed it with pliers, or something strong to make it no longer work. I strongly feel they used a scanner on her body to find it or else they would have never known it was there.

I can't help but feel she died because of me.

The guilt I harbor is overwhelming at times.

Whoever did this will die too. I will make goddamn sure of it. I'm fucking dying to spill blood over it.

I remember Lily telling me one time that computer geeks aren't supposed to have bloodlust, they aren't built to be involved in violence.

I'm unique, is what I told her with a smirk. If only she knew the computer geeks I do. She would see they very much enjoy violence and causing chaos whilst writing up some code for a kids' game and eating Skittles.

I've just described Bam. The same guy who proudly announces violence makes his dick hard.

"We are hearing rumors from our guy within the Saints that Pete is at a safehouse in Port Arthur, Texas. He's holed up with one of his top guys. Word is he's left a good number of Saints in town here and his righthand man is leading them in his absence. It makes me believe the attacks aren't over."

The two surviving top Saints from the morning of the massacre when we rescued Zharia and killed everyone in our path are who he's talking about. They're lucky they were off site with Panhead when it happened.

They are due their deaths soon.

"Do we know the exact location so we can go blow it up?"

"Yeah! What Slim said!" Bam shouts on the heels of Slim Jim's comment.

For once, I agree with Bam. I fully support blowing up shit right now. Hell yeah.

Rock throws his hands up, gesturing to Bam to sit back down. "As much as that sounds like fun, we still have to work somewhat within the law. A big ass explosion will lead to too many investigations. We're using plain ole fire. Much better excuse for how things started."

"Fuck yeah!" Bam grunts.

"We want nothing to point back at us. Trust me, I'm working all the angles to find a way to eliminate them once and for all," Rock finishes.

Danger steps up and addresses the small crowd of the Elite Team in our clubhouse. "We do know Panhead ordered the chaos from a week ago. It's retaliation for his wife's death. He doesn't plan on stopping either."

"A leader who's ruled by his heart is not a strong leader and he's vulnerable and weak. It's time to strike and strike hard." Rock surveys us as he stands with his large arms across his chest. "But we have to use our heads and plan this out. Panhead will expect swift retribution but we won't give it. Let's make them sweat and watch their backs for a little longer."

For an older man, Rock is just as built as my thirty-six-year-old ass. Rock definitely spends his share in a gym and it shows. I would not want to tangle with Rock and I can respect a man his age still being a bad motherfucker.

Danger speaks again, "We believe the Saints that were in town causing havoc have not left the city. They are going to lull us into a false sense of safety and let us think that it's done. We aren't stupid. As you heard from Sunday's meeting, there is a shitload of men wanting to go on a good old-fashioned raid like they did to us. Only we hit Houston. We hit them in the nuts, right at home."

Cheers go up in the room. "Fuck Yeah!" "Finally!" "About time!"

"Sunday is the raid. Plans were made Monday night and we are still following that plan. Let them think we aren't retaliating. Word has gone out to every man that has stepped up." Danger points to Gunney and Shadow and continues, "These two will be leading the raid while I stay back protecting Rock with a team of my men. We will be waiting for any retaliation in the city."

About fifty members are riding to Houston on Sunday with Shadow and Gunney. Main objective: Destroy all the small businesses of as many Saints members as we can find. We plan to hit them as close to home as we can. We will cripple their members, which will press back harder to their piss poor leadership. Enough to make numbers dwindle and lose more traction with this war.

You start fucking with how someone feeds their family and people start rioting within the ranks.

Because now, it's not just terrorizing the rivals and scaring the women. And for a good number of them not in on the bigger operations, this isn't what they signed up for but it's what they're getting. Now it's payback and answering the message they left behind regardless of who did it.

We've spent days tracking down, mapping, and learning routes to forty-four businesses of patched members of the Lone Star Saints in Houston.

Rock is all about bending the rules where he can and he doesn't like taking lives but he will if good triumphs all. He feels arson really isn't a crime, go figure. It's more like a punishment. It's crazy, man. Murder is a crime to him though. That's his hard criminal line.

I will never understand how his calculating mastermind works. He has held power over this area for over twenty-five years. Once he took over from his father, Rock grew this organization and his empire to the overabundance it is today. We all thrive from his master planning and vicious determination.

This means probably on Sunday night, Poppy will be staying with Birdie in the Ivory Tower while I work. I imagine Pierre will be there. And Zharia most definitely if Shadow and Gunney are going on the raid.

I'm glad Pierre will be there. I may not be happy with his choices right now but I don't want anything bad to happen to him. I'm not a monster.

My job is to monitor the police scanners and track Gunney and Shadow from here. Everyone has been advised it's mandatory to leave their cell phones with their Old Ladies or partners. We don't need us being tracked. We have a few burner phones that we've programmed with the men's partner's numbers for those wanting to call after the raid when they reach the safety zone.

We understand this is a lot for some of the guys going on the raid. Some have never had to deal with anything like this and they were content to ride and just do meetings and charity events. Until now. Until LSS fucked with the wrong people.

They are pissed. Understandably so.

No one is as pissed as me though. Their women and partners are still alive. These fucktards took my sister's life. As far as I'm concerned, they can all die and I'll be happy to drag them to hell.

Shadow takes up where Danger left off, "As always, if caught, deny and stay silent. We will have you lawyered up in a heartbeat and out as soon as possible."

Rock gives a half smile and a wink while pointing at Shadow, "What he said."

My laptop beeps and I quickly swing back to it. The program's red box switches over to green letting me know we are in. Yes baby!

Bam, knowing that sound, rushes over to me and props himself on the table, one arm bracing on the table while he leans over my shoulder to see my screen.

"Finally!" he claps me on the back.

"Which phone?" Rock asks as he makes his way through tables to get to me.

"Panhead's," I answer.

"Holy fuck, kid," T-Bone breathes out.

"That's my boy!" Slim Jim guffaws.

"We knew you could do it." Wild Bill whistles.

Somehow having the old birds' praise makes my heart quiver with pride. I have a half smile on as I pull up the messages on the phone.

The program is still running for his Vice President's and Sergeant-At-Arms' phones.

"Fuck, my laptop is out in the car," Bam says and pats himself for his keys.

I interject before he can run out, "No need, bro, I built a program for all the keywords we're looking for and it will scan the entire phone including all social media messages and emails linked up on the device. If those words are on there, it will produce a report. That's when we analyze data."

Bam calms down a bit after I say that. I know he's itching to choke someone out or stab someone in the head, or whatever gory shit he does.

"How long does it take to produce a report?" Shadow asks.

"Within fifteen minutes."

"Dang. That's really nice work, Dec," Rock says as he lays his hand on my shoulder and squeezes, "Damn fine work."

Most of the time bikers absolutely won't let another associate call them by their government name, the one ya momma gave ya. It's always by their road name.

But I don't have one. Being in the military I was always called by my last name and it stuck. I didn't want a road name or a nickname. Matter of fact, not a lot of people know my name is Declan. The older guys, the top five, and Bam. That's all I've ever told around here and we only use it in these meetings.

Shadow and I agree with having no road name, seeing as he doesn't have one either. Shadow is his real name and it fits him.

A file's being built since it unlocked the device. It's searching through tons of information right now at lightning speed. I can see the number of entries for the report escalating quickly. Goddamn it.

Another ding and I watch the red box turn green on the third-in-command's phone and immediately queue it up in the program to search it.

"Yes! Slidin' through like butter, brother!" Bam raises a fist in the air. "Let me go get my laptop to help go through the reports. I'll be back." He pats my shoulder as he jogs off.

"Those that want to head out can do so. We are done here." Rock takes the seat next to me and leans back with his arms crossed.

No pressure, Dec.

My damn leg starts bouncing from nervousness or is it giddiness? Little bit of both. So many fucking reasons I'm jittery nowadays, it could be anything.

I might finally find out who I need to kill.

God, it feels like I've been waiting forever to avenge Lily. There's no way in hell I'm letting that go by unchecked. Rock knows I'm not sitting by. I'm not waiting to strike.

I'm showing no mercy. I'm taking someone out. I'm acting on my own without orders from Rock.

The kicker is he's backing me. He wants vengeance as much as I do.

Short of tying me up in his soundproofed 'dungeon,' his abandoned warehouse two blocks over from the club house, he isn't going to stop me. He might as well go along with it.

The final ding chimes from my laptop and the green box appears just as Bam sits down.

I think we might be here for a while judging by how long these reports are taking. I watch the number of entries rise on all the reports and let out a sigh.

Time to get to work.

Chapter 31

Pierre

Wine Wednesday is interesting this week. Zharia and Tally are arguing about the latest season of some trashy, over-the-top reality show about numerous wives of rich people.

People I give no shits about, however one of the husbands is a client of mine. Small world.

Birdie sits next to me on the couch looking tired, nursing her bottle of water.

I've noticed for weeks her water bottle that sits close to her. Oh, she thinks she's getting one over on us. She's been putting water in a wine glass and adding those colored water juices to make it look like red wine, her favorite. I caught her doing it but said nothing. I was wanting to see how this played out but nahh, I wanna know now.

I lean over and bump her with my shoulder and ask, "So, how far along?"

Her eyes blow wide and her eyebrows climb into her hairline. She gasps, which makes her choke on her sip of water.

Immediately Zharia shuts her mouth and snaps her head in this direction as Birdie coughs. Eagle eyes laser focused on Birdie. Tally looks utterly confused as she must not have heard Birdie's sharp intake of breath nor my question.

"What?" Z's eyes narrow.

"What's happening? Someone tell me. I can't hear!" Tally leans closer to the camera like that will help. It only makes her face fill up more of Birdie's giant TV screen. I imagine this is what hamsters or goldfish feel like when we look through the glass at them.

Birdie tries to recover quickly. Her owl eyes blink at the rest of us. Cherry is hanging off the chair trying to get closer to hear what's happening. She fits in well here. She is always down for some piping hot tea.

"You just gave yourself away, babes," I smile at her.

"How long?" Zharia demands while crossing her fingers and smiling, bouncing in the chair.

"Oh my god," Tally breathes and brings her hands up close to her heart.

"Is this a good thing?" Cherry asks while looking from one of us to the other. Poor heart. She'll learn. I simply nod and Cherry lets out a sigh.

Birdie clears her throat and looks over at me. "Thank you, Mr. Lefèvre." Her eyes narrow slightly.

She draws her legs up by her butt and spreads her blanket over them, leaning on to me. "It's not like I'm keeping it from y'all. I was trying to make it to the second trimester before I said anything. Just trying to get in a safer zone."

"Oh my fuck! It's true." Zharia's breath rushes from her. "Holy fuck, it's happening!" Zhar jumps up and hugs her and bounces with Birdie back and forth like a ragdoll. It's comical to watch. Zharia acts like such a teenager sometimes.

"Birdie! I'm so happy for you!," Tally coos from the TV while she wipes away tears.

"Congrats!" Cherry says while she hugs Birdie too.

Birdie gazes back over at me. I smile, showing her all my pearly whites, "You're welcome, Mrs. LaFleur. Congratulations, sis. I'm really happy for you guys."

"Wow! This is so fucking awesome. Oh god…but wait, you've been drinking wine every Wednesday. Is the bean ok?" Zharia looks worried, her eyes almost frantic.

I chuckle at that and it earns me a dirty look from Zhar. I explain to them what I've been observing the past couple of weeks.

"How many weeks are you?" Tally asks. She's still wiping at her eyes with a tissue. She's our resident crier. Need something cried about? Our supremely empathetic Tally Belle will give a few tears up for it. She's a complete sucker for rom-coms and romance novels. ASPCA commercials will send her into an hour long spiral.

She sobs when she watches Titanic or All Dogs Go To Heaven and she hates going to pet stores where they have animals. There's been a few times I've refused to let her walk into one. She always wants to free the animals.

"I'm ten and a half weeks per the ultrasound a few weeks ago."

"You've known a few weeks?" Zharia is clearly upset she didn't know.

"I was going to tell you, I promise, just not yet. I've been so sick with this one, worse than with Denver. I've been spending a lot of time on this couch while Denver sits in that large playpen beside me happily playing, not caring his mommy is deathly sick." She's referring to the playpen right beside the couch that we've grown to accept as the normal décor now.

"You're due when?" Cherry inquires.

"September fifteenth."

"Oh no, you'll be pregnant through another summer. The first one was awful," I lightly jostle her shoulder again in jest.

"God, I know. I can't wait for my cankles to form again." Birdie giggles as she rolls her eyes and I know she's remembering her elephant legs, as we called them.

"When do we find out the gender?" Tally asks excitedly. "I want to make a few things."

A few things mean a lot of things.

I can only imagine the quilt Tally will make out of the expensive fabrics she has in scrap piles. The blue and green one she made for Denver is stunning.

"Not for another few weeks. We aren't sure if we want to find out," she replies then bites her bottom lip, cringing from the expected fallout.

"Don't put that evil on me!" Tally says horrified.

"I guess use neutral colors then," I supply. That earns me a shitty look but internally it makes me chuckle. The first thing Tally does is pick a color palette before designing anything and then sticks with the plan.

"Ok. Yeah. I can do that," she confesses then nods to herself. "It's going to be beautiful. I'm so excited!"

"Oh, me too!!" In her excitement, Zhar continues her bouncing on the chair. Suddenly she stops, "Gah! Denver already gives me baby fever. I'm not going to be able to fight against two of them."

I snicker and everyone else joins me. There was a day in the not-so-distant past where Zharia was very adamant about not having kids. Her men support her decision but she keeps flipping back and forth on the idea of having a baby. If she holds this next one of Birdie's…her willpower will *poof*.

"We aren't announcing we're expecting for a few more weeks so keep it under wraps, please. My dad knows and that's it. Well, now you guys."

"Oh man, I may burst." Tally shakes her head and breathes through the tears that threaten again. She fans her runny eyeballs but those tears still fall in fat drops. But hey, at least she's smiling.

I reach for Birdie's hand and she threads our fingers together. Zhar moves over and holds her hand over ours, sliding her fingers in where she can find a spot. She ushers Cherry over and places Cherry's hand on our pile. Tally chokes up and wiggles her fingers at the camera.

"We wish you a healthy and smooth pregnancy and birth. We will be here, right alongside you, every step of the way. I promise," I finish my declaration.

"I promise." Zharia nods as she says it.

"I promise!" Tally says on a small hiccup from her tears.

"I can only promise what I can do with going to school and working but yeah, I promise to be your friend," Cherry says with a shrug. It will do.

Another baby. Our friend group is growing. At least there are some bright spots in a world of darkness.

CHAPTER 32
TRAVARES

"Don't you have to take care of Poppy?" Bam asks me with raised eyebrows. Everyone has cleared out of the clubhouse after the meeting but me and him.

"Fuck." His words smack me upside the head as a reminder. Yeah, my life changed. I can't sit here and pull an all-nighter. I have a little girl to worry about and she's been at her sitters, a nice old lady named Mrs. Wallace, for about four hours now.

I need to pack up and go get her. Mrs. Wallace lives in the same apartment complex that Lily lived in. She's been a tremendous help to me. She was someone Lily was close to and counted on. She trusted Mrs. Wallace, therefore, I do too.

I have a standing arrangement with her to take care of Poppy on Wednesday evenings when the club meets. She was more than happy to take me up on the offer to see Poppy every week. The old lady misses her and is thrilled she can still spend time with Poppy.

I can't take advantage of her kindness though. I'm sure she wants to get on with her night. I sigh and shut my laptop before I convince myself to sit here 'just a little bit more' and next thing you know four more hours have passed.

"I gotta go, Bam. I need to pick up Poppy. After I get her settled in, I'm diving back into this."

"Do you need help? I can pull an all-nighter. I don't have class or work tomorrow." He must see the resignation on my face because he keeps at it, "I'll just do it. I want to help. Send me what needs done and I'm on it. I'll go home and shower and start back up. I got you, fam."

Bam gets up and takes the few steps over to me and grabs me up in a bear hug. Oh no, another crazy bonding time with Bam. He's a hugger and smothers you in his arms when they lock around you.

I hug him back because if I don't he won't let go of me until I do. I don't mind hugs, don't get me wrong, but Bam's hugs are like hugging a psychotic Care Bear that might bite you at any second. Sure enough, he turns up the vice grip until I groan.

Then he just drops me like a hot potato. My bones jar back into place.

He keeps a hand on my bicep, "Love ya, brother. We'll find him." One more nod and he's clearing out of the clubhouse too.

I make sure everything is secure and locked up before I set the alarm and lock up behind me. I look up at the darkened sky and say to myself, hoping like hell my words would carry to the intended faceless rapist and murderer, "I'm going to find you and then I'm going to make you beg for mercy. Bet on it, motherfucker."

"Did you know Russia is just two miles from Alaska? They are so close they could walk to visit each other. It looks much further apart on a map." Poppy shoves her toothbrush back into her mouth and goes to town sawing it back and forth.

I don't have it in me to tell her to slow down. She's excited. Mrs. Wallace bought her a new book. It's fun facts for kids. I'm going to know the entire book before she goes back next week.

She pulls the toothbrush out and runs it under the water while talking a mile a minute. "Do you know that some fish cough?"

That one does give me pause. I thought you needed air to cough.

I cock an eyebrow and say, "Nuh-uh. That can't be true."

After she's done swooshing the water around, she spits it out and says, "Ya-huh. It's in the book of truth."

"The book of truth is it," I chuckle to myself.

She wipes her mouth and steps back from the sink but stops to use the towel to wipe down the front of herself. Her pajamas are her favorite with cute little mushrooms and hedgehogs.

Yes, she's already asked if she could get a hedgehog. I told her I'd think about it.

We are definitely not getting a hedgehog. Hard stop.

"Horses and cows sleep standing up, can—"

"Nope," I quickly interject. "Humans lay down. We aren't trying that. That's how you fall flat on your face and break your nose."

Her mouth falls open in awe, "Did you fall asleep standing up before, Uncle Ducky?"

"A time or two, popsicle. What are we reading before bed?"

"Weehhellll…"

Oh no. This is never good when she does the butter-up *Well.*

I wait patiently for her to gather the courage to ask me for something. It's important I don't try to rush her or seem agitated.

But I am irritated. I should be looking for her mother's killer in all that data I need to skim.

Poppy is more important than vengeance. I remind myself of how grateful I am to still have my popstar.

When she doesn't seem to be forthcoming, I prod her, "Spit it out, Pops."

"Ok. Ok. Can I call Pierre?" Her face scrunches up in worry.

I hate that she's acting like this but I understand. Pierre's not been around as much anymore and she's picked up on the tension. Also, I told her we weren't friends any longer.

I have a split second to register her request before she goes on, "I miss him, ya know? He's my friend and I could really use my friend. I want to tell him fun facts that I've learned. Pleeease?" Her puppy dog eyes get me every damn time. I'm going to have to learn how to toughen up.

"I'll text him and see if he's busy."

"Yesss," she hisses under her breath and it makes my lips twitch. "Thank you."

"Yeah, yeah, gimme a few to clean up," I mumble as I whip out my phone and bring up Pierre's message thread.

Me: Hey, are you busy? Poppy wants to call you.

I know, I know dammit. Ugh. This is not what I need. I had decided not to let him back around her, but she just saw him at Lily's funeral a few days ago so he's still fresh in her mind. My plan is to stagger their interactions until the gaps are so long she just naturally forgets about him and we move on peacefully.

What I didn't expect was an almost instantaneous response.

☯ॐInk King: I'm not busy. You can video chat now.

Me: Handing over to Poppy now. She has ten minutes to talk.

☯ॐInk King: <thumbs up emoji>

I hit the camera icon and hand the phone over to Poppy, saying, "Ten minutes." I set a timer on my tactical watch and head to the bathroom as Pierre answers.

I don't need to hear this conversation. I trust him not to say some off the wall shit to my niece. He would never. He's too classy for that.

I'm grateful for whoever remodeled this old house with these huge bedrooms and installed a walk-in closet and full bathroom in every bedroom. One less thing I needed to do to modernize this place.

My timer goes off right as I'm finishing the cleanup and hanging her towel over the shower door and shutting the light off.

"Times up, popsicle."

"Wait, Uncle Ducky, one more!" She has her fun facts book in her lap and hurries to pick another one to tell Pierre. "Women's hearts beat faster than men's. That means I'm going to fall in love faster than you."

Pierre remains quiet for a few ticks. Meanwhile, my ass is clenched in so tight while my belly flips. "I don't think that last part's true. I did it faster than one heartbeat. Matter of fact, my heart skipped that beat and I just fell headfirst." He snaps his finger in front of his face and says, "And just like that, it happens, but you don't know it. When you fall in love with your soulmate, I want you to remember how fast it happens and make sure you recognize it for what it is before it's too late. When you're older and you fall in love, we'll compare notes but you have a good many years before that happens. We have to get through elementary school first."

"Yes, because boys are gross. Spencer eats his boogers."

And just like that her rock-solid reasoning only makes sense to her.

"Yes, Poptart, boys are gross," Pierre says on a laugh.

"Say goodnight, Pop." I remind her.

"Goodnight, Ringmaster. Sweet dreams." She snuggles down in her blankets while handing me my phone.

"Goodnight, Poppy. Sweet dreams." But before I can hit the disconnect icon, Pierre pipes up, speaking quickly, "Declan, before you hang up, can I talk to you, privately? Please?"

I grind my teeth. He's not helping the plan. The plan can only go down smoothly if he goes away and leaves us alone.

I pull the phone up and stare into the camera. I ignore how my breath gets caught in my chest at the sight of him. How my heart yearns to be with him, how my body reacts just to seeing him. I completely disregard how my cock twitches in my sweats. I full on deny the desire coursing through my veins over this man.

"Let me put her to bed and I'll call you back," I say thickly.

"Promise?" He has so much hope on his face.

Goddamnit. "Yes. I promise." Most begrudging promise I've ever made.

Chapter 33

Pierre

True to his word, thirteen minutes and twenty-four seconds later—psst, who's counting—Declan calls me back. Not video, only audio.

When I answer, he doesn't sound happy to be talking to me.

"Yes, Pierre, what can I do for you?"

Forgive me. Come back. Be with me again.

"I just wanted to check on you is all. How are you doing?"

"I'm fine. Look, I'm not sure why you care, but thanks for asking. Is there anything else? I'm sorta busy here." I hear his irritation. I can feel it through the phone.

"Declan…" I sigh his name.

"No, Pierre. Don't start. It's done. We're moving on. The only thing we now have in common is Poppy and pretty soon she'll grow tired of you, maybe even forget about you."

"That's not fair, Dec."

He chuckles darkly across the phone line, I can see his face in my mind, "That's rich coming from you. It's not meant to be fair."

"I adore Poppy. I still want to be her friend, Declan. Please don't take that away from either of us." I don't want to sound like I'm begging but goddamn it, I have to stay in this weird relationship we have going now so I cannot let Poppy down. I've already broken her uncle's heart by ghosting, I can't do the same to her again. She thinks I've just been really busy for the past couple of weeks and can't make it to get-togethers. I know I'm overstepping boundaries here but I can't help it.

Taking a huge leap, I press on in a rush, "Declan, please talk to me."

"I've got nothing for you, Pierre. I have to go."

Before I know it, he's disconnecting the call and my heart breaks even more.

I throw my phone down on the couch, grab the sides of my head and yell. Fuck, that felt good.

I'm so stupid. This should be the point that I give up.

I can't.

I sleep like shit nowadays, so I fully expect the same exhausted weight on my chest to hold me back every time I wake up. This morning is no different.

I'm the new poster boy for draggin' ass. No amount of coffee is going to help. Thank fuck I'm booked so it will keep my mind busy. No time to cry over a man if I'm getting handed money.

After the failure of a phone call with Declan a couple of days ago, I spent most of the night and the following two nights in my studio, hyper focusing on the portrait I've been working on in any free time I get this past week.

Declan talked about replacing the mirror that was above the very Victorian fireplace and mantle in his living room. It's a sizable canvas and will fit perfectly there. Now if he only accepts it...

In other words, I've been driving myself crazy with exhaustion, anxiety, and depression.

Today's been another mind-numbing day. I pretend to smile at my clients, listening to them rave on and on about their lives, all the while my heart withers like a rose on the vine. I'm constantly pulled back to regret.

I think it really is driving me crazy. I, for fuck sure, know this isn't like me. Maybe it's time I admit some hard truths. It's not that I don't see them, it's more about accepting them. Probably time for a counselor again too.

While I sit here in my empty living room in my t-shirt and jeans feeling sorry for myself—oh yeah, in my own self-induced land of misery and bullshittery, ha, yeah I recognize—Zharia video chats me.

The Universe has a wicked sense of humor.

What could Z possibly want on a Friday night?

Answering it takes a leap of faith because you never know what the hell Zhar wants. It could be a book recommendation, a new medicine she wants to discuss with anyone who will listen, literally anyone, or she just bought a baby elephant and needs vet recs. It's always a surprise. Some, not so pleasant.

Her face pops up, "Pierre Armond, where for art thou been, snookums?" Ahh, the sweet, silky purr.

I see this won't be a pleasant call either. I had such high hopes too.

"Zharia." That's all I have for a greeting in my current state of mind *aka* pity party. A polite reply. Honestly, I don't feel like talking to Z right now. I know that's awful of me, she's one of my best friends and all. I don't want to talk to anyone; it's not just her.

"How are you?" she asks.

"Fine."

"Hmm, fine is a very broad term. Care to elaborate, friend?" she hedges. Zharia is the friend that zeroes in and extracts information in the form of emotions from you, even if you are hiding it or you don't even know it's there, for fuck's sake. She will sniff it out and expose it for you to *deal and heal,* as she calls it.

"I'm ok. There's nothing wrong. I'm great." Shit. That sounded so fake. "What's up? That's a nice jacket." Deflection engaged.

I'll say anything I can say to throw her off my scent. She's as bad as a predator snuffing out the bleeding prey that's hidden in the bushes. Her love for her friends is immense but she has no concept of boundaries most times.

This is one of those times. Most people would have dropped it but not her. She will dig until you're raw and bleeding, pulling it out of you with her teeth and claws. But I have to admit, it always feels better after she's done it. I give her credit, her purges are cathartic.

"I've picked up on your energy the past few Wine Wednesdays and it's spiraling down. I'm looking out for you and your chakras. I'm reaching out because I'm worried. The worm in my gut compels me. Your smile doesn't reach your eyes anymore in case you are trying to fake it. It's not fooling anyone." Zharia sounds pensive and a little sad herself.

"I wish you wouldn't refer to your intuition as a worm in your gut," I murmur.

She gives an airy, fake laugh. "Ahh, not about me. Breathing, moving forward. Back to you. Do tell what's got you blue because it's making me sad too, babes, and I don't even know why we're sad," her voice cracks. "But I won't let you be sad alone!"

I guess I never figured into the equation how my depression over Declan affected others. I just tucked it down and put on a brave face. No one who's come into the shop the past month would be able to see how distraught I am, how lost I am without him, how much I pray to any god that he'll talk to me and just fucking listen for once. No one would know my heart is hurting and bleeding.

Definitely no one knows how much the guilt on my chest weighs.

I can play this one of two ways. Deny, which is usually my M.O., or confess and confide what's going on inside of me. It's barely contained inside my head. I feel like my chest has caved in.

I've started talking to myself as if I'm talking to him again. I stare at the lights of the ships trolling down the Mississippi while sitting on my balcony whispering to him how much I miss him.

I picture him wrapping me up in a blanket and holding me, cocooning us from the outside world, just me and him out there, making up stories about people milling about below. His fingers in my hair and his heartbeat under my ear, as we enjoy a beautiful night in the French Quarter.

How did I get to this point? I'm pathetic. The guy who was adamant about no strings, no feelings. All for me to catch hella feelings but not recognize what it was. All for me to freak the fuck out and cut him off and treat him like a forgettable piece of ass.

What a jackass move. I sigh to myself, fed up with my same ole pity party.

I sit down and run my fingers through my crazy hair. It's come out of its pomade nineteen-twenties gangster style cut and my locks are flopping in my eyes. The natural wave of my hair is starting to bend my hair back to its wavy will. Declan said he loved when I let my hair dry naturally and didn't try to straighten it so much. He loved how out of control it looked on me.

"Pierre," Zharia softly says. I stare into the camera at her. "I know you aren't ok right now, babes. Please talk to me."

If I talk to her, all of them will know. If I don't, she'll send them all one by one to make me talk about my feelings. I get it, I know where they're coming from, especially with my history. Maybe I need to reassure them I don't need hospitalization right now. I can hear that concern in Zhar's voice.

Finally, I blink and bring my hand up to rub my eyes with my thumb and forefinger. "You may as well pull the other ladies into this call."

It's evening so they should be available. Maybe not Cherry, I'm not sure her schedule. She works so many different odd jobs. I remember all too well what it was like to work in order to eat and scrape together a life while being a broke college student.

Zharia lights up in a radiant smile. She knows she's won. She's going to help me. Grudgingly I admit, this is exactly what my stubborn ass needs.

Pretty soon Birdie pops up in a small box.

"Hey! What's up guys?" Birdie's chipper greeting wraps around me like a hug. Just the sound of her soothing, motherly voice makes any one of us calm down and feel centered. She's in her kitchen with Denver on her hip. I wave at my nephew and blow him a kiss. He giggles and slaps his mom's head.

"Hey chicky-doos! What's happening?" Tally appears to be in her pajamas already. I look at my watch and see it's just after seven, then remember Tally acts like a crotchety old lady a lot of the time, so her wearing pajamas already is not shocking. I should be in mine but I hadn't made it that far.

Zharia clicks her phone into her phone holder at her desk in her home office. In a way, I know she's giving me privacy in her house. Her men are never far behind her, so I guarantee they are within ten feet of the closed office door.

Zhar clasps her hands together in front of her and leans on her forearms. She totally has the doctor pose down. I bet she delivers shitty news in this position.

"I've called this meeting as an intervention of sorts. Pierre needs us, but he won't ask us for help. And help he does need. Poor little button is about to explode with pent up aggression and depression. I can feel it rolling off of him, and you all know I'm an empath. He said to call all the girls then."

"Pierre, are you ok?" Birdie asks.

I look at the three beautiful women on my phone screen. Any one of them would take a bullet for me. I would lay my life in front of one of the Quarter carriages and let the horses trample me for any one of them. We are ride or die.

And there's no reason to lie to them. Don't start now, you never have.

"I'm not ok."

"I can be there in twenty. I'll be right over." Birdie is seen moving through their penthouse apartment, going to get dressed or whatever she plans on doing to get here in a rush. She calls for Lincoln.

"Birdie." She keeps moving. "Birdie," with a little more force, louder. "I don't need you here, darlin'. Thank you, but I'm not that bad currently," I call to her louder so she'll listen.

She stops still, hovering in her hallway, with her lips in a little O and says, "If you're sure…" Denver fights her for the phone. She's all over the place and it's giving me motion sickness.

"Yes. If it were that bad I would tell you ladies. I swear it upon my soul. I would reach out. We aren't there yet."

"I don't like the sound of yet." Zharia cocks an eyebrow and pokes, "Still. It means we have time. Let's start at the beginning. Leave *nothing* out. *Tell us everything*," Zharia is almost breathless by the time she finishes.

So, like any introvert, weirdo bestie would do, I spilled my guts to the girls. I left nothing out. Not even the parts where I look like a jackass. Every nitty-gritty fucked up thing I've done to him.

Zharia slides in an awed whisper, "I knew it was big daddy dom energy."

This is one of the very first times they've gotten a glimpse into my sex life. I've always been private about it when I was with Seven. Plus, there really wasn't a lot of sex to talk about since we weren't having any.

Exact opposite with Declan. I could never get enough, neither could he.

They sit transfixed, lost in the story being told. I tell them of how my insecurities cost me my second chance at happiness. How I thought loving someone else would destroy me so I shied away from it, deciding to play it safe, keeping myself at arm's length.

I failed epically.

Falling for Declan came so naturally, so sweet and carefree, like sliding down a water slide with excitement and thrill. The rush in your chest as you fly through the air and your heart lands in your throat became so addictive. I crave the breathless, the weightless feelings that overcame my soul when I was with my kindred spirit, my twin flame, my anam cara. I'm on the slippery slope that screams danger, but you do it anyways.

When the ride is worth the crash...just hold on.

"I've learned I still don't know what I'm doing in a relationship. I blew up one and now another."

"Pierre," tolerant, yet not listening to my self-suffering bullshit, Zharia says, "you were not the only one at fault for the first one. Can we agree on that? Seven played a huge part in this too. We aren't letting him get out of this scot free. He may never take accountability," small snort on her behalf, "but you can't keep punishing yourself for your dead marriage crumbling and dying out. You. Are. Not. The. Bad. Person. Here."

"I may not be Seven's villain, but I am Declan's. You hear it in his voice. He's just patient enough to listen to me now, but he's a breath away from bolting." My chest constricts as I sit on the edge of the bed.

My bed, where so much time has been spent with Declan. My bedroom that I can still smell him in. It makes me choke up and momentarily I forget I'm on camera.

The room is quiet. The call quiet. The tears stinging.

Fuck, it's so overwhelming to be in here.

I wish for one more time here. One more chance to reach him.

Give him every part of me.

Now I'm the villain in his story.

"Pierre..." Birdie tenderly says.

My eyes flick up to the screen. Zharia's hand lifts to cover her mouth but there's heavy concern in her eyes. Tally looks about the same, although she's not hiding her eyes filling up. Birdie's eyes shine with unshed tears like the others.

Birdie clears her throat, "You should show up at his house. Force him to see you," she pops off. "Listen, if you're as madly in love with him as you say, then make it known. Do the grand gesture! Get his full attention. Don't take the brush off as an answer. Stand on his porch until he hears you."

"Or the cops cart you away," Tally interjects.

Birdie shakes her head. "I don't think he'll call them on you. Let him decide from there after you declare your feelings. I know that part is hard for you but right now, that's a necessary evil. He needs to know. I can't stress that hard enough." Birdie locks eyes with me through the camera, "You need to release it. It's eating you alive and that's not how love is supposed to feel."

"Give yourself mercy, Pierre," Tally supplies softly.

"My biggest sin was ghosting him after using his body and his heart to make me forget how shitty I felt. I never expected this. I wasn't meant for a happily ever after. I thought I'd turn into an old cat lady." Zharia snorts a laugh and Tally and Birdie have a ghost of a smile too. "I thought I'd be alone. But I'm never alone. I have my girls, my brother, my nephew, my parents."

I look down at the rug on the floor while the tightening in my chest gets stronger, like a T-rex putting his whole weight on me.

I'm one big ball of anxiety.

Goddamn it. My chin wobbles.

"I'll drive you to his house," Birdie announces quietly.

Zharia gasps and says, "Not if I can get him in my car first!"

"Ack! Somebody just do it!" Tally says excitedly while clapping her hands.

Birdie's face lights up and has a mischievous sparkle, "Do it, Pierre. Be reckless, babes." Her eyes shine brightly. "Let love guide you. Don't let manners rule you this time. Show up unannounced, demand he speak to you, show him what he's missing and declare your intentions. I believe in you." Birdie makes it sound so easy.

"Fuck yeah, we do."

"Yes, fucking do it. Be impulsive." Zharia claps her hands and stands up as the background changes behind her. "I'm leaving to come get you. This is a mission for love!"

She's right. It's love. I should have recognized it for what it was back when. *Is* What it is. It is currently still on for me. I should not have feared how it would turn me inside out and I'd come running back, wanting more. That's the exciting part.

I feel my lips twitch at their excitement. They're determined. They have a plan. They have full faith this will work. They're banking a lot on me and my dorky inability to talk about my feelings.

I find myself saying, "Ok."

They let up a cheer and giggle. "We're doing the damn thang!!" Zharia declares with a smile.

I need to shower.

"Let me freshen up. Give me about twenty minutes," I tell them.

"I'm so bummed I can't go on this love mission," Tally says, pouting, complete with her bottom lip jutting out.

"Next time. We will plan a manic episode properly next time," I tell her with a hint of a smile.

"I'll hold you to that."

"Nineteen minutes and counting, bro," Zharia calls out.

"Love you all." I think for a second and make sure I say, "Thank you, ladies. From the bottom of my heart. I love each one of you. I don't know what I'd do without you. You are the stars in my sky."

"Oh god, Pierre, I'm trying not to cry even more over here," Tally whines as she does a small sob. "I love you too, sweetie."

Birdie's tears spill over, "You're welcome, brother."

Zharia clears her throat as I say, "And thanks for calling, Z."

She winks and says, "Anytime. Seventeen minutes."

I disconnect and all of a sudden it hits me with what I've agreed to.

Holy fuck. This is so not me.

Chapter 34

Pierre

"Uhh, our Pierre has been having quite a few *grow the fuck up* and *man up* moments here lately. I'm proud of you."

I'm not sure how to take that so I just nod and look out the window of Zhar's SUV. It's rainy and the streets have a shine to them from the lights.

I face forward and out of the corner of my eye I see Zharia just staring at me while we're stuck at this red light—still can't believe they talked me into this—then a smile unfurls on her beautiful face. "Growing up sucks, huh?"

I shrug. "In a way, I'm glad Seven made me wake up and grow up. Sure, he made me cry and feel dead inside but I feel like I came out on the other side better for it. There would have been no Declan if Seven were still around. I would never have had that kind of love. I don't think Seven knew how to give it. I don't think I knew how to accept Declan's love, but I'm ready now. Seven isn't going to hold me back anymore."

"That guy probably pinches his nipples when he cries."

"Zharia," I warn, stifling a laugh.

"I know, I know. I'm not sorry though. Maybe we should listen to this really great podcast I found on sound bowl healing on the way there."

I'm gonna have to change the subject or her self-help advice will start spilling out. Before I know it she'll have me offering up a cup of pomegranate juice under a full moon, while barefoot wearing a skirt made of fake coins, chanting some shit she found in a book, thinking it will help solve my problems.

Not knocking her witchy woo-woo, but if there were someone that it would backfire on, it would be Zhar. Personally, I don't want to get caught in the crossfire, so hard pass on working magick with her.

I wish her and Lily could have been friends. They would have gotten along well.

Freshly shaved, smelling irresistible—I hope—and looking rather dapper in my dark jeans and a black super-soft thermal shirt that wraps around my body snuggly. I'm going for alluring, disarming, magnetic. When I slide my leather jacket on over my shoulders before leaving, nervous about how this will play out, I realize my hands are shaking.

They haven't stopped. I don't normally have this problem, as a tattoo artist my hands are steady.

I'm just over here in the passenger seat trying out Zhar's newest fascination: manifestation. I'm manifesting him to reciprocate my feelings and talk to me.

I don't realize how close we are until Zhar says, "Almost show time, P. Knock 'em dead. Ehh well, not really but you know what I mean."

Suddenly my throat is dry, my lips cracked and I'm parched like a man lost in the desert.

Her hand lightly touches my arm, "You can do this, Pierre. I have every bit of faith in you. He deserves to know. You deserve to be heard. People are allowed to change their hearts. Hopefully he gives it a chance. If you don't come back, I'll just leave, but I'm waiting fifteen minutes out here first. Neighborhood looks pretty solid."

She has no idea there was a convoy of three vehicles that followed us here. She's not some sassy bad ass that's going to be toughening it up out here alone. She is never alone.

The phone tree of hearsay is alive and well between all of us in the message thread. I know from Birdie, who heard from Zhar, who was told by Shadow that Declan told him he was pulling all-nighters combing through the stolen info from the cell phones that we aren't supposed to know about.

Getting out, I turn to look at Zhar one more time. She gives me an enthusiastic thumbs up with a cheesy smile. Good gravy. I wave and shut the door and make my way up the steps.

Declan's house looks like one of those white Victorians that are splashed across the pages of a southern home magazine. And huge. It's a massive house tucked away in a spacious lot with greenery and plenty of shade trees. There's also plenty of space between his house and the neighbor's. Space like that is almost unheard of in this city.

You pay big money for that kind of breathing room. Which I'm sure Declan did. It's beautiful. The perfect place to raise Poppy.

I know he bought it with every intention of Lily and Poppy living with him eventually. But now, these are the most horrendous of circumstances forcing her to live with her uncle now.

It's late enough that Poppy would be in bed already. I don't want her to witness this.

This might be a total embarrassment for me, or trying to look on the bright side, the continuation of our love story.

I know he already knows I'm here. His security system would have picked up the car in front of the house while it sat there idling. It would have alerted him to us.

Most likely he's watched me walk right up to his house bold as can be. And he's watching me on cameras right now, from numerous angles, as I stand here. I guarantee.

His system has already picked up on my heat signature, my erratic heartbeat, and if I'm wearing underwear. His security measures are no joke. This is the reason he's such a hot commodity. He's a genius.

I have no intention of knocking. He'll be here soon enough.

I see his bulky frame barreling down the foyer through the white lace curtains covering the glass oval in the large oak front door. I resist wringing my hands in front of me. I shake out my fingers and lean my head back, looking at the porch ceiling, to let out a breath of anticipation.

Fuck, this was a bad idea.

Too late now, jackass.

I right my head as he opens the door and my eyes level with his beautiful green and gold gaze. I've missed looking at that colorful chasm.

"Declan…" I breathe, unable to believe for a moment I'm really here.

"Pierre? What are you doing here?"

I clear my throat. "Hi. I, uh, came to talk to you. Can I have a moment of your time?" Jesus, I sound like a Jehovah's Witness.

His eyes cut over to the neighbor's yard, staring off into the distance as his throat works.

"Please, Dec. Five minutes."

He looks at me again, the full weight of his gaze on me. I bask in his attention, even if he's mad at me. I just want to be near him. I'll sit in his anger with him, so long as I can be near him again.

He steps aside and opens the door, beckoning me entry to his home. I waste no time walking in. I may not get this chance again.

I wait for him to shut and lock the door, then follow him into the living room. He shuts off the TV, dropping the remote onto the coffee table where his laptop sits open, his glasses on the keyboard.

I finally take a moment to take him in. He looks exhausted. He's wearing a white V-neck t-shirt and a pair of baby blue sleep pants…that leave very little to the imagination.

F.u.c.k.

My heart starts thudding hard in my chest immediately and my knees grow weak. *I cannot get hard right now.* Oh god, how embarrassing would that be. I don't think it's possible with how nervous I am.

He stands by the couch, hands on his hips. I move further into the room, the coffee table between us. I'm not sure I want to sit for this. At this very moment I'm trying to pull my shit together and get this right.

This is my one shot. Zharia made sure to play music to pep me up on the drive over. She chose 'Lose Yourself,' by Eminem to play on repeat. I just went with it. I wanted to throw up from her driving and a little bit from my drama too.

"Five minutes. Start talking."

Like the loser that I am, I get lost in him and I freeze. I can't form words. My emotions are choking me, stealing my voice.

I barely remember to breathe. Time almost feels surreal.

I take a deep breath to steady myself and use it to speak, but not before Declan says—"

Crawl inside of Pierre's mindset right now. Listen to his heart upon being near Declan again. Hear his truth. Hear the music that flows through his soul. Let his love be heard.

Adore You – Miley Cyrus

Chapter 35

Pierre

"If you're looking to the Universe to have an answer for you, you're not getting one; you already know it. You know what this is." He swirls his finger around between us. "You've known since you fell into my arms. Keep denying it all you want and I will deny you until you can admit it. Say it, Pierre. That's what you came to do, right?"

Now or never.

"I'd rather die than hurt you again. I've been running from what I feel. That needs to stop. Declan, baby, I need you. I want you by me. Please." I clench my fists and squeeze my eyes shut against the hot tears burning behind my lids. This isn't like what I rehearsed in my head. I take a deep breath, filling my lungs, just trying to give me some semblance of stability that I need right now to get through this. The sliver of fear is growing as he throws his anger at me. It's well-deserved anger.

I'm a dick.

If I don't convince him we belong together, then I'll lose him right here, right now. I just feel it in my soul.

I can't lose him. Not again.

Say the words.

Say all the words, Pierre!

My heart's wrapped up in fear so much that it trusts no one. Fear of rejection.

But I trust him, my Prince Charming, my bad boy.

Steadier, "Declan. I was wrong. So fucking wrong. I should never have pushed you away like I did. I should not have ghosted you. I was stupid. It was the wrong thing to do but I thought I was protecting my heart." I wave those thoughts away, "It doesn't matter why, it just matters that I did it, I'm owning up to it, and I'm trying to fix it. I can't lose you. I'm sorry."

I watch him watch me. His chest rises and falls and his eyes are hard. It's not until this moment that the full magnitude of how much I've hurt him slaps me upside the head. I get it now.

This means I try harder. Beg more.

I shift my weight and throw out my hands, starting to negotiate with him, "What do you want me to do to prove it? Tell me and I'll do it. Name it," I say pleadingly, my eyes begging. "I want to be with you, only you. You're what I've been looking for my whole life. You're the reason my demons are under control. My soul needs you, Declan. The Universe gave me you and I was foolish enough to let you go but that will never happen again. I promise you. I will worship you. I will bow at your altar and give you any offering you want. Just tell me what it is. Just let me do it."

Fuck it.

Taking a few steps around the coffee table, it brings me closer to him. "Declan…" I say on a pitiful sigh as I drop to my knees mere feet from him. "Please, baby," I plead softly.

His breath hitches in his throat and his eyes flare wide in surprise. He makes no move towards me though. That's fine. I can do this from here.

"If there's nothing, *absolutely* nothing in your heart left for me, I'll walk away respectfully. But tell me how to get over you before I leave, because I will never…ever…get over you and what we had. I will die knowing what I did was unforgiveable."

Fuck, I feel the tears coming. The curse of having deep feelings. Sometimes they go out of control and I can't reign them in.

Now is one of those times.

I firmly believe this is the most important moment in my life.

Seeing the tears in Declan's eyes nearly destroys me. My heart aches to touch him. To hold him. Comfort him.

My body needs to be next to his. Skin to skin. Soul to soul.

His small sob that breaks the silence pulls my own from my throat.

"Declan, baby, I'm so sorry. I'm sorry. Say something, *please*."

He composes himself quickly and unleashes, "How can I believe you when you can't even admit what's truly between us? I love you. I fucking love you!!" he says in a repressed roar as not to wake up Poppy. "Do you hear that? I'm in love with you. I have been since the moment I saw you years ago. I've dreamed of you, Pierre. And then I had you. But then I lost you and it killed me inside."

He drags his fingers through his hair, "I thought what we had was special, it was going somewhere despite what we agreed to. It evolved. Then it went to shit and you tossed me aside like I meant nothing to you. And I know that's a fucking lie. I've known my worth this entire time. I meant something, goddamn it. I meant the world to you but you fucking refused to see it."

I know better than to interrupt him. He needs this release as much as I do. He needs to be heard. I hear him.

Declan levels me a look and says, "I have Poppy to think about now." He shakes his head, "I can't have you dipping in and out of our lives when shit gets too real for you. We're a package deal now and I remember well how much you never wanted to be around children."

I can't help but cut in, "Dec, I adore Poppy! I'm begging for you, but for her too. I want you both. I want a family with you. To grow old. Raise Poppy together. Get a dog, maybe a cat, or both. I want *everything* with you. Anything you'll give me." I finish breathlessly. My heart is pounding out of my chest. I'm a live wire about to go off. I need him to hear me, believe me.

"I trusted you once…"

"Trust me again!"

"You really, really hurt me, Pierre," the anguish in his whisper steals my breath and pierces my heart.

I hurt him.

Period.

Mic drop.

There it is.

My eyes fill and spill over as I look up at him. Hot trails of tears slide down my cheeks in pure, utter shame. I hate that I've done this.

"I know, and I'm forever regretful and sorry I did that. It will never happen again."

"You need to tell me how you feel. No more pussyfooting around. I deserve to know before you try to wreck me again."

I know what he wants. I know exactly what he wants to hear. It's in me. It ebbs and flows, swells and surges within me every second of the day. It makes me radiate happiness and it washes over me with some of the smoothest peace.

I love him. Undeniably. Wholeheartedly. Irrevocably.

"You are mine, Prince Charming, just as I am yours. I feel like I'm king of the world when I'm with you. Some of the best moments of my life were spent with you. You became part of me, intertwined with my soul to create something so beautiful and sacred between us. The very best thing I never saw coming was the love I shared with you. I crave it and I've been so cold without it. I love you, Declan. I do. I'm so deeply in love with you, I can't fathom it. More than the Universe." I throw my arms out and pull them back into my chest. "My mind is blown with how much I'm obsessed with you; how much I love and adore you. Please," I rasp. "Please forgive me and let me come home to you. Be mine again."

"'I never told you that you could have me." His throat works and his jaw clenches. He's going to break any minute.

"I thought it was implied when I said the words *you're mine*."

"And then you gave me up easily. Therefore, not yours."

I'm on my feet in a heartbeat and colliding with his body. My threshold has been reached and I'm tired of this fuckery.

I grip him by his throat, just hard enough to give a pulse of reminder. "You've always been mine and I never let you go, let's get that straight right fucking now, bad boy. I own that ass."

He sucks in air through his teeth in anger, hurt shinning in his eyes, "You have a funny way of showing it."

He can't hurt me anymore. His barbs won't get to me. I won't allow it. I expected this.

"You're absolutely right, baby boy, I've been a *horrible* boyfriend. I wasn't supposed to love you but I fell so hard and fast and didn't know how precious all of it was until it was gone. I'm a fool." His jaw ticks with astonishment of my accountability. His eyes grow a silver lining from either his anger or his heart speaking like mine is. His eyes turn glassy with the unshed tears. He's coiled, ready to unleash his hurt feelings. The feelings I've caused.

I can't do this anymore. I have to break the tension. I crowd into him making him feel! He remembers he's alive but he's forgotten what we're like together. Still, I push, getting this out in the open.

Begging didn't work, so I dare him while my hand grips his throat, "That's it. I'll be your villain, Prince Charming. Be angry, spit venom at me, spill all your hate into me, give me all that anger that's eating you alive...."

One last small squeeze and I pull back, taking my heat and my hand with me. I straighten, standing at my full height, yanking my leather jacket down and smoothing it out, never taking my eyes off his. With a little more force and authority, I tell him, "Then get the fuck over it so we can begin our epic love story where we left off, like it's always meant to be. I'm tired of waiting."

Declan's heart sings while it bleeds.
To forgive is to be set free.

Moon – Austin Giorgio

CHAPTER 36
TRAVARES

Oh my fucking god. It's like he finally knows exactly what to say. It's clicked.

My heart screams at me to forgive him, to give him another chance. My soul calls on me to be compassionate; he was wounded and vulnerable when we met.

His tender heart wasn't ready for everything I had to offer.

But I'm still big mad about how he went about all of it.

He's right. I have to get over it if I want a future with him. I have to trust him again. Will this erase weeks of hurt?

"Am I enough?" I ask, my voice hoarse with emotion.

"Abso-fucking-lutely," he growls. "You're everything to me. You're more than I deserve."

"Come here." I hold out my hand to him. I almost weep with relief as the center of rightness inside of me fills up at his touch when his hand slips into mine.

Pierre saddles up to me and his cologne washes over me, making my heart skip a beat. I've never been immune to his scent and he knows, that's why he's playing dirty.

I like it. A lot.

I actually like his bravery for coming here. For wanting me so much he dared my wrath. He's fighting for us.

Reaching for his neck, like he did me, I pull him close and stop a breath apart. I can feel my lips graze his, feather soft, when I command, "Say it again."

"I love you," he breathes across my lips like a desperate plea. The Pierre standing before me is not the same one I left that day in his apartment. This is a lovesick Pierre.

There's no holding back, no turning back now. I pull his mouth to mine and seal our lips together in a fiery, passionate kiss that claims my man back to me. His lips part when I lick into his mouth and try to possess every cell inside of him. I want him knocked breathless by what's between us. I want him to burn just as I do.

And I burn like the infernos of hell for this man.

How could he deny this? Even the man in the moon can see how good this is.

He whimpers into my mouth and I pull away, nipping his lower lip as I do. His breathing is ragged and his cheeks are flushed. He's beautiful.

"I love you," he whispers again.

"Be a good boy and drop back down to your knees. Show me how much." He sucks cock like a demon and I want this control before I give in, because right now I'm anything but in control.

He rolls his lips together. He's not used to someone giving him commands but damned if he doesn't do it.

He hesitantly drops to his knees, prepared to earn my forgiveness. He looks glorious at this angle. I stare into his icy blue eyes as he tugs my sleep pants down, enough to pull me out so close to his face. He inhales my musky scent and moans to himself, eyes fluttering.

"Open up, pretty king. Properly beg on my cock."

Pierre opens his mouth and I place my hand on the top of his head, fingers splayed, gripping his hair as I draw him to me. The second his tongue slides over my cockhead I almost lose my shit. His mouth feels like heaven. God, it's so fucking hot.

"Fuck," I hiss. "Make it count, Pierre. Your epic love story depends on it."

This spurs him on to the performance of his life. He grabs my thighs and pushes me down his throat. Pierre doesn't have a gag reflex until further down in his neck. Best thing in the fucking world. I'm to the hilt when he finally gags.

Pierre is breathing deeply through his nose, nostrils flaring, sounding like a bull rearing up to attack. It sounds fucking fire in here with his heavy breathing and my moans. And god-fucking-damn it feels so amazing.

"Oh fuck, Pierre…god, you feel so good." I rub my hand over his smooth cheek. Cupping under his chin, I make sure his face is lifted up to see me.

"So beautiful. You gonna let me come down that throat?"

Just for good measure, I thrust in, catching him off guard, making him gag again. It sends a ripple of happiness through me.

His lips pop off my cock and he grins, "If that's what it takes. Whatever you want." He spits on his fingers and my asshole clenches. We know who's really in control here. And it's not me.

"We'll start with this. Make me come, Pierre."

His lips lock around me again. He leans back on his calves and I step forward, leaning over him, dominating. I hold the back of his head in my palm, holding him close to me.

"You look beautiful on your knees like this, taking my cock. Like a fallen angel who's chosen sin over salvation. Am I your salvation, pretty king?"

His eyes stay on mine while he balances on his knees trying to nod around his mouthful. I love looking at him like this. He's so gorgeous with his lips locked around me.

"I think you were sent to steal my soul. I will gladly give it to you, Pierre."

He drives me crazy. He makes me feel like I've never felt before. I love how he makes me feel when we're together. This only proves that the flame isn't extinguished. We are still twin flames burning for each other across time and space.

"I love seeing you right now." I rasp to him. "Oh god, Pierre, you take my cock beautifully. I want to come down your throat so bad." I throw my head back, reaching my limit. I'm at the edge. He's not easing.

Pierre, bless him, who can suck the chrome off a tailpipe, hits that spot I love so much on the underside of my dick as he pushes his wet fingers up into me, past the ring of muscle.

My breath gets caught in my lungs, then releases on a harsh cry. I'm hypnotized by his stare eating me alive. The curve of his fingers inside steals my soul from my body.

My body lights up and it spreads throughout me. I come with a force that's almost painful. I hold his head to me as I cry out, sobbing from pleasure, drowning in his stormy gaze.

His arm reaches up and he slams a hand across my mouth, quieting me mid holler. Fuck, I forgot about Poppy upstairs! He didn't.

His mouth never stops working over me and his gaze never leaves mine until every last drop is wrung from me. I'm lost in his universe, in the depths of his mind. There's a look in his eyes that reflects the love I feel for him.

Finally.

He lets my softening member slide from his lips. He wipes the corner of his mouth as he stands, licking his lips.

"Can I come home, Declan?"

"Yes," I whisper.

He's on me before I finish speaking. His tongue invades my mouth and I taste myself on him. His hands are everywhere, gripping my shirt, rubbing my abs, pulling me to him. I feel his hard, hot body through my clothes.

He grazes his hardness against my hip. I feel exactly how much he wants me.

He allows me one breath, and I use it wisely. "Fuck me, Pierre." It comes out exactly how I feel: breathless, stunned and dazed. Every fiber in my body is buzzing with how much I want him. It will never be enough.

I've been living in a cold, lonely wasteland without him. Having him in my arms again is like stepping into a sunny day and being kissed by the light. The warmth is seeping back into my life.

I grab his hand and pull him to the stairs, towards my bedroom. He'll be staying with me tonight.

Currently thankful my bedroom is on the other side of the house from Poppy's.

I walk into my bedroom and pull him in. He shuts and locks the door. Walking backwards, I lock my arms around his neck, pulling him along and kissing him in between words. "You and me, in every life before and after." His arms wrap around me, pulling me close, "Every single time, I'm yours and you're mine, your soul remembers who it's meant for. It's me. Our epic love story transcends time. I'll be yours in every lifetime."

"And I yours," he growls into my lips. "Forever."

"Make love to me, Pierre," I whisper across his flushed lips.

"As you wish, Prince Charming."

Chapter 37
Pierre

Together, I feel at peace as his skin brushes across my lips which are making their way up his throat. "Strip for me, bad boy. Let me look at what's mine."

Oh baby, call me crazy but I think I'm going to explode or combust into flames. I've never been more turned on in my whole damn life.

I watch him do a striptease for me and it drives me wild. Piece by piece comes off and drops to the floor as he backs up, slowly making his way to the huge king bed behind him.

I drop my jacket on the chair in the corner. I whip my shirt over my head and toss it on the floor with his. I watch his eyes roll back with need as he groans.

Declan's eyes roam from my face down to the planes of my torso. My lean muscles dance with the shadows as I make my way slowly to him. I'm savoring the anticipation. I want to pounce, but I also want this special for him.

Whipping off my belt and tossing it, I rip open my pants and shove them down as I walk, stopping long enough to step out of them. I'm raging hard.

I reach him and take his face in my hands, staring into his eyes as I make this vow, "I'm going to love you like I've never been broken, I promise. I've got you and I'm never letting go. I'm all yours." I lean in and kiss and bite up his neck, pulling a gasp from his perfect mouth. "You deserve the world and I'm going to give it all to you, starting now."

My lips crash onto his as I feel the anger melting from him. My chest soars and my blood pumps hot like lava through my body. I embed my life force with his once again. Through this kiss, so possessive and all consuming, I lose my head and seal my promise.

Pulling back, I rest my forehead on his. "There's been no one else. I couldn't bear it."

Declan inhales sharply, "Nobody, only you," he says breathlessly. I believe him.

"On the bed. On your back." It's not gentle, it's not sweet. It's authoritative, taking back control. I gave him his moment. He gives in so willingly, trotting over to the bed.

He looks so glorious crawling across his huge bed, ass waving in the air, like a delectable, juicy piece of fruit. I want to bite it, rub all over it, get lost in it and find heaven on the other side.

It's been far too long since I was inside him.

The vicious need to claim him all over again rides high with me.

I come over and look intently down at him lying there. He's expecting this to be hard, fast, and it might just be in the end, but he wants love and I aim to show him just that by soaking all of him in and making sure every inch of him feels wanted. He's important to me and I need to prove it.

I am the biggest fool for ever letting him go but I'm going to fix it. Before I climb on the bed and situate myself between his legs, I grab the bottle of lube from the nightstand.

Once he's spread out below me, I take in the beauty that is my Declan. I hope he always looks at me with such reverence and love. A sense of happiness rains down on me and I let it shiver through my body.

My fingers find his back hole, eager and waiting for me, like it knows who its master is. Using two fingers, I spread the lubricant around good. He whimpers in wait and barely contains his want. It feeds my desire.

Slipping in both fingers, I stretch him, "That's it, baby boy, take me in. You're such a bad, filthy boy." His ring clenches down around me and he moans loudly. "I fucking love it, baby boy. God, I missed you so bad."

"Oh god," he croaks, "I missed you too."

I get him ready to be loved how he needs. Fuck, I need this too. My heart is soaring.

"Now you're ready to take me." Bracing myself on my arm, I use the other to line up at his back opening. "You still want me?"

"Every bit of you," he breathes out.

At his acquiesce, I press forward. He said yes to us.

"Fuck, how could I forget how tight your ass is," I hiss between my teeth, straining to push past his ring.

Below me his face is rippled with ecstasy, eyes locked on my face.

"Declan, you're so beautiful, baby," I tell him softly as I slowly slide in to hit bottom. He watches my face, enraptured by him. His face mirroring my own. Every moan and whisper is mine. I give him a moment to breathe, but that's all he's getting before I'm moving.

Slow, deliberate, soft. Long pulls out. Slow, gentle strokes in. Rocking our joined bodies together. I'm going to take my time giving him this.

I want to devour him but…patience.

I reach back and grip his thigh and bring it higher by my ribs. His hands come up to the sides of my face, pulling me down to kiss him passionately. Declan takes my breath away with the raw, brutal honestly in it.

Returning the same feelings, kissing him back, I rub my hand up his chest, lightly resting it at the base of his throat. Our tongues clash, his once again hard cock lays pressed between us, our stomachs caressing it between us as I move inside him.

I eat up every gasp, every moan, every loud grunt he gives me when my hips thrust into him. I absorb and give back a few slow rotating pushes I know he loves.

He's on the edge. I can see it in his wild, blissed out eyes.

I bury my face in his neck, breathing hard, whispering such filthy things in his ear about how much I love him and what I want to do to him to prove it. Dragging my mouth down to his collarbone, I lightly bite at him and he groans when I suck on his sensitive place on the side of his neck.

I don't stop until I mark him.

"I love you, Declan." His asshole tightens in response. I snap my hips forward, going a little deeper. "I fucking love you. Only you. The other half of my soul."

He lifts his chin and his eyes roll back. Wrapping his arm around my neck, pulling me closer, hoarse and ragged, he bears his soul in his words, "*Fuck*, I love you too, Pierre. Soo fucking much, baby. For so fucking long. Choose us, babe."

"I choose us. I choose you, Declan, now and forever."

We're both out of breath, not wanting this to end, pushing our bodies to make this last longer. The pants and moans of our lovemaking echo about in the room. It's the most romantic symphony I've ever heard.

I pull up, face to face with him, breaths mingling. We are as one and our souls are melded now. "I want you to come for me. Be my bad boy and make a mess. All for me. Come for me, Declan."

CHAPTER 38
TRAVARES

His words unravel me in the fiercest of ways. My body just obeys of its own will. As he commands it, so is it done.

It feels like every cell in my body has gathered to launch out in euphoria. I'm no longer in control of my own body. Pierre is.

I reside in his domain, his kingdom to share with me.

He pulls the climax out of me with a roar. An out of body experience, dragging me through space and time with him. I don't even recognize my own voice, yelling his name, sobbing into his neck. Holding on for dear life, my fingers digging into his flesh.

Near the end, I yell, "Pierre! Oh fuck! Come in me!"

Through the haze, I feel him grow bigger inside my small space, his body stiffening. "Declan," he groans, "Fuck! Oh god, baby." His helpless grunt beside my ear makes me shiver.

Pierre collapses on top of me, chest heaving. I cling to him still, even as I feel him slipping out of me. Our stomachs are slick with my seed. I can't believe I came like that, barely any stroking. All the sensations were too much. There was no holding back.

After a few quiet moments where it's just us breathing heavy, he gets up on his elbows, and his fingers graze my jawbone, "Are you ok?"

I smile looking up at him. "I'm perfect."

A smile appears on his delectable lips, crinkling the corners of his eyes. "Good. Me too." He kisses me, making sure I know how good it is between us. It's a permanent kind of kiss for ownership. I'm his once again.

And he is mine.

When he pulls back, he wiggles around on top of me, squishing my slippery dick between us. He laughs at my contorted face. "That feels so gross," I chuckle.

"I like when you make a mess of us. It's one of my favorite things." He pushes up over top of me, bracing himself above me to peel my sticky cock off his stomach. The air hits it and makes it start cooling now that our bodies aren't keeping it warm. Shrinkage is real.

He laughs and rocks our hips, "I'll be back in there later on, but I need a snack right now. It's been rough without my bad boy. I'll be downstairs raiding the kitchen." He leans down and kisses me through his big smile. "But first, stay put, I'll be back."

Goddamn, he's so sexy. Everything he says, everything he does. I can't resist it. I love all of it.

Pierre returns with a warm washcloth and cleans me up before cleaning himself. He pats me dry with a towel and I get up while he takes it all back to the bathroom.

"Thanks to Poppy, I have a vast supply of snacks, so you're in luck. We have an abundance of snacks for a picky kid."

He comes walking up. His bottom lip is caught between his teeth. He looks nervous. Unsettled. Not what I expect him to look like after that awesome makeup sex.

I finish pulling down my shirt just as he does. I walk over, putting my hand on the side of his neck. "Hey. What's wrong? Talk to me."

He looks up and I see the doubt briefly there. "I don't know how any of this will work. I don't even want to leave you to go back to my apartment. I don't want to be away from you." He finishes zipping up his jeans and grips my wrist. "I don't know where I fit in now."

My other hand comes up to caress his face. I hope my loving touch will ease some of his apprehension.

"Then move in here with us. We're starting over. Start here. With us."

It just popped out but it feels so right, asking him to live with us. It's the next step.

"Let's do it," I excitedly rush out. "You want it all, then let's go. We talkin' marriage, two-point-five kids? Done. We already have the white house with the white picket fence. Why wait, Pierre? We know what we want and we make our own rules."

"Yeah," he whispers, unsure of his voice. "Yeah, I want that. I want all of that. I'd marry you tomorrow if you'd allow that."

My heart is in the clouds. This is all I ever wanted. I wanted him, all in, wholeheartedly.

"Ok, it's settled. Tomorrow you're moving in. Call off work, play sick, I know the bosses."

He laughs and it's a shit load lighter than a few moments ago. Thank fuck. I thought he was backing out there for a moment.

"I have clients, goofball. I can't just call off work. Some of these clients have waited months. Tell you what, I'll start packing tomorrow and this weekend we can move some of my stuff. Until then, I'll stay here with you. That ok?" He bites his bottom lip again.

I kiss it and pull it out with my thumb. "Sounds like the rest of my life is falling into place." I kiss him again and then tug him out the door.

"You need to do quantum leaps with your electrons, Uncle Pierre—he's Uncle now?—so you need to get excited. It's science. Not old man excited alright." She flips her hand out as if to say I should know this already. "Happy like little kid on birthday cake and Mountain Dew excited. Almost pee yourself being happy. Mom would always say *shift your energy*." I love how her little kid voice became singsong mimicking Lily. "You should dance. It always makes me happy. If you see things from a different wavelength it makes miracles." She cups her mouth with her hand and whispers to him (it's not a whisper), "That's 'cause your music has cuss words in it."

I bet her breath smells like maple syrup and I guarantee that hand is covered in it since she keeps discarding the fork and using her fingers. Wild child.

That was a lot for a kid her age. I knew Lily dabbled in energy work but I wasn't sure if she was teaching Poppy those beliefs. Guess I know now. I should probably foster this way of thinking. I mean it couldn't hurt. "You sound exactly like your mother. I'm so proud of you. That's impressive knowledge for an eight-year-old."

"NINE! I'm nine now. Sorta. Almost a teenager, ya know." She crosses her arms across her chest in righteous indignation.

"Whoa! Slow down. First off you are *EIGHT.* You are *NOT* almost a teenager so get that right out of your head this instant. And yes, that was impressive advice. Maybe you can teach us how to do it, but right now…" I pluck her from the barstool and shoo her away from the table, "go get dressed, ya filthy heathen. Bah!! Be gone with ye, mortal! And wash your grubby hands!"

Poppy's giggles can be heard from the ornate stairwell as she runs up them to get dressed in her room upstairs. She yells over her shoulder, "I'll get my pet dragon to eat you!" Her little footfalls race down the hallway upstairs, sounding like a hippo crashing through the house.

Poppy was pretty happy this morning to see Pierre here when she got up for breakfast.

I was pretty happy for him to be here too, even if he's in my clothes but that kind of makes it that much sweeter. I can get used to mornings like this.

Since Lily's murder—that's exactly what we're calling it— her death was not natural, I let no one forget she was senselessly taken, robbed of a life because of a murderer.

Since that night, Poppy has not been back to her school. I can't take the risk. I refuse to risk it. She is guarded twenty-four-seven.

I've worked out with her school for her to attend classes and do homework remotely until we can make sure she'll be safe. The school was offended I thought they weren't a safe place for children, then they relented and allowed it when I advised them I had no problem taking this up through the school board for permission.

A tutor comes at ten every morning and uses the sitting room as a makeshift classroom. I supplied the tutor with everything they requested in the way of supplies. Boy, were they ever happy to have an unlimited supplies budget.

When my mini hurricane comes racing back in, we have the kitchen back in order and it's time to have a talk with Poppy. She's old enough to understand relationships.

"Hey Poptart? Can we have a chat with you?" Pierre says following her into the living room to sit on the couch with her as she powers up her tablet. She gets thirty minutes before school. I'm a stickler for screen time.

Ironic considering what I do for a living.

Her eyes get that look of dread, like she immediately thinks she's done something bad.

I hurry to cover where Pierre gave her anxiety, sitting down across from her, remembering he has no idea how to be around children and this is his first one her age. I put my hands up, "You did nothing wrong. We have a surprise to tell you."

She cocks her little head at me and her pathetic ponytail she tried and failed at, lists to the side. "Are you two getting married finally?"

Pierre's eyes go wide and he panics when he looks over at me across the couch. She looks between both of us, looking like she's watching a tennis match.

"Um, well, yes, we are, sometime, when…yeah eventually," Pierre tells her nervously. "Are you ok with that?"

"Of course I am," her face is so serious. Like we should already know these answers. Like this is no surprise to her. I have to give the kid credit. Lily needs kudos too. She's raised a great kid so far, one that's consistently showing me what a special person she is. It's my honor to raise her in her mother's absence.

I don't think I could have picked a better partner to do this with either. Pierre doesn't know it yet, but he's going to make a great dad when it happens. I'll convince him. I'd like a few more kids.

Then Poppy surprises us, looking at Pierre, she asks, "Does this mean I can call you Papa Pierre?"

She quickly turns to me, "I still want you to be my Uncle Ducky." She turns back to Pierre but he looks at me for help. He's not sure what to say, what I want, how I feel about it. It's not something we even thought about discussing beforehand.

"I am good with whatever you prefer. This is how we blend our family. Just let her know or she might explode." I grin at him and wink at my Popsicle.

"I..I guess I've never really thought about it." He clears his throat. "Poppy, why do you want to call me that? You just called me Uncle Pierre not even an hour ago."

She gets her little scientist pose. That's what I call her one where she crosses her arms and cocks her head like we are stupid and she knows everything, fuck, maybe she does. She seems to always be three steps ahead of us. From her lips she's almost a teenager and everyone knows they definitely know everything.

"I tried that out but my tongue said no, so my heart came up with Papa. It feels right. You're like a dad to me I get to visit, like custody that my friend Hector does with his dad, but with my bestest friend." She looks over at me and says, "Besides you, Uncle Ducky," back over to Pierre. "I already had a Dad, so it can't be that. I don't know why, the Great Spirit makes it happen." That's a lot to unpack there. Where does she come up with this stuff? Furthermore, what the hell was Lily teaching her? I can't continue shit I don't know. Guess we are all learning about the Great Spirit here soon.

Pierre's eyes fill. Oh god, it's making mine fill too. We're overhydrated here lately; it's just leaking out whenever it can. I blame invisible onions. If I'm not careful it will turn into a flood since my heart is so overflowing with emotions.

"That's the most beautiful thing anyone has ever said to me, Poppy."

"So, can I? Papa or Grandpa, you pick."

I bark out a laugh. That escalated quickly. She knows how to negotiate what she wants.

Pierre holds out his arms, beckoning her to him. "Com'mere."

She happily crawls over to hug him. They look so happy together. Like family. It would have been tragic and cruel of me to take Pierre from her too. I see their bond now. I was too blinded by my own feelings to see what was best for her, what he meant to her.

I never saw this coming. I don't think he did either. I know kids have a *person* and I always thought I was her person, but I can share her attention and affection with Pierre.

He kisses the top of her head and murmurs in her hair, "I would be honored to be your Papa."

He doesn't get to see the look on her face, but I do, I can see it perfectly. It's pure joy. Something I thought I wouldn't get to see on her pretty face for a very long time.

For that, I'm thankful.

Another piece of my life falls into place.

CHAPTER 39
TRAVARES

Somehow in the past twenty-four hours my life's puzzle pieces all slipped right into place, making the picture whole.

I'm in a video call with Rock, Danger, Shadow and Gunney, our Top Five, in my home office that has been soundproofed for such things. Our line is also impenetrable and hacking into it is just not possible. All the guys take huge precautions so as not to be overheard.

I'm sharing my screen, showing them screenshots of messages, texts, social media messages. Every single one of them is coded between the three phones we 'file shared' with. Well, they shared with us unwillingly and unnoticed. We liberated their information for our own use.

We've easily dismissed the messages from family members and other friends outside of the club. Nothing hokey happening in them.

But the other shit…

It's not like it's an easy code either. It's gibberish. "No clue these idiots were this high tech." I pull up another text that literally reads: @73u'0[1<9

"What in the actual fuckity fuck?"

I nod while typing and say, "Yeah, what Shadow said. If y'all think you can crack it, please help, give it a gander. We're stumped."

I show another one: <01[901<92>3|3~

Gunney's frustrated growl echoes my own when it comes out of me every moment I comb through this infuriating information. There's no rhyme or reason and none of the cracking programs I possess has figured it out either.

"Who the fuck can figure that shit out?"

"No one, that's who. They've went through great lengths to ensure the best two hackers in the country, even the world, can't break their code," Rock says with a sour face. Everyone can clearly see how much he hates the Lone Star Saints.

I mean, what's there to love of them?

Nothing. They're scum of the earth.

"What about our men inside?" I ask. "Can they maybe find a key to unlock this bullshit? I'm sure there's got to be a handwritten one somewhere. These fuckers didn't just all memorize this shit. I wonder if there's more than one out there. I'd say there's at least three, one for each of them."

I bring up the final picture. It's of an incoming text to Bear, Panhead Pete's second-in-command, from a phone number that's a burner phone. It's already been disconnected. The picture is of the alleyway where Lily was found.

I shock them with this one. "Whoever sent this to Bear was at the scene or is even the killer. The timestamp of the message matches the timeframe in which the coroner said Lily's time of death was."

I'm working every angle until the rape kit comes back with a name for the DNA.

The VP knew what was going to happen in that alley that night. He was expecting it. He waited for them to report in. He waited for the confirmation.

"That night there were dozens of texts, from tons of numbers with one word: Term."

"A few say *'Terminado'* in your pics," Gunney points out.

"That's means completed, finished, done in Spanish. Bear is of the Latino community, as is a healthy number of their organization. They have been accused of being part of the cartel, at least in cahoots with them. We can only assume these were confirmations of their terrorizing acts on the women and partners that night."

Danger jumps in, "So that means that night, these were planned out. They were probably organizing this for weeks right under our noses."

"Motherfuck."

I agree with Shadow.

"They're idiots. He had all those men text his personal number that they completed their fucked up assignments. Sloppy." Danger shakes his head like he can't believe they were this messy.

"That's a *them* problem. Our problem is cracking this code. I fully believe all our answers lie within that code. All other parties texting their phones don't use this code. Only these three, together. But the others are very vague, picky with their words. They do make a lot of outgoing calls to each other, which I haven't tracked from trying to figure out this shit." I finish, then sit back in my gaming chair. Sighing, I run my hands down my face. I look at my screens and see the grim faces of our Top Five team staring back at me, silently asking questions I don't have answers to.

"Are you able to hijack the phone while they are using it and record the calls in real time?" Shadow taps his chin and asks. Him and Gunney are sitting next to each other in their home office, calling from the same laptop.

Why didn't I think of this?

Because I've been burning the candle at both ends? I'm exhausted. Clearly, it's affecting my brain. Staying up making love with Pierre all night didn't help my already exhausted brain. But I'm not going to complain.

"Yes, Shadow!" I smile really big. "This is why I need you guys. Y'all keep me grounded and see the things I can't. I should have thought about that, I apologize."

"No need to apologize," Rock says, "Any way we can have that up and working here soon? ETA?"

My hands are flying over the keyboard. I'm clicking through windows, lost in the thrill. Tracking them like a hunter through code. Reaching my long arm out through the ethernet and finding them, wherever they may be.

I'll find you, then pluck the meat from your bones one sliced morsel at a time.

"We're live," I breathe.

"Now?" Rock asks, dumbfounded. "That quick?"

I nod. "Uh huh, right now. Starting with the next call we will be able to hear the phone calls in real time, live on Panhead's phone. Good idea, Shadow, thanks brother."

He nods, giving a half smile, then asks, "Should we take shifts listening to the calls? That way it's not all on you, Dec. You need a life too. By the looks of it, you need rest."

"I agree," Both Rock and Danger say at the same time.

I swallow the lump in my throat. Technically this is not club business. This is a personal vendetta. Rock has graciously made resources available to me left and right to track Lily's murderer, without asking for anything in return.

I'm so touched these men, my chosen family, are ready to jump at a moment's notice to assist me on my path to justice. Whoever did this is going to die a very long, drawn out, torturous death. I guarantee it.

I clear my throat, "Ok. Thank you for offering. Yeah, I can whip up a quick schedule for us to go by. You'll have to do your shift here at my home where the set up is. I have snacks though! Poppy makes sure of it." I shrug like snacks are not a big deal, when in fact they are a huge motherfucking deal apparently. Ask the tiny terror living in my house and the five different kinds of apples on the kitchen counter.

"Text it out to us within the hour. Anything else before we part, gentlemen?" Rock gathers up his notes he's always taking.

Now's a good time to drop this bombshell. "Yeah, I got something before we sign off. I wanted you guys on this call to know that Pierre and I are together. Going forward, well, immediately, he will be living here at my house, formally moving in this weekend. The wedding will be in two weeks if I have it my way. A spring wedding in City Park."

I stop fidgeting with my pen and look up at my quiet screens. There are so many different reactions. Danger sits blinking at me like I've spoken another language.

Shadow and Gunney smile at each other and giggle between themselves. Gunney puts his hand out and Shadow slaps his in it for a shake. "You owe me fifty."

"Oh, yeah," I snap my fingers, remembering the important part, "You can't say anything to your women because Pierre wants to tell them first, on his own. Good luck keeping that locked inside you. That's all. Have a good day."

Pure evil.

Chapter 40

Pierre

Saturday morning, I gathered the girls at my house under the false pretense of having breakfast together. My eight-hour tattoo scheduled to begin at ten called to cancel. They've tested positive for flu A. I'm not trying to get sick so I was ok to reschedule. They were doing me a favor anyways. Which brings me to breakfast with the girls.

Oh, there's breakfast, but it's bagels and cream cheese.

They are here to help me start packing. But they don't know that yet. I also have to break it to Birdie I'm leaving her apartment.

The first to arrive is Cherry. She seems a little flighty but that's her usual I've come to learn. She overwhelms herself with school and then all her odd jobs. Zharia told me she is a shoo-in for top of her class and she's very diligent in her studies.

Birdie arrives next, then Zharia. They are all wearing huge smiles because they think they are getting some confirmation of the surprise visit last night, perhaps they are.

I call Tally and prop her up against the candle on the island. That's a good place for her. She can see and hear. She's gonna wanna hear this next part.

I pick the moment they all have their faces stuffed. It will be quieter that way.

"I just wanted to say thank you for all of your support and friendship. But I lured you here to help me pack my belongings. Birdie, I regret to inform you I shall be moving, babes. I'll be moving to Declan's today and living there full time. I think I'm getting married in two weeks too. That's a maybe. Let's just say that's Declan's timeline. I'm iffy on a May wedding at City Park."

"Omehgaww!" Zharia straight spits her bagel into her napkin and jumps up and down. She rushes over to hug me as Tally breaks into joyful laughter, "I had a feeling!" Here comes the tears.

Birdie swallows and says, "This is fantastic news! I'm so happy for you!"

Cherry, not as reserved now that she's been around us more, comes over to hug me and say, "I love this for you, Mr. Pierre." God. She makes me feel like such an old man sometimes.

"You did it. I'm so proud of you." Birdie's smile says how happy she is for me.

"Thank you, ladies." I admit, I have to wipe a tear from my eye too.

"Of course we'll help you. I have nothing else to do today. Do we need Shadow and Leo?" Zharia is looking around, assessing what all we need to do. There are shelves of books, and some knickknacks here in the living room. Plenty of art everywhere you look.

I may have a small obsession with buying local art.

I know one of the first things I want taken over is the portrait I've done for Declan. I finally finished it. Along with the one hanging in my bedroom. I did what I said I wanted to do, I painted him in bed with the sunlight filtering in. He has a sheet pulled up over his midsection and beckoning me to bed.

"The kitchen and my bedroom, specifically, my closet is what needs started today." I look at my watch, "The boxes and totes should be delivered any minute."

"Argh! Another damn mission with friends I can't do." Tally pouts from the phone.

I know it has to hurt her to be so far away from us. Distance never kept us from being close to her emotionally, but sometimes you just need to be around your people in person. Tangible hugs are needed, not just ones sent across the internet.

As if the supplier heard, the door downstairs rings. Me and Zhar head down the steps and see the big pile growing at the doorway. The delivery guys are going back for more.

I look over at Zhar. "I may have bought too much."

"Ya think? How much shit do you have Pierre? I know you have a fuckton of Prince's wardrobe in your closet but other than that I can't imagine all those rooms are full. Are you a secret hoarder?"

"Christ, Zhar. No, I'm not a hoarder. I don't have that much and you really think I look as good as Prince?"

"That's what you picked up on most? Sheesh, let's get this done."

She starts dragging plastic totes towards the stairs and that's when I feel it. Eyes on me, burning across my skin. I stand up and start looking around Jackson Square.

My eyes jerk around, straining, seeking out anyone standing and watching. I have suspicions of Seven since I won't sign his papers, but I can't discount LSS and them wanting to harm partners.

Just as fast as it came on, it went away.

Zharia hollering at me jars me back to the present. "Are you coming?"

One last look around and I grab up my totes and head to where she's holding the door open.

Definitely was an odd feeling.

Once we get the tunes grooving and assignments dished out, we go to work. By noon we were all in need of more food so I ordered in po'boys for everyone, their favorites. I remember sitting in the living room eating these sandwiches with Declan and getting to know each other. Good times.

"Where is all this going?" Cherry asks around a bite.

"Ya know, I'm not really sure. Probably Declan's garage or a spare room. I was told to go through the kitchen and anything he didn't have but I do, leave it out. Since he cooks better than me we are excited to join our kitchens together." I wipe my hands with a napkin and take a drink of sweet tea.

"We might be able to pack this place up in one day with all of us working at it. We're over halfway through," Birdie confirms.

After we eat, we throw on an old rock playlist and get back at it. Some time later my phone alerts me to a visitor at the door downstairs. I pull up the camera and see it's Seven again.

Why the fuck?

I would ignore it but Zharia has already peeped over my shoulder and saw him.

"Oh, hell naw!!! This motherfucker's got balls showing up here. Audacity in leaps and bounds. Fuck him."

Birdie and Cherry come running from my bedroom and Birdie breathlessly asks, "What's happening?"

Zharia yanks my phone out of my hand and shows her Seven on the screen, standing at the door like he's welcome there.

"Are you letting him up?" Cherry asks, wide eyed.

"Of course not," Zhar snorts.

"No, but I am going down there to see what he wants."

"You've got to be fucking with me, Pierre," Zhar deadpans. We can clearly see she's upset about his presence, but she has to remember, I still have a pending divorce that is gearing up to be a battle.

"I'm not letting him in." It's like she doesn't trust me.

She holds my phone up and looks at the screen. Her hands gesture from her eyes to the screen, meaning she's got her eyes on Seven. And quite frankly, I'm glad someone has my back right now.

I'm depleted emotionally where Seven is concerned which makes it easier for him to get under my skin and take advantage.

Zhar hands my phone back and crosses her arms, "I'll be at the top of the stairs."

Birdie crosses her arms too and juts out her hip. Ut oh. "Me too," she says.

Cherry just shrugs and says, "Same, I guess."

I head down the stairs to see him standing there casually, with his hands in his pockets, like he doesn't have a care in the world.

Like he isn't out here trying to destroy lives.

Moments like now, I look at him and wonder what the fuck I was thinking? And why the hell was I so blind?

I open the bottom door and stand there with it propped on my body.

"Seven."

"Pierre."

"Why are you here?"

"I came to pick up your signed papers and thought we could divide up our furniture."

Z's right. Audacity is at an all-time high.

"That won't be happening."

"Sign the papers, Pierre. Quit dragging this out. I could take more but I feel my terms are more than fair."

Behind me the door yanks open, causing me to lose my balance, but not before Zharia tries to force her way through the doorway.

"You don't deserve a fucking dime you free-loading, greedy piece of shit. If it wasn't for you leeching off of him for *YEARS* he could have been happy a long time ago. You don't deserve the dirt he walks on, you rotten pussy ass bitch." Then she spits at him. Spits! Jesus fuck, I should have known she wouldn't stay put. She's like a mama bear protecting her cub right now.

"You're letting her talk to me like that?" He wipes his face off with his hand and smears it on his jeans. I watch his fists clench as his teeth gnash together in anger.

"He don't *let* me do nothing, fucker. I do what I want and right now I'd like to fuck your shit up, starting with your ugly face but I see the security is about to escort the trash outta here." I look up in time to see the guards trying to get through the people milling about the Square.

Doesn't stop Zhar, "Do yourself a favor, stay the fuck away from Pierre. We're all happy he finally moved on. I can't wait to plan his wedding with him. I feel sorry for you, never knowing the happiness he does now."

Killshot engaged.

Zharia hit him where he's most vulnerable. He thought I would wallow in self-pity and he's mad I'm not pining over him still. He got off on it. He got off on my pain. I realize that now.

"Go on, git, Seven. Go fuck yourself, there's nothing here for you." Look at Birdie jumping into the madness. Danger's going to kill me, so is Gunney and Shadow.

"I can't believe you let these bitches talk to me like this," Seven yells incredulously.

"I told ya, I fuckin' told ya, who you calling bitches, skanky ass ho," Zharia puffs up and launches herself out the door. I barely catch her in time before she scratches Seven's face off. She has a hold of his shirt in her claws and she's pulling him to her, yelling, "Come here you festering coward. I'm gonna show you *let*. Fucking pig. He should have left you a long time ago. Dead fucking weight." She takes a breath and keeps going. "You're nothing without him, that's why you're here. You're nothing, Seven."

Zharia is causing quite the scene.

"Pierre, what the fuck is going on?" Declan's voice. I look around and then realize it's coming through the security system.

By now the security team surrounding the apartment has been alerted and they have grabbed Seven, hauling him back. Zharia is still in my arms, fighting, squirming to get her hands back on Seven. He looks absolutely terrified. I can't help but smirk at that.

Zharia is a firecracker, no, more like an atomic bomb. She is a lioness that will stop at nothing to protect her friends. She's proving it.

I hear Declan again over Zharia yelling at me to let her loose. She's trying to pry my arms from around her where I have them like a vice grip. Birdie comes around us trapped in the doorway and places her hands on the sides of Z's face to try to calm her down.

God, I knew Zhar didn't like Seven but I didn't know it was at the point of violence now.

"You'll pay for this bullshit, Pierre, mark my words. I'll take everything you have by the time I'm done. You can thank your little whore friend here."

"Whore? Face me like a man, you scurvy pirate whooooore!" She tries to swing, barely missing him, but elbows me in the jaw nearly making me bite my tongue off.

This is all happening so fast and I've lost all control of the situation.

"Is that Seven? What the fuck is he doing there?" Declan yells over the chaos. He sounds mad.

"Zhar, please stop," Birdie begs.

"Try me, Seven. You bird brained shit sniffer." One big breath and her two fingers point at his head, Zharia screams, "I curse your junk that it will never work again, I curse you with bad sex for the rest of your miserable life and I hope you die a lonely, painful death."

Everyone falls silent except for Zharia's maniacal laughing and pointing.

Here in the Crescent City, surrounded by the hoodoo and vodou practitioners, we don't joke about curses. We never joke about the magick that thrives in our Quarter. It's an unspoken rule that you give the magick here the respect it deserves. It's in the air now, the heavy words are close enough to land on him. He immediately recoils in the security guards' arms.

It's out of my hands now. The word gauntlet has been thrown down. I watch as horror spirals across Seven's face while he's restrained by two armed men. He's struggling, the same as Zhar is.

Seven actually screams like a banshee in rage. "You take that back right now you fucking brown bitching harpy!"

"Neverrrr!" Mwahaha!

Something has to be done. This is ridiculous. I don't know whether to laugh or be pissed. We can't stand here screaming at each other. We are a spectacle to behold, I'm sure.

I double down and haul Zharia over my shoulder. She yelps and starts threatening me, "Pierre, so help me *gawd*, if you don't put me down right fucking now."

I've been lax on my gym time lately, but I'm still in shape enough to drag Z back upstairs. I hear Declan telling the two guards to escort Seven away and make sure everyone knows he is not to be allowed around there anymore.

Once Birdie has the door shut behind me, I drop a huffing and puffing red-faced Z on her feet.

Jesus fuck.

"You do yourself a disservice by not letting me beat his ass," Zhar states as she straightens her clothes. She pushes her messy bun out of her face, then unties it so she can redo it. Her hair reaches past her ass so it's a feat to trap all that hair.

I'm a cross between being pissed and being astonished by her loyalty and her fierce desire to get vengeance for me. She gave not one fuck about her own welfare. She was out for blood. For me. Has this Zhar been in there the whole time?

Cherry stands with her mouth open, starstruck, "Zhar, I think you're my spirit animal. That was amazing. Remind me to stay on your good side. Rock on, sista."

Wonderful.

My phone is ringing in my pocket again and *I just know* it's either Declan or my brother.

Zharia stalks off to the bathroom with a fitful Birdie trailing behind. Cherry looks from them to me and back to them, then skedaddles after the girls. Pulling my phone out, I answer Declan.

"Hey, honey!" I try to sound like I haven't went ten rounds with a tiny Mike Tyson but it comes out flat.

"What the hell is going on? I'm working and I have alerts going off like crazy. Are you ok?"

I'm relieved he doesn't sound very mad. "I'm ok. I only took one elbow to the face trying to hold Zhar back."

"I didn't realize what a wildcat she is," Declan says laughing.

"Me either. She keeps that locked up tight apparently. I assume you saw he's been taken away."

"Yes, my pretty ink king, I saw everything. It won't happen again. Because you'll be with me, in our home. How is packing going?"

I bite my thumbnail and look around. Not too shabby. "We need a few more hours. You're going to owe these girls a nice dinner. They are trying to keep to your timeline. We aren't getting me moved in one day, Dec."

"Then I'll hire a team for tomorrow."

"Where are we storing all this?" It didn't dawn on me until Cherry said something and I looked at the size of the growing stacks of totes and boxes. Yeah, where is it going?

"For right now, upstairs in the empty bedroom next to ours. You can decorate, move things around, store stuff wherever you want in the house. My house is now your house. Do whatever, babe." I hear a faint clickity clack of his keyboard in the background and know he's still working.

I've distracted him. Technically it's not my fault. I didn't bring Seven here.

"Are you going to be ok there the rest of the day or do I need to come down?" Clickity clacking stops. I have his full attention.

"I should be fine but thank you for offering. Could you send for a moving van to take some of this over? Like my clothes. We are growing quite a pile." Looking closer I just now notice scrawled on the sides of numerous boxes are the words

'Prince's clothes.' It looks suspiciously like doctor handwriting. The topper of it all, she drew Prince's symbol. This bitch…

"Yeah, no prob. Anything else?"

"Not right now, but later. I need some more of that." In my pants my cock twitches.

"Anytime you want. I'm all yours, my love."

"I'll pencil you in for nine-ish. After the kid's in bed."

"I love you."

This is the first time I've said it over the phone.

"I love you too." Comes so naturally now.

CHAPTER 41
TRAVARES

"I'm sorry, Mr. Travares, the male sample is not in the national database."

My heart deflates. Not the news I wanted to hear.

"Can you send me the police files?"

"You know I can't do that."

"Ok then, thought I would ask nicely first. If I have any questions about them, I'll text." I disconnect the call with Detective Laurens. No need to speak to her grouchy ass any longer.

I need to think on this. I'll get the file by any means necessary with a keyboard and mouse as she well knows, as usual, and sort through what they have. Again. It's not like their cyber security is locked down tight. A child could hack the police department's crime files. It's literally like a plastic food container and lid, except the lid has huge cracks in the top, letting anything into the food. I can't believe we pay tax dollars for this.

Maybe I should offer to redo their cyber security once all this is done.

It's not like I haven't been following their investigation like a hawk from the very beginning. I know they have nothing we don't have. I've swiped the autopsy report, the tox screen, the rape kit details and any other notes and pictures they have from the scene.

The only thing I don't have are the DNA results. And as we speak, they are being transferred over to my computer.

So, nothing in CODIS, the nationwide database housing DNA profiles managed by the FBI. It's a powerful system designed to help local, state and federal forensic labs compare DNA samples in unsolved crimes.

If the male DNA found on Lily is not in CODIS, then he's not been arrested or a sample taken before.

This search just got a lot harder but not impossible.

I had high hopes about the DNA sample though. I thought it would have all the answers. Never fear, I have an idea and watching all those hours of Paula Zahn with Lily are going to pay off. Royally.

Pulling my cell phone over, I text my friend, Bethany, who leads a team of experts in forensic genealogy. Kim, her counterpart, is the brain of building the family trees. Bethany is the savvy business end of the empire they've built together.

The use of forensic genealogy has become a huge selling point for people to find loved ones they never knew existed.

But the other side of the coin is that law enforcement can use it to build a family tree to investigate further through relatives, hoping to find the person responsible.

This is what we are about to do. The girls owe me a favor. This is a 'drop-what-you're-doing and build a tree for me' kind of repayment. I know how busy they are.

While I wait for them to get back to me, I check in on Pierre again since it's been a few hours. He should be wrapping up here soon.

Needing a break, I step away from my computer and stretch. I take up my phone one more time and text my love.

Me: Hey lover, how's it going?

Slipping my phone in my back pocket, I head to the kitchen. I hear Poppy giving a book report of the book she's been reading for class. Her voice is loud and clear and she seems to know exactly what she's talking about.

Good. I was really worried about the shift in her education. I know she needs the social interaction with other children but that's not something I can afford her right now. My number one job is protecting her. This change in schooling is most likely temporary. Once we kill off all the Saints, there will no longer be a threat.

I can't wait for the day they all die.

Going through the kitchen cabinets proves useless. I'm hankering for something, but I don't know what. I hate this feeling. I don't want any of those snacks. Let me just open this fridge and see what we have.

I hire a housekeeper to come in once a week to stock groceries, do laundry and clean, sometimes cook. Since Poppy moved in I've had to up the services to twice a week.

The housekeeper, Mrs. Thompson, a lovely local older lady who is widowed with three older children living nearby, is scheduled to come tomorrow with groceries. She has been my housekeeper since I've lived here. It was a blessing to find her. I've never had one complaint about Mrs. Thompson.

She absolutely adores Poppy. She is very good with her and has made no complaints about the messes Poppy leaves. Mrs. Thompson says it's like taking care of one of her own grandchildren and she doesn't mind.

We are going to see if there's anything good in the fridge left over from hurricane Poppy. The kid eats ten times her weight in Go-Gurts and cheese sticks. How did Lily afford to feed her?

Oh wait, I did. I sent food there too. I never looked at the order though. Oh snap, that's another service I need to contact to cancel. I forgot all about the delivery service that's probably wondering why they haven't received Lily's weekly orders.

I'm in luck today.

There're ingredients to make a turkey sandwich. I know Poppy will have already eaten lunch but it's encroaching upon snack time, signaling the end of the school day.

When I put everything back, I see there is a cup of Jell-O with mandarin oranges and two cheese and pepperoni stick combos on the lowest shelf with a note attached that says, *'Great job on the fungus report! -Mrs. T.'*

Ahh. The fungus report she needed a mushroom hat for. Have you ever tried to hunt down a mushroom hat in the stores? The entire time Poppy told me to just order it online. The whole thing was infuriating.

After the third store, I gave up and ordered it online. I let her pick it and now we have a big red and white spotted mushroom balancing on her head. It's tied on with a ribbon of wide lace.

She's worn it for a week. I wouldn't be surprised if she has it on currently.

My phone chimes with a text message:

☻ॐ**Ink King:** Hello sexy xoxo We are about finished loading the van and we will be headed that way soon.

☻ॐ**Ink King:** Also, side note, I feel like someone is watching me. I have the heebie jeebies. Are you watching me through the cameras outside?

Well, if that doesn't just sound warning bells in my mind.

Me: Not at all. I have eyes on you all around you. Possible you feel one of our men?

☻ॐ**Ink King:** Could be. Immediately made me on high alert. Maybe I'm just jumpy but in my defense it was before Seven got here. It could have been him but even standing out here typing this, I feel eyes on me.

Me: Be done now. Come home. Don't wait any longer, gather the girls.

Already I'm starting to feel the edge of panic. This can't be good. I send out a text to the Security Team Leader of the unit in the French Quarter watching the girls and Pierre. They need to know how Pierre feels.

There are about thirty armed undercover guards in street clothes strategically placed around Jackson Square. They are within steps of our loved ones. Which makes me wonder why it took so long to reach Seven on the doorstep.

I knew I should have gone over there. If anything happens to him, or one of the Old Ladies, I won't forgive myself.

I hear back from the Lead man in the Quarter and he confirms Seven has not been seen since. Whoever it is, they are perceived as a threat and we will continue that line of thinking until proven otherwise.

No sooner did I lay my phone on the counter than Poppy comes zooming around the doorway into the kitchen, beelining to the refrigerator for her snack. When she reaches in and sees the handwritten note from Mrs. Thompson she lets out a little squeal and does a tiny dance.

I chuckle to myself.

"Uncle Ducky, when is Papa Pierre going to be home?"

I pick her up and plop her down on the island so she can look at me without jacking up her neck.

"He's on his way home right now actually."

She nods gleefully and around a bite, with pepperoni breath aimed right at me, says, "Good, I need help on my art project."

"I can't help you?" Trying not to be jealous here. Not even twenty-four hours and he's replacing me with things.

Breathe. This is to be expected. I shouldn't be jealous. I should be ecstatic she loves him as much as she does and has accepted him into our lives. It could be much worse.

So much worse.

I'm truly grateful for her resilient soul. She's doing amazing since Lily's murder. I didn't know what to expect, but the child counselor I began taking her to says this could be shock, or she's hiding it well, or she really is ok.

It's a wait and see situation from here on out. I think having Pierre around will help.

"Because he's the artsy fartsy guy. If I was doing a report on cussing at computers I would pick you."

Out of the mouths of babes.

I love the mischievous twinkle in her eyes when she says shit like this.

Poppy's tutor, Laura, pops her head around the entryway to say goodnight.

Once she's gone, I turn back to Poppy. "How're you doing, popstar?" I lean my hip up against the counter, facing her and rest my hands on the cold surface.

I do these every other day check-ins with her per the counselor. It would devastate me to lose Poppy in this to depression and sadness. You never know how kids are going to handle something. I'm trying everything I can to help her through this.

She shrugs.

Ut oh. That could mean a number of things.

"Do you want to talk about the details?"

She hesitates and won't look at me. I put my fingers under her chin and tilt her head up, softly I encourage her, "Hey, I'm here for you. You can talk to me about anything, I promise you that."

"Can I say whatever I want during our talks?" she quietly asks.

"Yes," I assure her.

"I think it's really fucked up someone killed my mommy."

Then she promptly bursts into tears, covering her face with her hands, her little shoulders shaking.

I can't imagine holding all this in.

Immediately I have her in my arms, her tears soaking my shirt. I rock her like I did when she was a baby, side to side. Rubbing her back, I whisper back to her, "Yes it is, honey, I agree."

Her sobs grow louder with every heaving inhale. I squeeze her harder. That's when I hear another sob and my gaze jerks over to the entryway.

There stands my soon-to-be husband, hands over his mouth, crying, and his best friends fanned out around him, crying too.

I didn't hear them come in, but I was also focused on Poppy.

Lifting my arm, I hold my hand out to Pierre. He hurries over to us, throwing his arms around Poppy, onto me too.

"Hey, *sha bébé*, Papa Pierre's here too. I'm right here with you. I miss your momma too and it's ok to cry and be sad about it. You're allowed to be mad, sad, lonely; however you want to feel. Let it out, Poppy. Don't let the tears inside drown you."

Pierre lays his cheek on her head. Eventually, Poppy calms down and her sobs subside, but her small body still jerks with the shivers that come after a good cry.

My gaze goes back to the entry and I see the girls are no longer there, giving us privacy. I'm grateful for it. I'm not sure how Poppy will feel about other people seeing her breakdown.

"I love you, Popsicle," I whisper softly in her hair and I rub my hand down her tangled hair.

Sniffle. "I love you too, Uncle Ducky." Sniff. Shiver.

If Pierre loves her, this would be the time to tell her. She needs us. He just admitted to loving me last night, maybe saying it to her is a line he's not ready to cross.

He surprises me. "I love you, Poppy," Pierre quietly tells her. "I promise I'll always be here for you. I'll cry with you," he sniffles from crying too, "I'll listen, I'll give hugs, I'll sit with you in silence. Whatever it takes to help you."

Now I'm going to cry, damn it. I've done great thus far holding it together. Sorta. There's been a few leaks here and there. But he's going to make me bawl like a baby.

He really does love my baby girl. From the moment I held her, I never thought there would be another man besides her dad and me that would love her more than anything. I managed to find another man who will fight for her and love her for all that she is.

God, how did I get so lucky?

"Is there anything else we need to get out?" I ask her.

I can't tell her how every time I close my eyes I see her beaten and dead mother.

I can't tell her every time I hug her I silently scream inside.

"Will you tell me the truth?"

"Of course I will."

Pierre steps back some so she can lift off my chest. He rushes over to get a few tissues. I imagine she's one big snot bubble after that.

She takes them and does her thing and hands them back to Pierre. I see the revulsion in his eyes and think to myself, *better get used to messes and germs, here's the beginning test.*

Resignation flickers over his features and he takes the snotty tissues and tosses them in the bin. He moves back close to us, hovering just enough to remind her he's here.

Poppy looks up at me with her red blotchy face and bloodshot eyes. "When you find the man that killed Mommy, what are you going to do with him?"

Well, fuck. I did not expect this question when I promised honestly.

I'm not sure what to say in this instance.

So, I go with my gut.

"I'm going to kill him."

She looks thoughtful for a minute, quiet and still. Soon she nods and with complete affirmation, she says, "Good. I would too. I promise I won't say anything ever to anyone, but good, that's what I want." She crosses her heart with her child sized fingers and then puts her pinky out to promise with.

Huh. She shocks me. Didn't expect that response either.

Maybe my niece is a little demoness that believes in revenge too.

Chapter 42

Pierre

So much is happening in such a short space of time that it's really hard to keep up with.

Declan has been working all day monitoring the raid preparations (that I'm not supposed to know about.)

Sundays are my days off and I was hoping to spend it with him. I understand he has to work and he holds unconventional hours. I get it.

Instead, I seek out Poppy. I'm not going to say I'm bored, but sitting idle is never good for me. My thoughts are a beast on their own and no one needs me to spiral right now from made up scenarios of paranoia that drop into my head randomly. I wish my spicy brain worked normally.

Sometimes being a doomsdayer sneaks up on me when I least expect it and it's a royal battle to fight the intrusive thoughts away.

My main goal is to have less depressive episodes and take my medicine regularly. Same goal every day. Sometimes I slack on my meds and I need to stop doing that. Now that I have something happy to look forward to everyday, that goal should be attainable. Declan will help me, I know he will. I just have to have time to talk to him about it.

I find Poppy in the library. Of course, the house has a fully stocked library.

When he bought the house a few years ago, the previous owners had died and they left all the books in the library and a lot of the antique furniture. It seems Declan just absorbed it and used it in the décor. I love it.

"Hey, Poptart, whatcha reading?"

I sit on the chair catty-corner to hers. She looks up from her book and holds it up for me to see the cover. *Harry Potter and the Half-Blood Prince.*

"Good choice." I settle back and clasp my hands in front of me, resting them across my stomach. "Have you read all the previous ones?"

"Yep. So far I still love Goblet of Fire. I'd like a Horned Tail to train and ride. Me and Mom used to read them together. Have you read them?"

"I sure have, a few times. I love the movies too."

"Mom said I wasn't allowed to watch the movies until I finished the series." Her face turns sad for a moment at the mention of her mother.

"Lily had a great idea. We can watch them together when you're finished, if you want. You have to read the books to see what all the movies left out. Tell me, how did you like S.P.E.W?"

Her face lights up at my knowledge. That makes a difference to me. I hope she grows up to love reading. The excitement, the adventure, the emotions it brings forth. I hope whatever she reads she enjoys it immensely.

"I loved it! Slavery is bad. I'm team Hermione all the way. I hope I'm as smart as her one day."

"I think you already are. You have a knack to see things at a different angle than most. That's a very good quality to possess. And look at all the random facts you know." She's always spouting something she's read in her books or learned at school. It's one of the highlights of my conversations with her. I think Declan should get her tested for gifted or advanced classes.

"How much longer are you going to read?"

"Another hour or so. I'm in a good spot in the story." She licks her lips in anticipation. I know what it's like to be interrupted in a good part, so I'll leave her be.

"I'll leave you to it." I pat her leg, "Come find me when you're done and we'll play a game or something."

"Ok, Papa." Then her nose is buried right back in the book. Her term of endearment for me makes my heart tingle. Is it too soon for her to call me that? The doubt would imply that I second guess what Declan and I've built and the stability of our love. There's no doubt where our feelings are concerned and like with any relationship, no one can predict the future. Only time will tell.

Walking out of the room I tell myself I can't get disgruntled at her for not wanting to entertain me. It could be worse; she could be plotting world domination. Actually, I'm not so sure she isn't.

I take my ass upstairs and continue where I left off putting my clothes away. It needs done anyways. I have twice as much as Declan but his walk-in closet is ginormous. He barely takes up a quarter of it!

I was shocked but strangely expected that. He's a man of few needs.

A couple of hours later I come up for air. I hadn't realized I'd worked so long. It enters my brain that no one's come to find me, so I assume that means they've been busy too. But the growling in my stomach can't be ignored any longer.

I check my watch and see it's past lunch. Did Poppy eat? Declan?

I head downstairs and go to find Poppy. She's still in the library but she's sound asleep, curled up on the small couch. Grabbing the blanket off the back of the settee, I cover her up.

She's been having nightmares Declan said, and she's having fitful nights. I'm sure her body needs this nap. I'll leave her here for another hour but if she doesn't get up by then she might not sleep tonight.

My new direction is Declan's office. While approaching the partially cracked door, I hear Declan telling someone it's imperative we get the family tree built as soon as possible. Family tree? Whose? What?

I rap my knuckles on the door a few times before pushing it open.

Declan looks up from his monitors that are sitting on his desk and beckons me to enter. He has an entire wall of monitors on the wall beside his desk. He has his eyes on so many things at once. It's fascinating how fast his mind works.

"Tonight would be optimum, tomorrow by noon is pushing it."

Declan pauses as if he's listening to someone talk on the other end of the line.

"That works. Thank you, Kim. Tell Bethany I appreciate all your hard work on a moment's notice. I wouldn't have asked if it wasn't important. It's personal."

He sits quietly nodding his head.

"Yes. She was my sister."

"Thank you." "Yes, you too."

Then he hangs up. He looks so tired, worn out.

I cross the large area rug to his desk and lean against the edge. He scoots closer and wraps his strong arms around my midsection. My hands automatically caress his back in comforting, slow circles.

"Wanna hear something cool?"

"Yes, I do." And I find that I really, really do.

He explains to me all about forensic genealogy and how he's trying to use it to solve Lily's murder.

"I'm shocked by the advancements of DNA. I had no idea that was a thing. You're right, that is cool."

"I have a few friends I went to college with become Investigative Forensic Genealogists with fancy degrees and big brains. They will be able to hunt me down people related to the killer. Once they do that, I contact those people. I'm a few steps closer than before."

I hug him to my body and tell him how wonderful and truly intriguing that all sounds. Sounds like a nightmare to build but I'm intrigued enough to follow this process with him.

Declan moves his face to lay in my crotch, dangerously close to my cock that's already half-mast from touching him.

I can't help it. Every time I'm around him my body reacts.

He slides his hand across on my body and makes it to the button on my pants. He looks up with a grin, then raises his eyebrows in question.

"You may, but we are locking this door. We have a kid now." I get up and shut the door and lock it, the click loud in the silent room. A room that's going to be filled with so many filthy sounds soon.

I slowly turn around. Hunger written across his face. Desire thick in the air.

"Kneel for your king, Declan. You've been a bad boy."

CHAPTER 43
TRAVARES

Tingles ripple down my arms and thighs. My cock twitches in my boxer briefs. It feels like it's been forever since we were together. I know it's roughly been fifteen hours.

Still. I crave him every waking minute.

Slipping off my glasses, I lay them on my desk on the open ledger I was working on as my duty of Treasurer for the club. I'm multitasking today.

Stepping from behind my desk, I lower myself to my knees on the rug. There's a lightness in my chest when I see his look of approval. I bask in the light of his love.

"You've been too busy today. I missed you."

"I missed you too," I breathe out, the anticipation making me salivate.

Pierre undoes the button on his slacks, ripping the zipper down next. When he finally stands in front of me with his gaping pants, he commands, "Take me out, bad boy."

Wasting no time, I dig in and pull him out. Now's when I drool. To behold his majestic cock is the highlight of my day. I know he's going to take care of me.

My hands slide up and down, over the barbells piercing his shaft.

Pierre reaches down to cup my jaw and squeezes. He tilts my face up to his, "Take a deep breath, I'm fucking that throat hard."

Love so strong it can't break radiates off of him. He doesn't see the ugly scar on my face, the hurt and lost man from his sister's death, the determined killer vibrating under this skin; he sees me, who I truly am and loves that part of me.

My heartbeat speeds up. I get lost in his bright blue eyes. The intensity simmering in his eyes makes me forget the rest of the world. It just falls away when he holds me captivated.

He runs his thumb over my bottom lip. "Open, baby."

His words may be nice now but soon he's going to show me who's boss.

Opening my mouth, I shiver when his cock first touches my tongue. Not about to waste time, I want this so bad, I close my mouth around him and swirl my tongue over his metal.

He grinds into my mouth slowly at first, letting me warm up and get the juices flowing. In and out he slides across my lips. I hollow out my cheeks.

I pay special attention to the spot right above the barbell on the underside of his rod. It's his favorite. His knees knock as he tries to keep standing.

"You feel so good. I love fucking your face. Your mouth is so hot. Your tongue is pure magic." He runs his fingers in my hair, gripping me in the back of my head.

"Take your cock out, Declan. Stroke what's mine. Make yourself feel good."

Quickly I undo my belt and then my pants, whipping me out in record time. All without removing my mouth from him. It was getting painful in my pants. I stroke up the length, then back down to the root. There's precum hanging off my slit already.

"Are you ready, my dirty little Prince Charming?"

Wildness courses through my blood, hauling ass through my veins. Burning hotter than a Louisiana moon. Arousal courses through me so hard it steals my breath.

Fuck yes I am. I squeeze his thighs giving the signal that I'm ready.

Using my hair, Pierre plunges into my mouth, hitting the back of my throat and just as quickly he pulls out, sliding down my tongue.

Again, and again. Deeper and deeper down my throat until I gag.

"Oh, Declan," Pierre stands in front of me, head thrown back in pleasure, lips parted, hand fisting my hair and the other caressing my cheek. He looks like a god riding his pleasure high above me. I rub my hands up his torso and back down, relishing in the feel of his hard body.

With a low growl, Pierre shifts his hips and picks up his pace.

"Unlock your jaw, baby," he rasps. I comply. "I'm so close, Dec. I want to fill your throat. Make you choke on my cum. Claim you every way I can. You want to be my bad boy again?"

I can only whimper. God, yes, do I ever.

He's close. I have him to the brink. Then he suddenly pulls out.

"Not like this, I changed my mind," he pants. He flicks his hand towards my desk and says, "Bend over your desk, Declan. Just as you would for work. I have to get inside that sweet ass."

Oh god.

I'm up and over there in a heartbeat, quickly pulling my pants and boxer briefs down, shutting the ledger and tossing it on the floor. I shove my office chair out of the way so I can bend over the desk ass out, my cock jutting into the ornate oak desk's cold surface.

Pierre walks around me, slowly caressing me with his eyes. I feel the heat from his gaze, burning all the way down my body. He bites his lip and it's the sexiest thing I've ever seen. Oh fuck, I'm so in love with him.

"Please, Pierre."

Walking up to me, he answers by a resounding smack to my ass that makes me jump and groan. My breath catches in my chest. I fucking love when he spanks me.

"I missed this ass, Declan. My ass. Mine. Say it." A small love tap with hardly any heat to it.

"Your ass," I whimper.

"Yes, mine," he firmly says, making sure I don't forget it with another smack to the other cheek.

The air whooshes out of my lungs with the sting. "*Oh my god,*" I whimper softly.

"My bad boy loves it, doesn't he? You love when I take control of your body. "

"Yes, god yes." My knees are weak and shaky.

"Chest to the desk," he says as his hand pushes me down until my ass is sticking up in the air. I clench in need. "Good boy."

Pierre opens the drawer to the left, which I know has lube. There's lube stashed all over this house. It's best not to snoop too much. We're going to have to get creative with Poppy around.

The cap snaps open and next thing I know his fingers are circling my entrance. The lube is cold but quickly warms up. I concentrate on my breathing that's running out of control. I might hyperventilate at this rate.

Two fingers slip inside of me, scissoring, loosening me up.

"I'm taking this ass fast and hard and you're going to love it, aren't you?"

"Yes," I pant. Third finger. "*Yesss*." The burn is settling in as he stretches me. I could lose myself in this moment.

He stands and I feel him move into position. He reaches up and pulls one arm behind me, laying my hand on the small of my back. He reaches for the other and pulls it back too, clasping my hands. My cheek is pressed into the calendar on top of my desk. I hope I don't end up with ink all over me. Right now, I could care less.

He slides in, not waiting for me to adjust. I clench my jaw and groan feeling every nerve in my body come alive. I cry out as the discomfort gives way to pleasure and then the moan erupting out of me comes from my gut. Full, loud, guttural.

Pierre doesn't let up on his pace, "Shhh, baby boy, we have a child now. Can't have her thinking I'm hurting you." He snaps his hips hard, going deeper, "Am I hurting you?"

"No..oh god, no it feels so good. Please let me come."

The only thing that slows him down is my phone ringing, right next to my head on the desk.

Pierre says, "We're answering this phone, Declan, but I'm not stopping." He swipes the green button to answer.

Trying to sound like I'm not getting railed within an inch of my life, I take a breath and say "Hello." I hear it, my voice sounds off, shaky.

Danger starts talking, "Do we have anymore earpieces? I can only find about thirty of them? Are they kept somewhere else in this clubhouse?"

My chest keeps getting tighter from holding back my deep breathing caused by my boyfriend's cock shoved so far up my ass it punches my lungs and steals my breath.

I'd like more please.

"Uhh…" A breath puffs out of me. Oh shit. "Umm…I can see where they are in the inventory." As I'm talking my voice warbles and I can't hide it.

"Are you ok?" Danger asks.

I inhale to steady. Does no fucking good.

"Yep." This is when Pierre thinks it's a good idea to punch his hips hard and dig the edge of the desk into my thighs. It makes me grunt.

Right into the phone.

"Oh man, is my brother there? Goddamn it."

Pierre purrs, "Hello, brother dear."

"Fuck, shit. You gotta be shittin' me."

"Paybacks a bitch, bro."

"Call me when you're done." And hangs up.

I blink a few times and definitely don't have time to analyze what just happened because Pierre reaches around and settles his hand around my cock.

"It's time to come, bad boy. I want you to come all over this desk. When you sit here next you'll remember this very moment. Come for me, Declan."

His hand feels so good, too good. "Pierre," I grunt from deep in my throat.

"I'm so close…oh god," I fuck into his hand as he pounds away at my ass. The tingle spreads like wildfire through me. The explosion of pleasure barrels through me and I come in his hand with a yell.

"Fuck yes. Declan, my baby," Pierre stiffens and releases in me while I feel him pulsate.

I'm gasping for air and so is he. He bends and kisses my back through my shirt. "I love you, hacker."

"I love you, my pretty ink king." It comes out breathless, like someone who's just been freshly fucked.

He's already pulling out before I know it. I feel like all the bones in my body are jelly. Standing even makes me dizzy. Pierre's cleaning up my desk with tissues as I stuff myself back in my pants.

Once I'm cleaned up and my clothes are situated, he kisses me and says, "That was just a teaser. I want all your darkest fantasies later. I want the most wicked of cravings unleashed. I want to make your dreams come true, Declan. Office sex crossed off the list." His words rush over my lips before he kisses me again.

"Let's go check on our kid. Last I saw she was asleep in the library." He holds his hand out for me and with a side eye to my laptop, I take his hand and follow him out.

I'm antsy and I can't shake the willies off of me. Earlier Pierre had told me it was such a nice spring day I should go for a ride. Blow off some steam. He said he had a game date with Poppy and I should use this opportunity to ground my spirit.

That's how I find myself soaring down the road, headed outside the city limits.

The distractions of the city fall away as open spaces take over the buildings. The city is too cramped for what I need. Give me the open road and some wind in my hair. Pierre is right, today is a perfect day for it.

I'm almost jealous of all the Devils heading to Houston for the raid riding in this beautiful spring weather. They should all be on their way by now.

At the long-closed storefronts, I look over and see my reflection in the glass as I pass through a small town.

I look at my beautiful brute, cleaned up, shined out, razor sharp with style. His chrome shining with outlaw pride, blinding when the sun hits it just right.

My roaring demon of a bike, Hades, keeper of the gates. The same as me as I guard the gates into Rock's empire. Me and Hades fit together like peas and carrots.

I ride for some time before I allow thoughts of Lily to overcome my mind. I find the pain isn't as intense when I'm pushing the pedal, zooming down the highway. Goddamn, my thoughts are so loud, but the machine is louder. I can't loosen up my grip but I reason with myself and eventually settle into a much safer speed. I don't want Poppy to be left without me. I know Pierre will take care of her, even Birdie would, but still I slow down and quit being reckless.

I'm like a parent now. I can't be doing stupid shit.

Hades growls down the open stretch of road and the vibrations feel good throughout my body. This is where I'm going to find my peace. It's about letting go of the ghost of regret as it fades into the wind. Time is a thief. I wish I had more time.

I'm catching myself more and more staring off into space, being enveloped in memories of Lily. It's becoming obsessive. I can't drag myself away from it. I won't stop until I find her killer. I owe it to her and Poppy. There's this overwhelming drive to never give up until it ends.

I'm not taking this ride to forget her. I'm taking this ride to help me deal with her gone. To come to terms. To accept.

It's throttle therapy. Every biker craves it. Needs it. It's our balance, our relief. Nothing says freedom like screaming down the open road. It's the calm in the eye of the hurricane in our chest.

It's amazing what this bike can heal.

Forgiveness is waiting for me in the rumble of chrome pipes. The truth is heavy.

I must forgive myself for Lily's murder. I've skinned myself alive from the inside out over the guilt. If she hadn't been related to me…If I hadn't joined the Devils…If I'd had more security on her…

I finally make up my mind that I'm not responsible for this. I did not cause it. Vile, evil men caused this. Men that deserve to die. They will die. I promise you.

The wind tickles across my exposed skin. The edge of freedom from worry embraces me as I put more distance between me and home. As the sun shines on me and warms my leathers, I fill my lungs with the fresh air outside the city and just breathe. Just be.

Maybe breaking down's the only way to make me whole, I think to myself as the first tear slips out, caught by the helmet

There's no real direction. Just a ride. To clear my soul. Like I said, it's throttle therapy. Road recovery.

I'll carry the weight of her loss for the rest of my life. I serve her to the highest good by doing right by Poppy and raising her how Lily would have wanted.

One hippy dippy kid coming up.

Everything doesn't feel as wrong now. The knot in my chest is easy to breathe through. Thank fuck for Pierre telling me I am allowed to cry, to feel, and still be a bad ass biker. Sometimes the feelings of sadness overwhelm me and I feel embarrassed. Pierre gives me the space to mourn with no judgement. So has my other brothers in leather.

I don't need all the answers, I'm just tired of pretending like I have it all together. Clearly I do not since I'm hiding my broken heart and ripping up miles today.

But Pierre sees right through me—his annoyingly accurate gift—and he's pushed me to come out here which I grudgingly admit has relieved a lot of pent up emotions.

Oh, how he knew exactly what I needed. This is why he's perfect for me.

CHAPTER 44
TRAVARES

The forensic family tree doesn't come in until late Monday afternoon and now Bam and I are going over it right before supper. I check my watch again. It's after six and Pierre was supposed to be home half an hour ago.

"You good, man?" Bam asks.

"No, I'm not," I say gruffly.

His eyes grow wide, like he expected me to blow off his concern.

"Pierre was supposed to be here some time ago and he hasn't called. You'll have to excuse me." I pick up my cell phone, looking for his contact and calling.

It rings three times before he says, "Hey babe." It sounds like he's in a vehicle. "I'm so sorry! I got to talking to Birdie and neither of us were aware of the time and we were not anywhere near our phones."

My heart slows down now that I know he's safe. I can take a deep breath and the cold fingers of panic can recede. To be used at a later time I'm sure.

"Ok," I quietly say. "Just making sure, babe. After last night…"

"I know. I should have paid more attention. It won't happen again. I promise. Birdie just got her ass ripped too so I'm not alone in this and I totally get it. I didn't mean to worry you."

I bite my thumb nail and try not to move to my cuticle. I've been so nervous today.

Last night was the big raid. It went smoothly. They were able to torch twenty-seven places. Today's been a shitshow of chatter on the hacked phones.

More gibberish.

Then comes in the pics from members. Pictures of their trashed businesses asking them what Panhead was going to do about this. Lots of cries for retaliation. Lots of calls to give up being a Saint, they didn't sign up for this.

There's discord all through the ranks, rippling out into the outer edges. The buzz on the street is all about Houston today. Our ears are to the ground, eyes in the air, head on a swivel.

"Come home to me in one piece, my love."

"Always, baby boy. Love you."

"Love you too."

After I hang up with him my chest doesn't feel as heavy. Rolling my shoulders and loosening my neck, I walk back into my office.

Bam looks up and says, "Everything ok?"

I nod and tell him Pierre lost track of time with Birdie.

"Gotcha. Glad he's ok." He looks over at me as I sit back down at the table. "Hey man, I can't blame ya. I'd be a basket of nerves too."

I cock an eyebrow at him.

"Seriously. I'd be paranoid as fuck. Hell, I'm already paranoid today. Has it been off for you today too?"

"Yeah, man, it has." The day's had a completely weirded out vibe. Like something's coming. And we won't like it.

As they say, the night is young.

After another fifteen minutes, Bam clears his throat and says excitedly, "Hey man, I think I got something finally."

I'm moving so fast I make myself dizzy. I stand over him and watch his screen scroll to a picture of a man.

"Who's that?"

"That is the brother of your rapist. More specifically this is his mugshot from Harris County, also known as Houston, Texas. It's at least ten years old though."

The air leaves my lungs like someone punched me in the ribs. Motherfuck!

This is our tie.

"So, who is Mark Stiltner?"

He shrugs. Just because we have a grainy picture of a face doesn't mean we know the person. If he is a Saint, they go by road names and hardly ever legal names. It could be no one in the Saints knows his real name except the top tier. I find it hard to believe but it's a possibility we can't ignore. Most of them have kept their real identities to themselves.

However, I know every Devils' real name in our organization. It's my job to know.

Whipping out my phone as fast as I can, I dial Shadow. He should be up by now. I'm sure every one of those men have slept the day away after calling off work.

But for men like us, there's no rest for the wicked. The things I plan to do to this bastard is beyond unholy. It, for damn sure, will be cruel and unusual.

"What's up, D?"

"Hey man, do you know a Saint by the name of Mark Stiltner?"

"Uhhh, that sounds familiar. Wait…Is that Bear? From the Saints? The guy that owns a couple of car lots across the state? His stuff is all in a bogus business name and almost untraceable."

Second-in-Command. That son of a bitch.

"Yes, it is. I'm certain of it. That would explain the pic from the text, the one from the alley that night. It was his brother who sent it and…If we find Bear we find his worthless brother."

"Jesus, Dec. Good work. Call Danger, explain and he'll get Slim and T-Bone out in the streets hunting them down. I'm sure there're Saints in town still. I think they're waiting on something." Shadow sounds like he's on edge too. We're all just waiting around for the fallout.

I doubt Panhead is going to take this sitting down. It was a direct hit to his organization. I'm sure he's heard of my revenge being served up. We would do more but people still got lives to live and besides, we have a whole separate military-style division armed and ready to be dispatched where needed.

"Honey, I'm home!" Pierre calls through the house as he comes in through the kitchen.

"I'll call Danger. Thanks man." I hang up and quickly call Danger. I walk over to the window and look out at the dying light of day while it rings.

"Yeah, Dec?"

"I know who killed her."

There's a gasp from the doorway and at the same time there's a sharp intake of breath on the other end of the phone.

I turn to see Pierre standing there with his hand over his mouth. This is the moment we've been waiting for. He slowly enters, holding my gaze, as I tell Danger, "It's Bear's brother. Their VP's brother."

"Motherfucker," he growls. "That's great we know who we are looking for now."

"I don't have his name yet, only the brother's, but Shadow seems to think they're still in town and if we find Bear, we find his brother." I put it on speakerphone.

"That's very possible. I'll send a few of the old fuckers out but you know it's close to their bedtimes. Although, they do have their underlings. We can get this city to shaking in a matter of an hour and sus him out. Send me the mugshot. I'm on it Dec, hang tight, brother."

My heart is pounding out of my chest and I feel lightheaded. I'm so close to getting this fucker.

"Thanks, Danger." I hang up and Pierre envelops me in his arms.

"Oh, Declan, I'm so happy for you. So much closer, baby."

I nod my head and let it hang for a moment. Pierre grips the back of my neck and brings my mouth to his as he lights up my soul with his lips, his touch, his essence.

A throat clears. Bam.

I pull away from Pierre with a half grin. "I'm going to get to kill someone soon," I say across his lips. A truly wicked smile spreads across my face.

Vengeance will be mine soon.

Chapter 45

Pierre

By the time we drop off Poppy at Birdie's tower in the sky—at Declan's insistence—the city is alive and all the Devils have come out to play. Hell has burst open. They're on a scavenger hunt of life and death.

One mission: Find Bear and his brother.

Every available associate is on the street scouring every dark corner for Bear. His picture is being passed around. Every bar in the greater New Orleans and Lake Charles area is shown the picture. Whispers with back-alley bribes are raking in the information.

The vibe has shifted. This is no longer scare them. This is a Devil seeking justice and an act of all-out war in the midst of a battle.

The Lone Star Saints Vice President will die tonight.

What a message to send!

Every one of these men know exactly what happened with Lily. They're enraged! They've sworn to honor their patch and brotherhood and go out to the haunts and start looking. Rock made it club business. For Dec.

It's hunting season and all Saints are fair game. Shit's going down tonight. It's a test of my willpower to wait. Watching him pace like a caged animal at home isn't helping.

A few Saints have been taken to the warehouse around the corner from the clubhouse for questioning. The guys all call it 'The Dungeon.'

Questions about my morals keep popping up. Seeing as how I'm still going about this with him by his side, I seem to be somewhat more than ok with this. Any other time I don't think I can condone this type of violence.

Maybe I just needed a really good reason to tip over to the dark side. It appears Lily's murder was the catalyst.

Plus, Birdie baked cookies and sent them with us as snacks, saying *'Killing takes a lot out of you, fuel up.'* So yeah, the dark side really does have cookies.

"If you don't want to be with me for this you don't have to."

"No, I promised you we'd see this thing though, together. I knew from the beginning what the plan was. I'm going in with eyes wide open."

He grabs my hand and squeezes. "Thank you." With the other hand he maneuvers us through the Commercial Business District to the dungeon.

We reach a fenced off warehouse that has two armed officers from Danger's security team at the front gate. Men stand around the premises all holding big guns with scowls on their faces. They look like intimidating assholes. Not someone to mess with.

When we walk up to the main entrance, a metal non-descript door, a member of the security team reaches out to open the door for us. Declan nods to him as the man tips his chin back and says, "Sir."

My eyebrows raise. Then I remember I'm dating one of the Top Five of the Southern Devils Society, the notorious and wildly popular and publicly followed national biker gang.

Club. It's a club, Pierre. So Dec says.

More like mafia.

Semantics.

I'm here to help support Declan. It's not my place to judge but I'd be lying if I said I wasn't scared shitless for what I'm about to witness. I'm not some manly man who is used to a mafia-like lifestyle or aggression, loud noises, or brutality. Some elements of this are shocking, I admit. I'm damned sure it's going to get worse. So much more.

I'm trying to steel my stomach. I guarantee there's going to be screaming and blood by the end of this.

In a way, I have to be ok with this if I want to be with Declan. This is a huge part of his life. He basically works for a real living breathing mafia king. I'm just along for the ride. I'm the moral support with questionable morals. The irony is not lost on me.

Rock will allow Declan to do whatever he wants to these guys and smile the entire time in approval. I've known Rock for most of my adult life and respect him beyond measure but I never forget in the back of my mind, this man can make me disappear in a heartbeat if he so chooses.

We make our way through the maze in the warehouse to a darkened, more closed off area. We walk through a set of double doors and to the sides of us are doors down a long hallway. We pass by them and I can't help but wonder how many prisoners have been held here and no one outside of this organization knows anyone is kept in here. They could drive by this place and no one is ever the wiser.

We reach a room on the right with a metal door that swings open to reveal Slim Jim, Rock, Danger, Shadow, and Gunney. There's more than one of them surprised to see me here but they cover it quickly and roll with it.

I see I'm overdressed in my black dress shirt, slacks and a pair of Prada dress shoes. These guys are dressed like they're going to get bloody. Shit. I never thought about blood splattering on me. Next time I'll remember to wear cheaper shoes for the torture session. My bad.

I hover on the wall a few feet away from Shadow, who is standing by Gunney. Declan walks around to face the guy whose back is to the door. The man's been beaten and his face is bloody.

My eyes jerk around the room, wondering which of my friends whipped this guy's ass before we got here.

The man looks up at Declan and his shoulders stiffen. I see he recognizes Dec.

"You know who I am."

"Yeah. The keyboard warrior, the ghost, the pussy who hides behind a computer." He spits at Declan and the bloody mass hits his leather vest.

The only indication of what's about to happen next is a flicker of hardness that takes over Declan's face right before he punches the guy. The guy's body jerks and he groans, echoing off the concrete walls.

"Where is Bear?"

The guy laughs. What kind of psychopath acts like this? These guys are hella better than me at taking pain. When the Saints kidnapped me and beat the hell out of me, I thought I was going to die it hurt so much. I am not meant to be a fighter.

"Come on, Lucas, we know you're friends with Bear. We know you're here with him. Tell me where him and his brother are and I won't kill you."

He scoffs, "You're not going to kill me."

Declan leans down and says, "Not yet, my precious, but I never promised I wouldn't love torturing a Saint. That's the thing about us quiet computer boys, we love a good pain session."

Declan walks over to Shadow, gesturing to his bowie knife on his hip and says, "May I?"

Shadow smirks and says, "Be my guest."

Dec takes it back to the guy and faster than a blink of an eye he spins the long bowie knife in his hand and slams it down into the guy's thigh, sinking it into the wooden chair beneath him, effectively securing him there.

Of course, the guy is screaming his head off and it's loud as fuck in this room.

Cheap shoes- check

Ear plugs- check

Anti-nausea meds- check

I'm racking up quite a list of items I'm going to need to be able to watch more torture happen.

That little move by Declan has my stomach in my throat. I am not cut out for this life. I'm fully aware of that now. There is no romance to this lifestyle, no calm, or rest, or sanity. There's no way I could live constantly alert and looking over my shoulder. I have to hand it to these guys; they're pretty bad ass.

When the wounded man's cries slow down to whimpers, Declan says, "Just making sure you aren't going anywhere. So, you were saying where Bear is…"

"Fuck…you," he hisses, chest heaving.

Wrong answer, man.

What an idiot.

"I'm going to give that knife some time to throb but I'll be back. I'm looking forward to working with you." With that he pulls out his pocketknife and slams it down on the man's shoulder.

More screaming.

"I'll be back for this in a bit." Then pats him a good three times right beside the blade making the guy groan and clench his teeth.

Then Declan walks around the chair and holds his hand out to me. I take it, I don't know what else to do. He's my lifeline here.

We make our way out of the room and back down the hallway to the double doors, where we turn right and walk into what looks like a conference room. This is all so strange and frighteningly fucked up to me. Is this when we regroup and plot?

"Gentlemen, brothers, thank you."

Rock walks up to Declan and claps him on the bicep as he shakes his hand, "Anytime, son. Whatever you need. We're right here with you."

Declan's mouth stretches into a thin line but he nods with his hard eyes softening for Rock. When Rock leans in to speak to just Declan in a low, quiet hum, Declan hangs his head and nods. Rock pats him on the arm a few times and steps away. I know Declan is trying to keep his shit together.

Declan comes over and grips my hand again. Maybe I'm his lifeline, tethering him to reality, reminding him of humanity. Our joined hands signify his need for me to be here with him. I'm where I'm supposed to be. I can't walk away now. *Man up, Pierre.*

Danger's phone rings in the quiet room. He answers and he has a series of grunts until he abruptly says *thanks* and hangs up.

He looks right at Declan. "Bear and his brother are on the way here."

CHAPTER 46
TRAVARES

Those words zing through me and it feels like my chest is going to burst open with excitement.

"Finally," I breathe out.

The adrenaline courses through me, preparing me for what I need to do.

Danger steps forward, puts his hands on my upper arms, gripping them, "At any time you need one of us, holler. I mean it."

Shadow comes up next and hugs me, clapping me on the back. "Right here, man." He pulls back and drills his gaze into mine, "For Lily." He pulls me forward and touches our foreheads. "Right beside you, brother."

He's making me choke up and it's getting harder to keep a lid on this overwhelming rage and tears.

Gunney comes over and wraps me in one of those handshake hugs and tells me, "At any time, it's ok to cry. It's ok to feel. Let it out. Walk out of the room if it gets too much. We ain't letting them leave until you're done with them and we cart their carcasses out." Gunney ends with a pat to my cheek.

You can clearly see how much my brothers love me. This is beautiful to watch them rally around my revenge and grief. Even if it is for dark and sinister reasons, their support means the world to me.

"Y'all motherfuckers are gonna make me cry and I can't be snottin' up a storm while this youngin' breaks bones, damn it." Leave it to Slim to break the tension of the moment, a small laugh escapes me.

The other guys get a soft laugh out of it too and Shadow looks at him and says, "We'll get you some tissues, old man."

Danger's phone rings again.

He stands with his hands on his hips, looking at the floor. "Bring them to the back bay. Yeah, the one with the drain….Roger that," he says into his earpiece then disconnects.

His eyes swing over to Pierre. "Hey P, you up for this?"

I watch Pierre lick his lips nervously. I gave him an out before. He's decided he's my ride or die through this whole thing. "Yeah, I'm good," he hesitantly says.

I asked him not to love me differently after he sees the dark side of me. The side of me that spills blood and tortures people. He said I will be a hero in his eyes. There'll be one less piece of shit roaming the Earth looking for more victims.

"How are we working this?" Danger claps his hands together and rubs them around each other like an evil genius. If I didn't know better, I'd say he was excited too.

I shrug. "I thought I'd start with a way to shut him up and work my way to fingernails and then…"

"No, no, Dec," Danger laughs. "Are you wanting to do this alone? Who do you want in the room? Do you want help or we just stand and watch?"

Oh.

My brain is already so far ahead.

"You guys can stay." I look over at Pierre. "This is your out. You don't have to go in. Last chance."

I look deep into his eyes, to his heart and beyond to his soul, so I know he's sincere when he says, "No, I'm right here, all the way. Even if I puke and maybe pass out, do not remove me from your side. To the bitter end, for Lily. And for you and Poppy too."

"Goddamn, I love you."

I drop his hand and grab his face, pulling him to me to kiss the holy hell out of him. I need this kiss so much right now. I need to feel alive with him before the cold meanness takes over, before the killing machine inside me takes over.

My tongue lashes out with his and after a few heartbeats and one well-placed moan, we hear a throat clear and a few giggles.

I come back to Earth, blinking back into my body and draw back, looking at Pierre. He smiles and the world melts away.

For just a second.

He kisses my lips one last time and whispers, "I love you too."

I reluctantly pull my hands away and have no idea what to do with them. I'm jumpy again. He solves that by holding my hands in his.

Pierre jiggles my hands and squeezes. His icy blue eyes look at me through his devilish grin. "Now tell me what you're raping him with first."

Chapter 47

Pierre

"You can have one chance to apologize before I kill you."

"Fuck you. She screamed for you at the end, begging for you," Zach, Bear's brother spits out with such hatred and venom.

"Ok then," Declan nods while looking at the floor, humming *uh-huh uh-huh*, rubbing his fingers over his prickly chin. Impeccable control. I would have killed him with that comment alone.

"Open, bitch." Declan, shockingly quick, sinks a knife into Zach's cheek from the side, causing him to scream, opening wide and just as soon as he opens his mouth, Declan slams a ball gag with barbs in his mouth.

Holy fuck.

He secures it around Zach's head and leans down and tells him, "Now you can't clench your teeth through the pain."

The ball gag does not deter Zach from trying to talk. It sounds like he has a fat cock in his mouth.

That is warped shit. This isn't my sweet, loving boyfriend right now. This is a stranger to me, wrapped inside the man I love with all my might. A dark foreboding angel hellbent on ripping apart his enemy.

Declan's demons are emerging from their depths and it's powerful to watch. Hot as fuck too.

Bear looks traumatized sitting in the chair catty-corner to his brother's demise, tied up and gagged for good measure. I pick up on the one glaring look in his eyes: it's absolute shock. You can tell this level of violence is below his pay grade. He's never done this.

Mr. Billy Badass isn't as bad ass as he thought he was.

He's too chickenshit to get his hands dirty. How the fuck he made VP I'll never know. My brother is the strongest man I know and he clawed his way to the top, proving every step of the way he was worthy. This fat fucker paid his way. No honor.

This is why he had his brother do it. He didn't have the guts. He's a pussy.

"Did you know the human body has thirty-two adult teeth? My niece told me that the other day." Declan rests his hand on Zach's shoulder and leans down smiling to speak to him,

"That means we have that many times to knock out each one at a painstakingly slow pace. It makes me giddy to think about all the fun we're going to have in the name of cold, hard revenge. My rage dies with you today."

Zach fights against his bindings and muffled cries can be heard in his throat as he drools all over himself with the ball gag lodged firmly in place.

"That's three."

More yelling from Zach. His brother tries hollering through his gag, his throat straining and face turning red. Oh god, the veins in his face popping out look nasty.

Bloody drool and snot drip down Zach's chin where Declan broke off three teeth already. It's quite disgusting. It was so hard to watch. I had to keep reminding myself of what he did to Lily.

He deserves this. Eye for an eye.

Declan shoves a hand into Zach's shoulder, laughing like a loon. He's moved onto ripping off Zach's fingernails with a pair of pliers. "You know what the fun part is here?" Declan gestures up and down Zach's body. "We have seventeen more times to do this between your hands and feet. Buckle up buttercup." And then pats Zach's chest like they are best buds.

Something I've learned today: my boyfriend is a maniac.

All the other men in the room watch on with focused intensity. I realize they're monitoring the room. Each one of them in a different way. Danger's focused on Dec's state of mind. The other four are making sure this happens how Declan wants it.

No one's going to interrupt this for him. I'm sure there's guards heavily positioned down that hall and through the entire building, fanned out, keeping watch while Lily gets her retribution from the grave through Declan.

I take a deep shaky breath. *Keep going.* Jesus fuck, I don't know if I can. My boyfriend is scary as fuck. Right now, in this element, no one would believe he's a fun loving, quiet nerdy guy who loves reading and playing video games.

I still want to bend him over any surface after seeing this display. A huge part of me inside is highly attracted to his aggression and madness in the situation.

I think Zach passed out again.

"Y'all want to help me get him on the table. Face down, spit roasted. Legs open, please."

I watch as these men work together like a well-oiled machine. Very efficient, very quick. They know how to maneuver an unconscious body around.

Like they've done this a hundred times before. They probably have.

Watching my brother lift an unconscious man onto a table for torture makes me see him in a brand-new light. I knew he was ruthless, but this? I have a new respect for all the times he's glossed over the dangerous situations he finds himself in. Shadow too. All the times we'd spend at the camp house back home, just the three of us, drinking, tattooing and talking bullshit.

They never once let on their lives were this bloody and dark. I guess without the details they just expected me to make up something. Maybe they figured with all the gory movies out there I'd know what to expect.

Those are movies!!

It's not real life.

If anything, today I learned THIS IS REAL LIFE!

People actually do this shit.

My boyfriend is one of those kinds of people.

He assured me this may be the only time he ever gets his hands this bloody.

Dec's usually the snarky asshole on the mic stationed far enough away from the action, better suited to watch over everything. He is the demon ghost walking through the battle by others' body cams and communications.

I watched him in his element the night of the raid. I sat on the couch in his office, very quietly out of the way so as not to be disturbing and watched him with rapt fascination as he guided dozens of men through a city he didn't know.

At the same time, he was monitoring the Houston police scanner, calling out where Devils would cross paths with a cop.

Impressive shit.

He slaps Zach back to reality.

"Ready for number four?"

Zach starts screaming and shaking his head back and forth. His brother seems to have given up trying to be heard through his cloth gag. He hangs his head, heaving and crying.

Bear is a sorry excuse for a human.

Bear's brother, who is much worse, is laid out with his arms tied over his head and his legs spread and bound where he can't close them. His pants ripped off of him in the moving process.

While they were moving him he came back around and Danger slapped him in the face and told him *welcome back*. Zack just started whimpering and passed out again.

Declan walks around the surgical table, trailing a bloody finger on Zach's body. *Ohmigod*, I mutter to myself where only I can hear. He's humming *'Pink Pony Club'* as he walks and plots torture. Poppy keeps playing this song nonstop and for the life of us, we can't get it out of our heads.

He comes to stop at the top of the table with the pliers he's been using. He leans down as says, "I'm going to ass rape you now, Zachy Boy," Zach starts screaming, "so every fingernail I rip off, every time your ass clenches….Mmmm. Can you imagine anything more painful than that?"

Declan stands to his full height, like he's stretching out some tension in his body. He rolls his neck and takes one step, "Oh, did I mention it has metal spikes? It will feel like spirit finger razors up your ass." Declan laughs like that's the best joke ever.

I'm not sure if I should go try to ground him, help him find his center, or let him go stark raving mad, descending into the darkest of places. Pushed to the brink of madness.

But fuck if he isn't glorious in his madness. Splendid. Radiating. He has the finesse of a doctor, the patience of a saint, and just enough crazy to pull it off well.

Did I mention after the fingernails come off, he's dipping Zach's fingertips in pickle juice they found in the fridge in the breakroom?

Diabolical.

I don't know if it's the endorphins or fear but I have to work really hard at not being hard during this. Fucking crazy, I know! Watching Declan unravel like this is calling to something deep and depraved inside of me. Something primal seeking the brutality and justice right alongside him. It only makes me want him more.

"See, I've had some time on my hands. I built you your very own sex toy, fitting of a filthy rapist."

My eyebrows shoot up. Declan's at the counter and I can hear the jingle of something metal being laid out. He made something? When does he have time for this?

"I've been waiting for you. I'm so thrilled you're finally here to test it out with me."

How Declan sounds so calm and cool with his customer service voice is a wild thought I can't imagine doing. The hint of his condescending intent is heavy.

He loves the psychological warfare as much as the pain.

Declan turns around and holds up an apparatus in front of Zach's face, table level. Zach immediately starts sobbing. It's a metal butt plug. One on the larger side. That's not something you start off with on an ass virgin. This is going to hurt.

"Now, now, we haven't even gotten to the best part. This part will go in your ass…" He points to the rounded tip that flares; it's the kind of item that can cause damage if an ass is not properly prepared.

I have a feeling Declan's not getting him ready for it. I'm ok with that.

"It has this special nifty button at the end." Declan pushes it and dozens of razor blades pop out and then Zach's screaming again. So's his brother. Declan quickly puts away the razors. "Gotta save the rest of the surprise."

Holy shit. That is vile. Declan is creative, I'll give him that.

"I hope you don't mind, Zachy boy, I'm going to use Carolina Reaper hot sauce for lube."

Savage.

All the guys chuckle at that.

At this point Zach and his brother shouldn't have a voice left after so much screaming. I give them props though, I'm utterly terrified for the level of pain Declan's about to introduce to him.

Zack's screams turn into full blown sobs, like body wrenching and hyperventilating. My eyes drift over to Bear, yep, he's crying too.

He's had a front row seat for all of his brother's comeuppance.

Declan smacks the guy's ass with his gloved hand, narrowly missing the shit that's slipped out from the pain, and says, "I hope you like prickly boys. I've learned they give the best head but it's not going to be as enjoyable for you." He nonchalantly parts the man's ass cheeks with his hot sauce covered butt plug of annihilation and shoves it in with all his might.

The roar coming out of Zach's chest is like nothing I've ever heard before. It's scary, makes your skin crawl. It is brutal, raw, and full of pain.

Good.

You deserve nothing less you piece of shit.

However, yes, I am going to stand here and gag behind my hand.

If Poppy can't stand here to watch the exquisite and violent rape of her mother's rapist and murderer, I will gladly stand witness for her as her representative. I can't guarantee the contents of my stomach will stay down though.

Zero percent. That's how much I care about this man's pain. Human or not, compassion and morals, I guess I don't value human life as much as I thought I did.

He gets everything my boyfriend gives.

Zach's body is heaving, trying to breathe around the ball gag and guttural sobs. Snot and drool drip everywhere.

"I haven't even hit the button yet, silly." Declan slaps Zach upside the head, "Oi! You still with us?"

Zach can't stop his body from shaking violently. He is definitely not dying quietly.

Dec walks back by the man's ass. I can't take my eyes off Declan. He moves with a purpose.

Vengeance.

In its most purest form. Malicious. Villainous. Vicious.

"Can we flip him over guys? Dick up. He can keep his legs spread."

His brothers move in and do as asked almost reverently. Watching Declan is unnerving but it's an eloquent tragedy unfolding. This feels like a small intermission to the show.

For the first time in a while, his eyes rise to meet mine. I see such clarity in his green fathomless depth. He's in complete control of his emotions and he's high on the bloodlust. He blows me a kiss.

I stop gnawing on my nails long enough to return one. I'm straight chomping these fuckers down, wondering what part's coming next.

God, I feel like I've ran two marathons back-to-back. The adrenaline ebbs and flows. I think I'm a little high with the bloodlust too.

First, I was scared I'd be a pussy and pass out but this has been excruciatingly grotesque and I can't look away. I can't find any sympathy for him. There will never be sympathy in my heart for any man like him.

I hope Declan drags this out. We have all night. Zach deserves no less.

Declan returns beside the table and rips Zach's shirt open. Holding up a scalpel over Zach's chest, Declan feigns confusion. "What was it you carved on my sister's chest? LSS?" Dec shakes his head. Zach's eyes track him like a terrified rabbit, his chest rapidly rising and falling from his trembling pants of air.

"I made sure I got some isopropyl alcohol to clean it with." He splashes it across Zach's chest. Then starts carving on Zach's body.

And down goes Zach.

"Do you want him awake, Dec?" Gunney asks.

"Nahh. I got a surprise for him. Let him rest up." Declan looks across the room at Bear sitting in his soiled chair. "Don't think I've forgotten about you, older bro. I'm just working my way over there."

Declan waves his hand around, "You know you brought all this on him. Your own baby brother. Damn, I bet the guilt is eating you alive right now. It's all your fault he's at my mercy, in so much pain. And please don't think I'm showing mercy. I've forced it out of my vocabulary tonight."

He goes right back to carving Zach's chest. He's very focused. Blood is running everywhere. The metallic smell grows stronger.

Shadow and Danger both stand with their arms crossed over their chests, intensely watching Declan, with what amounts to pride shining in their eyes. Rock leans against the wall, one leg braced and his phone in his hands texting someone with a grim look on his face. He keeps glancing up at the freak show in front of us. I'm sure he had to move around a lot of things in order to be here right now to stand in solidarity with Declan. He finishes, slips it into his pocket and resumes watching over Declan.

Gunney watches on the other side of Shadow and I noticed when the butt plug shoved home, Gunney flinched into Shadow's back and hid. No shame man. I would have done it too if I could have taken my eyes off of Declan.

Declan tosses the alcohol across Zach chest and Zach wakes up screaming. Or what's left of his throat and voice.

"Her name was Lily and you tried to erase her. I want you to be assured, no one, absolutely no one is going to find your body. But you'll feel this burn for eternity and know it's in her name that I kill you tonight and send your soul straight to hell to have all of this done to your body every day, all day, day after day for, well, forever. I made a deal with the devil."

More alcohol tossed on the incisions. Christ. That has to burn something fierce.

"See, I have a child now thanks to you. I need to still fit in your brother over there timewise." Declan wiggles his fingers at Bear. Zach's terrified eyes squeeze shut in anguish. "I'd like to get home at a decent time and play Kid's Jeopardy with my niece. Spoiler, she'll win. And then I'm going to take my husband over there home and make sweet love to him knowing my sister's soul can now rest knowing that your soul was forfeited for her eternal glory across the Universe and beyond."

"Her name was Lily." His voice rings loud and clear in the momentary silence in the room. Declan tips the bottle again, only this time he shoves a gloved finger in a slit. My stomach turns.

Declan reaches between Zach's legs and put his hand on the butt plug and Zach starts whimpering.

The button is pushed with no preamble. He just does it.

Zach's eyes go wide a split second before his voice goes out completely from screaming.

"I forgot to mention there's hydrochloric acid seeping off all those razors. Slowly. I don't actually know how long it will take to melt your insides and die. I bet it hurts though." Declan grabs Zach's chin and pulls his face to look at him, "Just think, one day, you'll see me again. I'll crawl through Hell on my knees to kill you again and again."

Zach's sobbing stops and so does his whimpers. His glassy eyes stare at the ceiling. His chest stops rising.

Declan staggers and drops the scalpel to the concrete floor with a clatter.

"Dec…" I reach forward, into thin air, taking a step begging with my eyes. I don't even know what I'm begging for. I just want to hold him to my chest and make all this go away for him. Make it all better. My eyes fill up and my nose burns. Oh, god.

But this is how he feels better.

Be steadfast, Pierre.

"Pierre," He quietly says before he has eyes on me. "One down."

"One down, baby."

He turns to Bear, strangely calm and says, "I wish I knew necromancy to bring your brother back so I can fuck his ass again and again. But you'll do instead. You don't get mercy either."

Bear still has some screams left in him after all.

CHAPTER 48
TRAVARES

I roll over and my head throbs. Fuck, what's happening? Did I get drunk and not remember? Sure feels like a hangover or I got hit over the head with something. I don't remember that happening.

Flashes of torture. Memories of my soul being set free. Pierre driving us home. Bourbon. Shower.

I did drink.

Fuck me.

I know better. I can't handle liquor.

Pierre's side of the bed is long cold. The light streaming in the windows is at a different angle than I'm used to. I roll over and check my phone. It's full of texts but I do see it's after ten.

Double fuck me.

I calm myself down. Pierre is here. He doesn't go in today until noon. I rub my hand down my face and sit up. We have at least one more day of calm before the storm.

Pierre goes to court for his divorce tomorrow. It's supposed to be the final hearing. Money can make your divorce fly through the court system.

His lawyer said the magistrate ruled sixty-five percent of Pierre's worth is tied with Birdie and the business and therefore Seven's not allowed to gain from it. Sixty-five percent wiped off the table instantly. I can only imagine the fit Seven threw. He's not getting the payout he's expecting.

He tried to call Pierre numerous times from numbers that weren't blocked.

Then you have Pierre, who through knowledge and advice given by Rock and Danger, has hidden accounts, hidden wealth that he doesn't declare and Seven doesn't know about. I had no idea my quiet, reserved gothic man-candy had it in him to defraud the United States government. Yet here we are.

I've done the exact same things with my money too. The same people advised me of it. I listened.

Pierre said he calls it intuition when he took their advice and did it back then. Even if Pierre had no money, like I would care, it's not a dealbreaker, I could still take care of him very comfortably for the rest of his life and then some. I would love nothing more.

He would make a fine house-husband.

I know he would never do it. He loves creating art and tattooing too much to quit in his prime. I would never want to stand in the way of his art.

My head swims a little when I sit up. Oh, this isn't bad. I've had worse. This is just a twinge.

I flick my eyes to the door to make sure it's closed before I swing dick over to the closet and pick out a band shirt and a pair of sweatpants. I know these white ones are Pierre's favorites.

I have to take into account closed doors and muffled moans since there's a child living here now. I'm sure in the coming years she'll be more traumatized by physical displays of affection around here but it will give her a thick skin living with two handsy men in love. It's no different than a straight couple showing their love in front of people and kids.

Striding into the kitchen, I see my man sitting at the dining room table, looking divine, with his tablet in his hands, drawing something. He looks so breathtaking in the morning light by the window.

My savior. My rock. My world.

I remember him holding me last night in bed. I laid across his stomach, my arms clinging to him as sobs wracked my body. Pierre just held me close and let me cry it out after we got Poppy to bed.

No judgement.

No questions.

Just blissful silence. Comfortable quiet. My mind coming down from the all-encompassing high.

He's dead. Both of them are.

It's done.

After I slit Bear's throat while he gurgled and screamed God, Danger sent me home. Said he would take care of everything.

After a good scrub down in the dungeon's industrial bathroom, and my clothes handed off to Shadow, I let Pierre lead me out into the night in clothes Danger brought me. It was only a little after ten when we picked up a very excited Poppy. She thought we were on a date.

She went to bed yapping about some nail polish Birdie promised her. God, she's growing up so fast already. We aren't going to be able to keep up with her.

"Hey, baby," I drop a kiss on his lips when he looks up at me. "Thanks for letting me sleep. Poppy get off to school ok?"

"Good morning, Prince Charming. Yes, our girl ate a good breakfast, told me that the United States and Canada shared the longest border in the world, and then brushed her teeth and got dressed. Mission accomplished."

My heart settles down. I knew Pierre would handle it. I'm grateful I have someone to share this with, someone who I can count on.

Someone who loves my niece as much as me.

"What do you have planned today?" Pierre inquires as he shades a spot on his drawing, with his tongue tucked in his cheek, rolling it around.

It's cute.

My coffee finishes and I bring it over to the table and sit down with him, trying not to gulp the blessed bean concoction. I like morning coffee with Pierre. I feel very domesticated. Very much like a family man.

Very different from the man I was last night.

"Listen, Pierre, I want to thank you for last night. For all of it. For everything." I clear my throat to ease the lump in it, "It means a lot to me."

Pierre watches me through his clear starlight blue gaze, "You're welcome, Declan. I love you."

"I'm pretty sure that was over and above love."

"Not for me. There's nothing I wouldn't do for you."

"I just don't want you to think I'm a mistake now. Like it's too much and you bolt because you see me as some kind of monster."

"I promise you, we aren't a mistake and I don't think you're a monster. Our life, it's not a mistake. The biggest mistake I have made in my life is letting shitty people stay in my life far longer than they deserved, and you my love, deserve the most important place in my life, for however long you'll have me. I'm not going anywhere, Declan, and I plan to keep you around a very long time, like forever."

"You sure you want me that long?" I tease him, feeling more alive with each gulp of coffee.

"Ten times as long as infinity."

He leans over across the table and my lips meet his halfway. So sweet. So loving. I get swept away when he kisses me and I desperately needed a Pierre kiss this morning.

"Do you want to sneak upstairs and crawl back into bed with me?" he asks, feather soft across my lips making me shiver.

"Absolutely, I do." I nibble at his lips and get turned on even more.

It's a scramble for us to get out of our chairs fast enough to jog to the bedroom, laughing all the way. Pierre is the last into the room and he shuts and locks the door.

He turns to me, breathing heavy, enjoying the chase. He rips his shirt off over his head and stalks to me across the room. I got my shirt off and my sweats are low on my hips, hanging off my thumbs. I can't pick up my jaw watching Pierre stride across the room towards me.

He could fucking wreck me again and I'd still love him with all my heart.

Pierre wraps his hand around my neck and purrs, "Slow or hard today, Declan? Pick how you want fucked, baby." He inhales deeply up the side of my neck, dragging his hot tongue across the delicate skin.

Lordy lord, my legs are already shaking.

I whimper with an excited shiver, "Sweet then hard." My breath catches in my throat. I'm already hard. The minute I saw him this morning, the second I woke up. I stay hard for this man.

He bends over in front of me, sliding my sweats down. While he's eye level with my cock, he swirls his tongue around the head.

"*Ohhh fuck,*" the air punching out of my lungs.

Pierre's hand comes up to cup my balls as I step out of my pants. He takes me deeper into his hot mouth and I can't stop the moan that comes out of me.

My hand grasps the back of his head, "Pierre.." My hips are steady swaying with his movements.

He pops off and stands to look at me, a beautiful sexy grin on his lips. "I'm going to fuck you on the balcony."

"In broad daylight?" I ask incredulously.

"Yes. I want you bent over the railing."

Holy fuck. "Pierre, we can't…the neighbors, babe.."

"The balcony is secluded by two-hundred-year-old oak trees. No one's seeing us and if they did, either enjoy the show or go the fuck on." He opens the French doors and gestures me out of the doors onto the covered balcony.

Oh shit. I've never had sex on this porch. Hell, I've never had sex outside until him.

I take a deep breath and tip my chin. Ok. This will be fine.

"Let's do it." I boldly take a step forward.

"You obey so well," I lovingly tell him, swatting him on the ass as he walks out the door.

We really are secluded back here. They are going to have to really be looking in order to see us through the ancient canopies. And they live far enough apart…we can be discreet and quiet, but enjoy the public sex.

Which I know is one thing on Declan's sexual bucket list we've talked about before.

I memorized them all the night he told me and mentally started planning for each one.

If this balcony won't do, I'll take him to the apartment in the French Quarter and fuck him out there like Lestat did Louis. In front of everyone. The people around here expect that kind of debauchery from the Quarter. I'll even bite his neck like the vampires he's so fascinated with if that will help turn him on more.

Coming up behind, my hands tingle to rub his sweet cheeks. He's so beautiful leaning on the railing. Waiting patiently for me. He has an air of nervousness about him. Soon he'll forget all about it.

Especially when I make him come out here.

I open the cap on the lube I swiped off the side table on the way out here. Once I have my cock and fingers lubed up, I rub them over Declan's sensitive back hole. He clenches in anticipation.

I slide in a finger easily. He's so ready. His body trembles with the thrill.

"I know this is what you want. The thrill of being caught. The shot of adrenaline straight to your dick thinking about it. You love it, Declan. You're panting with desire," I state.

"Oh fuck me," he moans at the second finger entering him and he pushes back to gobble up more. So greedy.

"Oh, I plan to, baby boy." Third finger. I watch him arch his back at the burn. He gasps when I yank them out and replace them with my cock at his entrance. "That was the sweet part. This is the part where you beg me to make you come."

I enter him in one swift thrust. He cries out and it echoes in between houses. Huh, maybe they can hear. Still don't care.

"Don't you dare shut your mouth, let me hear how good I make you feel." I pull back and slowly thrust in and out, making him moan.

I pull him up, my bare chest up against his shirtless back. Skin to skin. My arm comes around his front, across his chest holding him to me. I reach around and wrap my hand around his weeping cock.

"Oh my god, Pierre," Declan cries.

My hips continue to grind into him from behind. His legs are shaking. His head finally falls back in pleasure. So long as he stops looking around nervously.

"Pierre, fuck.."

"Does it feel good out here, Declan?"

"Yeah…" he whispers.

"Where anyone can see you. In all your naked glory. You're beautiful, baby. I love showing you off."

His moans turn to heavy pants the closer he gets. If I pick up my pace, rubbing against his g-spot deep inside his sweet honey pot…I shudder. Oh god, I'm fucking addicted.

He gets louder at the increase. I'm right there on the edge and I know he is too. I bite his ear and command, "Come for your king, Prince Charming."

I slap my hand over his open mouth right before the yell breaks free. He comes with a mighty war cry, his body jerking, chest heaving. I hang on for dear life.

He clamps down so hard, I have no choice, my climax is ripped from me. I can't see straight. "Declan, oh god," I choke out as I come harder than I ever have in my life. It's almost painful.

I never.

Declan falls forward, catching himself on the railing and bracing himself there. I take big gulps of air and try to steady my heartbeat.

I move a bit inside his ass and he groans. "There's no way..I can't..I died.." He can barely stand up.

I chuckle at that last part. "Same." I grab his hips, "But I have to get ready for work. Let me slide out." I say like it makes it better. I mean I love to watch my cock slip from his ass. I love watching my cum seeping from him. That's my mess. Our mess.

I plan to do it again and again. For a very long time. As long as he'll have me.

"I just wanted to remind you that I'm madly in love with you. My heart and soul is literally addicted to you. My favorite place is you. My home. Don't ever forget that, Declan."

"God, you can't just fuck me and then make me cry," he says.

I pull him up once I'm out and kiss the side of his neck. "Come on Prince Charming, let's go shower. I feel like spending time on my knees. You can cry then."

"Dinner was amazing, Poptart."

She beams at the compliment. She helped Declan make dinner tonight. It was a very good shrimp scampi with angel hair pasta.

I resist the urge to anxiety-tap the table with my fingers while they clear off the dishes. My nerves are a little jumpy tonight, what with court and all tomorrow.

I just want to be done with it. I have a very good chance of getting that closure very soon.

That door needs to be shut so I can move forward in this life with Declan. Where I was always meant to be.

Poppy comes over and hugs me. I wrap my arms around her and hold her close to me. I get choked up every time she loves me like this. How fortunate am I to be in her life? My cup runneth over.

"I love you, Papa Pierre. Thank you." She straightens and doesn't miss a beat, "I'll be back to whip your arse in rummy before bed."

"Poppy!"

"What? I didn't say A-S-S." Spelling it out like that makes it ok. "I put an R in there. I'm covered under the tri-lingual treaty of oh-twelve."

She skips off to the stairs, humming to herself. God forgive us when the teen years hit…

"Babe…" I try.

"What the fuck are we going to do now? She's starting to make sense, for fuck's sake." He just shakes his head with his hands on his hips staring off after her.

I make my way over to him and slide my arms around his hips, pulling him to me. I reach over and kiss the scar on his cheek. He hates it but it makes him flawlessly beautiful. "Kiss me."

He sighs when our lips touch, softly at first. His annoyance quickly receding. That was the goal.

I quickly deepen our kiss. His hands land on the sides of my neck, slowly sliding up to hold my face at my jawline, his fingers gently rubbing tiny circles behind my ears.

I groan with arousal. I can't get enough of him.

My grip gets tighter on his waist. My tongue assaults his mouth and his ragged breathing is loud in the quiet room.

I'm enjoying myself, so of course, it's time for my cell phone to start ringing. We know it has to be family. Not many people have my personal cell phone number.

He pulls back and whispers, "Go ahead." He moves away from me so I can reach over and answer the call. The caller ID says it's my lawyer.

At seven at night?

I answer, switching to speakerphone while I hold Declan's hand. "Hey Marcus, what can I do for you this evening?" I'm a slight bit annoyed to be taken away from my time with

Declan, but I know this has to be important if he's calling this late.

"Hi Pierre, sorry to bother you so late but I just received word from Seven's lawyer." My gaze cuts to Declan's face. His eyebrows shoot up in question, just like mine are, I'm sure. "He signed the papers we sent over. He did it an hour ago."

The giant sigh of relief that just left my body. Indescribable.

It's done. Just like that. Over a decade of my life signed away.

"My divorce is done?"

Declan's heated gaze burns down my body and back up. I know what he's thinking. I'm that much closer to being his, soon, very soon.

He'll have me at the courthouse tomorrow to marry me before the ink is even dry on my divorce decree.

I watch him shift from surprised to molten lava running through his veins.

I throw up a finger to ward him off.

"Yes, sir, all done. The magistrate will sign off on it in the morning. You won't need to appear."

"And Seven can't come back any time after this, asking for more?"

"No. He's settling for one-hundred-and-twenty-five-thousand dollars. His lawyer must have advised him on this. We both know he expected much more."

I scoff, "Yeah, he did. I appreciate you letting me know, Marcus." My hands and legs are shaking. It's done. It's really, really done.

As soon as we disconnect, Declan has my face in his own shaking hands, smothering me with kisses. "Marry me, Pierre. Marry me and make me the happiest man in the world," he murmurs across my lips, looking into my eyes.

"I was going to ask you first." I chuckle.

"I beat you to it, big guy."

"I see."

"Marry me, Pierre," he whispers.

I act like I'm thinking on it, letting him hang on pins and needles just for a moment. We both know my answer already.

"As long as you'll marry *me*, I'll marry *you*."

He actually hoots loudly right before he kisses me within an inch of my life. I wrap my arms around his body and melt into him.

I am his. He is mine.

I haven't been this happy in a long time.

Nothing can stop us. I'm really looking forward to the life we are building together.

He pulls back and his shining eyes stare into mine, glistening with happy tears, "I had this big thing planned out, I know I should have done that big gesture to make it special for you, but that exploded out of me, I'm sorry, but not really." He laughs and his smile lights up the room. I can't help but return a big smile of my own.

"Of course, I'll marry you. I want to spend forever with you." I rest my forehead on his and continue giving him all the pretty words his greedy little heart wants from me. "I want to wake up beside you every morning and lay my head down next to you every night. I want your love to fill my darkened life with your colorful light. I love how you paint the colors of the galaxy across my heart in my mundane gray world. I crave your love, I'm hungry for it. I'll never get enough. I need you like I need air. There will never be anyone else for me, you're mine, Prince Charming. And I am yours, mind, body, and soul. You're everything to me. I want to teach you how forever feels." I lean in and kiss his lips softly, yet hungrily.

A lone tear escapes his eyes and runs down his cheek. I lean in, kiss it away and lick it off my lips.

"What are you doing tomorrow after the ink dries?" he asks hopefully.

"You," I breathe.

"Do I have to spend the rest of my life watching you two suck face all the time?"

My heart leaps into my throat just as Declan and I start laughing. I look over at the door and Poppy stands there with a workbook from her schooling.

"Yes, now get over it. We're madly in love, there's plenty more coming your way," Declan tells her, laughing at her face. Yeah, she's going to be traumatized by the PDA.

Then again, maybe if it's normalized around her she'll know what to expect from her partner and never settle for less, thus surviving in a cold, lonely relationship. We can teach her about love and give her standards and show her how to thrive under the right kind of love.

She rolls her eyes, "Well, ok then, happy for you and all that but I'm going to need a dog to emotionally support me through my scarred childhood."

Where the fuck does she come up with this shit?

Declan drops his hands from my face and swipes at his cheeks and eyes while turning to her.

"Damn, you're such a hustler," he tells her.

"There's more where that came from, get over it," she throws his words back at him.

Good gravy. This kid.

"Tell you what, tomorrow we'll go to the shelter and pick out a dog but you're on poop detail, every day, feel me?"

She considers it. I can see the wheels turning. Her mind works just as fast as Declan's so I know she's going through all the scenarios in her head.

She must settle on an outcome she likes because she holds out her hand and says, "You have a deal, Uncle Ducky, but I get to pick the dog."

He puts his hand in hers, "Deal."

“Oh, brother,” I mutter under my breath. This is my life now. My, how it’s changed.

I love it.

CHAPTER 50

TRAVARES

Keep that smile plastered on your face, I remind myself as I walk through kennels of barking, excited dogs of all ages and sizes. Great job, Declan.

This is a huge responsibility and I don't know if I'm ready.

You have a kid now…come on, what could be harder than that?

Poppy is in heaven, skipping around, while she holds Pierre's hand, pointing in kennels and ohh'ing and ahh'ing at all the fluffballs. It's refreshing to see her so happy about something and enjoying herself.

After she thoroughly went through all the kennels four times, she comes back over to this stately guy I'm eyeballing.

He's a lovely tan Golden Retriever. His name is Zeus but he doesn't appear to be as wild as his namesake. Quite the opposite. Hence why I like him.

Poppy looks at Pierre with her own puppy dog eyes, her childlike I-get-whatever-I-want-with-this-face look, and says, "Papa Pierre, can I have this one?"

Why are we asking just him?

I'm chopped liver around here now.

The way Pierre is staring, stars in his eyes, he will give her anything she asks for. Stars? Done. The moon? Done. God, he's such a sucker. He's even started calling her our little princess. And, *and!* she actually allows it, preens under his attention, she does. I tell ya.

I have been around her her whole life and all of a sudden someone new comes along and rips the moon right out from my hands and hangs it for her instead of me and she loves it. Perhaps I am a little jealous. Like I've been here longer, dude.

Although, who knew she was missing someone like Pierre in her life?

The volunteer, Gregg, says, "Excellent choice. Zeus's previous parents had a baby and the child was extremely allergic to Zeus, so he ended up here this past weekend. He is here by no fault of his own, simply circumstances. His hold just came off today and he's available. You're in luck."

Damn. That backstory hurts my heart. Imagine how lonely he is, missing his family, the only home he knew. He's probably scared and confused. My chest constricts.

Oh no, I'm hooked. I'm caving.

Gregg goes to unlock Zeus's door and the dog finally stands from where he was perched on a cot, assessing us right back. He stands slowly wagging his tail, watching Poppy closely. He's a big dog. I bet if he stood on his hind legs he's way taller than her.

"Is he aggressive?" Suddenly I think to ask this.

"No, sir. Zeus is a total sweetheart. He's three years old, quiet, house trained, neutered and up to date on shots. He has no known health issues and has a lot of life left in there." Gregg leans in closer to me and puts his hand over half his mouth to secretly tell me, "He's actually quite lazy."

I feel it, doggo.

The cage door swings open and Zeus surges to Poppy, who's on her knees, arms wide open, waiting on this dog, the happiest smile on her face.

I jerk, reaching for her, but I don't need to worry because Zeus excitedly covers her in doggy kisses and shimmies and shakes with happiness to be around her. She positively vibrates with excitement, her arms all over him, trying to hug him but he's dancing in place too much.

"I think we found our dog," Pierre says, his eyes looking a little misty.

Ok, so are mine, damn it. It's such a wholesome sight.

Gregg smiles and says, "Great! We can go fill out paperwork and get your new fur child home with you."

"Yay! Yay! Yay!" Poppy cheers from the floor, still wrestling to hug Zeus.

"Yeah, let's do it." I swallow past the lump in my throat. I look over at Pierre watching me. I would have given her anything she asked for too. I can't be even a little bit upset about this change.

All of my life is changing and I never want to go back. *Embrace, Dec, accept and go with the flow.*

Once we get home, Poppy takes Zeus out to run around with her in the spacious back yard.

Good thing I bought this house with that giant yard in mind for her.

You can tell Zeus is having the time of his life jumping and dancing around with her and her giggles can be heard clear into the house. A little bit more of my heart heals.

Pierre stands by the back door, arms across his chest, head tipped to the side. He's far away mentally watching her.

I let him have his moments. These are his 'visions' of the life we're building where he's looking at his future, mapping it out, envisioning. That's what he's told me before about the zoning out moments that he sinks into. I know Pierre, sometimes he just needs some alone time to think. I go to my office to let him process.

After a few hours, I come up for air and realize it's almost supper time. Downstairs I hear Pierre, but I can't make out the words. It's a low, soothing hum.

I find him with Poppy curled up beside him, under her favorite blanket. It's a blanket of chaos with a cat in body armor, complete with a lightning bolt sword, riding on the back of a huge T-Rex. The T-Rex has a tutu and crown on.

Where do people find things like this?

Of course, Zeus has made himself at home. He's lying on the entire bottom half of Poppy's body.

Pierre's perfect cadence continues to speak softly. He makes a funny voice and I recognize the passage he's reading. They're reading *Harry Potter* together.

The day couldn't possibly get any more wholesome. It's like I live in a sitcom now.

Not wanting to disturb them, I skirt around to the kitchen and grab a water bottle out of the fridge. I have the thing over half gone when I hear Pierre from the couch in the other room, "Hey, baby, you want to sit in with us?"

I stride into the living room. I ruffle Poppy's hair and then drop to kiss Pierre's upturned face.

No commentary from Poppy this time. The doggo bribe worked.

I sit back into the overstuffed chair near the couch they're on. "I was thinking, how about we go to your favorite restaurant in the Quarter tonight?"

Pierre's smile is instant. "Oh yeah?"

"Yeah, let's take Poppy."

"Ok. Yeah, let's go. Poptart, get up and get dressed. We're going out."

"I'm going to eat the biggest plate of salad." Umm, ok. She scrambles out from under Zeus, as he just lays there dead weight. Pierre ends up helping her.

When she runs off, I stand and hold my hand out to him. I lead him to our bedroom and go to the closet to help him pick out one of his silk vests I'm so crazy about.

I never ever in my life thought I would fall for a prissy, Victorian, ruffle wearing man covered in tattoos, but fuck, if it isn't the best thing ever.

I turn to ask him what color he was feeling tonight but I recognize the look in his eyes as concentrated panic.

"Pierre?"

"What are we going to do Declan? It's almost time!"

"For what?"

"Her to have a nine and three-quarters party. We will pick her Hogwart's house then. It will be a grand event. It's important. But the planning must start soon!" His voice rises with his panic.

"Ok, chill out for a minute. Let's talk about this." I try to reason with him.

"What do you mean chill out? We only have three-quarters of the year to get this together, Declan. She has to be celebrated. She has to get her Hogwarts acceptance letter in three years! Her first trip to Universal is next year! I refuse to let any kid of mine not get all that magic. Like *all* of it."

Alrighty. "All I'm saying is it's just now her ninth birthday. In like a week, babe. We have a while to plan a nine and three-quarters party."

He's still lost in his thoughts, mumbling something about Slytherin, "I want it to be a family vacation. Next year. A whole week. I want to take her to Universal to have the *Harry Potter* experience."

I can get down with that idea. "Absolutely, let's go. We'll plan it, but maybe we'll start in a few months, ok? Plenty of time there, Papa Pierre." I chuckle and pat him on the shoulder. I cross my arms, watching him with a grin. He's really gone all gung-ho over this. All of this. Me, Poppy, the move. He's proving how all-in he is.

I grab his chin with my thumb and fingers, caressing his cheek. "Hey," his eyes flick up to mine. "I love you."

His eyes focus, "I love you too."

"Let's get through dinner first and then me and you will sit down and talk about this life we're creating. We need to talk about a lot actually. Sound good?" I search his eyes and see his panic receding. God, it feels like I've been with this man for decades already.

"I'd love that," he whispers.

"Let's go take our princess out to eat a shit ton of vegetables," I offer and hand him a blue and gold satin vest. He's going to look delicious in it.

CHAPTER 51
TRAVARES

"Let's show Poppy the shop while we're in the Quarter," Pierre says wistfully.

We're walking back to where my car is parked after eating at one of the finest restaurants in the French Quarter. It's actually Birdie's restaurant, Evangelina's. Technically her father owns it, but it's really hers. She designed everything about it.

"I think that's a great idea. She's seen where I work, but not you. It might help the separation anxiety she's developing with you."

"Popstar? Wanna go see Papa Pierre's studio?"

"As if I'll say no to that ever. Lead me to the Ministry of Magic where the Ringleader dwells daily."

She reads too much. This vocabulary. It's out of control for a kid. That has to be where she gets this shit from.

I grab Pierre's hand, who has a hold of Poppy's and we head off in the direction of Jackson Square, where his studio and old apartment are located.

The evening is that twilight between time and space, where everything's soft and romantic. Poppy is prattling on about some history of the French Quarter she learned in school, when I hear my name being yelled.

We are right in front of Pierre's studio, under a streetlight, about fifteen feet from the front door. We still have a handful of men stationed around this area, watching over Pierre and Birdie's business.

There's movement up ahead of us in the dusky light. The hooded figure screams my name this time. My full government name. He rips his hood off and behold, Seven is here. In front of us. Angry, enraged. Crazed.

I almost don't catch his arm flying up, brandishing a gun.

My first thought is he won't shoot. People panic. They get torn up by morals at the last minute. They hesitate.

But he doesn't hesitate.

He shoots.

The first bullet lodges in my right thigh and staggers me. I'm momentarily shocked by his accuracy and action. In a flash, I reach for my gun that's always, always, always on my hip whenever I leave the house. The world is too fucking crazy to leave home without it.

Point proven by this jackass.

The second bullet hits my left bicep. Fuck, getting shot hurts like a bitch!!

I grunt in pain. I vaguely hear Poppy screaming. I feel Pierre moving away from me.

I get my gun out and as I swing it up, his third bullet goes wide and hits the tree two feet to my right. Close to my head.

I hurry and sight in on him and pull my trigger as his fourth shot hitting my ribs. Fuck, fuck, it hurts to breathe.

At first I don't think I hit him as a drop to one knee, grabbing my ribs, listing to one side. I pant through the pain.

His face is caught in a shocked expression. The bullet hole in his forehead drips a line of blood down the center of his face as he crumples to the stone ground.

Holy fuck. I just killed my boyfriend's ex-husband.

Then I feel myself falling, hear Poppy and Pierre screaming and yelling, and swing my gaze over to them. Poppy is red-faced, tucked into Pierre's body as he covers her and protects her as a shield. I fall the rest of the way to the ground with my head turned to them and see Pierre rushing at me, yelling my name with tears in his eyes.

Seven just tried to kill me. Poppy's safe. Pierre's coming.

I have no choice. Darkness takes me and drags me down.

Chapter 52

Pierre

Danger rushes into the waiting room with Birdie following close behind. Poppy is wrapped up in my arms, my hands dried with Declan's blood rubbing her back as she hiccups from crying so much. Poppy holds her hand out to Birdie and flexes her fingers, wanting her comfort too.

"Hey princess, I need to talk to my brother," I whisper to her just as Birdie reaches us and immediately has Poppy in her arms in a heartbeat, "Oh you poor baby, com'mere."

Birdie pulls her from my lap and holds Poppy in her arms, rocking her on her lap, whispering things to her as Poppy cries.

I barely hold back the sob in my throat and swallow past it. Walking over to my brother, I take his arm and tug him over into the hallway with me. Before I get a word out, Lincoln grabs me in a tight hug. When we gruffly part, I quietly tell him his brother's still in surgery and what happened. Word for word, every detail.

Declan got super lucky. Seven hit nothing major shockingly. He's lost a lot of blood and he has a big hole in his thigh, a few broken ribs and a shit load of astonished looks from nurses but he'll live. It's not critical. How the fuck being shot is not critical I'll never know.

I let him know there are hushed tones whispering about in the halls and breakrooms that the Gulf King's ghost was brought in all shot up.

Staring down at the floor, I blow out a harsh breath, running my fingers through my disastrous hair.

Danger pulls me to him in another bear hug, "Hey," he says gruffly, meant to be soothing.

I can't stop it, my chest heaves, my shoulders shudder. I held my shit together this long. It's too much.

"Hey, brother, he's going to be ok." He pulls back and grips the sides of my head and forces me to look into his intense gaze, "You heard them, he's going to be ok and so is that little girl. You protected her. You were willing to give up your life for her. She needs you, in one piece. You can't fall apart, not yet, no matter how strong the urge is. She needs to feel safe and she gets that when she's with you. Be her rock, cry when she can't see. I love you, I'm glad you're still here. *Fuck.*"

He pulls me back in, holding the back of my neck to his shoulder. I can feel his chest rumble when he talks to me. "Thank fuck, you're still here. I thought I lost my brother. Two of them really. I was so scared. I am so scared for Dec, but I know what a fighter he is. You have to believe that. He's coming back to you."

He steps back and drops his arms from around me. "Now," he sniffles and coughs, "Go get yourself some fresh air. Splash some water on your face. Clean the blood off your hands." I look down and see there really is dried blood caked on my hands. Declan's blood. "Birdie's got Poppy. Zhar will be here soon to help and I'll check in with the nurses. I got it, brother. Take care of you, they need you."

I nod and bite my bottom lip before I start crying again. I can only nod.

"I love you, Dec."

"Love you too, Linc."

Taking his advice, I take myself off to the restroom. Sounds like a perfect place to start.

Once I freshen myself up, I take a quick walk where I calm myself down, then I grab Poppy and myself a snack and drink.

When I arrive back, Lincoln tells me Declan is in recovery and is doing great. The vise grip on my chest is loosening. I finally have some breathing room.

Gunney, Zharia and Shadow show up ten minutes later. Poppy loves Zharia too and crawls into her lap next. For once it stuns me wholly aware; Poppy will have the very best circle of women overseeing her life. She will have her own tribe of amazing women to lean on. They will never replace her mother, but where Dec and I fail or lack, my beautiful best friends will pick up where we leave off.

Another building block inside of me clicks into place. This life is going to work. I just need Declan to survive.

The guys stand off to the side talking quietly amongst themselves. Probably discussing my ex-husband.

I knew Seven had mental issues but I honestly don't think that played a major role in this. It was greed. Pure and simple.

He thought I was going to set him up for life. As suspected, he's furious he had to settle.

And we mustn't forget about how jealous, how vividly green he was with it. He hated the idea of me with Declan; it was written all over his face.

He didn't want me, but he didn't want me to be happy with anyone else either.

As I sit here and watch Zharia and Birdie tell her stories about their childhoods, I take assessment of my own heart while I have a small moment. I haven't had time to do an emotional body scan and see where I'm at mentally. I just pushed through because that's what needed done.

I wish I could erase every bit of it from Poppy's memory.

No child should have to see evil things like that. Hasn't she had enough already?

I'm trying to find it in me to pity Seven, to feel something for him, but I can't. I won't, I refuse. He's been so far removed from my mind for months now. I don't even remember what life was like with him. Declan's replaced every bad feeling, changing it into something spectacular. There's no room to feel anything for Seven.

However, he intentionally hurt someone I love.

That's unforgivable.

I didn't wish him ill will. I simply wanted to move on. I was indifferent. That's how I feel in my heart, I'm still feeling that way. I don't care about him. Not even about his sudden departure from this Earth, I feel indifferent.

I'm angry. I find that inside, simmering underneath my skin. How dare he? Hadn't he put me through enough? I'm disgusted I was ever with him. I wish I had left years ago.

I wish I had seen who he was long before now.

"Mr. Lefèvre?"

I raise my hand and stand up. The lovely nurse who's watched me pace for what seems like days now, says, "Your husband's been moved to a room. You can see him now."

Poppy scrambles to her feet. I look back at her and see her tearstained face. I don't know how much more I can take.

"Can she come with me?"

"How old is she?"

Poppy puts her hands on her hips and says, "Nine."

The nurse's eyes soften, like she's about to deliver some shitty news, "I'm sorry, sweetie. You have to be at least twelve to come back."

Oh fuck.

Poppy's bottom lip wobbles.

I look back at the nurse frantically I ask, "What will it take to get her back there," I look at her name tag, "Adeline."

Her mouth flies open and she snaps it shut and swallows.

"Ten thousand cash? Delivered to your house tomorrow. Let me take her back. Five minutes." I beg and bargain.

Adeline looks around nervously. Zharia glides her way over to the nurse, and puts on her customer service smile, "Adeline, I'm Dr. Zharia Davish."

"Like the name of the hospital Davish?" Adeline asks, shocked.

Zharia gives a little slow shrug and a sickly sweet demure smile, "I don't like to brag or bring it up." Zhar leans down to speak to Adeline, although I can still hear. "Twenty thousand for you to hand me your badge and go to the café for a coffee for like five teensy minutes. Maybe not even that much time, right, Pierre? I'm good for the money."

"I-I don't know," the nurse breathes.

"Fifty. That's my final offer before I just cause a scene." Zharia smiles and bats her eyes.

Sometimes I think Zharia could have been the lead tigress of a powerful underground mafia, ruling a city or even a region like Rock.

I see the exact moment Adeline can be bought. She almost looks relieved for the bargain. She slips her lanyard off and says, "Room two-C. Two doors in, on the right. I'll be right back."

As Adeline walks off, I spin around and hold my arms out, "Come on, princess, let's go see our prince."

We only have to pass one nurse's desk and none of them are paying attention to us walking by in a hurry. I find the room with no trouble.

As soon as I open the door, Poppy gasps. Declan is hooked up to all kinds of machines. The steady beeping of his heartbeat shatters the silence.

I quietly pick up Poppy and rush over to the bed.

Declan's coloring is off, he's too pale. I see there are a couple bags, including one of blood, hanging on his IV bag holder.

God there was so much blood everywhere. It was a nightmare. A big brutal nightmare.

"Uncle Ducky?" Her little voice cracks.

"I think he's sleeping, *cher*. He needs lots of sleep to heal."

Leaning over, she braces herself on the railing of the bed, looking down at him. "I love you, Uncle Ducky. Please don't go see Mommy without me."

Je-he-sus Christ.

I clear my throat so I won't cry. Few quick, swallow breaths to get me through. "He's staying here with us. He wouldn't leave us."

"But he won't wake up," she cries. "It's me, your favoritest person."

"Shh, honey, listen, the doctors have him on a lot of medicines to make him sleep. He needs to sleep so his body repairs itself. Kinda like when you're sick and you sleep a lot."

I shift her weight in my arms, "I'm going to have you stay with Aunt Birdie tonight while I stay here with him, ok?"

She nods.

"I want to kiss his forehead like you do."

Be still my heart.

I manage to balance her and hover her over him for a quick peck then set her down.

She rubs his arm and whispers to him, "If you die, I'm putting your spirit in a moving picture on the wall in the living room by the TV where Papa put our painting." She's referring to the canvas I painted of Declan, Poppy and Lily and hung over the fireplace. "And you can haunt us that way. You can do Sunday brunch as a ghost."

I don't think I was meant to hear any of that.

Epilogue – Pierre

"Come on, let's go get the mail." The vet says he's chonky and could use the exercise. He tends to disagree with the vet, with a huge pissy attitude I must say.

Zeus does not live up to his name. This one's never been a thunderbolt wielding anything. Maybe a marshmellow. Or a brick.

He's in his bed laying down, paws crossed in front of him, as he regally stares at me. I forgot to mention he's a pretentious asshole when he wants to be dramatic.

He huffs, his doggy lips vibrating out as if to tell me, *'You're good on your own.'*

One squirrel. That's all it took for him to be afraid of the driveway. One warrior squirrel.

Zeus thought it was a good idea to chase a squirrel. But this wasn't any ordinary squirrel. Oh no, this squirrel was Jet Lee. This one had ninja training. Instead of running, it bows up, squaring up with Zeus's huge incoming body.

The moment Zeus was within range, the squirrel—not even hesitating—launched itself in a ball of angry fur and claws at Zeus's head. Zeus's eyes widened right before impact.

It was at that moment he knew he fucked up.

Too late.

A life lesson was being learned. Trauma created.

The squirrel crawled up the side of his head, then threw his tiny head back and bit Zeus's ear. Zeus yelped and in a panic, whipped his head around to dislodge the crazy squirrel. It's was a fiasco. Entertaining chaos.

So, now, a few weeks later, Zeus still refuses to walk down the driveway. Honestly, I can't blame him. He took an ass whoppin' from a feral squirrel head on. Literally.

The driveway is Zeus's back alley he's leery as fuck about.

This is how I find myself trying to make him get some exercise. This is usually Declan's thing with him but he still can't bear too much weight on his bad leg. Even though it's been a few weeks, the tiny piece of bone the bullet knicked, has to grow back. They prefer him sitting and he's getting cabin fever.

"You know you have to do this."

Every rumor or stereotype you've heard about Golden Retrievers is true. They are dramatic and lazy.

Well, ours is.

"You got one more week to mope about." I point over to him, swirling my finger in the air, as he just rolls his eyes, "I'm tired of looking at your pathetic ass. It happened, move on."

Outside of the kitchen, happily drawing in a sketch pad, sitting on the library bench window, Poppy has no idea her 'favoritest thing in the Universe' is acting like a scardy cat and being an all around pain in the ass. Or arse as she likes to say.

Frequently.

Loopholes, man.

She's going to have to coax him back down the driveway and make him get over it. I smile at him as that thought dawns on me.

"I'm not above using the kid to make you do it. You catch my drift." I'm going insane, arguing with this dog. I have to work in an hour, I don't have time to fight over a walk of death apparently.

I quickly jog down the driveway and grab the mail without the moody dog.

I'm getting dressed for work in our bedroom and Declan hobbles out of the bathroom fresh from a shower. He's still a little shaky on that leg. He's going to make a full recovery but says the twinges of pain from the nerve damage gets to him sometimes.

"Hail to thee, my pretty king," he says with a huge smile, coming over to the dresser by me. He looks like a rogue pirate sometimes with his scar running down his cheek into his short beard. He has a flare for the mysterious with an air of danger swirling around him.

It's what drew me in at first.

I noticed him years ago too.

I should have left Seven that first time another man turned my head and made my cock twitch. I gave my head and heart to Declan a long time ago it seems.

"Hail there, Prince Charming," I say, wrapping my arms around him. "I got you a present."

"Oh yeah? I bet it's good."

Confused, he picks up the package and I raise my eyebrows at him. He turns it over in his hands, inspecting it.

"Open it," I tell him.

He rips open the packaging and pulls out a box. It's a black box, fits in his hand.

Setting it on the dresser, he proceeds to open the black silky box and pull out…a butt plug.

"It's a remote power thrusting prostate plug. It vibrates too. I want to see if I can get my prince to break while he's working tomorrow. I'll be sitting naked on the couch in your office, stroking my cock while you wear that on your video call." My eyes eat him up with hunger.

We haven't been having as much sex because he's healing, but that doesn't mean I haven't sucked a lot of cock or bent him into a comfortable pretzel.

He loves the twisted way I smile at him. He will enjoy every minute of his first day back to work. Rock made him take these past few weeks off. Bam has been filling in for him and covering.

Declan leans forward and kisses me, his tongue doing a quick lazy sweep across my lips. "Tonight, you're mine. Have a good day at work, baby. I look forward to you *coming…* home." Then he winks at me.

I know he's remembering last week when I gave him a tattoo and then afterwards sucked his cock like a banshee while he sat in my tattoo chair. I made sure to tell Danger to shut the cameras off.

I finish buttoning up my dress shirt and he says, "Yeah, about that one thing…"

I know what he wants. He wants a damn cat. Says he's wanted one since he was a kid.

I did some research and the experts say you should really get two so they have playmates. Lovely. I haven't told him that yet. It will be two cats and a dog now. There's going to be fur everywhere and all my black clothes will be covered.

"Ok, I'll agree as long as it's a black cat. I don't want to wear light colored fur everywhere I go."

"Really?" He smiles so big. "Like for real we can get a cat?"

I shake my head with a ridiculous smile, "You're so spoiled, you know that, right?"

"Nope," he chirps from where he's nestled in my arms, vibrating with excitement. "I'm a well taken care of man. Big difference. Spoiled alludes to me feeling entitled to it. Well taken care of means I deserve it. I know what I deserve."

I nuzzle into the warmth and comfort of his neck. I inhale a deep breath, "You deserve the world and I aim to give it to you every chance I get. One animal at a time apparently." We both chuckle in contentment.

At the empty studio with Birdie, both of us waiting on our clients scheduled for their sessions in an hour, I'm finishing up the final details on the custom piece I'm about to do while she wipes down her station. My phone rings with an incoming call from Tally.

I answer with a simple '*Hey Tal*' but as soon as I see her alarm bells start lighting up in my brain. She's walking, outside, in the city. She's holding the phone angled up from chest level, so my angle to see isn't head-on but I can clearly see up her nose and tell she's upset. Her hair is wild flying around her as she walks with a purpose. Her nose is red like she's been crying.

"Tally?"

Then I hear it over the city scene. Her sob. Not the kind where she cries because her heart is full. This is the very opposite.

This is heartache. True, deep, mournful despair.

Birdie rushes over and leans over my shoulder, looking at Tally march to wherever we're going with her.

"Tally, baby, you're scaring me," Birdie says hesitantly.

In a brief angle I see the mascara tracks down her face. Just as fast the angle changes.

She turns into a building, an apartment building it looks like. I remember seeing this when I visited her in New York. She's home. Immediately I feel some bit of relief that she's somewhere safe. Tally slams into her apartment and stops. I hear her erratic breathing, ragged. We can hear the thud of her body against the wall. Then her utter stillness.

Her hiccup is a tell, she's going to let loose soon. We have to find out why.

"Tallulah…" I say with a tad bit of firmness. I need to pull her out of this. "Talk to us."

She moves the camera up to her face. Her makeup is smeared everywhere. It's wrecked. She's been through something. She's devastated.

Birdie is already crying. She feels it in her gut too, something is seriously wrong. We both share in the pain with our sister. We lift her up every way we can to help ease the burden.

"Please, Tally," I quietly beg.

She licks her lips, preparing, "My mom has stage four inoperable breast cancer," deep shuddering breath, "and she doesn't want chemo." Tally's face crumbles.

Oh my god.

Oh fuck.

She must be devastated.

"I'm coming home," she whispers before breaking down as her whole world crashing around her.

The End.

   Whew!!! That story was fire!! I love Declan and Pierre's love story. Coming up next, Tally Belle has to come home to New Orleans, but she doesn't know the most dangerous man, is also the man of her dreams and he is relentless to make her his. Watch her summer fling heat up and sizzle while she battles grief and coming to terms with her mother's impending death.

   Please consider leaving a review. Even if you didn't like it. I give you kudos for being honest. If you want to discuss, I'm more than happy to. My email is author.brandyrife@gmail.com If you loved any of my stories, please share them with others 😊

THANK YOU!

   First and foremost, thank you to all my readers! Y'all make it so worth it!! I appreciate every one of you. (((HUGS)))

   Immense thanks goes to my patient husband, Bryan, who listens to me bounce ideas off of him with very little context, expecting him to keep up with little to no direction lol. Especially the torture scenes. He told me I was fucked up. Yes, I am, in all the best ways. Thank you for your endless support in achieving my dreams. To infinity and beyond, ilu xoxo

Thanks to my groupies (our inside joke) Kim and Bethany for hyping me up whenever I feel down and making me believe I might actually know what I'm doing. Plot twist! I really don't know what I'm doing, but you girls give me courage. I appreciate our friendship, honesty and support<3

Thank you Laura for taking a chance on a stranger and coming to book club at my house. I love having you as a friend. And extra thanks for all the emojis you send when you read my books. I love them and they make me smile.

Lastly, thank you James Lay @Gymjym for giving me the ideal body type for my MMCs in this series.

www.ingramcontent.com/pod-product-compliance
Lightning Source LLC
Chambersburg PA
CBHW071737110726
47908CB00006B/1613